A Family Recipe

Veronica Henry

ORION

First published in Great Britain in 2018 by Orion Books,
an imprint of The Orion Publishing Group Ltd
Carmelite House, 50 Victoria Embankment,
London EC4Y 0DZ

An Hachette UK company

1 3 5 7 9 10 8 6 4 2

A CIP catalogue record for this book is
available from the British Library.

ISBN 978 1 4091 6662 7

Typeset at The Spartan Press Ltd,
Lymington, Hants

Printed and bound in Great Britain by Clays Ltd,
St Ives plc

www.orionbooks.co.uk

To Paul and Lucy – key ingredients in my family recipe

Acknowledgements

The biggest thank you of all to Claire Collins for the inspiration for this book. We've known each other since we were eleven, which is a pretty firm foundation to build a friendship on. I am in awe of her wonderful work as an interior designer and property developer and this book would never have happened without her. Also to Claire Lewis, the third in the Royal School triumvirate – our Annual Reunion fills my heart with joy. I'm not sure Bath is quite as happy about it . . .

I'd also like to thank Marian McNeir for her Bath insight but mostly her encouragement – sometimes new friends are as good as old ones!

I could not get through life without:

Alice Wilson for dog walks, wine and the sagest advice on the planet. Claire McLeish for cocktails, evil plans and reality checks. Julia Simonds for being in my heart on a Friday night with a bottle of Isabel. Teresa Mcdine for kindness and cream cakes. Fanny Blake for wisdom and writerly support.

My mother Jennifer and my three boys, Jacob, Sam and Paddy – I'm prouder than proud of you all.

But most of all my little brother Paul for knowing me better than anyone. Thank goodness for FaceTime!

I

1942

The night sky was quiet and watchful, as it always was these days.

The full moon slid out from behind a cloud to check up on the city beneath, like an anxious mother with a newborn baby. Bath was settling down to sleep: people were drawing up their bedcovers, reflecting on the day that had been. Prayers were said, thanks were given, and everyone hoped for sleep untroubled by nightmares, or worse.

At Number 11 Lark Hill, the back gate opened. A figure stepped out onto the little lane that ran behind the terrace. Jilly Wilson drew her coat more tightly over her jumper and tweed skirt: late April still had a bite to it once the sun had gone. She would have worn something prettier, but she didn't want to arouse suspicion. It was Saturday night but there was no call for her to be wearing her lilac dress again. It was still on the back of her chair from last night. It smelled of contraband Black Cat cigarette smoke and him.

She and her parents had had supper at seven and by now she should be in bed, if not asleep. Her mother was already snoring lightly, her current read spread on her chest where it had fallen from her grasp. She would hardly read more than a page before conking out, worn out by her primary school charges whose ebullience never failed to both delight and exhaust her. Her father would still be in his study, reading through his patients' notes, writing referral letters, all the administration of a busy doctor, though there was no light to be seen from his window.

There was no light to be seen anywhere. The hills around Bath were filled with looming shadows, black under the pale moon. The magnificent crescents and terraces made themselves as inconspicuous as they could. In daylight, they could do nothing to hide their beauty and splendour, the yellow stone glowing in the spring sunshine. But come dusk they hunkered down, crouching fearfully, like every other city in England.

Jilly crept along the alley behind the row of Regency houses that made up Lark Hill. Their front gardens were hidden behind a tall stone wall that reached to head height, the houses standing to attention behind, rows and rows of sash windows staring out over the road that swept down into the city. Once she was on Lansdown Road she relaxed a little. If she kept her head down and her hands in her pockets no one would recognise her or question what she was doing at this time.

Halfway down the hill she darted off the main drag and along a side street, the houses here less grand, Edwardian rather than Regency and tightly huddled together, with only a small front garden each. Jilly's legs wouldn't move fast enough. She was breathing heavily now. She couldn't wait to get there.

Until yesterday, she'd had no idea it was possible to feel the way she did. She hadn't had a chance to speak about it to anyone else. She wasn't clandestine or duplicitous by nature, but she hadn't even told Ivy. She didn't want to break the spell by making it public. For the time being, she wanted to keep the wonder of it all to herself, which only added to the thrill she was feeling. And he felt the same. They'd agreed to keep their meeting secret.

And to think that she nearly hadn't gone to the dance! Ivy had egged her on – Jilly really hadn't wanted to go, but Ivy wasn't going to take no for an answer and when she was in that mood it was easier to say yes. Jilly had had every intention of making herself scarce as soon as Ivy homed in on a likely victim, which she always did within ten minutes of arriving at a social event. Boys – men – loved Ivy, and she loved them. She bubbled over in their company, even more than usual. Ivy was the fizziest person Jilly had ever met, an electric shock of a girl. Tiny and skinny as a rake but star bright. Next to her, Jilly sometimes felt lumpen and staid. No one had ever accused Jilly of being shy, but compared to Ivy she was the ultimate wallflower, a role she found interminably dull.

The church hall near the Assembly Rooms was full to bursting on that Friday night. The onset of finer weather had lifted everyone's mood. The boys had a swagger about them, and twinkling eyes, as if they'd all been reading Tennyson and the spring had turned their thoughts to love – though Jilly doubted that many of them were familiar with the poet. The girls had dug out their prettiest frocks, because it was lovely to have a reason to dress up. The band put a bounce in everyone's step. A fruit cup laced with ill-gotten dessert wine was intoxicating and sweet. Within those four walls, just for one night, you could forget there was a war on.

Ivy threw her arms up with a whoop and was swept up

in the mass of whirling dancers. She had no inhibitions, as giddy as the mirror ball twirling above that threw shards of diamond light across everyone's face. The room soon became hot with music and laughter and a peculiar energy that didn't reach Jilly. She felt panicked by the mood of the crowd, unsure. Her shoes felt as if they were made of lead, whereas Ivy was dancing on air. She could see her friend waving at her, gesturing to her to come into the melee. Jilly watched as a lithe young soldier took her by the arm, and Ivy threw back her head and laughed up at him. White-gold hair, red lips, no shame. Oh for just a smidgeon of her confidence, thought Jilly.

A persistent drum beat began, then the band burst into an exuberant tune that was impossible to resist. The soldier and Ivy began to dance, all elbows and knees and smiles, in perfect time, some secret signal between them synchronising their movements. Jilly had no such signal inside her, she knew that.

'You just need to stop thinking and feel it,' Ivy had told her repeatedly, but the more she tried to stop thinking, the more she thought, and the less her feet did as she asked. It had been the same on the netball court and the lacrosse pitch. She was, she decided, more cerebral than physical.

She decided to head for the cloakroom, more for respite than any particular need. There was a young man of about her age leaning up against the wall in the hall outside. He flashed a smile and raised his glass to her in a gesture of conspiracy.

She stopped in her tracks and smiled back, putting a hand up to smooth her hair. Ivy had set it into curls, with a roll at the front that was larger than she was comfortable with. It made her feel awkward and foolish. She preferred her shoulder-length hair loose. She wanted to run her fingers through Ivy's handiwork and become herself again.

'You look, like me, as if you wish you were somewhere else,' he said. There was a sombreness about him as if something weighed too heavily on him to shrug off. He was tall and slender, his auburn hair swept back, his eyes Malteser brown.

Jilly nodded. 'Anywhere,' she told him. 'Dances aren't my thing, but I don't want to be a stick in the mud.'

'One always feels such pressure to be jolly at these dos.'

'I know. I think you're either a dance person or you're not.' She gave a rueful smile. 'I'm not.'

'Snap.' He held out his hand. 'Shall we be stick-in-the-muds together?'

She hesitated for a moment. She felt drawn to him. He had dark freckles on his pale skin. His eyes were roaming all over her, asking questions. There was something about him that unsettled her, though. Maybe it was to do with the glass of whisky? Was he drunk? He had the confidence of one who was, though he still seemed in control. But he made her tummy flip; made her feel not quite sure what was going to happen next. It wasn't a feeling she was used to, but she rather liked it.

'So what sort of a person are you?' he asked.

'Well,' said Jilly, thinking. 'A book person, mostly. I like books. I like people too, but I prefer talking to them than dancing with them. One to one.'

'One to one,' he mused, and she blushed.

'I'm not keen on crowds.'

'Why did you come, then?'

'My friend forced me. Ivy won't take no for an answer.'

'You look perfectly capable of saying no.'

'Of course I am,' Jilly laughed. 'But you don't know Ivy. I'd never hear the end of it.' She watched him drain his glass, though his gaze never left her face. 'What about you?'

'Same. I'm staying with a friend. He insisted. As a guest, it would have been rude to say no. This is much more his sort of thing than mine.'

'So what's your sort of thing?'

He looked wary, as if it was a trick question, as if there was a right answer and a wrong one and he mustn't get it wrong.

'I like girls who like books,' he said finally. He took out a cigarette case and offered it to her. She shook her head. Ivy smoked like a trooper, but Jilly couldn't take to it. There was enough to worry about without trying to fit in a smoke as often as you could, which is what seemed to happen to everyone who took it up.

She heard the whir of flint and smelled oil as he lit the end of his cigarette and drew on it.

'Would you like to go for a walk?' His full mouth wasn't smiling, but his eyes were.

Jilly gulped. Was it wise, to wander off with someone you had only just met?

'A walk? It's nearly pitch black.'

'I want to explore the city. By moonlight. It's my only chance.'

'Only chance?'

He blew out a ribbon of smoke. It left him in curls, drifting into the air. 'I'm leaving on Sunday.' His smile was tight. 'I'm training to fly.'

'How exciting.' She could imagine him in a flying jacket. He looked like a fighter pilot. Some people looked

6

like their jobs, she'd noticed. Her father looked like a doctor – suited, studious, concerned. Her mother looked like a teacher – round, kindly, comforting. Ivy looked like a hairdresser – glamorous, always done up to the nines, with red lipstick. Jilly didn't look like anything yet. There was no point in her embarking on a career in wartime, even though she had done well at school. She was far more use helping her father in his surgery for the time being – making appointments and keeping notes – because it seemed the most patriotic thing to do.

'Perhaps.' He didn't sound sure. He seemed perturbed. Perhaps he was just losing interest in their conversation. Jilly didn't want him to lose interest. She needed to make more effort, she realised. Fizz a bit, like Ivy.

'Come on then,' she said, holding out her arm. 'I'll give you a tour.'

He grinned, dropped his cigarette as they left the building and crushed it beneath his shoe, and placed his glass on a window ledge. Then he took her arm. She could feel the warmth of him under the wool of his suit jacket. It stirred something in her.

There was silence for a moment.

'The Circus is just round the corner,' she offered.

'Circus?' He looked surprised. 'With elephants and clowns and acrobats?'

'No.' She laughed. 'Not that kind of circus. Just buildings. In a circle.'

He feigned disappointment. 'Oh. Doesn't sound like much.'

'You might be surprised. Come on,' she said, leading him out of the hall and into the night air.

The music from the band followed them as they walked

along the street. The golden buildings had turned to grey, but they could pick their way along the pavement by the light of the moon. Moments later they were at the Circus: a solemn, silent circle of buildings around a green lawn. Jilly felt straight away that it was something of an anticlimax.

'You're right. I think a real circus would have been much more exciting,' she said eventually. Handsome boys like this probably didn't get excited about girls who admired architecture.

'Shush,' he told her, and led her across the grass to the cluster of plane trees in the centre of the lawn. The night breeze teased her skin. He sat down and leaned his back against a tree, then patted the space next to him for her to sit too. They sat for a moment, in silence. There was a stillness and a quietness and a gravity to him that she found alluring, and she wondered if he was always like that or if it came from the knowledge that this was his last weekend of freedom; his last chance to be carefree before he entered another world over which he had little control.

'Talk to me,' he said eventually. 'Talk to me about things I can remember, when I'm up there in the sky.'

Her mind raced. Her heart thumped. What on earth was she supposed to tell him?

'The Circus was designed by John Wood the Elder.' She began gabbling to fill the silence. She was nervous as she wasn't sure of the rules or what exactly she was supposed to do or be. 'It was his grand vision. His masterpiece. But he never lived to see it finished . . .' She trailed off. This part of the story never failed to sadden her. And suddenly people not living to fulfil their potential seemed a tactless thing to mention. Presumably he had wanted her to tell

8

him something to take his mind off his mortality, not remind him of it.

He turned to face her. She could just make out his smile in the darkness.

'Are you some sort of tour guide?'

'No!' She laughed. 'I've lived in Bath all my life, that's all. I know everything there is to know about it. The Romans, the Georgians, Beau Nash, Jane Austen . . .'

'Tell me something about *you*,' he said, taking her hand. 'Something interesting about you that will give me something to think about. A reason to survive.'

She blinked. That was a tall order. Nigh on impossible. What on earth could she tell him about herself that could possibly be of interest?

'That's a bit unfair,' she said.

'Well, if you can't think of anything to say . . .' His fingers danced on the back of her hand. 'Then think of something to do.'

The night breeze shimmied in the branches overhead but Jilly remained still. What did he mean? She thought she knew. His eyes hadn't moved from hers. She wasn't going to tell him she had never kissed anyone. It was a source of exasperation to Ivy. There was barely anyone Ivy *hadn't* kissed.

'It's the only way you find out,' she'd told Jilly. 'What sort of a man they are. When they get it wrong, it's enough to turn your stomach. But when they get it right . . .'

Jilly stared at his mouth. It would have been perfect on a girl, yet it didn't make him look like one. A full lower lip and a curved top one. It was the same with his eyes: the thick dark lashes looked as if they'd been painted on. Yet put together with a straight nose and a strong chin, the combination was devastating. The more she looked, the more handsome she thought he was.

For God's sake, Jilly, she heard Ivy tell her. *You'll never get this chance again. Not the way this war's going. It's only a kiss.*

She shut her eyes. It was worse than plucking up the courage to dive into the water off the cliff at Maiden Cove, when they went to Cornwall on holiday.

When her mouth found his, she knew straight away what sort of a man he was.

His lips were soft and sweet. It was like devouring a firm, ripe peach, and kissing him felt as natural to Jilly as breathing, her body responding in a way that made her understand every book she had ever read and every song she had ever heard. She pulled him down onto the ground, the chill of the grass unnoticed. Their kiss seemed to last for ever, yet was over in a flash. Eventually they broke away, arms still round each other, eyes locked, their breathing ragged but in tandem.

'Will that do?' she asked with a shaky laugh. 'Will that give you a reason?'

'I think it will do very well,' he replied. He stroked her hair away from her eyes and ran his hand over her head and down to her neck and she shivered in delight.

'Are you very scared?' she found the courage to ask him. They both knew the risks a fighter pilot took. Him better than her, presumably. He must have given what he was about to do some considerable thought. She had nothing but admiration for his valour.

It was a while before he replied. 'Some people say the risk doesn't change, every time you go up. That the roulette wheel has no memory.'

'That can't be right, surely?' She wrinkled her nose, trying to work out the logic, trying to remember probability from school. 'You must increase your chances—'

'I don't want to talk about it.' He cut her off abruptly.

'I'm sorry,' she said, panicking she'd upset him as he looked away into the shadows, his expression dark. 'Let's talk about something else. Tell me something.' She paused. 'Tell me your name! I don't even know your name.'

He seemed to be giving the matter some thought. Maybe he didn't want her to know who he was? Maybe he did this to girls all the time? Maybe she wasn't special? Maybe he made everyone he kissed feel the same?

'Harry,' he said. 'Harry Swann. And you?'

'Jilly.' She didn't give her last name – Wilson sounded so plain next to Swann.

'Jilly. Jilly and Harry.' He hooked his arms round her neck and pulled her to him. 'It sounds perfect, wouldn't you say?' he murmured, kissing her again.

Jilly and Harry . . . The words sang in her head from that moment onwards. Like a nursery rhyme.

And now here she was the following evening, approaching the entrance to Hedgemead Park, the great oaks in a cluster like a crowd of girls gathering in the playground. As she plunged deeper in among the trees the darkness enveloped her and for a moment she doubted the wisdom of the rendezvous they had planned the night before. They had wanted total secrecy. No chance of being observed. The opportunity to be just themselves, uninhibited by the curious glances of friends or onlookers who might make assumptions.

She didn't think for a second about what her parents might say. They weren't particularly disapproving or strict, but they did love her, and if they knew what she was doing they would worry that she might get hurt. Harry Swann was going the next day, to an airfield in Devon, to learn how to fly a plane. Everyone knew what that meant. Every day brought rushed engagements and hasty marriages. The war conflated life. Everything happened more quickly and had a sense of urgency that was contagious. She felt it now as she rushed through the park, searching for him in the tenebrous ink. This was their last chance to be together for who knew how long. He would get leave, of course, but not straight away. Their future was as uncertain as it could be.

There he was, waiting in the bandstand. She imagined the ghosts of musical notes drifting around him, untethered crochets and quavers, searching for an audience. She smiled at herself. Love was making her quite fanciful.

Love. How could you call what you felt for someone you had only just met 'love'? But she didn't know what else to call it, that hot, overwhelming certainty that someone held the key to your future. When she thought of Harry Swann something molten rushed through her, urgent and sweet and unstoppable. And it wasn't unrequited. That was what was so intoxicating, the sense of being complicit: the way their gazes had locked that evening as they explored each other, looking for clues, little crumbs of information to turn into memories. The depth of a freckle, the length of a lash, the curl of a hair. They didn't have long to commit each other to memory, after all.

Sunday. The very next day. Never had she felt such dread. She imagined being inside a giant grandfather clock, holding on to the pendulum to stop the hands moving round. She had never felt less in control of her destiny.

Even war didn't fill her with this sense of panic. Though of course the whole situation was the fault of the war.

Everything was the fault of the war.

'Jilly.' She could sense rather than see his smile as he reached out for her and she moved into his arms at the top of the bandstand steps.

Harry Swann. A hero's name, she thought. In less than forty weeks, he could be a pilot, flying off into battle...

The cloth of his sports jacket was rough, rougher than the suit he had worn the night before. She slid her arms underneath and felt the solid warmth of him beneath his flannel shirt, breathed in his smell, so familiar already. It made her slightly unsteady on her feet, that scent of cedar and tobacco and leather. The smell of a man, not a boy.

They barely spoke. They both knew any words would be almost meaningless. What they had each done that day, since they had met the night before, was irrelevant. Talking about the future was pointless, for no one knew what it held. They were living for the moment, this very moment, not yesterday, nor tomorrow.

His mouth found her mouth. Her fingers twisted in his hair. His lips were on her neck. She felt the button on her skirt undo and the rough tweed slither down her legs; the softer wool of her jumper rode upwards, leaving her milky paleness exposed. But he soon warmed her, leaving her breathless, speechless, barely able to stand. And she explored him too, peeling away the layers, with no reticence, no inhibition.

Soon all that was left was skin on skin, their discarded clothes flung to one side.

There were no warning voices in Jilly's head. No stern parent or forbidding teacher or shocked friend telling her to stop. Not even her own conscience, which was usually quite vocal. Jilly wasn't a reckless girl by nature, but the pull she felt towards Harry was stronger than her moral compass.

This was the first and last chance they had. She wanted to get as close to him as she could. She knew it was madness, but the need was overpowering. He paused for a moment, uncertain.

'Are you sure?' he murmured, the whispered words making her quiver inside.

She couldn't speak. Instead, she urged him on with her body. It was a primal response, but her answer was quite clear.

She felt the roughness of the wooden floor beneath her and the warmth of him above her and the hardness of him inside her and she could hear the roaring of her blood. It was momentous, more than anything she could ever have imagined. And somehow her body knew what to do, when to yield, when to take control, how to dictate the rhythm. She felt sinuous and confident, pulling him deeper inside her until she felt a triumphant explosion and they laughed and cried, the tears on their cheeks mingling as they kissed each other.

'Oh!' was all Jilly could say, softly.

'You're beautiful,' he whispered in reply. 'I don't ever want to let you go.'

'Then don't,' she whispered back. 'Hold me for ever. Let's stay here for ever.'

He was still inside her. He began to move again and she felt him grow hard, and the tingling warmth that still hadn't subsided spread through her veins and she cried out with the wonder of it.

'Shhhh,' he laughed, kissing her. 'You'll wake the whole of Bath.'

She laughed too, kissing him back. 'I don't care,' she breathed, locking her legs round him to stop him moving away, and the sensations charging through her body seemed to make the whole bandstand shake and the pounding of her blood roared in her ears.

Suddenly he stopped, alert to something she wasn't. The bandstand was still shaking, and her ears were still roaring, but there was another noise. A very real one.

'Shit. They're bombing us.' He rolled off her, and suddenly everything was clarified. The roaring wasn't her blood. It was the bombers – she was used to them flying overhead every night, on their way to Bristol. Only this time they weren't heading for the port. 'They're bombing us! The bastards.'

Jilly sat up. She could see the flares falling from the sky, dozens of them twirling in the moonlight, deadly silver ballerinas. And then the awful sound of dead hit after dead hit all around them – north, south, east, west – as the sirens began.

'They can't be bombing Bath!' It must be a mistake. A bungled mission. Bath wasn't strategically important or heavily populated. Never for a moment did they think they would be a target.

'They bloody are,' said Harry, leaning his hands on the bandstand rail and peering out at the sky. His naked body was like a silver ghost in the moonlight. He bent down to grab his clothes.

'My parents. I need to get to my parents.' Jilly began pulling on her skirt and tugging her jumper back over her head. She pushed her feet into her shoes, not doing up the laces. He reached out for her as she made for the steps of the bandstand, pulling her back.

'You've got to stay here. They won't go for open spaces. They'll go for buildings. It's not safe to leave the park.'

He was holding on to her from behind, his arms pinning hers. She twisted round, pulling at his hands, prising at his fingers. Only moments ago, she had wanted to stay in his arms for eternity.

'Let me go,' she protested.

'No. It's far too dangerous.'

She realised he was much stronger than she was. She stopped struggling for a moment.

'Don't worry. I'll keep you safe.'

She nodded, breathing heavily with the exertion, leaning against him until he finally relaxed his grip. She stood still for a moment, watching from the corner of her eye until he bent down to put on a shoe. Then she made a run for it.

'Jilly!' He was still half-naked. He stood at the top of the bandstand steps, anguished. He grabbed at the rest of his clothes. 'Wait!'

She darted into the undergrowth. She knew the park like the back of her hand – she'd been playing here since she was tiny. He would have no hope of following her through the twisted trunks of the trees. She wove her way among them, back to the streets she had come from. She heard him shouting after her but she ignored him. No one was going to stop her. She lost a shoe but she didn't pause. Instead she kicked off the other. It was easier to run with none than one. And all the lights were illuminating the night sky, while the bombers were screaming above her, filling her head with a terrible noise. She'd read about bomb attacks. They all had. Listening to descriptions on the wireless or reading accounts in the papers didn't even begin to match the reality.

As she reached the main road, she could see people running for shelter, each face a rictus of panic, women holding babies tightly to them, men with toddlers under each arm. Her lungs burned with the effort of running, her feet were scraped raw on the tarmac, so for one moment she stopped and looked back down the hill. In the distance, the sky was crimson with flame. More flares were falling, spinning silver. The noise was hellish. The pounding of her heart, the moans of the sirens, the buzzing of the planes—

Suddenly she saw one swooping low, coming towards her. She heard cries of warning. Surely it wasn't going to land on the road? There was a gunman staring straight at her, illuminated by the searchlights. He was aiming to shoot her down. Couldn't he see she was just a girl? A frightened, desperate girl? She threw herself into a doorway as the bullets strafed past her.

She crouched down in terror, too terrified to cry. An ambulance hurtled past, siren clanging as it headed down the hill. She breathed to calm herself, then emerged, cautious, trembling.

She carried on up the hill. She smelled burning, the air thick with charred soot. Her beautiful city, she thought. They couldn't destroy it. Surely it was sacrilege, to decimate centuries of history? She turned a corner and saw a row of houses, one in the middle knocked out like a skittle. It had spilled its guts out onto the pavement and was now a pile of bricks and splintered wood and rubble and dust. She had no way of knowing if the people who lived there were underneath. She wondered if she should stop and help, then thought of her parents. She could see a fire engine turn the corner and felt relief. There was nothing much she could have done in the face of such destruction.

Further, further, up the hill she ran, her chest tight with exertion. Again she stopped for breath and looked back down into the city, at plumes of black smoke, cherry-red flames and the moon looking down in astonishment.

At last she reached the end of her road. Lark Hill. A dozen houses, as familiar to her as her own fingers and thumbs. She couldn't see past the first three for the smoke. The terrible sound of bombs dropping was beginning to subside as the planes disappeared, though there was still shouting and sirens and the roar of nearby flames. Bedlam, thought Jilly. This is what Bedlam sounds like.

'Jilly!' Her neighbour Mr Archer stepped into her path. He was the air-raid warden for Lark Hill. She'd known him all her life. His wife used to take Jilly for walks in her pram when her mother was working. She would pretend to let go when they walked down Lansdown Hill to the park: Jilly remembered squealing with horrified delight, sitting up like a princess in her Silver Cross.

'I need to get home.'

'I'm sorry, love.' He grabbed her by the arms and pulled her back.

'My parents.' She writhed in his grip, sobbing, but like Harry he wouldn't let her go. This time she had no strength left to fight him or outwit him. 'My parents...'

'There's nothing you can do,' said Mr Archer.

In that moment, she knew.

2

September 2017

Willow had asked for nachos for her farewell supper. Laura was pathologically incapable of doing what most normal people would have done: plonked a saucepan of chilli on the table with a packet of tortilla chips and got everyone to help themselves.

Instead, by five o'clock the evening before Willow was due to go to university for the first time, a huge cauldron on the hot-pink Aga belted out a cloud of steam scented with cumin and cinnamon and chilli. On the worktop were bowls filled with grated cheese, soured cream, guacamole, jalapeños, spicy beans, finely chopped coriander and chargrilled sweetcorn salsa. Wedges of lime were waiting to be stuffed into bottles of beer – 'cerveza', Laura teased herself with a Spanish lisp.

She had stopped short of making margaritas because no one would want to face the next day with a hangover: it was a six-hour drive to York and it was going to be a difficult enough day without a thumping tequila headache.

She'd put a row of tiny cactuses in pots down the middle of the slate-topped island and empty milk bottles filled with bright pink, yellow and orange gerbera. A donkey piñata hung from one of the hooks in the ceiling. She'd managed to refrain from filling it with sweets. This wasn't an actual party, after all, just a goodbye to Willow from her family and her friends, and a few neighbours, and ... well, Laura didn't know exactly who else, but by eight o'clock the joint would be jumping. That was how things rolled at Number 11.

It was Laura's schtick to go to immense trouble, but her efforts on this occasion were doubled, masking the fact that tomorrow was the day she had been dreading more than any other in her life – and there had been a few. She stood for a moment in the quiet of the kitchen.

This kitchen was her safe place, where she felt love and gave love. There was always a sense of calm underlying the chaos. No one else knew how she did it.

'How do you make it look so effortless? I always have a nervous breakdown when I'm entertaining. Nothing looks right, nothing tastes right, and I worry myself to death.' Her best friend, Sadie, was eternally mystified by her entertaining skills.

'Because I love it? Because I don't have a career? Because I don't look as if I've just walked off the pages of *Vogue*?' Laura teased.

Sadie owned La, the most fashionable boutique in Bath, and always looked incredible. 'But you're naturally gorgeous. You don't have to spend hours making yourself look ravishing. You just *are*,' she complained.

It was true, with her eyes the colour of maple syrup and her tousled dark mane. Laura, however, thought she was overweight and unkempt, as it was all she could do to pull a comb through her hair. She wore skinny jeans, because her legs were like matchsticks, and had a selection of linen shirts and sloppy sweaters that covered her embonpoint and her tummy, about which she was unnecessarily self-conscious. She didn't see her own beauty.

'I'm top heavy,' she complained. 'Like a robin – far too big for my silly little bird legs.'

She felt distinctly unglamorous at this moment, her hair tied up on top of her head with the elastic band the postman brought the letters in, a blue and white apron wrapped round her and a wooden spoon in her hand, dishevelled and covered in tomato sauce. She was also finding it desperately hard to stop herself from seeing how Willow was getting on with her packing.

The back of the car was already loaded up with everything a new student could possibly want, mostly courtesy of Ikea to keep the cost down. But Laura had spoiled Willow with a few things. A luxury mattress topper, essential for making a strange single bed comfortable. A fleecy blanket to snuggle up in when it was cold and Willow was missing home. And some Jo Malone bath oil, because Laura believed in the power of smell to comfort you.

Willow, however, was a girl who liked to leave everything to the last minute. Even now her favourite sweatshirt was rolling around the tumble dryer because she'd only fetched it from her friend's house this morning. Laura, who laid everything out on the spare bed a week before they went on holiday, found it nerve-racking.

Dom told her not to worry. If Willow forgot anything she could do without until she came back for the weekend.

'I probably won't come back till Christmas,' Willow had pointed out. 'York's miles and I won't be able to afford the train fare.'

Laura's stomach lurched at the thought of three months

without seeing her daughter, but she squashed the feeling down. Instead, she sat down at the island and picked up her Berol pen. She couldn't remember the last time she'd written a proper letter, but she wouldn't be able to say what she wanted to say without blubbing. As she began to write, in her best handwriting, she relished the satisfaction of forming perfect letters, the ink running smoothly across the paper, the loops and the circles and the curlicues.

Number 11 Lark Hill
Bath

My darling Willow,
Apologies in advance for doing one of those embarrassingly sentimental mum things. You know how good I am at those! But I wanted to send you off on your adventure with something to remind you of home, and I couldn't think of anything better than these recipes. They all come from the little recipe box I keep in the pantry. You and Jasmine have used them often enough over the years because they still have your sticky paw prints on them!

The oldest recipes go all the way back to your great-great-grandma — the flapjack and the Yorkshire pudding come from her (also good for toad-in-the-hole!). The crumble and the tea loaf come from Kanga — she used to cook them during the war for the people she had living with her at Number 11. The avgolemono and the spanakopita are from my mother, from her travels in Greece . . . I was not the only thing she brought back!! You can taste the sunshine in them — they are for when the wind is howling outside and you want to feel warmed.

The rest are from me: things I have made for you over the years. Brownies and pancakes and sausage rolls for

*sharing. And your favourite suppers: spag bol and chilli
and Thai curry. I know you probably know how to cook
them, but I wanted you to have a keepsake, a little bit
of family history to keep with you. And I know you will
probably live on Cheerios and Cheesy Puffs and Chinese
takeaways, but maybe from time to time you might want
some proper home-made comfort food to share with your
new friends.*

*I'm so proud of you, darling girl. I know you will fly, and
make the most of this wonderful opportunity.*
With lots of love and kisses
Mum xx

Laura looked down at the letter, the inevitable tears blur-
ring her eyes, then folded the sheet into three. She tucked
it inside the Moleskine notebook she had bought specially.
Each page held a different recipe, carefully copied. It had
taken her over a week to write it, as she'd had to hide it
from everyone. She wanted it to be a surprise, but she was
also a bit self-conscious. Was it too sentimental?

'My goodness – it smells absolutely wonderful in here.'

'Kanga! You made me jump.' Laura put a hand to her
chest. 'I was miles away.'

Kanga walked through the kitchen, lifting the lid on
the pot and smelling it appreciatively. She looked around
the room.

'What is this? Fiesta time?'

'You know me. I can't help myself.' Laura grinned, sliding the notebook into a drawer. 'I'm sure Willow would
much rather go to the pub with her mates.'

'She did that last night. Tonight's for family – she
knows that.'

'Yes. I want it to be a good send-off, though.'

'You're a good mummy.'

'I had a good role model.' Laura smiled at her grand-mother. Kanga had brought her up from the age of four, when Laura's mum had died. The tiny, thoughtful Laura had decided that she didn't want to call her 'Granny' any more, as she was so much more than that, and had christened her Kanga, after her favourite *Winnie the Pooh* character.

At ninety-three, Kanga was still more than just a grandmother – though she looked barely seventy-three. She was in a pale-pink linen shirt and black trousers and soft boots, her bright white hair cut close to her jaw, her dark-grey eyes with their hooded lids missing nothing. Of course Laura worried she was too thin, but Kanga had laughed that her appetite had gone with her libido many years ago, and she was much happier for it. 'I have so much more time now I don't have to think about sex or food,' she claimed. Laura wasn't sure what else there was to live for.

'No Dom?' asked Kanga, taking a seat at the island.

'He's got a meeting with the quantity surveyor this afternoon. So he's bound to stop off at the Wellie on the way home.'

The Wellington Arms was Dom's favourite watering hole, where he and his property mates cut deals and watched rugby and sneaked in dirty pints on a Friday afternoon.

Kanga frowned. 'Even on Willow's last night?'

'It's fine. He'd only drive me mad if he was here. It's always much better if he turns up five minutes before everyone else and doesn't interfere.' Laura pulled the elastic band out of her hair, wincing as it caught. 'Can I leave you to keep an eye on everything while I get changed?'

'Of course.'

'There's wine in the fridge.'

In her bedroom, Laura tipped her head upside down and sprayed dry shampoo onto her roots then ran her fingers through her curls. There was no time now for a shower. She pulled off the sweatshirt she'd been cooking in and rifled through her wardrobe for something to wear. Sadie was incredibly generous and always gave Laura things from La for her birthday she would never dare choose for herself. She pulled out a pearl grey shirt with pintucks and pearl buttons, pulling it over her head. It looked perfect – it fitted in all the right places, as expensive clothes tend to.

'Hey, Mum.' Willow sauntered in. Laura's heart squeezed. Every time she saw her she wanted to hold her tight. All her fears whooshed in – a runaway bus, an insecure balcony, a virulent strain of meningitis... Oh God, had Willow actually had all the jabs she should have? Laura knew she'd checked a trillion times, but what if she thought she'd arranged it but had forgotten? The familiar dry mouth of anxiety hit her and she worked her tongue to get some saliva.

'Have you finished packing?'

'I think so. I'm going to do make-up and stuff in the morning.' Willow flopped on the bed.

'Are you excited?'

'I don't know about excited...'

Of course. Excited wasn't cool. 'Looking forward to it?'

'It'll be what it is, won't it?'

'Well, I think it's exciting. York's lovely. We can explore tomorrow. Maybe an open-topped bus tour if it's sunny.'

Willow laughed.

'What?' asked Laura, hurt.

'You're so funny, Mum.'

'I'm not trying to be funny.'

'I know. That's why you are.'

Willow jumped up and put her arms round her. Laura breathed her in. Sugary, powdery perfume and Wrigley's and the awful incense she insisted on burning in her bedroom. Not like Jasmine, who was driving back to her third year at uni in Loughborough by herself the next morning, who smelled of chlorine and talc and muscle rub.

Laura had always been grateful for Jasmine's love of sport. It had given their life structure at a time when everything else was chaos. Asthma was nothing if not disruptive. They had never really known when Willow might have an attack. There'd been a team of mums ready to help whenever she did: the netball mafia were fiercely loyal and supportive, taking Jasmine home for tea or for a sleepover or dropping her home. Laura could never repay them as long as she lived, but they didn't want repaying. Of course not.

Jasmine could have told her she was going to Timbuktu on a skateboard and she wouldn't have worried. They were close, but in a very different way. When Jaz had gone off to Loughborough, Laura had treated them both to a day at the spa in Bath, swimming on the rooftop and sitting in the Roman steam room and the ice chamber and the celestial relaxation room; a physical treat for the physical Jaz, who rarely sat still for a moment and didn't really need nurturing.

But Willow . . .

She felt tears fill her eyes. She didn't want to go down

to the kitchen and share Willow with everyone else. She wanted to curl up on the bed with her, watch a few episodes of *Gilmore Girls* on Netflix, eat a bowlful of M&M's, let her daughter fall asleep in her arms, like they always used to when she was recuperating.

'Do you think I should take Magic?' Willow asked.

Magic. The white toy rabbit whose fur had worn away to nothing, he had been hugged so much. So called because he was the Magic Rabbit who helped her fall asleep in a plethora of strange hospitals. Laura felt fearful for him. What if he got lost or stolen or thrown out of the window as a student jape?

'If you want to leave him here, I'll look after him.'

'I kind of want him, but I don't know if you're supposed to take your cuddly animals to uni.' Willow made a face. 'Of course Jasmine didn't, but we all know Jaz doesn't need looking after.'

Jasmine's teddy was as pristine as the day it had been bought.

'I'd leave him here,' said Laura, not wanting to admit that Magic had been as much a talisman for her as Willow. 'You will look after yourself, won't you?'

'Mum.' Willow sat up and fixed her mother with a stern stare. 'Will you stop worrying? I'm not an idiot. And it's been nearly eighteen months.'

'That doesn't mean you won't have an attack. Anything could trigger one.'

York, thought Laura. If something went wrong, she couldn't be there quickly. Even London would have been nearer. But maybe Willow felt the need to escape. She knew she'd been guilty of smothering, but what mother wouldn't?

Let her go, her inner voice told her.

She turned and picked up her mascara wand. They must have had this conversation a thousand times, starting from the moment Willow filled out her UCAS form. If it had been up to Laura, she'd have chosen Bristol.

'Mummy. I will be fine. I promise you.'

Her daughter's voice was kind and understanding. Which made her want to cry even more.

There was a tap on the door and Jaz put her head round.

'Are you OK? Is there anything else you want me to do? I picked up a bag of ice from the garage when I went to fill my car up.'

Laura felt grateful. Jaz was a practical girl, and often thought ahead – not like most young people. She put down her make-up and turned.

'Come on in. Come here, both of you.'

The two girls tucked themselves under her outstretched arms.

'Group hug,' said Jaz, and they all squeezed each other tight.

'I'm so proud of you both,' said Laura, choked. 'What am I going to do without you?'

'We've talked about this, Mum,' said Jaz sternly. 'You've got plans, you know you have. And I said I'd help you with the techy stuff.'

Laura gave her eldest daughter a squeeze, appreciative of her reassurance. Practical Jaz was never phased by anything. Laura thought it was probably Kanga that Jaz got it from. She didn't have her daughter's confidence, though as an adult and a mum she often had to pretend.

'Go the Griffin Girls,' she said, giving a cheerleader's

punch to the air. It was their team name, the name they invoked when they needed some family solidarity.

'The Griffin Girls,' echoed Willow and Jaz.

Laura grinned.

'Come on, then. Let's get this party started.'

An hour later, Laura thought the party had been the right thing. There was no time for her to dwell. Sadie had turned up first, with a shoebox for Willow. Inside was a pair of silver sequinned sneakers.

'Oh my God, these are perfect!' Willow squealed with delight.

'They'll bring you good luck whenever you wear them,' said Sadie. 'There's a pair for Jaz too.'

'Darling, that's very generous.' Laura smiled at her friend. Sadie always showered Willow and Jasmine with presents as she had no children of her own.

Mike and Daphne from next door turned up with a popcorn machine. Then came Edmond, the owner of the bar Willow had been working in all summer. The Reprobate was a glamorous cocktail bar with a reputation for being rather decadent. Edmond, with his pale face, large grey eyes and emerald velvet suit, looked just that, but Laura knew that underneath his glittery exterior he was extremely kind and was also very good to his staff – part of the reason for the bar's raging success.

He gave Willow a Gustav Klimt card with two fifty-pound notes tucked inside. He only had to phone when someone rang in sick and Willow would cover at a moment's notice, and he appreciated the fact she was reliable.

'I don't know what I'm going to do without her,'

he told Laura. 'I hope she'll come and help me out at Christmas.'

'I'm sure she will. She'll be needing the money.' Laura smiled at him.

He lifted up a tendril of her hair and tucked it behind her ear. 'What about you, darling? The dreaded empty nest. What are you going to do?'

She was touched by his concern. He wasn't the sort of person you'd expect to be empathetic about the things that affected middle-aged women. 'I've got a few ideas,' she said. 'It's about time I contributed to the coffers, for a start.'

Edmond frowned. 'That's not Dom speaking, I hope?'

'God, no. But let's be honest. I haven't done a day's work for as long as anyone can remember. I've got no excuse now.' She smiled brightly.

'So what are you going to do?'

Laura had mentioned her idea to the girls, but only in passing to Dom, because he was so busy and had enough business worries without hearing her paltry plans. But she thought she'd test the water with Edmond, whose opinion she respected.

'Actually, I was thinking about doing Airbnb. I've got two rooms at the top of the house. They're just full of junk at the moment. They'd be perfect.'

Edmund nodded. 'You'd make a killing. Honestly, it's money for old rope. You've got this bloody great house. You wouldn't even know they were there. You could almost charge what you like. Just lob them a croissant at breakfast and give them the bill. Job done. Kerching.'

She laughed. 'It can't be that easy.'

'It is! Honestly, everyone's doing it. I'm telling you,

Laura. You could clear a couple of hundred quid in a weekend just for making up the beds and plonking a few freesias in a vase. Check-in early evening, leave by elevenses next morning. And you're such a great cook – you could charge another fifty quid for a couple of plates of boeuf bourguignon and a slice of roulade.'

'Do you think?' She was delighted by his enthusiasm.

'Absolutely, yes. This town is crammed with visitors, all looking for somewhere to stay. You could have people booked in by the next weekend. No stags or hens, though.' Edmond curled his lip. He didn't allow them in the Reprobate. 'They're sucking the soul out of Bath. They might spend money but they make a mess.'

It was true – the city was an incredibly popular destination for pre-wedding knees-ups, and they were definitely a double-edged sword.

Laura felt excited. Maybe she'd run it past Dom as a serious proposition, rather than an idle fantasy. It had just been a germ of an idea, as she had long been meaning to clear out the attic rooms. Now she had actually vocalised it, it made a lot of sense. The perfect way to ease herself into doing something constructive and potentially lucrative. Dom never ever complained about being the breadwinner, but he had worked incredibly hard over the years. Maybe she could take some of that pressure off him with an easy source of revenue. And she and Dom might meet some fun new people as a result. She loved having the house full of laughter, and with the girls going . . .

She looked at her watch. Surely Dom should be here by now? It was gone eight o'clock. A few more friends and neighbours had arrived, and some of Willow's friends from school. Sasha, Poppy and Emma were heading off on their gap year in a month's time. Laura felt grateful that she wasn't having to face the horror of Willow going to Colombia. She couldn't even imagine the fear of your kids loose in South America. York held enough terror for her.

'I swear I never had a send-off like this,' Jaz grinned, but she didn't mind. Everyone knew it was a miracle Willow had got through her A levels and got the place she wanted. She'd lost a lot of school time over the years, but had worked valiantly to catch up. There had once been a suggestion that she stay down a year, but she was desperate to stay with her friends, and it was her determination that had kept her on track. So this was a celebration as well as a farewell.

At half past eight, as Laura was handing out warm plates for everyone to start helping themselves, Dom turned up. He looked strained.

'Everything all right?' asked Laura.

'Eventually. I had to do a lot of sweet-talking to release the next tranche of money. I'm sorry I'm so late. But it was time well spent.'

Laura knew Dom was under a lot of pressure with his latest development: three apartments converted from a seven-storey house in Wellington Buildings, a grand eighteenth-century terrace in a prime position near the Royal Crescent. It was the biggest project he had done so far. The financing was complicated and the building itself beset with problems – the vagaries of Georgian drains, the logistics of keeping the Listed Buildings people happy, the conundrum of future-proofing. Every day brought a fresh set of challenges. Not least keeping the bank sweet so the money to do it was available. So Laura wasn't going to moan about him being late. She knew Dom would have much preferred to be at home than schmoozing but it was a necessary evil.

She hugged him instead, her big bear of a husband. People often mistook him for Will Carling, with his thick dark hair and dimpled chin. Dom had given up rugby after uni, though he was a familiar fixture at the rugby ground on match days.

'Shall I get you a plate of food?'

'Thanks.' He grabbed a bottle of beer, held it to his lips and drank thirstily. 'What time are we off in the morning?'

Laura felt a flash of irritation. If she'd told him once, she'd told him ten times. She ladled some chilli onto a plate for him.

'Seven.'

He puffed out his cheeks and rolled his eyes. Laura felt guilty for being irritated. He was tired. She knew he lay awake at night worrying about the apartments. He needed to get them on the market in the New Year if he was going to stay on target, and there was still a long way to go. Time was money: every day he was paying interest on his development loan. She decided she'd try and drive the next day. She wasn't keen on motorway driving but he could nap in the car if he needed to catch up on sleep.

When everyone had finished eating, Willow stood up and tinged a fork on her glass. She was usually quite reserved, but she smiled around at everyone.

'This is such a massive deal for me. I never thought this day would come. So I want to say thank you to a few people. Firstly, to my big sister, Jaz – for never complaining when I upset everything because I was ill, not even

33

when we had to cancel our trip to Euro Disney. And for making me awesome playlists to listen to in hospital, and letting me watch *Skins* in her bedroom when she knew I wasn't allowed.'

Laura's mouth dropped open in mock shock as Willow and Jaz grinned at her, scheming sisters.

'I'm proud of you, Willow,' said Jaz. 'But if you've nicked my Jack Wills hoody, it's war.'

'I swear I haven't. You can check my bags.' Willow turned to her great-grandmother. 'Thanks to Kanga, for being a brilliant great-gran and holding the fort at home when Mum was with me in hospital, and for encouraging me when I was behind with my work and thought I would never, ever pass an exam. You are the reason I know all my irregular French verbs and how the digestive system works and what an allegory is. Thank you for believing in me.'

'I always believed in you, darling,' smiled Kanga.

Willow went and burrowed herself under her dad's arm.

'Thanks to Dad, for always coming to see me in hospital as soon as you got off from work – your hugs are the best. Thanks for the piggybacks whenever I got tired and for teaching me to ride a bike and to swim and to ski, even though I thought I was a weakling and I couldn't do all the things other kids were doing. Thanks to you I know I can do whatever I want.'

'You can do anything. You know you can,' said Dom, beaming with pride.

'But most of all . . .' Willow turned to Laura and held out her arms, 'thanks to Mum for being all-round totally amazing and always there. I know how much you've given up to look after me and I know you say it's your job but I don't know anyone else who has such an incredible mother who never complains. *You* are why I'm going off to York tomorrow. I never dreamed I would go to uni, but you made it happen.'

As she stepped across the room and into Willow's arms, Laura wondered how on earth she was supposed not to bawl her eyes out after such a heartfelt speech. Luckily everyone else was a bit teary too, so it was acceptable, but the difference was that Laura wasn't sure she would stop once she'd started.

'That was the most wonderful speech. I can't tell you how much it means. Thank you,' she murmured in Willow's ear, struggling to keep her composure but somehow managing.

'Thank you, Mum,' said Willow. 'I meant every word.'

As the evening started to wind down – everyone had been told they had to leave by half ten; a first for Number 11 – Kanga touched Laura on the arm. 'I'm going to slip away. I've already said goodbye to Willow. I won't come and wave you off in the morning. It'll be a bit emotional.'

'That's very thoughtful.' Laura kissed her grandmother's cheek. 'And thanks – I know you've given the girls some money.'

'A little bit extra won't go amiss.' Kanga smiled at her, aware that her granddaughter was anxious. 'And don't worry. It'll be Christmas before you know it.'

Laura didn't want to think about it. Christmas was over three months away. How on earth was she going to survive?

3

Just after midnight, Kanga was woken by Dean Martin singing merrily about marimba: one of the girls had made *Sway* her ringtone, knowing it was her favourite song.

Kanga had embraced her iPhone completely. She had every app going. She sometimes saw people staring at her with astonishment as she scrolled through her messages or tapped out a reply with speedy fingers.

She reached out to answer it. Middle-of-the-night calls were never good. Was it a distress call from Laura? No – she would come and knock on her door. Kanga's house was only at the bottom of the garden. It had happened often enough over the years: Dom and Laura bundling Willow up in her duvet to carry her to the car so they could take her to hospital; Kanga coming over to Number 11 and slipping into the spare room to look after Jasmine.

She peered at the screen to see who was calling. It was a number she didn't recognise. A wrong number? If she didn't answer she wouldn't know.

She pressed the green dot.

'Hello?'

'It's Beverley,' a hoarse voice replied. It had an edge of panic. 'I got your number off Mum's phone. Sorry to phone so late, but I thought you'd want to know.' Her voice wavered. 'Mum's had a fall.'

'Oh no.' Kanga snapped on her bedside lamp, fully alert. 'Is she all right?'

'No. She's broken her hip.'

'What happened?'

'I don't know, exactly. I'd popped in with her lottery ticket – she'd been lying there for hours. She was nearly unconscious – I couldn't get any sense out of her.'

'Where is she?'

'I'm at the hospital with her. In Intensive Care –'

'I can come. Straight away.' Kanga swung her legs over the side of the bed.

'What if she dies?' Beverley's voice went up, tinged with hysteria. Kanga knew Beverley could be a bit of a drama queen, but now was not the time to judge. She'd be able to assess the situation for herself.

'She won't die. Stay calm. I'll be there as soon as I can.'

When you got to ninety-three, you'd had your fair share of bad news. You became stoic about crises. It wasn't that you didn't care; you just got used to dealing with them. But this was the one call she had been dreading. Dreading but half expecting.

Kanga had been strong all her life, a coper, a doer. But her friend had always been right there beside her. Kanga thought of her as a bright buttercup in the dull greyness of her darkest days. She'd had her fair share of grief, after all, over the years. You were lucky if you got that kind of loyalty in your life. It was harder than finding true love. Some people never had it: a staunch, lifelong friendship that withstood everything.

She got ready as swiftly as her body would allow. She

was still active and mobile but she wasn't the whirlwind she had once been. She had to take things slowly and surely. 'More haste, less speed' was her mantra. She moved through life now with a deliberate care.

She pulled fresh clothes out of her cupboard. Twenty years ago, when Dom and Laura had built Acorn Cottage for her in the garden of Number 11, she'd had wonderful fitted wardrobes put into the bedroom, with special shelves and shoe holders and drawers and hanging rails. Everything was in its place. The move had been a timely opportunity to sort through all her possessions, to bring with her only what she either needed or loved.

It had been the perfect arrangement: a cottage purpose-built to her specification in return for her giving Number 11 to them. She'd been recently widowed, rattling around the huge house and feeling her husband, Jocelyn's, absence keenly, and Laura and Dom had been squashed up in a little house and about to start a family. She hadn't needed all that space. Besides, even now Number 11 was still her home, in a way. The door was always open to her, although she was mindful not to pop in with too much regularity. She lived in dread of being thought a nuisance.

She pulled on clean underwear – she'd taken to pull-on bras with soft seams and stretchy big pants and pop socks that came up to her knees: not a good look but she felt comfy and snug. Then jeggings – like the iPhone, she had embraced jeggings as one of the great luxuries of the twenty-first century: streamlined and forgiving, they were part of her everyday uniform. Over that she slung a long, fine-knit jumper and slipped her feet into the low-heeled ankle boots she'd worn earlier. There was no time for make-up. She went to the loo quickly, rinsed her teeth to freshen up, then found her bag and car keys.

She wasn't going to worry Laura by waking her. She and Dom needed to sleep, to be ready for their journey to York the next day; the next milestone in their life. She knew Laura would probably tell her off when she found out she'd gone out in the middle of the night without telling her, but this was an emergency. Kanga slipped out of her front door and into the alleyway behind the house where her car was parked.

It only took half an hour to get to the hospital at that time of night. The air was clammy and cold as she hurried through the car park and in through the automatic doors, searching the signs for the right floor – it was always impossible to find the way; the layout seemed to be deliberately disorientating – following the arrows along endless corridors that were half-lit, presumably to conserve energy at night-time. Occasionally she would pass a shuffling patient – an insomniac escapee in a shabby dressing gown – or a purposeful porter. She reached the double doors of the intensive care unit, pressed the buzzer and squirted her hands with sanitiser. She knew the drill. She had been in one ICU or another often enough over the years: this was the same hospital where her beloved Jocelyn had slipped away, nearly twenty years ago now. She still missed his strength and his kindness, but she felt him with her. He was always with her.

She went into the reception area, with its unique hospital smell of soup and disinfectant, helpful posters on the wall giving advice, photos of the consultants and doctors you were likely to meet during your visit. There were three nurses chatting at the station, conferring over paperwork.

Behind them she could see the shadowy outlines of beds on a dimly lit ward. She scanned the whiteboard for the name she wanted.

There it was, written in blood red.

'Can I help you?' asked one of the nurses.

She pointed.

'I'm here to see Ivy Bennett,' she said. 'Her daughter's expecting me.'

She was ushered onto the ward with reverent urgency, of the kind given to visitors who weren't going to like what they found when they arrived at the bedside, but as she walked towards the bed the machines were steady and reassuring rather than alarming. Under a thin cellular blanket was a tiny figure, no bigger than a child. All that was evident was a veiny wrinkled hand containing a cannula, and a pink scalp with a smattering of snow-white hair.

At one side of the bed was Beverley. Beverley was defiantly overdressed and over-made-up for her age, her hair dyed cherry red, in tight shiny clothing and high heels, rings on every finger. She had a big mouth and a big heart, like her mum, although Kanga thought she was a little selfish. She had often thought that Beverley wasn't as attentive to her mother as she could be, and this situation was a case in point.

Ivy had become more frail over the past few months. She would never admit to it, but Kanga had noticed she was finding things she had once taken in her stride more difficult, that her confidence was faltering, and she got tired very easily. Of course, because of her forceful personality you had to know her well to notice. Kanga had asked Ivy if perhaps she should get some help at home, but Ivy had brushed away her worries.

The problem was, thought Kanga, it often took a crisis for people to change their lifestyles in old age. She was annoyed that Beverley hadn't been more proactive. Surely she'd seen that her mother was struggling?

Though perhaps she shouldn't judge. It was, after all, easy for Laura to keep an eye on Kanga when she only lived next door. And Beverley still worked full-time in the hair salon that Ivy had passed down to her. Beverley didn't do hands-on hairdressing any more, but ran the salon with a rod of iron. Her daughter, Nadine, and two of her granddaughters worked there, and Kanga knew it was hard work keeping them all in line.

Beverley stood, a balled-up tissue in her hand.

'Thank goodness you're here,' Beverley said.

'How is she?'

'She's sleeping. She's had a CT scan to check if she banged her head – it seems to be all right. She's broken her hip and she's very dehydrated, which is why she's on a drip.'

'What happened?'

'I'd called in to see her, to bring her lottery ticket. She'd tripped over that silly rug she insists on having in the kitchen. I've told her about it a million times.' Beverley tried to laugh then gave a sob. 'I don't know how long she'd been lying there. I couldn't get any sense out of her. I called the ambulance straight away.' Her face crumpled. 'I haven't phoned Kim yet. I mean, what can she do, all the way over in Australia?' Beverley's older sister had emigrated years ago. 'Anyway, I thought you'd want to know.'

Kanga put a hand on her shoulder. She understood that Beverley needed someone with her. Her sister was the other side of the world; her daughter, Nadine, was a terrible worrier and not much use in a crisis.

'Of course I want to know. Thank you.'

Beverley nodded. She was trying desperately hard not to cry. 'I'm so scared. Look at her. That's not my mum. She looks so tiny . . .'

Kanga stood over her friend.

'Ivy. Ivy, darling, it's me. It's Jilly. I'm right here, and I'm not going anywhere. So don't you worry.'

She sank down into a spare bucket chair next to the bed. She picked up Ivy's hand. She couldn't stroke it because of the drip, but she held her fingers. Next to her the machine gave a beep and flashed up another set of figures that seemed to cause the staff no alarm.

'You're going to be all right, my love,' she whispered. 'We're fighters, remember, you and me. Neither of us are going anywhere. Seventy-five years since the Germans tried to get us. And we didn't let them, did we? Do you remember?'

4

1942

All Jilly could remember of the rest of that night was being terribly cold and everything happening in a blur. Nothing made sense. No one was where they should be. Everything was upside down and out of context.

Mr Archer, the warden, had hurried her into a cellar after he found her. She had no idea whose it was or who else was in there. She'd huddled herself into a corner until the all-clear had sounded, then let someone guide her out into the cool pearlescent dawn and back to her own house.

Number 11 stood there as if nothing had happened. She wanted to scream at it – *why didn't you look after them?* – but it wasn't the house's fault.

She was shaking, her bones filled with ice, her teeth chattering.

'She's in shock, look. Poor duck.'

Firm hands guided her to a seat. There were endless cups of warm liquid held to her lips. Tea, she recognised, but it scalded her so she pushed it away. Then something that tasted vaguely of beef. This was cooler and she managed to sip at it. There were gentle voices all around, whispering, conferring. Then one more urgent.

'Jilly. Are you able to speak to me?'

She could make out a uniform, but she had no idea if it was police or army or perhaps a nurse of some sort. The light was still dim, so she couldn't tell what time it was. She seemed to be wrapped in a thick blanket that smelled of dust and mould. She wrapped it more tightly around herself. She looked up, taking in the familiar sight of the white Aga and the pale-blue wallpaper covered in drawings of vegetables: carrots and onions and cabbages. She was at home, in her own kitchen. She should feel reassured, but instead she felt anxious. Something wasn't right.

Then she heard Mr Archer's voice.

'She weren't at home when it happened, I don't reckon. She came from Lansdown Hill direction.'

His observation made her stomach lurch. She didn't want to go into her memory bank. Sleep. She needed to sleep.

'I want to go to bed. Please.'

It was her own voice, loud and clear. Perhaps if she lay down in the peace and quiet she could make some sense of it all?

'Well, of course,' said the original voice. 'And you shall. But we can't leave you here on your own. Is there anyone you can have with you?'

The voices conferred again as Jilly searched through the muddle that was her brain. All she could think of was Ivy. Ivy would know what to do. Ivy would send them all away and help her.

'Ivy. I want Ivy.'

'That'll be Ivy Skinner,' said Mr Archer. 'She lives down Bear Flat. Her mother used to do for the doctor. The girls used to play with each other. They've always been friends.'

There was a slight tone of disapproval in his voice. There often was, when people spoke about Ivy.

'We'll see if we can get hold of her.' Two warm hands wrapped themselves round hers. 'Jilly – you know what happened, don't you?'

Jilly shook her head. Not because she didn't know. Because she didn't want to hear any more. As soon as someone voiced it, it would be real. While it was tucked away in the back of her mind, she could pretend.

'Your parents. They were both killed last night. In the air raid. They were out in the street. They were by the church wall and it fell on them.'

She took in a sharp breath. There. It was out. The truth. Ugly and terrifying.

'No . . .'

She put her face in her hands, though she had known straight away. As soon as she'd arrived at the top of the road and Mr Archer had stopped her. The look on his face had said it all. Distress and sympathy and horror.

'We don't know why they didn't go straight down to the cellar. But they didn't.'

The cellar at Number 11 was all kitted out with blankets and candles, bottles of water and tins of food, ready for any eventuality. Her parents had been prepared.

Jilly shut her eyes. She knew only too well why they hadn't gone down to the cellar. They had been looking for her. When the air raid started, they would have gone to her bedroom and found her missing. They would have had no thought for their own safety, only hers. She was the reason her parents had died. If she had stayed at home that night, they would have all gone down to the cellar together. And they would be up here now, making a cup of tea and discussing it all, the bloody sneaky Germans taking them by surprise.

But she'd wanted thrills and adventure. She'd wanted to sneak off behind their backs to see Harry Swann. She could have told them where she was going. They wouldn't have stopped her. She was eighteen years old, perfectly old enough to go and meet a boy for the evening if she wanted to, and they weren't prudes, or overprotective.

But it wouldn't have been half as exciting, to have gone out with their blessing. The thrill had been in the secrecy of a clandestine liaison; the urgency of a final chance to meet before Harry-the-hero went off to take to the skies. She'd wanted to go out under cover of darkness and sneak back in again through the back gate.

She was a fool. A selfish little fool. She shuddered with the realisation and gave a moan.

'Try her again with some hot sweet tea.'

More wretched tea. What was that going to do? Jilly turned her head away and closed her eyes. She wanted to empty her mind of everything. Of here. And now. And her parents. And him.

'It's going to take more than hot sweet tea to get the city back on its feet,' said someone.

Jilly half listened as the events of the night were discussed. No one had predicted it or seen the raid coming, but it had been devastating. Dozens of houses and churches and shops blown apart by several hundred incendiary devices scattered at random, like icing sugar over strawberries. The targets seemed to be haphazard; a blow to Bath's pride rather than its infrastructure, as no strategic buildings had been hit. Nevertheless it was a timely warning to remind them that, no matter how beautiful and ancient the city was, it was vulnerable to attack.

'Lübeck,' said Mr Archer, with gloom and doom in his voice. 'We weren't ever going to get away with that.'

Bomber Command had carried out a brutal attack on the German city that left many dead and razed its historic buildings to the ground. It wasn't hard to see the logic of the reprisal. An eye for an eye, everyone was saying. Bath for Lübeck.

As dawn crept over the devastated city, Jilly began to shiver uncontrollably. She felt so cold. Her eyes were burning, as if they were filled with dust. Someone was bathing her feet, dabbing at them gently with warm water, towelling them dry.

'Your feet are bleeding. Where were you, love?'

She wasn't going to tell anyone. Where she was didn't make any difference. She wasn't going to think about it ever again. The thing she had thought so wonderful had been a trick. A trick to cover up the most terrible thing in the world. She just wanted to sleep. She shut her eyes, but as soon as she did all she could see was the plane coming towards her; the terrible noise of the engine and the strafing bullets. She whimpered.

'It's all right, love. You cry. Come here.'

Mrs Archer. She recognised the meaty pong of her underarms mixed with talc. She recoiled. She had never relished an embrace from Mrs Archer, even when she was tiny, even though the woman was kind.

Then she heard a *tap tap tap* on the stone floor, the familiar sound of high heels that lifted her heart just a fraction.

'Where is she?' the husky voice demanded. 'Oh, Jilly.

Jilly, love.' And then Ivy's skinny arms were round her neck as her friend pulled her to her, crooning and rocking her. 'It's all right, my darling. I'm here. I'm here to look after you. It'll be all right.'

'It was my fault,' whispered Jilly. 'It was all my fault.'

'Don't you dare say that.' Ivy's tone was sharp. 'It was the dirty stinking Germans' fault. Don't you ever say that again.'

Then she turned to the others in the room. 'I'm here now. I'll look after her. She'll be all right with me.'

Mr and Mrs Archer looked doubtful. Ivy's bright blonde hair was all over the place, and she looked as if she had pulled on the first clothes she could find. Jilly gathered herself together and stood up.

'It's all right.' She was surprised to find her voice quite strong. 'I'll be fine with Ivy. She'll look after me. Thank you so much.'

She didn't want these people in her home. She knew they meant well, but she wanted privacy, to take in what had happened. She didn't understand why she couldn't cry. She felt cold and empty and full of dread, but there were no tears.

Ivy wasn't as polite as Jilly. She chivvied everyone out as quickly as she could, herding them towards the front door.

'They're just nosy,' she said as she came back into the kitchen. 'I've never liked that Archer bloke. He looks at me funny. Like he wants something but he's not sure what.'

She pursed her lips and pushed at her hair. Jilly almost smiled. She knew what Mr Archer probably wanted from Ivy. That's what she did to men.

Ivy was looking at her. Now they were on their own, Jilly was surprised to see tears in her friend's eyes. Ivy was tough. She didn't cry easily.

'It's not fair,' said Ivy, wiping her cheeks, furious. 'Your dad and mum were two of the best people I ever met. They were kind, and they never thought they were better than anyone. Even though they *were* better than most people.'

Jilly nodded. They were her parents so of course she thought the world of them, but she also knew how much impact they'd had on people: patients and pupils particularly, but also anyone they came into contact with on a daily basis. Ivy putting that into words made what had happened a reality: her beloved parents, both of them, were dead and were never coming back. She would never smell the scent of her father's spicy shaving balm through the steam seeping under the bathroom door or the noise of the wireless as he made himself a pot of fresh coffee and a poached egg in the morning – he had always been up before her mother. Her mother had loved her bed; had always stayed under the covers for as long as she could get away with then made a mad dash to get ready for setting off for school. She was happy to sacrifice food for a few more minutes' snooze. Jilly used to bring her a cup of tea as soon as she got up. Her mum never touched it and it always went cold, but she brought her one every morning nevertheless without fail. It was their tradition. It would never have occurred to Jilly *not* to bring the tea.

'What am I going to do?' she asked Ivy, her voice very small. 'What am I going to do without them?' And the grief engulfed her, an unstoppable wave, and her knees went from underneath her as she fell to the cold tiled floor. Ivy rushed to her side, kneeling beside her, desperately trying to console her, but she was sobbing herself.

Eventually Jilly cried herself out. There just weren't any tears left inside her. She got up and sat at the kitchen table, laying her head in her arms, limp with exhaustion; lack of sleep, adrenaline and grief had taken their toll.

'Cocoa. That's what we need,' said Ivy, decisive as ever, and pulling a small saucepan from one of the kitchen cupboards, she found the milk and a tin of cocoa powder and a spoonful of precious sugar. And although she watered it down so they could eke it out, the sweetness gave Jilly a little bit of colour back, and made her feel stronger.

Then her friend led her up the stairs to her bed, put her into a fresh nightie, plumped up her pillows and slid a piping-hot water bottle in between the sheets.

'We need to tell people,' said Jilly. 'My aunt. And my dad's brother . . .'

'Don't you think about any of it, my darling,' Ivy soothed. 'It can all wait. Get in there and sleep. I'll be here. By your side. Now take these.'

She handed Jilly a pair of tablets and a glass of water.

'What are they?'

'I got them from your dad's bag.'

Jilly looked down at the tablets in Ivy's palm. She thought of the bag her father took with him everywhere he went. A magic bag full of everything and anything his patients could want. She knew, quite often, he would give them a placebo of sugar pills. He understood people better than anyone. Understood when they wanted to feel listened to and looked after, and if all it took was a pretend panacea he was happy to give it to them.

Oh, her wonderful father, with his patience and

kindness and wisdom. And her mum, with her energy and optimism and no-nonsense brio.

'What will I do without them, Ivy?' asked Jilly, yet again.

'I don't know.' Ivy's voice was gruff, tight with anger that she couldn't show just yet. She put her arms round Jilly and squeezed her tight. 'Swallow them down and get into bed. I'll be right here beside you.'

5

The day after Willow's leaving party dawned bright, a golden autumn morning with a sharp chill that foreshadowed the frosts to come. There was a gentleness to the light that was comforting after the dazzling harshness of summer; the sun still coaxing ripeness into the fruits of autumn.

Laura looked out of the floor-to-ceiling Crittal windows at the back of the kitchen and into the back garden, breathing in the mellow September scent of dead leaves nestling in the warmth of the earth. The last of the blue agapanthus were fading; the lavender was turning grey. Deep-purple plums gleamed through the twisted branches and the very last of the raspberries hung heavy from the canes.

Dom was outside the front of the house, loading stuff into the car. It was so early that Willow wasn't even on her phone as there was no one else up to communicate with. Jaz would come out in her pyjamas and Uggs to wave them off – she was leaving for Loughborough much later and would no doubt go back to bed as soon as they had driven round the corner.

Laura stood in the hallway, wanting to hold on to the last precious moments of them all being together. *There is nothing to panic about*, she told herself. *This is a natural part of Willow's growing-up process. Don't spoil it for her.*

Dom came in. He seemed subdued this morning. She wasn't sure if it was because he was as unsettled by Willow's departure as she was or because he had stayed up until one o'clock with Sadie, finishing off a bottle of wine. Sadie was always the last girl standing at any party. Laura had offered her a bed, but she had teetered off back to her flat in her high heels. And she would be up at seven and in the gym or doing a park run. Laura didn't know where she got the stamina.

'Do you want me to drive?' Laura asked Dom, hoping he'd say no.

'Nah.' He pulled out his phone and checked it out of habit, then shoved it back in his pocket. 'Have we got everything?'

Laura waved the lists she'd printed out and ticked off.

Willow stood in the doorway. 'As long as I've got my inhalers, my bank card and my phone, that's all that matters.'

Laura gritted her teeth and smiled. She'd spent the last four weeks organising everything Willow needed. 'Pop and say goodbye to Kanga.'

'We said goodbye last night. I don't want to wake her up this early.'

Laura hated the thought of Willow leaving without kissing her great-grandmother once more. What if...?

What if what? She was getting on her own nerves with her sense of impending doom. They had a road trip ahead of them, a night in York, and a bright new future for Willow. She should be up, not down.

*

In the end, the journey was painless, and they swept into their hotel car park just after lunch. It was a comfortable three-star by one of the city walls; nothing swanky, as they couldn't afford to throw away money at the moment, but it was perfectly adequate.

'Can't we just leave her and drive back tonight?' asked Dom. 'It would save a couple of hundred quid and you can see she's desperate to get rid of us.'

Laura frowned. They'd agreed they were going to make a night of it weeks ago, when she'd booked the hotel. York was bound to be full of other parents staying over.

'The halls aren't open till tomorrow and it's too late to cancel the rooms. And I want a wander around York. I didn't get a chance to look properly when she came up for her interview.'

Dom just gave a shrug. 'Fair enough.'

'It'll be fun.'

'Yeah. Sorry. I've just got a lot on my plate.'

Laura bent down to pick up her bag. She wasn't going to get drawn into an argument. Nothing could be more important than settling Willow in, surely?

'If we eat early tonight we can get cracking in the morning. We can be on the road by midday.'

'Midday . . . ?' Dom's face said that was far later than he was hoping. Again, Laura didn't rise. They'd leave when the time was right and not before.

'Any ideas about where to eat tonight?' she said instead. 'I saw a review of a great place on the river.'

'Just cheap and cheerful, eh?' said Dom. 'We don't have to go mad.'

'Course not,' said Laura, thinking she had never heard Dom utter the words *cheap and cheerful* before. He was much more of a *to hell with the expense* sort of person. Not in a reckless way. He just knew how to enjoy himself and wanted to extend that to his friends and family.

She knew the pattern. This was the darkest hour before dawn, the couple of months when the project came together before it went on the market. It was always a race to finish and there was a lot of whip-cracking and breath-holding. Dom always got twitchy and panicky. In property, you had to hold your nerve, because there were so many variables: interest rates, economic climate, politics, world events – anything could affect the saleability of a property, and its value.

In a few months' time, she told herself, once Christmas was over, the flats would be on the market, maybe even sold with the money in the bank, she would be used to Willow being away, and they could relax and enjoy themselves. Perhaps slip off for some winter sun or a ski trip. She'd look at some possibilities next week.

Laura found York profoundly reassuring: solid and ancient, bustling with tourists and staffed by kindly locals who seemed proud of their city and couldn't do enough for the endless stream of visitors. Thick stone walls and cobbled streets, the magnificent cathedral, welcoming pubs, tea rooms serving scones and fat rascals and Eccles cakes: it didn't seem a place where anything bad could happen. The streets were filled with couples like Laura and Dom with their offspring, all nervous and excited about the next phase of life. Laura wanted to hold on to the day for ever. She could feel the dread of tomorrow lurking just above her stomach. She knew when she woke the next morning it would have nudged its way upwards into her heart. She was determined not to spoil their day together. Instead she watched fondly as Willow wheedled a hoody from Jack Wills out of her father, just like the one she hadn't stolen from her sister.

'Expertly done,' Laura teased.

They had dinner in a Caribbean restaurant decked out in bleached wood and scaffolding and splattered with luminous graffiti. It was pumping out reggae which did nothing for the headache Laura was trying to hide. She sipped at the too-sweet rum cocktail and toyed with her jerk chicken. She could sense that Willow was longing for the evening to end so the next day would come and she could get on with her new life. She didn't hold it against her. She envied her standing on the brink of an exciting future, with new friends to be made and challenges to be met.

She could sense Dom was on edge too. He was tired after the drive, and drank three beers in quick succession, then finished Laura's drink as well. He had the clenched-jaw look of someone who was trying not to check his mobile phone. He was on it all day during the week, keeping in touch with contractors and suppliers and workmen. Once or twice he smiled at Laura, trying to look relaxed, but she wasn't fooled.

The three of them wandered back through the streets, past the city walls and the towering cathedral and back to their hotel. Not for the first time, Laura wondered if Willow had chosen York deliberately because she knew her mum couldn't just pop up to see her on a whim. *Don't*, she told herself. *You're being paranoid.* Willow had chosen York because it was a good university, with a great course.

And she'd got in against the odds. She hadn't quite got her grades, but they'd offered her a place anyway. A tiny, tiny, tiny bit of Laura had secretly hoped she wouldn't get in and would have to reapply, so she could have Willow for another year. After over ten years of being on high alert, of constant disruption and fear, Willow hadn't had a full-scale asthma attack for nearly eighteen months, and Laura selfishly wanted more time with her daughter free from anxiety. But she knew that was ridiculous and, to be honest, a little unhealthy in itself. It was time to cut the apron strings.

As they got ready for bed, Laura found a small box on her pillow. She presumed it was chocolates, and went to put it on the bedside table.

'Open it,' said Dom. He was smiling.

It was a silver charm bracelet with a 'J' and a 'W' dangling from it.

'So you've got your girls with you all the time,' he said.

Laura slipped the chain over her wrist and held out her arm for him to do up the link.

'I'm never going to take it off,' she said, and put her arms round his neck, kissing him, incredibly touched by his thoughtfulness. She realised the bracelet was his way of telling her he knew how difficult she was finding this, and that he would always be there for her, and he was sorry for being grumpy.

She pulled him down onto the bed, kissing him harder, laughing, because there was something about a hotel bed that always made her feel a bit naughty. She slid her hand into the waistband of his boxers.

He nuzzled her neck for a moment, then rolled onto his back with a sigh, putting his hands behind his head.

'God, I'm knackered,' he said. 'That was quite the drive.'

Laura was rather taken aback. It wasn't like Dom to turn down sex. She felt a little crestfallen, but she wasn't going to make a big deal out of it. He must be shattered and she knew what it was like having physical demands made of you when you were tired. So she just snuggled down next to him and put her arm over his chest, closing her eyes and breathing him in.

Five minutes later Dom was fast asleep and Laura was wide awake. She found it difficult to get to sleep, after years of keeping one ear open for Willow. She'd been woken so many times, either by her coughing or calling out. She'd had a constant sense of dread in her stomach, dread of hearing that awful struggle for breath, the gasping and wheezing which, when it didn't respond to an inhaler, meant a hospital visit for a nebuliser. Sometimes they'd be home the same night; sometimes Laura would have to sleep in a slippery chair for three nights running.

And all those years she'd had to manage her own anxiety. The terror she couldn't control that took *her* breath away. She had been petrified the first time it happened, one night in the hospital when Willow was worse than usual. She had felt the very air squeezed out of her own lungs. She stood in the corridor, her hand on her chest, desperately trying to pull oxygen in.

Surely asthma wasn't catching?

'You're having a panic attack,' the nurse told her, and talked her down, helping her to calm herself until she could breathe easily, and afterwards she had felt rather foolish, as if everyone might think she had been looking for attention.

From then on the anxiety would visit her when her stress levels were high and her resistance low, particularly if she'd not had enough sleep. She'd resisted medication and learned to control it herself, but it was hard. She tried to hide the extent of it from Dom, but that added to her stress levels and he'd found out in the end. Life seemed to become a cycle of asthma and anxiety, with some brief periods of respite in between. Until Willow's symptoms had eventually settled, thanks to better medication and management.

Yet Laura felt sad. She had wanted a little more time to be *normal* with her daughter. To have a few extra months that weren't fraught with worry. The majority of Willow's childhood had been so high octane and dramatic, and then for the past year it had been coursework and exams and the dread of results.

There would be the holidays, she consoled herself. This wasn't the end.

She could see by the digital clock on the television that it was gone one. The hotel room was hot and stuffy, but she couldn't quite be bothered to get out of bed and open the window. She began to sing the soundtrack from *The Sound of Music* in her mind. At last, by the time she reached 'My Favourite Things', she managed to fall into a fitful sleep.

6

Laura woke with a start at six the next morning to see Dom staring up at the ceiling.

'Hey,' she whispered.

He turned to face her.

'I woke up at four and couldn't get back to sleep,' he said. 'Typical, isn't it? When you really need to, you can't.'

'What's the matter?' She brushed a lock of hair away from his eyes.

'Oh . . . nothing in particular. Just life. Work. Willow. Overtired.' He smiled at her.

She held out her wrist.

'I love my bracelet,' she said.

'Good.'

'Want a cup of tea?'

'No – I think I'll try and get another hour.' He burrowed down under the duvet and plumped up his pillow, turning onto his side away from her.

She slid out of bed and went to fill the kettle. She knew she wouldn't sleep now. She looked over at Dom, wondering what he'd been thinking about, then wondered if Willow was awake yet. Probably not.

She looked out of the window, at the ancient red brick

of a bigger, grander hotel than the one they were staying in. *Be good to my girl*, she told the city.

The three of them went down to the hotel dining room for a full English breakfast: huge plates of bacon and egg and black pudding, with mugs of Yorkshire tea, served by a cheery waitress who couldn't do enough for them.

'Take note,' said Dom. 'You can't beat Northern hospitality.'

Laura had mentioned her Airbnb idea, and he'd thought it was a good one. Now wasn't the time to discuss it, though.

'Here,' said Laura, putting a parcel wrapped in silver tissue paper on Willow's side plate. 'This is for you. Don't get too excited. It's just something silly.'

Willow opened it while eating her toast and marmalade. Inside was the notebook. Willow flipped it open and as she began to read, she realised what it was.

'Oh, Mum,' said Willow. 'That's so lovely.'

'What is it?' asked Dom.

'Our family recipes. Mum's copied some of them out for me.'

'There's a letter too,' said Laura. 'But you might not want to read it until I've gone.'

'I'm going to read it now,' said Willow, unfolding it.

Laura watched her face as she read.

'Are you trying to make me cry?' teased Willow, and wiped away a tear.

Dom picked up the notebook and flicked through it.

'What a lovely idea,' he said.

Laura shrugged. 'She probably won't have time to use it.'

'I so will,' Willow contradicted her. 'This will make me friends. The way to a student's heart is through their stomach. Everyone knows that.'

Dom looked at Laura in admiration.

'Why didn't I think of something like that?'

'Cos you're a bloke, Dad,' said Willow. 'Blokes aren't thoughtful and sentimental.'

'Yes, they are,' said Laura, shaking her charm bracelet.

'Oh yes!' said Dom, looking proud. 'Get me, in touch with my feminine side.'

After breakfast, the three of them headed out from the city centre to the university campus, driving past the huge lake with its colony of ducks and through the maze of roads until they found the right accommodation block.

The car park was already buzzing with arrivals. The other fathers looked resigned, lugging suitcases and boxes of books. The other mothers looked as if they were swallowing down their hysteria, just like Laura, and were scrutinising the other students for tattoos and indications of substance abuse in case they were to lead their little darlings astray. The new students all looked fresh-faced and optimistic and reassuringly normal.

Willow's block was square and modern, and housed a dozen or so students with a communal kitchen. Her room was on the ground floor – Laura had requested this when they filled out the accommodation form in case she ever needed to get to hospital quickly. It was small, equipped with a single bed and a desk and a tiny cubicle with a sink, shower and loo.

'Well,' said Laura, trying to see the best in it, like

someone faced with an ugly baby in a pram. 'It's small, but we can do a makeover. Come on. All hands.'

Laura made up the bed with soft bedlinen sprinkled with pale-blue stars. Dom strung up fairy lights and set up Willow's computer and docking station. Willow unpacked her books and pictures and put Magic Rabbit in his rightful place on her pillow. She had decided it was OK to bring him. She could always hide him if necessary.

Laura tucked the first-aid cabinet she'd bought from Ikea on the bookshelf and made sure all Willow's emergency medication was inside. She'd checked for triggers, but everything seemed very clean. There was no dust or mould spores; no crouching cats; and there were plenty of 'No Smoking' signs so there'd be no passive smoke drifting into Willow's bedroom. All her bedding was hypoallergenic.

Her brain was racing, trying to think of every eventuality. She knew she was feeding her anxiety, but she couldn't help it. She'd done this for years. It was her default setting. She could tell Dom knew she was getting jittery. If she got overanxious, he would step in. He knew the signs as well as she did.

She felt calmer when she saw how delighted Willow was with her room.

'Thanks, guys. It looks awesome.'

Laura thought how very far it was from her light-filled bedroom at home, with its creamy walls and stripped oak floorboards and the pretty French wrought-iron bedstead. But everyone here was in the same boat. The rooms were all identical.

'Let's go and check out the kitchen,' she suggested.

'Shouldn't we head off? Willow can do that,' said Dom.

'Course I can,' said Willow.

'It won't take five minutes. I just want to see.' Laura could sense Willow and Dom exchange glances, but it was important to her, to know exactly what her daughter's life was going to be like.

The kitchen was huge but a little stark, with strip lighting and grey lino. There were three stainless-steel sinks, five fridges and plain white cupboards for the students to share, as well as a number of bins, which would no doubt soon be filled to overflowing.

Laura looked around the kitchen, telling herself it was fine.

'Do you want to choose a cupboard?' she said brightly to Willow, who rolled her eyes with a small smile and indicated the nearest, not bothered which one she had.

Everything looked spartan and municipal at the moment. By the end of the week it would be in glorious chaos. Laura could imagine everyone sitting round the table and the sinks piled high with cups and plates.

She unpacked the plates and the mugs she'd bought for Willow. There had been no point in spending a lot – they'd soon get broken or find their way to someone's else's room – but she'd bought the prettiest she could find: cream with pale-blue and green spots.

Then she took all the things she'd been making over the last few days out of the cool box: Tupperware boxes full of roasted vegetable couscous and Coronation chicken to keep her going. She'd brought some jams too, and some lemon curd and marmalade. A jar of granola made with honey from up the road went into the cupboard. Finally, she pulled out the tin of red velvet cupcakes she'd made for Willow to share as an ice-breaker with the other students and put it on the table.

'Oh my God, did you make all this stuff?' another mother asked. 'You've put us all to shame. I just brought Pringles and Jaffa Cakes.'

'I'm a bit of a feeder,' Laura grinned ruefully.

By this time there were half a dozen students in the kitchen. There was one particularly sensible-looking girl, in navy-blue track pants and a hoody – sporty and healthy and smiley and a bit like Jaz. Laura wanted to draw her to one side and whisper to her: *Willow has asthma. Chronic asthma. She'll have an inhaler on her and there are spares in her room. Please watch out for her.*

But she didn't. Because that was inappropriate and very possibly a trigger in itself, given the potential embarrassment factor.

She caught Willow dart a pleading 'get her out of here' look at her father, and felt hurt.

'Let's go, darling,' said Dom. 'Let's hit the road. We can be home in time for supper. And I need to check in on Wellington Buildings. Make sure that pipe hasn't burst again. I can't afford another setback.'

'OK,' squeaked Laura. There was no room for breath in her lungs alongside the panic. She needed to go now if she wasn't going to make a fool of herself in front of the other mothers. There was no point in lingering. She darted forward to give Willow a hug.

'Text me,' she managed. 'Maybe FaceTime later this week?'

'Sure, Mumbelina.' Willow used the family pet name and gave her sweet, attentive smile. 'Thanks for everything. Thanks for driving me up. And thanks for the book.'

65

'If you want anything, just say and I can post it.'

'I'm going to be fine. There's shops. Loads of shops.'

Dom put a big hand on his daughter's shoulder and stooped down to kiss her on the head. 'Take care, sweetheart.'

'Cheers, Dad.'

Willow stood on tiptoe to hook her arms round her dad's neck and kiss his cheek. Laura couldn't tell what she was thinking or feeling. Did she feel sad or was she thinking *hurry up and go*?

She turned and walked away down the corridor before too much emotion overwhelmed her and made her do something embarrassing. She pushed against the bar that opened the glass door of the block and hurried to their car. There was a gnarled lump in her throat and the TCP sting of tears behind her eyelids; a heavy stone in her chest and an uneasy sick feeling in her stomach. She tried the breathing exercises that usually worked when she felt panic or anxiety rolling in: that heavy, claustrophobic mist. She breathed and breathed and blinked away the tears and swallowed down the lump, pulling open the car door. She sat back in the passenger seat, closing her eyes. She prayed Dom would just get in and drive off without saying anything. Which, thank God, he did. He knew her so well, bless him. She wanted to get out of there as quickly as she could.

As they left the campus and joined the road that would take them back to the motorway he put a gentle hand on her leg, patting her. He didn't need to say a word.

Laura tried her voice. 'She's going to have such fun.'

'Of course she is,' said Dom. 'And so are we. It's time to think about ourselves. When's the last time we had some fun?'

Laura looked at him, surprised. 'Well, we can't. Not while you're doing Wellington Buildings.'

'But we should. Otherwise what's the point? Let's think about somewhere exciting to go when it's all done. Morocco? I've always fancied Morocco.'

He seemed slightly fevered and overexcited.

'Have you had too much coffee?'

'No. I just think it's time for some changes. It's been a tough few years. We've got no responsibilities now.'

'I haven't. You have.'

Dom squeezed her leg again. 'You've been a fantastic mum. But it's your turn now. Time to find out who you are.'

Laura laughed. 'Have you been watching *Loose Women*?'

She put her feet up on the dash. Her anxiety was beginning to subside and she felt warm inside. It was lovely that Dom understood and was being so supportive. She was so lucky. She had a wonderful husband, a beautiful house, two children out in the world doing their thing and a fresh new page in front of her.

'I've got loads of ideas,' she told him. 'The Airbnb, for a start. I'm going to get going on that as soon as I can. Edmond reckons we can make a small fortune. A few hundred quid in a weekend.'

Dom whistled.

'Great idea,' he nodded. 'All revenue streams gratefully received. And it's what you do best. Making people feel at home. Looking after them.'

'I suppose it is.'

Dom was right, Laura thought, as she twirled the silver bracelet round her wrist. It was what she did best, so she might as well make a go of it. Five minutes later her eyelids closed and she was asleep, dreaming of all the things she might do.

She woke as Dom pulled into the service station at Gloucester.

'I was hoping to make it home in one go but I need a coffee,' said Dom.

'My God, are we here already?' She peered at the sign. 'I must have been asleep for hours.'

'You were snoring.'

'Oh dear – how unattractive.'

'It was sweet. Snuffling really.' He demonstrated a snuffling noise.

Laura giggled.

'Why don't I take over the driving from here and you can have a snooze?'

'Nah. We're nearly home. I'll be fine.'

They fell into step, holding hands as the glass doors slid apart to let them through.

'I need the loo,' said Laura.

'I'll get us coffee.'

'Tea for me.'

'Cake?'

'Date slice.'

She grinned at him over her shoulder as she headed off to the Ladies. She felt warm, and optimistic for the future; the dread she had been feeling had dissipated. She was going to be all right.

Dom joined the straggly queue for hot drinks.

It's got to stop, he thought as he pulled his wallet out of his pocket. *As of today, it's got to stop*. 'Quit while you're

68

ahead' had always been his motto in business, so it should be the same in his personal life. You always got out while the going was good and before disaster struck. That was how you survived: it was the reckless and greedy who came crashing down. The cautious and the risk-averse reaped the benefits long-term. It didn't make for such a good story, but who really wanted stress and drama? The media was always full of rags-to-riches tales of mavericks who'd lost everything only to go on to make a fortune, but they were, Dom knew, the exception rather than the rule.

As he picked up the juiciest-looking date slice for Laura from under the cake dome, he felt filled with resolve. It would only take one meeting (he wasn't crass enough to do it over the phone – he owed her that much). He wouldn't need to explain because they both knew it was wrong and they'd been on borrowed time. And then he could carry on the life he *should* be living, rather than the lie. He smiled to himself at the prospect. It would be so much more relaxing. Maybe not as exciting, but definitely more relaxing.

He bought himself a piece of tiffin to celebrate – though it didn't look as nice as the tiffin Laura made – and took their tray over to a long wooden counter with high stools. As he sat down to lay out the cup and saucers, he took out his phone and saw he had a text. It had been sent much earlier that day, but he hadn't been able to check his messages in the car.

He frowned when he read it.

Never communicate at the weekend. That was an unbroken rule. *Her* unbroken rule.

He kept one eye on the corridor that led to the Ladies, deleted the text and put the phone to his ear.

Laura went to the loo, came out to wash her hands, then couldn't help checking her phone to see if Willow had texted yet. Of course she hadn't. But she couldn't help wondering about her. What was she doing? Who had she met? How was she going to survive Freshers' Week? Urban myths about drug-taking, alcohol poisoning and casual sex floated into her mind.

She'll be fine, she told herself. She took some calming breaths, washed her hands again and put them under the industrial-strength dryer, willing her anxiety to be blown away with it.

She headed out into the food area, looking for Dom among the melee of Sunday travellers, and spotted him sitting on a stool at a high counter, her pot of tea and date slice waiting. She hurried over and sat on the stool opposite him.

'Thanks for this. I'm really thirsty. That snoring must have dried me out.'

Dom was eating a piece of tiffin. He had his mouth full. He pointed to it.

'This is nowhere near as good as yours.'

Laura gave it an appraising glance.

'No. It won't be. I use Valrhona chocolate. And pistachios. And apricots.'

A girl just along the counter was spooning the froth from her cappuccino and staring at them. She had the pale washed-out pink hair that seemed to be fashionable at the moment, a nose ring and a big army jacket. She was going for the beautiful-but-intimidating look. Brimful of bravado. Young and ready to change the world. Laura pushed down the shadow of Willow that tried to enter her mind.

'I'm sorry.' The girl leaned forward. She had a strident tone, and the kind of attitude that would make a university lecturer's heart sink. 'I've got to tell you, because you look lovely and kind and it's not fair.'

'Not fair?' Laura frowned.

The girl pointed her spoon at Dom. 'He's having an affair.'

For a moment no one spoke. Laura frowned. Dom rolled his eyes.

'Oh for God's sake,' said Dom. 'Are you coming down from last night or something?'

'I heard you on the phone while your wife was in the toilet.' The girl's eyes were blue and cold. '*I've been thinking about us too. All last night.*'

Dom scrumpled up his napkin. 'She's a nutter. Let's go.'

Laura didn't move. The girl waved her spoon again.

'*Laura's going to be all over the place for a few days because of Willow, but I need to see you.*'

Laura's mouth dropped open. The detail in what the girl had said was all the proof Laura needed. She stared at Dom.

'*Come to the house first thing. There won't be anyone there until nine.*'

Laura looked incredulous. She grabbed her bag and jumped off her stool.

'Have you got any idea what you've just done?' Dom asked the girl, who shrugged.

71

'Given her a chance to find someone who's not cheating on her?'

'I was talking to my *lawyer*.'

The girl just raised an eyebrow. Dom turned to Laura, desperate.

'Laura – she's taken it totally out of context. I was talking to Antonia Briggs – there's conveyancing stuff we need to sort out before the flats go on the market. The leaseholds –'

'Trust me,' said the girl. 'She might be his lawyer but she's going through more than his fine print.'

'This is ridiculous,' said Dom. 'Come on, darling. Let's go. You're lucky I'm not calling security.'

He took Laura's arm but she shook it off.

'I know you're a flirt,' she said, her voice trembling. 'And I know you've probably got a higher sex drive than I have. And I know you come into contact with loads of women. But do you know what? I always trusted you. I never doubted you for a moment.'

'You are seriously going to believe some stalky drug-crazed weirdo at a service station? She twisted everything I said. I told Antonia to come to Wellington Buildings because there's stuff she needs to look at. I told her to come early because I don't want the team hearing my business. Surely that makes sense? It's not some seedy hook-up, which was what she made it sound like.'

'*Laura's going to be all over the place*?' Laura quoted the girl back at him.

'I was concerned. I know how anxious you are about Willow and what a big deal this is for you. She made it sound as if I think you're an inconvenience. I meant that I might be a bit preoccupied for a week or two.'

Laura thought for a moment. What Dom was saying sounded plausible. It was certainly the version she wanted to believe. It had been wrong of the girl to interfere, and she did look like a troublemaker – someone who thrived on drama.

'Give me your phone.'

'What?'

'If you really expect me to believe you, you'll let me see your phone.'

Dom sighed and handed his phone over. Laura examined it.

The last number he had called said **A Briggs**.

Laura flipped through to see if they'd exchanged any texts. There were none. Dom swallowed.

'You see?'

'Maybe you're just very efficient at deleting incriminating evidence?'

She went to hand him his phone back. He laughed in semi-relief and went to take it, but at the last moment she snatched it back.

'Wait.'

Laura typed in a text and sent it.

'What have you written?' asked Dom. He looked tense. More tense than he should be if he was innocent.

'Never mind,' said Laura, staring at the screen.

The seconds seemed eternal while they waited. Nothing. No response.

'Come on, Laura. This is silly.' He held his hand out for the phone, just as it chirruped a reply.

Laura read the reply and blinked. Dom couldn't tell anything from her expression. Then she held the phone up so he could read the exchange.

Dom: Can't wait to see you xx

A Briggs: See you later xxxx

'You're nothing but a cliché,' said Laura, and stalked off.

'Well done,' Dom said to the girl. 'That's a twenty-year marriage you've just stuffed up.'

'No,' said the girl. 'You did that quite well for yourself.' She swung her canvas bag covered in badges onto her shoulder and slid off her stool, disappearing into the crowds.

Laura stumbled back into the toilets, pushing past two other women and heading for an open cubicle. She would never usually queue barge, but she needed to barricade herself in.

'Hey,' said one of them, but she slammed the door shut.

'How rude,' she heard the other one say, but she didn't care.

She folded her arms against the cubicle door and rested her head on them.

She tried to remember what she knew about Antonia. She'd heard her name, of course. There were lots of people on Dom's team. Most of the actual workmen were blokes: the carpenters, the electricians, the plasterers. But there were plenty of women involved too. His bank manager, for a start. His web designer, his garden designer, his planning officer . . . She'd never worried about any of them for as much as a second. She had thought their marriage was as rock solid and watertight as the house they lived in.

She knew Antonia had worked pretty closely with him

74

on the conveyancing of all his deals. There were endless issues: searches and covenants and indemnities. Laura had heard her name bandied around for at least three years. She felt a bit sick as she racked her brain for clues as to when the relationship could have gone from personal to something more. Had she misread the signals or hadn't there been any? Had she been totally unobservant or just too trusting? She felt her past reconfigure, every moment called into question. Had everything been a lie? She felt foolish, and had no idea how she was supposed to proceed.

All around her she could hear people talking, the sound of flushing and taps running and dryers blasting out hot air. She couldn't stay in here for ever. But what was she supposed to do? She just wanted to un-know what she'd learned. Carry on living in blissful ignorance. Her initial reaction was to call Sadie, who was after all her best friend, and an expert in affairs of the heart, including extra-marital ones. Although Sadie had never been married, she had certainly been the other woman. Not recently, but when she was much younger, and she had been badly burnt on more than one occasion. She would have opinions, of that Laura was certain.

But Sadie was fiery and tended to stoke fires rather than put them out. Laura wasn't sure she could cope with the inevitable drama. Then another, more terrible thought occurred to her.

Maybe Sadie knew about the affair. Maybe the whole of Bath knew, except Laura. She felt her cheeks flush. Was she the only person not to know her husband was playing away? After all, wasn't it usually the wife who was the last to find out? She'd heard of other instances. Bath was rife with dinner-party speculation and school-gate insinuation. She usually ignored the whispers. She certainly never passed any of them on. Laura wasn't the type to thrive on tittle-tattle. It made her feel uncomfortable. If people started talking about others behind their backs, she withdrew from the conversation or changed the subject.

'You're such a saint,' Sadie would complain if she chose to ignore a juicy snippet. 'Everyone loves a gossip.'

'Well, I don't.' She would remain firm.

Now, she imagined the rumours that might have been circulating about Dom and . . . Ugh. She couldn't give the woman's name headspace or even begin to imagine what she looked like. The very thought made her heart start to hammer.

She looked up at the ceiling. Oh God. Here they came. The symptoms she dreaded. She tried to empty her mind of what had just happened and focus instead on something positive: a still, calm lily pond, tranquil and verdant, a waxy white flower opening its petals. She couldn't lose it in here, in a public toilet with no one to help her. She certainly wasn't going to call on Dom for assistance.

Breathe. Stay calm. She kept the voice in her head firm and steady. She'd been doing so well. It had been months since her last panic attack. She wasn't going to allow them back. It was all in her mind. She was in control. She had the power to dictate how she felt.

Eventually, as she breathed, she felt her pulse subside and her nausea settle. Shaking slightly, she pulled the car keys out of her bag. Dom was in the habit of giving them to her rather than putting them in his pocket.

She left the cloakroom and slipped out of the service station by a side door, then hurried as quickly as she could to the car. Before she could think about it too much she reversed out of the space and headed for the exit.

As she drove through the hordes of people heading back to their cars, she passed the girl who had dropped the bombshell. Her head was down and she was texting as she wove through the car park. Laura slowed down and wound down the window.

'Hey.'

The girl looked up.

'I don't know if you did the right thing,' Laura told her. 'You've either done me a huge favour or ruined my life. But I don't think you should make a habit of interfering in people's lives like that.'

The girl looked defiant. 'If any man cheated on me, I would never forgive them. I'd want to know.'

Laura looked at her pale face, her bitten nails, her tattoos, and thought, for all her principles, she hadn't a clue. 'Life's not always that straightforward, you know. I've got two daughters about your age. How do you think they're going to feel?'

The girl opened her mouth, then shut it again, and for a moment she didn't look as sure as she had been. She was obviously headstrong and used to voicing her opinions. And not used to someone like Laura questioning her.

Laura wound the window up. There was little point in carrying on the conversation. The damage had been done. The exchange had made her feel anxious again, and she felt tears nudging their way out of her eyes. She wiped them away with the heel of her hand. She wasn't going to cry. Not yet. All she could think was thank God the girls weren't at home. She wouldn't have been able to hide what had happened from them. She felt sick all over again at the thought of them knowing. They worshipped Dom. All of them did.

Then she spotted Dom coming out of the automatic doors. She saw him clock the car and begin to run, an expression of anguish and panic on his face. He waved at her wildly, but she put her foot down, holding her breath until she reached the inside lane of the motorway. She was going to drive home without him. At least that way she could think about what had happened and make a plan. She wasn't worried about leaving him stranded at the service station. That was his problem.

She didn't look back.

7

Antonia had woken up that Sunday morning with a heavy heart and a slightly sick feeling in the pit of her stomach. Today was the day she had to put her decision into action. She knew from experience that once her mind was made up it was best to get on with it.

She was proud of quite a few of her achievements. She was proud of the four A levels she got despite her school being in special measures and being endlessly bullied for wearing glasses and being a spod.

She was proud of getting her Duke of Edinburgh Gold Award. She had gone to St James' Palace to collect it: a four-hour bus journey from Somerset to London and back. Her parents didn't come because they couldn't leave the shop, and Antonia didn't protest that surely, just once, one of them could have left the other to manage. It was a small pet shop in a small seaside town. The worst that could happen was someone might have to wait in a queue to buy their cat litter. But no one in the Briggs family ever imagined they might come before anything with four legs.

She was proud of her job as a conveyancing solicitor. She was proud of the flat she had bought in a leafy square in the centre of Bath. She was proud of the Ikea kitchen she had put in herself with just a tiny bit of help from an electrician.

She was not, however, proud of her affair with Dom Griffin.

Whenever she saw Dom, she felt an extraordinary clash of conflicting emotions. There was a top note of shame. In the middle was a deep affection, fed by her desire to nurture and protect him, because she knew better than anyone he wasn't all he pretended to be and he needed looking after. And the base note was the most powerful feeling of all – the one that made her giddy and quite unsteady on her feet. It blazed through her, hitting her in the guts (or perhaps not quite her guts; the feeling was a little lower than that), taking her by surprise every time. If she were to put a name to it, she supposed it was lust. Whatever it was called, it was dangerously addictive and overrode all of the other sensations.

Antonia wasn't the type of girl to sleep with a married man. Prior to Dom, her lovers had all been carefully considered, and even then the word 'lover' was something of a misnomer, as love hadn't come into it. Her last tryst had been the dullest of relationships: occasional trips to the theatre or dinners out, with the evening ending in perfunctory sex which had left her baffled as to why they bothered. Or, indeed, why anyone did.

Now she knew.

People would be surprised if they knew the truth. On the outside, Antonia was navy blue and buttoned up. Even her name was buttoned up: Briggs, a hybrid of brisk and priggish. She never wore clothes that were too tight or too short or heels that were too high. Knee-length skirts, white blouses, nude tights and low-heeled court shoes. Brown hair tied back in a ponytail. Tortoiseshell glasses for reading the smallest of the small print. Antonia was entirely appropriate in everything she did. She was efficient, ambitious and happy in her own company.

Apart from choosing a manual Golf over an automatic (traffic in Bath was terrible, and an automatic was almost essential if you weren't to drive yourself mad), Antonia rarely made mistakes. So it was ironic that the mistake she made this time last year was such a monumental one.

It didn't affect her work because Antonia had an enviable ability to compartmentalise and the minute she walked through the door of her office she switched to business. Her personal phone stayed in her bag and her mind didn't wander.

But yesterday afternoon, she had finally faced the truth: she had fallen in love with Dom. And she knew that, because when he had told her he was driving to York with Laura, she had felt jealous. Jealous that he and his wife were going to be exploring a strange city together and sharing a hotel room. Even though the reason for them going there was entirely practical and reasonable.

Antonia had been shocked by the depth of her jealousy, and by the fact that she had spent all of Saturday wondering what Dom was doing, if he was having fun, where they were having dinner. It was as if while Laura was in Bath, in the family home, she was no threat. But take her out of that place and she became competition.

Jealousy was a new experience and was infinitely worse than the shame Antonia already felt, and it helped make up her mind. She already knew someone – or more than one someone – was going to get hurt if this affair continued. It didn't matter if it was her, because if she got hurt that was her own silly fault. But there were likely to be innocent victims and she didn't want that on her conscience. Added to which, the relationship could go nowhere other than where it already was – she had never *ever* hinted to Dom that she wanted him to leave Laura. Because she didn't. The idea of being responsible for breaking up a marriage appalled her. And every day that went past was a day nearer to the day they got caught out. So it was time to stop.

What she was going to have to do was going to be painful, because the love she felt for Dom was a deep, caring love. It wasn't an electric, fizzing, superficial passion. It had far more meaning and stamina. It was a *good* love, and that was going to be difficult to sacrifice.

She had felt her love more deeply than ever in the past week, because Dom was dreading Willow going away to university and she had been desperate to take his pain away, but she couldn't. Twice in the past fortnight he had cried in her arms at the prospect, because he couldn't cry at home, he told her. He couldn't admit to his wife how terrifying he found it. He had to put on a brave face for Laura, who had a tendency to be highly strung. Antonia knew much of Dom's life was spent heading off his wife's anxiety.

She longed to be the person who made it all right; the one that he turned to in order to fill the hole left by Willow. But it wasn't her place, and the fierceness of her longing brought it home to her once and for all.

It had to stop.

She got out of bed straight away – one of her rules was to get up as soon as she woke up; she just didn't see the point of lying there unless you were actually ill – then made her bed, shaking out the duvet, plumping the pillows, smoothing the bottom sheet and tucking it in firmly. She had read somewhere that making your bed straight away set the tone for the day. And then when you came to bed at the end of a long, hard day it was a pleasure to climb into.

As she plumped up her pillows and settled them back into place she thought: *We all deserve better. Laura deserves better. I deserve better.* Not better than Dom, because she thought she would never find anyone who came close. But a better situation. And Dom deserved to be set free. She knew he would never have the balls to end it, that she had become a habit he didn't have the strength to break.

They both recognised they couldn't get away with a clandestine relationship for ever. They had a strict regime. Once or twice a week, at about six o'clock, just after she got home from work, she would buzz him into the building, where he could be visiting any of the people that lived in the six flats. He always made sure the stairway and hall were empty before tapping on her door. Antonia knew categorically that no one had ever seen him go into her flat. And before he left, she checked the stairway again before letting him out.

Nevertheless, more than one of her neighbours had given her a knowing look. Perhaps she was being paranoid, but Bath was a small place. Everyone knew everyone and everything about them. One day someone would say something to someone else, and they would repeat it someone else, and it would get back to Laura. They were on borrowed time, and Antonia believed that she should neither a borrower nor a lender be. Having someone else's husband on loan was against everything she stood for.

So today was the beginning of the end.

After she had made her bed, she put the kettle on and texted him. It was breaking another of her rules, but she had to get the plan underway.

Can you please give me a ring at your convenience? A.

A perfectly acceptable message to receive from one's solicitor. Not one that would arouse suspicion if it was intercepted.

She would ask him to meet her at Wellington Buildings the next morning. By the time she got to work the relationship would be behind her. A fond memory to be tucked away. Taken out every now and then to be looked at, then neatly folded and put back again in a faraway corner of her mind. There was no point in being sad or regretful. She should be grateful for the time they'd shared. She'd learned a lot from him, about life and love.

She sighed. It was going to be difficult telling Dom, she knew that. He would probably cry and she probably wouldn't. He was surprisingly emotional and sentimental. And she had taught herself not to show her feelings long ago. Her parents hadn't run to affection for humans, so she had trained herself not to expect it.

Once she'd sent the text she sat down on the sofa with her coffee.

Her flat was like a show home. The walls were painted in Egyptian Sand, a warm but neutral beige which had none of the heat or promise of its name, but was so understated it was barely there. The carpet was a pale wool twist; the sofas cream linen; the Roman blinds at the deep sash windows the same. The kitchen area had white high-gloss units with touch-close drawers and not a handle in sight. A bookcase held a row of novels, and she arranged them in the order she had read them (she had to fight the urge for alphabetical order), and they made quite a pleasing display: Barbara Kingsolver, Anne Tyler, William Boyd...

Fiction, Antonia realised, was about as much as she let go. With a book, you had to let the author take control and follow them wherever they led.

Antonia didn't allow anyone else to take control in her life. She didn't allow mess. Or disruption. Or chaos. Every day when she woke up, she was certain what the day would bring. Of course, she couldn't allow for calamity or catastrophe or weather conditions, but as far as possible her days were timetabled and she rarely deviated. Dom had been the only exception.

Sometimes after they'd been to bed together she had looked in the mirror at her wide eyes and dishevelled hair and flushed cheeks and thought she looked *almost* pretty. Not that she was ugly, but she always felt her features rather severe: a somewhat bony face, with a very straight nose, hollow cheeks and eyes that were just, well, *eye*-shaped, as a child might draw them, with sparse eyelashes and thick eyebrows (quite the wrong way round) that she'd never had the nerve to pluck. Or indeed have plucked, by an expert. Antonia was a stranger to that kind of indulgence.

Dom had once told her Laura had a hot-pink Aga in the kitchen. Antonia had an induction hob, and thought their respective ovens said it all. Laura was vibrant, ever-warm and glowing. Antonia was just a blank hard surface, impossible to read or turn on unless you happened to know how.

She told this to Dom one night, who laughed.

'Yeah,' he said, 'but Agas go out when you least expect them to, and with no explanation, and then need coaxing back into life, and in the meantime the whole kitchen is thrown into disarray, with soot and dust sheets and bloody men with rods sucking air in through their teeth and shaking their heads and no one can get anything done. And then you get a whopping great bill for servicing and parts.'

Antonia nodded. Yep. She was an induction hob. Steady and reliable. No drama.

By mid-afternoon she had signed up to do a charity bike ride along the Great Wall of China.

It ticked lots of boxes. It would be an adventure. It would get her super-fit. And she'd be raising money for a good cause. She didn't much care what the cause was – she had no personal experience of any disease; there wasn't one particularly close to her heart – but anything that focused on scientific research appealed to her.

The ride was advertised as tough, which was good, and she could reward herself with the promise of a trip to a panda sanctuary. She would buy a bike in the meantime, to console herself. Maybe she would go and buy one this very afternoon. She could start her training right away.

Then she looked in the mirror and thought *Seriously? A charity bike ride? How worthy and dull can you get?*

She sighed. She was reverting to type yet again.

She jumped as her phone rang.

'I'm nearly home,' Dom told her. 'I'm at the service station. Is it urgent? What's the matter?'

He sounded worried. She placated him.

'I need to see you first thing, that's all. About a couple of things.' No need to tell him it was personal. She didn't want to ruin the rest of his weekend.

She asked how Willow had got on. She wasn't one of those needy mistresses who pretended their lover didn't have a wife and children. She took an interest in them. They were part of him. Maybe she shouldn't. Maybe that was where she had gone wrong. She'd crossed a line by being too invested in his daily life.

He'd rung off, quickly, after they agreed to meet at Wellington Buildings. She had keys. They always met on the top floor as they could hear if anyone came into the building and it took ages to climb up all the stairs and gave them time to get their clothes on.

'I'm not this sort of person,' he had said, the first time.

'Neither am I,' she agreed.

That's what made it so irresistible, that it was so unexpected. So unlike either of them. He told her he'd never looked at another woman during his marriage and she believed him. Although she found it hard to fathom that it was she who had tempted him. She had never felt like a temptress. She had never so much as kissed someone she shouldn't.

Her eyes filled with tears at the memory as she realised she wasn't going to feel his hands on her ever again. Not even tomorrow. Tomorrow she would deliver her pre-prepared speech and leave, before he had time to protest or dissuade her.

She thought about going to the swimming pool and doing her hundred lengths. She knew it would distract her, because her mind always focused on making sure her strokes and her kicks were as perfect as they could be.

Before she could find her swimming things her phone rang. Dom again. Was he going to cancel on her?

'Are you busy?' He sounded strained.

'No. What's the matter?'

'Can you come and pick me up?'

'Where are you?'

'I'm still at Gloucester Services.'

'Have you broken down?'

'Not exactly.'

'It's going to take me an hour to get to you.'

'Just be as quick as you can. I'm on the southbound.'

'Dom – what's happened?'

'I'll explain when you get here.'

Antonia grabbed her keys and headed out of the door, not even stopping to put on make-up. She was still wearing her Sunday-morning lounge pants. She had a feeling this was a crisis and what she had on wasn't going to be of any import.

Dom was pacing up and down outside the entrance, looking like a man who didn't want to be seen yet who needed to make himself reasonably obvious. Antonia pipped her horn and he hurried towards her.

When he opened the car door, there was a look on his face she hadn't seen before. He looked shattered. Not as in tired, but as in broken into a million tiny pieces. Her first thought was that something had happened to Willow. But if it had, he wouldn't be here with her. He'd be with Laura.

Her second thought was that what she'd been planning to say to him the next day was probably superfluous. Something had happened to supersede it.

88

'Laura knows,' he said, confirming her suspicion.

Antonia rapidly processed all the possible outcomes of this announcement with her solicitor's brain: practical, financial, emotional. Dom slid into the passenger seat next to her, running his hands through his hair in a filmic gesture of despair. She smelled the rank scent of panic underneath his Diptyque aftershave. The two didn't go.

'*How* does she know?' she asked. Which part of their watertight regime had a chink in it? A nosy neighbour? An eagle-eyed builder?

'Some girl overheard me talking to you while I was in the service station. She told Laura. Repeated our conversation. Well, my side of it.' He looked despairing. 'She had some sort of feminist idea that telling Laura was sisterly solidarity.'

'You've got to be kidding.' Antonia was horrified. Not least because she was mortified for Laura. What an undignified way of finding out: at a motorway service station, over cappuccino and cupcakes. 'But what did you say that was so incriminating?'

'It wasn't that so much. It was the texting afterwards. It was Laura who texted, not me. You sent back four kisses.'

Antonia groaned. Four kisses. Solicitors didn't send kisses to their clients, even in this world of disingenuous x-ing. It had been automatic – she had suspected her single kisses were rather bloodless, so had saved four kisses as her predictive text rather than keep having to remind herself to show her affection.

Instinctively she started to think about damage limitation. Not for her – she was brave enough to face the music – but for Dom. His marriage was far more important than she was. There was much more at stake.

They didn't speak much as they sped back down the motorway towards Bath, then turned off and drove along the A-road, meandering down through the green hills towards the city, the pale-gold buildings laid out like a toy town below them.

'Am I dropping you home?'

'I can't go home!'

'Where, then?'

'I thought I could come to you?'

'Is that a good idea? Shouldn't you go somewhere else?'

Dom shook his head. There was a faint sheen of sweat on his forehead. The late-afternoon sun was making the car warm, but the sweat was a result of panic.

'Everyone loves Laura. I won't be welcome anywhere. I'll be a . . .' He searched around for the word.

'Pariah?' suggested Antonia.

'Outcast. I'll be an outcast.'

'Well, Travelodge then. Isn't that what Travelodges are for? Men who've been kicked out of home?'

He looked sideways at her. 'That's a bit harsh.'

'I'm sorry. I don't mean to be.'

She knew she was terse when she was stressed.

They were coming into the outskirts of Bath. The Sunday-night traffic was building up. They queued along the London road, the square terraced buildings ranked either side of them. Antonia felt as if they were folding their arms, observing them with disapproval.

She sighed. How had this happened? She was furious with herself for not coming to her senses sooner. She would have made it a clean break. She would have been ruthless, for both their benefits. Her ability to compartmentalise was very male. She supposed it came from years of not feeling as if she mattered. Of causing as little trouble as possible.

Dom was looking at her beseechingly, like a little boy pleading not to be told off. She couldn't just cast him out. She was, after all, complicit.

'Laura won't be happy if she thinks you're staying with me, though? I mean, that really does make you look guilty.'

'I won't tell her.'

Antonia raised her eyebrows. He wasn't that naive, surely?

'Women know these things, Dom.'

'But I can't afford a hotel. Not at the moment. Every penny I've got is in that wretched building. It's bleeding me dry. Even the bloody doorknobs are nearly a hundred quid each. I need all the spare cash I've got.' He looked desperate. 'I couldn't even really afford that hotel last night.'

Antonia inched the car forward as the lights up ahead turned green. How was she going to rescue the situation? Obviously the most important thing was for Laura not to be hurt any more than she needed to be, and if she found out Dom was shacked up with Antonia she would be mortified. But he had to sleep somewhere.

'You can stay with me tonight,' she told him. 'But you'll have to find somewhere else.'

'I suppose it's not your problem.' His voice was tight with agitation.

'Dom, of course it's my problem. I'm not turning my back on you. But we're occasional lovers. No more than that. I don't want Laura to think this is any bigger than it is.' She didn't want Dom to think it was any more than it was, either. She couldn't tell him the depth of her feelings. 'And staying with me makes you look culpable...'

'Don't talk to me like a solicitor.'

'But that's what I am. I'm being objective. Not emotional. You must have a friend with a spare room? Or you'll have to sleep at Wellington Buildings.'

'I can't sleep in a building site. The showers and loos aren't plumbed in yet. I'm not using the bloody Portaloo. And what will the builders say?' Dom gave a groan. 'I hope that girl's happy. Does she realise what she's done?'

'You can't blame her. What we were doing was wrong. You know that. I know that.' She paused. 'The terrible irony is I was about to tell you I couldn't do it any more. That's why I phoned. That's why I wanted to see you tomorrow.'

'Really?'

She nodded. 'I should have done it last week.'

Dom's face was craggy with misery. 'Every time I left you I used to tell myself it was the last time.'

'Same here.' Antonia put her foot down, going through the lights just as they turned to red behind her, then cut down along her favourite road, with its bohemian bars and antique shops and boutiques that made you want to buy everything in them. She wished she could be more like Walcot Street, with its relaxed and confident style.

She hit the centre of town then negotiated a few side streets before coming to a halt in a small cobbled square, outside an antiquarian bookshop. The old-fashioned lamp posts were just coming on as dusk approached. It was quiet and still in the cold of late afternoon and there was no one around.

'Get out here. We can't be seen together outside my flat. Head over to mine in ten minutes and I'll let you in.'

Dom looked at her in admiration. 'You'd have made a great spy.'

She gave a wry smile and pretended to lift up her collar. 'There's probably still time.'

He leaned over to kiss her but she jerked her head away. 'No kissing! For heaven's sake. This is it, Dom. There's no more between us.'

'Of course. Sorry.'

He got out and slammed the door. She watched him in the rear-view mirror as she drove off. He was standing on the pavement looking utterly lost. She knew deep down that what she should do is cut him off now, for his own sake.

If he'd been a bastard, she'd have given him the chop and let him sort himself out. But he was a good man. Yes, what they'd been doing was wrong, but despite everything he belonged with Laura. Of that she was certain. And she knew Dom didn't have the guile to save his own marriage. He was going to need her help.

Twenty minutes later, she let him into her flat. He was pale and shaken.

Antonia moved towards the kitchen. 'Coffee? Tea? Wine?'

'Strychnine.'

He walked over to her sofa and slumped into it with a deep groan, tipping his head back with his eyes closed, his arms and legs out like a starfish.

She looked at him. The warmth and solidity of him made her want to cry; to hug him. The broad shoulders, the strong arms, the stomach kept flat because he was hands-on at work, lifting and carrying and shifting sand and rubble and bricks, up and down stairs all day long.

The thighs like iron. His sleepy smile. His kind eyes. The lock of brown hair that fell over his eyes when he was on top of her – he would try to blow it away, then laugh. She put a Kirby grip in it once. They'd both laughed at that.

Yes. She loved him. But she was going to lose him. She knew that. She had to make things right. She had to mend his marriage. The wonderful, warm, chaotic marriage that she was so deeply envious of, because she knew she would never have one like it.

She knew enough about it. They'd been working together for three years now, ever since his conveyancing file had been handed to her when he was selling a small barn conversion out near Box. The purchasers had dropped their offer by fifty thousand on the day of exchange. He was anxious for the deal to go through because he was buying another property to renovate.

'Hold your nerve,' said Antonia. 'They'll pay the full price. It's a beautiful conversion in a stunning location. They won't find somewhere else like this in a hurry.'

'But I can't cope with the stress.' Willow was in hospital again. Laura was sleeping next to her in an armchair. He didn't want to compound the situation by being distracted by the deal. So what if he lost fifty grand? He'd make it back somewhere down the line. 'I don't care about the money.'

'OK. I'll tell them.'

Antonia, however, did care about the money. She wanted the person who deserved it to have it, not the greedy buyers who were trying it on and taking advantage of the fact they were right up against the wire. So she had taken a huge professional risk. She'd gone back to the purchasers and said *asking price or no deal*. As the clock ticked by, she felt more and more calm. She was going to get the money for Dom if it killed her.

At midday their solicitor phoned. 'Split the difference.'

'Which part of full agreed asking price don't you understand?' Antonia replied, not missing a beat.

By three o'clock that afternoon the exchange took place for the original amount. When Antonia called Dom to tell him the money had gone through, he was amazed.

'Why did they do that? When I'd agreed to drop? What did you do?' asked Dom, suspicious.

'Just my job.'

He had sent her a huge bunch of flowers to thank her.

She handled all of his sales and purchases from then on.

When he was about to buy Wellington Buildings, he asked her to come and look at it, to flag up anything she saw as a potential conveyancing issue. They had spent three hours together on site as she listened to his vision of the building. She was smart and eagle-eyed. Hundreds of deals went through her hands. She kept up to speed on every sale, every planning application. She knew all the surveyors, architects, planning officers and every estate agent.

'I'd make it three apartments, not four,' she told him. 'As high a spec as you can make them. So each one has the sense of being a proper house, rather than just a slice of a house. If you're buying in a prestige building in Bath, you want grandeur.'

'But I'll make more money on four.'

She shook her head. 'No you won't. Look. You can get much more exponentially for each apartment if they're big. A higher price per square metre.'

She did the maths in the dust on an old table. He looked at her in awe.

'You're in the wrong job.'

'Maybe. I've thought about it more than once. But I don't have the capital to go into property development yet. I need my salary to pay my mortgage.'

He looked at her thoughtfully. 'You think out of the box, though. That's smart.'

'I can assure you I don't. I think into the balance sheet.' Antonia laughed. 'I get an inside view of so many property deals. It's mostly common sense. And spotting trends and patterns. What people want from their property and how they like to spend their money.'

'Well, I value your advice hugely. It's good to have someone to talk it through with. I hate worrying Laura. She has enough on her plate with Willow. And you know what the property business is like in Bath – everyone's after the golden project. If I talk about things, I worry people will go behind my back.'

'I've seen that happen more than once. It's ruthless.'

'Yes, and sadly I'm not.' Dom made a self-deprecating face. 'I don't know how I've survived.'

'Sometimes being sharky can backfire. Slow and steady wins the race.' She gave him a mock punch to the arm and he jumped back in alarm.

'Sorry,' she said, but their gazes locked. She cleared her throat, wanting to step away from him, scared of the way the atmosphere had changed. But he had reached out and taken each of her hands in his, and instead of stepping away, she had stepped closer.

That had been the first time, and it was history now.

8

Number 11 Lark Hill was tall, slender and elegant, in Bath stone the colour of crumbly, sugary fudge, with deep sash windows that glowed pewter in the lamplight. On the first floor two sets of French doors led out from the drawing room onto a delicate wrought-iron balcony with a leaded roof. Above that were the shuttered windows of the master bedroom. Above those, the tiny attic windows of what must have been the servants' bedrooms. Laura always imagined a Frances Hodgson Burnett heroine peering out onto new arrivals. It was a house of stories. Some of which she knew; one of which was yet to unfold.

An ethereal late-afternoon mist had fallen as Laura opened the gate to the front garden. The house loomed through the silver wisps, looking down at her sternly. She shivered, her hands shaking as she wrestled with the latch. It had never seemed forbidding before, but she could sense disapproval, which felt odd, as she was hardly the transgressor.

Though perhaps, on second thoughts, the house was empathising, but didn't know how to express itself. It often happened, when you went away somewhere. That your home felt different when you got back. Because wherever you had been, you had come back a slightly different person. And it had to adjust to your new aura. You had to get to know each other again.

And she was entirely different from the person who had left the morning before. Then, she had been squaring her shoulders in an effort to be brave. Now, she thought she was probably in shock. She felt sick and shaky. All she wanted was to get inside and hide away. It had taken all her efforts not to fall apart on the drive back, but as soon as she saw the familiarity of home, the impact of what had happened started to close in.

She stumbled slightly over the pale chippings that led between the low box hedges, planted in neat squares. Inside them were drifts of eryngium and alliums, now past their best since the tail end of summer had passed. They had kept the long, narrow front garden simple and formal, to save mowing. Her favourite thing of all was the twisted wisteria that insinuated its way up the wall by the porch. The heavy purple blooms were splendid in early summer, with a narcotic scent. Now, she could smell the peaty sharpness of dying leaves. It wasn't unpleasant, just a reminder that the nights were drawing in and the temperature was dropping, for as soon as the sun vanished from the sky any heat it had provided dissipated straight away.

She fumbled for her keys and unlocked the front door. As she stepped into the house, a chill settled on her shoulders. Almost a reproach, as if the house knew she was the bearer of bad tidings and was reluctant to let her over the threshold. It was that gloomy time of day when the light starts to fade and everything looks dreary and grey.

The hall echoed with emptiness, the rattle of her keys

sounding unnaturally loud. She had been in such a hurry to get everyone on the road yesterday that she hadn't noticed the evidence of the girls' absence. More than half of their paraphernalia had gone: Converse, Nikes, Hunters, Uggs, Crocs, Havaianas had all been cleared from the floor. Coats and hoodies and beanies and scarves were missing from hooks that hadn't seen the light of day for years. Once Laura had fought for hanging space – now there were several hooks to choose from. She saw Dom's wax coat, the one he wore to work.

On impulse, she went to search through the pockets. She would never have done that before today. She found a tape measure, the stub of a yellow pencil, a half-eaten pack of Polo mints . . . She almost laughed at herself. What had she been expecting? A lacy handkerchief with an initial in the corner? Scanty knickers? A lipstick? Condoms? People didn't carry evidence around with them. They just didn't.

A lawyer. His lawyer. What did a lawyer have that she didn't?

Brains, she supposed. Money? Power? Influence? Inside knowledge? Lots of things Laura certainly didn't have. She imagined a tall, forbidding creature in a tailored suit and black stilettos, with glasses and red lipstick. Predatory. Although that wasn't really Dom's type.

Or was it? She had no idea about him any more.

She took her coat off and hung it up. There was no noise in the house at all, and it added to her disquiet. She longed to hear a voice or footsteps on the stairs or a door bang. She put her face in her hands and stifled a sob. It was too much. The awfulness was too much.

She went into the kitchen. There was an unfamiliar chill. She frowned. The kitchen was never cold. She put a hand on the Aga and realised it had gone out, a trick it played every now and again. It had been in the house for generations and was very demanding and capricious. She would have to phone Sam Budge. He and his dad before him had looked after it for years, lovingly servicing it to keep it alive despite its grand old age. It had been Sam who'd suggested re-enamelling it in bright pink and she had clapped with delight when she had seen his handiwork.

It seemed symbolic, somehow, that the beating heart of her home had gone out just when she needed it the most. She shivered. What was she supposed to do now? She felt a surge of anger towards the girl at the service station. Did she know what she had done to Laura's life?

Yet would she have preferred to carry on living in blissful ignorance? To unknowingly live a lie? Was this affair just a phase or was it the tip of an iceberg? The beginning of the end of her marriage? She didn't want to know, any of it. She sat down at the table and put her head in her hands. It was throbbing, and she couldn't marshal her thoughts. She still wasn't sure if she was dreaming. Perhaps in a moment she would wake up in the hotel bed and the day would start properly, with a different story.

She stood and went to the other end of the kitchen, and looked out at the back garden. She could see the glowing orange lights coming from the little house they'd built for Kanga. Acorn Cottage was tiny, as they had only been able to get planning permission for just under a thousand square feet on the corner of the orchard, but Kanga had insisted, when she'd handed the main house over to Laura and Dom, that it was big enough. Lots of her things were still in the attic or the basement. Kanga thought she had cleared everything out, but there were masses of her things left. Laura didn't mind being the custodian. It was a small price to pay for being given the house of her dreams. The only house she had known since she was four, when her own mother had died and she'd come to live here with her grandparents. They'd been so wonderful, and Kanga still was. She was gracious and generous and always so dignified.

Her stomach curdled at the thought of Kanga knowing what had happened. She couldn't even begin to imagine telling her that Dom had been unfaithful. That he was having an affair. Had she been a complete fool not to notice? And to think that on the drive home she'd thought that there was an adventure for her around the corner. Had he been laughing at her? Hoping she'd find something to fill her time so he could carry on carrying on behind her back?

Instead, she was left with nothing. On Friday night this kitchen had contained everything she wanted. Friends and family; music and laughter. Now it was echoing with emptiness. It had been the last time her life had been perfect and she hadn't realised. It would never be the same again.

Despair swirled up inside her, dark and overwhelming. And underlying the despair was fear. Fear of the future, but also fear of finding out what had been wrong with the past. What if the past wasn't what she'd thought it was? Had Dom been unhappy? If so, why on earth hadn't he said?

She picked up a mug from the dresser. She was going to make a cup of tea. Tea: that was normal, wasn't it? That would make her feel safe and secure. She gazed down at the mug in her hand, pink and pretty and as perfect as the life she thought they'd had. Suddenly rage replaced the despair. She drew her arm back and threw the mug at the wall. The smash made her jump: it was louder than she thought it would be. And the fragments of china flew everywhere.

She picked up another and threw it. Then another. Until every single mug on the dresser was lying on the floor. Not even the most dedicated archaeologist could piece them back together.

She never knew she had so much rage inside her. She'd never thrown anything like that in her life before. She wasn't sure if it made her feel better or worse. Either way, it had made a terrible mess. Her former instinct would have been to get down on her knees straight away and clear it up. She'd had a lifetime of clearing things up and making things better again.

Then she looked at all the shattered fragments and thought: this is my life. Everything has been smashed into tiny pieces. Her face crumpled as all the events of the weekend swirled around: the image of Magic Rabbit on Willow's pillow, the face of the girl at the service station, the fridge in the student kitchen with the Tupperware boxes she had so lovingly filled for her daughter, the incriminating text with its treacherous kisses...

The charm bracelet that had touched her so deeply. The charm bracelet that had clearly been bought out of guilt, not love.

She couldn't bear it. No amount of controlled breathing could keep her feelings at bay. She sank into a chair at the kitchen table, put her head in her arms and let out a low, keening wail of despair.

'Laura?' Kanga appeared in the doorway. 'Oh, my darling.' Kanga moved towards her. 'Of course you're upset. It's been such a strain, and I know how much you've been dreading Willow going . . . It's horrid. I know.'

She slid her arm round Laura's shoulders. Laura tried to pull herself together, but now she'd started it was impossible.

'It's not Willow,' she sobbed.

'What's happened?'

Laura couldn't say it. It was sordid and terrifying and totally bloody unfair and she couldn't bear the thought of her grandmother knowing.

She composed herself while she thought about what to say. She wiped away her tears with the heel of her hand.

'Dom's been . . .' She had to choose her words carefully. Nothing too crude for Kanga. 'I don't know what to call it. Having an affair? With his solicitor.'

'His solicitor?' Kanga looked startled, as if this was the shocking part of the revelation. 'James Kettle?' James was the family lawyer.

Laura managed a strangled laugh.

'No. Not James. Someone else from the practice. His conveyancing solicitor. She's a girl. Woman. Female. Antonia.' Laura spat out the name like a mouldy cherry.

'Are you absolutely sure? That doesn't seem like Dom.'

'Oh yes. They were texting each other. Arranging to meet.'

'But that doesn't mean anything, does it? Perhaps it was business?'

'She sent him four kisses.' Laura gave Kanga a look to cement how much that signified. She held up four fingers. 'Four!'

'That's hardly *in flagrante*, darling. Are you sure you're not jumping to conclusions?'

'His face said everything.' Laura covered her own with her hands. 'He as good as admitted it. He certainly didn't deny it.' She could see Dom's expression now. Horrified guilt. He had never been any good at poker. She was surprised he'd managed to keep it quiet this long.

'It just doesn't seem like Dom. There must be an explanation.' Kanga shivered. 'It's freezing in here. Has the Aga gone out?'

Laura sighed. 'It's a portent.'

'No, it's not.' Kanga had her no-nonsense voice on. 'The wicks need replacing, that's all. Now come on.' She held out her hand to help Laura up. 'You need to clear all this mess up, then find Dom and get him to come home so you can talk to him.'

'Talk to him?' Laura shook her head. 'Oh no. I'm not talking to him. I've got nothing to say. There's nothing I want to hear.' She shook her head again. 'I can't face him, Kanga. I just can't.'

'Well, then you must go to bed. You've had a long and tiring weekend. If you're tired, everything will seem worse.'

Kanga found the electric kettle in the larder, made Laura a cup of tea and sent her up to bed.

As Kanga swept up the last of the china she looked around the kitchen, the scene of such a warm and happy family occasion only two nights before.

Oh, Dom, she thought sadly. *You absolute fool.*

She hadn't mentioned Ivy's fall to Laura. There was no point in adding to her worry. She had stayed at the hospital with Beverley until about three yesterday morning, and they'd met at the hospital again that afternoon, while Ivy had her hip operated on.

Ivy had come round after the operation, but had been very confused. The nurse had told them not to worry: she was bound to be fuddled, a combination of shock and the anaesthetic and the painkillers, and they still couldn't be sure how hard she had hit her head, although a scan had shown no sign of injury. Ivy needed to sleep.

Kanga cursed herself for not intervening sooner, for not insisting that Ivy should get some help at home. She phoned her regularly and they met up once every couple of months for lunch. The last time she'd seen her Ivy had been done up to the nines and full of verve, so it had been easy for Kanga to reassure herself that her friend was back on form.

But hindsight, as ever, was a wonderful thing. And they were of that generation that put up and shut up. They were stoic. They were copers. They didn't ask for help.

They had, after all, been through more than most people in their lifetime.

9

1942

Jilly slept and slept: a deep and dreamless sleep that took her right down. When she woke she was puzzled. Something didn't feel right. The clock told her it was early afternoon. Ivy was sitting on the bed looking at her. She seemed strangely subdued. Usually Ivy would be dancing around the place, making a plan, luring her into something she probably wouldn't want to do.

Then the memory hit her hard in the chest.

'There's been people calling all morning, to pay their respects,' Ivy told her. 'I've sent them all away.'

Jilly nodded.

'Come on. You've been in bed long enough. Get up and get dressed.' Ivy pulled back the covers. 'We're going into town. See if we can help.'

'Help?'

'It's what your mum and dad would be doing, isn't it? No point in lolling about in bed.'

Ivy looked at her, defiant, but Jilly could see her fists were bunched and she was trembling with emotion, trying to hold in her feelings. She was right, though. Her mother and father would have been first on the scene, not giving a thought for their own safety.

'You're right,' she said. 'They would.'

She pulled on her clothes and looked for her shoes. She remembered: scrambling up the hill like diddle-diddle-dumpling before discarding the remaining shoe. She searched for another pair more suited to a rescue mission than a night-time rendezvous.

For a fleeting second she wondered about Harry Swann. Where had he gone, in the midst of the bombing? Had he stayed in the bandstand until it was over? A memory of his silver body, lean and perfect, flashed into her mind. But now was not the time to think of Harry Swann and what he had done to her. Or what she had done to him.

In the kitchen, Ivy scraped a thin swipe of margarine over some bread, topped with raspberry jam.

'You need to eat,' she told Jilly.

'I'm not hungry.' Jilly shook her head. Her stomach was too full of feelings to accommodate food.

'An army marches on its stomach.' Ivy forced the bread into her hand. Jilly nibbled at it, swallowing it down. Perhaps Ivy was right. She did feel a little stronger: like the cocoa earlier, the sweetness of the jam lifted her spirits.

'It hasn't been on the news properly,' Ivy told her. She had ventured out to talk to the neighbours. 'In case the Germans hear and start getting all cocky. But the word is there's hundreds dead and half of Bath flattened.'

'I still can't believe it,' said Jilly. 'But you're right. We must go and help.' She stood up. 'Let's face it, the worst has already happened. And there's people out there who need us.'

It should have been a glorious spring day, a day to lift your heart and listen to the birds sing. But as Ivy and Jilly walked down the hill, their arms linked for comfort, the truth of what had happened the night before dragged their hearts down into their boots.

There was no rhyme or reason to the devastation. A terrace of houses would stand true but for one house razed to the ground in their midst. The air was acrid with burning and thick with ochre brick dust mixed with soot. Everyone was subdued but determined. Determined to restore order. Yet underlying that determination was the fear the Germans would return the next night and wreak yet more havoc. There was no way of knowing whether they would or they wouldn't. It was a game. A game of cat and mouse.

There were people everywhere, but there was a kind of grace to the activity, a sense of purpose. There was a hierarchy of helpers, from firemen putting out blazes, their long ladders perched four storeys up, down to messenger boys who flew through the streets on their bicycles, puffed up with pride at the import of relaying vital information. People who had lost their homes had teams of neighbours helping them to retrieve what they could from the wreckage. Everyone they spoke to had a story to tell: of a narrow escape – or no escape. The bombs did not discriminate, it seemed. The homes of the rich took as many hits as the homes of the poor, from the gracious curves of the crescents to the Georgian slums piled up by the town centre.

They walked on further into the centre of the town. Cats coiled themselves among the debris on an eternal hunt for mice and rats. Houses stood with their fronts peeled away: there were walls inside with the pictures still hanging on them; a mantelpiece with a clock still telling the right time. A piano stood on the pavement, saved from the wreckage but with nowhere to go. Ivy ran her fingers up and down the keys, plink-plonking an unidentifiable tune.

'Don't!' said Jilly, feeling it was disrespectful.

Ivy nodded to the ruined house it must have come from. 'They won't have any need for it now.'

Jilly pulled her on.

They went into a church hall that had been commandeered as a rest centre. Volunteers were pumping endless cups of tea from urns, sustaining the dazed and the injured while they waited for guidance. It felt surprisingly calm and ordered, with just the occasional crying child indicating something was amiss. It was as if no one wanted the Germans to know the chaos they had caused.

'We're here to help,' Ivy told a woman with a clipboard who seemed to be in charge.

'Are you any good at administration?' She looked at them both.

'Not me,' said Ivy. 'I'm a hairdresser. But I'm not afraid of blood.'

'I am. I work for my father. He's a doctor.' Jilly stepped forward, then realised she should have said *was*. *Was* a doctor.

'Excellent. We need people to help co-ordinate accommodation. We've got hundreds of people without a place to stay. We need you to take names and details; size of family; where they would like to be billeted. Not that there's much choice.' She looked at Ivy. 'You can help in the kitchen. They're sending soup over from Bristol, but it will need heating up again.'

Jilly watched Ivy in admiration as she went about her task. She seemed undaunted by the situation. It was almost as if she was handing out teas at the village fete.

Her chirpy, cheery attitude put a smile on people's faces even amidst the loss. Ivy was truly kind, thought Jilly, even though she was as tough as boots and took some getting used to. She supposed working as a hairdresser taught you how to talk to people, and Ivy always said the stories her customers told her were beyond belief.

'Honestly – it would make your hair curl! Sometimes I think I don't need perming lotion.'

Jilly busied herself with taking names and addresses, murmuring her commiserations when talking to people who had lost someone. The only advantage was she didn't have a moment to think of her own loss. All that spurred her on was the thought that her parents would want her to be doing this. She wondered how many of these people were her father's patients. She recognised a few of them, but didn't tell them the sad news. She hadn't yet spoken of it to anyone. And there were people who were worse off than she was. People who had lost their homes as well as loved ones. People who had lost children.

Cars, trucks and wagons arrived to drive people off to their temporary accommodation. Gradually the queues subsided and as dusk approached the city became quieter. There was a palpable tension.

Would the bombers come back?

Bath was as vulnerable as a newborn baby, with no anti-aircraft to defend her. But what could anyone do? They just had to sit tight.

As dusk approached, Ivy and Jilly left the church hall to make their way home. Never had Lansdown Hill seemed so steep. It was always a tough climb; although Jilly had done it every day on her way home from school, it still made her calves scream. But today it seemed interminable. They barely spoke, just put their heads down and walked on. The impact of the night before and everything they had seen that day was sinking in.

Jilly both longed for and dreaded going home. It was where she wanted to be: in the kitchen, chewing on a piece of bread and dripping and making up a hot-water bottle. But the empty chairs at the table, the absence of her father's pipe smoke, without her mother turning up the wireless because she was deaf in one ear after her brother shoved a dried pea in it when she was small ... how was she going to bear it? She looked sideways at Ivy, whose painted eyebrows were drawn in towards each other in a scowl of fury.

'What is it?' Jilly asked, though her question seemed superfluous.

'Everything,' Ivy replied. 'It's everything and I feel as if there's nothing I can do. I wish I had a Spitfire. I'd fly it over the sea and drop a bomb on Hitler while he's having his dinner.' Her little fists were clenched as if she was holding the controls. Jilly wanted to laugh. Ivy would be a fierce and deadly fighter pilot, she was sure of that.

And for a moment, yet again, she had a flickering image of a boy – no, a man – wrapped in sheepskin, auburn hair flying back in the wind, his face intent on his mission, his determination to defend his country ...

He was gone, she reminded herself. Harry Swann had never happened to her. He wasn't going to swoop in like a hero and gather her up in his arms. He wouldn't come to find her because he didn't know her name or where she lived – they hadn't talked about that kind of detail.

Harry Swann had been a mirage. That was all.

Jilly rushed out to feed the hens when they got home, before the light went. They were still there, roosting in their little wooden house, just half a dozen of them, but they'd laid a few eggs, despite the horrors of the night before. Hens didn't understand war, it seemed. Jilly gave them some feed, shut them away safe from the fox, then brought the eggs in, putting them gently in the basket on the dresser, a little reminder that life went on. Then she went back out to feed Mungo.

Mungo had been given to her father by a patient as a thank you for lancing a tricky boil. The farmer had assured him that when the time came he would do the necessary and they would never want for bacon or sausages or pork chops. But Mungo turned out to be something of an extravagance: pig feed was expensive and scarce (the ships that feed came in on were given over to munitions), and the current fashion for kitchen economy meant there were few leftover scraps to be boiled up for his consumption. Jilly suspected that it had suited the farmer to get rid of him in a gesture disguised as generosity. Since then Mungo had gone from a potential food source to a much-loved pet whose good nature melted everyone's heart. He was good at listening, Mungo. Half an hour spent chatting to him in the sunshine, scratching his back with a stick, could restore anyone's spirits.

Mungo lay half in and half out of the brick piggery that had been built to celebrate his arrival. It was tucked away at the very end of the garden, so his piggy smell wouldn't waft up and bother the neighbours. Being at the end of Lark Hill, the plot at Number 11 was the biggest and the longest, and her parents had done their best to turn it into a small market garden worthy of a country estate in an attempt to be almost self-sufficient. Jilly had watched her father dig up his beloved dahlias and rose bushes and throw them on the compost heap, to make room for rows of carrots and cabbages and potatoes.

'Oh, Mungo,' she said. He stared at her with wise eyes through ginger lashes and gave a gentle knowing grunt, and in that moment she knew he would never adorn her plate, no matter how tight things got. He was an expensive luxury, but somehow he embodied the spirit of her father, and because of that he had earned his reprieve.

That evening, the two girls made their way up to bed early, exhausted and grubby.

The city was on high alert after last night's raids, but there was no point in sitting and waiting for the next one. They'd hear the warning soon enough, and in the meantime it was important to try and get some sleep. They didn't get undressed, in case they had to get up. It was almost inevitable that they would. The Germans would have got the layout of the city from their mission the night before and have a better idea of what targets to hit. The railway, perhaps. Or the Abbey, one of the grander crescents or the Circus. No one could be sure if they would go for the useful bits or the pretty bits. Jilly imagined a room full of Nazi officers poring over a map. She shuddered as she pictured a nicotine-stained finger prodding at potential targets. They were ruthless but, of course, so had Britain been. War was dirty. War was about doing the unexpected and taking people by surprise; a battle of wits and nerves.

Bath was prepared tonight. Hundreds of people had

left the city already, begging a bed with friends or family in the countryside or even further afield, not willing to take the risk. Everyone else stood their ground.

'We can't all be cowards,' said Ivy. 'That's what they want, everyone running around like headless chickens. I'm not afraid. Balls to Hitler, I say. He's not going to win. He thinks he will, but he won't. I'll tell him if he wants.'

Despite her mood, Jilly couldn't help laughing at the thought of the Führer confronted by Ivy. She knew who she'd put money on.

'I might as well sleep with you,' said Ivy as they brushed their teeth and combed the dust out of their hair in the bathroom. 'I don't like to think of you on your own. But I'll have no snivelling and no snoring.'

Jilly didn't like to protest that she would rather be on her own. She had a feeling that Ivy would probably wriggle in her sleep, with all that restless energy. But she knew she was being kind, and it didn't have to be for ever, so she didn't shun her offer.

And when she started drifting off to sleep and the tears started to come, she was grateful for the warm little hand that patted her, and Ivy's comforting whispers.

10

Laura had lain awake until five after Kanga sent her
to bed, replaying yesterday's horrible events, then had
fallen into a deep sleep until she woke with a burning in
her stomach – a nauseating slurry of panic and sadness
and bewilderment and, oddly, shame. Why did she feel
shame when she'd done nothing wrong?

The bed was cold and empty. She remembered a song
from her youth, 'The Bed's Too Big Without You'. She
lay there with the lyrics going round and round in her
head, realising that she had never slept in this bed without
Dom, never woken up without his solid warmth beside
her. The only time they'd slept apart since they'd got married was when Laura slept at the hospital.

She wondered where Dom had slept last night, then
thought she didn't want to know. Was he snuggled up
gleefully with his brief? Telling her it was all going to
work out in the end, that Laura would survive...

Her phone pinged. It made her heart jump. Was it
Dom? Willow? She grabbed it.

Sadie: So how did it go yesterday with Willow? All
settled in?

She texted back.

Laura: It was fine. Until I found out Dom's been
screwing his solicitor.
Sadie: WTF? Actually really?
Laura: Yep.
Sadie: OMG. I'll be with you in ten.

Laura knew she could share her revelation with Sadie and it would stay with her. They had been best friends since they had sat together in the back of the Maths class at school. Sadie would bring in fashion magazines and they'd leaf through *Vogue* and *Harpers and Queen*, sighing over the couture dresses and ignoring their quadratic equations. Laura had always been convinced Sadie would jet off to Paris or London as soon as her exams were done with, but to her surprise she had stayed in Bath, starting out selling velvet scarves and diamanté earrings on a market stall. Despite their different lifestyles, they were firm friends and shared all their secrets. Laura had spent many an evening mopping up Sadie's tears after a relationship disaster.

It would be strange for the boot to be on the other foot.

Quarter of an hour later, Laura opened the front door, still in her pyjamas, her hair tangled, her feet bare. Sadie swept in with the fresh autumn air, wearing calf-length pinstriped trousers over high boots and a red polo-neck sweater, her white-blonde bob artfully messy. She threw her arms round Laura's neck, her silver bangles clanking.

'Where is he?' she hissed in a stage whisper. 'Is he here?'

'No way.' Laura shut the door and padded back into the kitchen.

'You've kicked him out?'

'Well, not kicked him out, because he wasn't here when I found out. I just left him at the service station and he didn't come back.'

'Oh my *God*. Where did he stay last night?'

'I haven't a clue.' Laura flicked on the kettle. She was trying hard not to sound as if she cared too much.

'How did you find out?'

Laura mimed her thumbs texting with a wry face.

'A text? What a cliché.'

'Actually, it wasn't just that. A girl at the service station overheard him talking to her, then told me. Repeated their entire conversation.'

Sadie winced. 'That's *terrible*! But I can't believe it. Dom? He just doesn't seem like the type.'

'I know.' Laura sat down at the table. 'I feel such an idiot.'

'Aren't you going to talk to him about it?'

'I can't face it.'

'But you have to.'

'I don't. I don't want to talk about it. I don't want to sit there and listen to his reasons and his justifications and his excuses. What can he say that will make me feel better about it? *Your arse was getting a bit big so I fancied a skinnier version*? *You're getting a bit boring and I wanted some stimulating conversation*? There's nothing he can say that will make me go *Oh, OK, I get it. No problem. Come home and let's try again.*' She looked at the dresser. 'Bugger. There's no mugs.'

'Where are they all?' Sadie looked askance at the empty hooks – there were usually at least six mugs hanging there.

Laura looked shamefaced.

'In hundreds of tiny pieces in the bin. I smashed them all last night.'

'What? Laura! What did you do that for?'

Sadie was shocked. Laura was always so placid.

Laura got up and burrowed about in one of the dresser cupboards for some spares.

'Because I was furious. Because I didn't know what else to do. Because I wanted to slice his balls off. And feed them to whatever-her-name-is.' Sadie winced as Laura banged two cups down on the work surface. 'Sorry. I'm ranting. But I think I'm allowed to rant.'

'Of course you are. I've just never seen you like this before.' It was true. Laura was always first to see both sides of the story. She was always calm and measured and quick to pour oil on troubled waters. 'So who is she?'

'Antonia Briggs. Have you heard of her?' Sadie knew everyone who was anyone in Bath, but she shook her head. 'She works at Kettle and Sons. She does Dom's conveyancing. He's known her for a while, I think.'

Sadie wrinkled her nose. 'A solicitor? She must be as dull as ditchwater.'

'Presumably not as dull as me.' Laura looked at Sadie, her eyebrows raised as she spooned fresh coffee into the pot.

'No one thinks you're dull, Laura.'

'Then *why*? What's the attraction?'

'I don't know. How long's it been going on?'

'I've got no idea.'

'Loz, you've got to talk to him. Get to the bottom of it. Maybe there's been a misunderstanding?'

'What – you mean he *accidentally* shagged her?'

'Are you sure he actually has been? Maybe they're just . . . ?' Sadie sighed, knowing she was being unrealistic.

'Just what? Sade, it was written all over his face. He looked properly guilty.' Laura poured water onto the coffee. 'It's so unfair. I'm supposed to be moving into the next phase of my life. I've got loads of great ideas for things I want to do. Things for me. And us. But I can't think about any of it.'

'I know, darling. But this is just a blip. Loads of people have blips.'

'A blip? I've put Dom and everyone else in my life first for over twenty years and he does this to me? That's not a blip. Antonia bloody Briggs is not a blip.'

Laura forced the plunger of the cafetière down. Hot coffee spilled over the edge, scalding her hand. She grabbed a tea towel and wiped off the boiling liquid and felt hot tears threaten to spill over too. She was not going to cry. She was not going to turn into the archetypal wronged wife: a blubbering mess. She was not going to be a cliché, like her husband.

The tears spilled over anyway. They had no truck with her attempts to be brave.

'Damn. I wasn't going to cry . . .' She did a half-laugh, half-sob. 'He can bugger off with his fancy-pants lawyer. I hope they'll be very happy together.'

'I'm sure that's not what he wants. You know what men are like.' Sadie pointed at her head and then her crotch. 'Brain in pants. It doesn't necessarily mean anything.'

'It means a lot to *me*. It's undermined everything I have done for this family.'

Laura was properly crying now, wiping her face with one hand and trying to pour the coffee with the other.

Sadie jumped up to hug her friend. She couldn't handle the thought of the Griffin family falling apart. They were her constant. They were *her* family. They were the one good thing she held on to when she was having a crisis or had done something she was ashamed of. They were her refuge, her comfort.

'Come on,' she said to Laura. 'Sit down and drink your coffee. Have you had breakfast?'

'No. I'm never eating again. It's because I'm fat, I expect.'

'Don't be bloody stupid. You're not fat for a start.'

'No. I know. I just want a reason, I suppose.' Laura sat down, looking utterly miserable.

'I'll make you some toast.'

'The Aga's out. You'll have to use the Dualit.'

Sadie pulled a loaf out of the bread bin and stuck two slices into the toaster. She knew the kitchen at Number 11 like the back of her hand. She'd spent more time in here than she had her own, almost.

Stupid Dom. She understood far better than Laura how it might have happened, because she was a cynic. She got all the gossip at the boutique. Plenty of wives came in to spend money when they found out their husbands were up to no good. Though it wasn't always the husbands who strayed. Sadie could spot an incipient affair in a customer a mile off: there was always a renewed confidence; a sense of daring; a frisson. And a need to buy new clothes. That was to start with. Affairs were beguiling and intoxicating, but inevitably ended in disaster. Sadie didn't judge or comment when she spotted the signs. She was there to make a living, not give marriage guidance.

She hoped that when Laura calmed down she would see sense and talk to Dom, and that Dom would have the strength and backbone to fight for his marriage. She hoped he wasn't in too deep with this Antonia. She hoped Antonia didn't have long-term designs on Dom. He was a very attractive option: successful but not arrogant, attractive but not narcissistic, fun but not irresponsible. She'd always thought him well-balanced. She felt quite sick to think of him being unfaithful to Laura. It shook her belief in what was good and right in the world.

She decided the best thing she could do was listen and be there. And make sure Laura didn't make any rash decisions.

She put the buttered toast on a plate in front of her friend.

'Darling, just stay calm and take it easy today. You've had a big weekend and you're probably still a bit up in the air about Willow going. Be kind to yourself.'

'How?' Laura looked miserable. 'All I want to do is go back to bed.'

'Have a long bath with loads of bubbles. Put on some nice clothes.' She pointed at her. 'I'm not having any skanky victim outfits. Then go for a walk. It's a gorgeous bright autumn day – the leaves look amazing...' She trailed off. 'Yeah. OK. I'll shut up.'

Laura looked deflated. 'Do you know what I usually do when things are rubbish? I cook something. But what's the point? There's no one here to eat it.'

'Laura. Don't go under. You need to stay positive and

121

calm and clear.' Sadie picked up her bag. 'I've absolutely got to go to work now. I should have opened up five minutes ago. But I'll call you later and I'll pop round when the shop shuts.'

Laura shut her eyes and nodded. Everything was closing in. Suddenly it was all too horribly real. And she didn't feel angry any more. She felt scared. And bewildered.

'I'll be fine,' she told Sadie, her voice tight. Sadie had to go to work; she didn't want to worry her. 'Thank you for being here.'

Sadie hugged her, picking up her bag and her keys.

'Call if you need me.'

Then she was gone, bangles clanking, high heels clicking over the limestone, leaving a cloud of Coco Mademoiselle and emptiness behind her.

Laura refilled her coffee cup and looked down into its depths as she chewed on her toast. How on earth was she going to face life on her own, if that was the outcome? For a start, what could she actually do? She had no CV, no experience. She hadn't had a job since she'd been a chalet maid, the winter she met Dom. Over twenty years ago now.

She remembered the first night she had met him. At a loss as to what to do with her life at the age of nineteen, with unimpressive A levels, she was spending the winter season looking after a rental chalet in the French alps in the hopes of finding direction and inspiration.

Le Chalet Rouge was perched in the middle of an Alpine village near the Trois Vallées, and she had immediately felt at home there. It was a traditional wooden house, decked out in cheery red tartan with cosy rugs and wood-burning stoves, comfortable rather than luxurious.

Her job was to provide a substantial breakfast, a restorative tea and a three-course dinner, make the beds and keep the place tidy. It suited her down to the ground. The fresh air and the beauty of the location, all-day cooking and the occasional chance to ski, as well as a lot of jolly socialising on her night out with the other seasonaires: sometimes she thought that perhaps this would do as a career. She loved nothing better than to look after people and fill them up with heart-warming, rib-sticking fare. Her toffee-apple cake was legendary.

Dom and his mates arrived on a crystalline February afternoon, full of bonhomie and Becks. The ten of them had been on the rugby team at Exeter University together. The chalet owners didn't usually allow big single-sex groups but there had been a connection, a friend of Dom's who vouched for them all.

'He's supposed to be a good bloke,' the owner told Laura. 'They're rugby players, so they'll be party boys, but my friend assures me they're quite tame and well-brought-up.'

And when they turned up, they were charming. Well-mannered, high-spirited lads who wanted a hard day's skiing followed by a hard night's eating and drinking. Laura wasn't fazed. She knew they needed treating with firm, matronly kindness.

'I don't clear up sick,' she told them. 'And I don't want any cling-film-over-the-toilet-seats shenanigans. The bottom two shelves in the fridge are no go – they'll be the ingredients for supper, so if you eat them, there won't be any. And please hang your wet towels up.'

'You're very strict,' said Dom, who was the tallest of the group. 'We brought you this, from the airport.' He held up a huge bottle of Badedas and a box of Ferrero Rocher. 'We know the way to a girl's heart.'

He smiled and his eyes twinkled, and looking back, that was the moment she lost her heart to him, because she knew instinctively that it was he who had instigated the gift. The others would have been too busy downing pints in the airport bar. And he had shown lots of thoughtfulness throughout the week: helping her butter brown bread for the smoked mackerel pâté, clearing away the plates, offering to wash up. And he kept a watchful eye on his friends, reining them in when they got too loud or looked in danger of getting out of control.

On her day off, he asked if they could ski together. She'd been there three months so was pretty accomplished and knew the runs well.

'So the black run that goes down the back of the valley – is it hard?'

'Not if the conditions are good. If the sun's been on it all day and then it gets cold, it can get tricky. But it should be fine.' She'd only done it once, and it was scary. But her heart was pumping and she felt exhilarated by the challenge.

The accident had been one of those things – as accidents so often are. A momentary lapse of concentration, a lumpy mogul, the wrong decision... Then the blood wagon, an air ambulance, an operation on his knee. Laura was distraught when she went back to the chalet that night. Dom's friends gathered round and were surprisingly kind to her.

'Don't blame yourself. Dom's a big boy, and a good skier. He knew the risks. Accidents happen.'

Nevertheless, she did blame herself. She'd wanted to

show off to Dom. Show him what a good skier she was; that she wasn't just a skivvy.

Dom was in the hospital for days afterwards, until he was fit to fly home. She visited him every day, bringing him cake. At first it was guilt that had taken her there, guilt that she'd underplayed the difficulty of the black run, but it wasn't long before he was the first thing she thought of when she woke, and she hurried to get the breakfast things cleared so she could rush to his bedside.

Laura sipped at her coffee. She'd put too much milk in and it was lukewarm. She pushed the cup to one side. The kitchen still felt cold too. She needed to phone Sam Budge and ask him to service the Aga. She'd be lucky to get him. It was autumn. Everyone would be after him. She dialled his number and he promised to fit her in at some point during the day if she waited in. She told him she'd wait until the end of time if necessary.

Now that had been done, Laura sat at the table, not knowing what to do. Her sense of purpose had evaporated. There was no one to do anything for. Rather than liberating, it was totally inhibiting. She could barely breathe. She didn't want to phone Willow or Jaz – they would know something was wrong and she didn't want to have to tell the truth or to lie. She didn't want to think about Dom, let alone talk to him.

She sighed. Where was the manual that told you what to do when your husband had been unfaithful? What were you supposed to think/eat/do/wear? Because she had no idea.

She wondered where her grandmother was. It was odd that Kanga hadn't been in to see her after last night. Maybe she'd wander over to Acorn Cottage and find her.

She stuck on her Uggs and grabbed a cardigan from the hook in the hallway. She still couldn't be bothered to get dressed. She went out of the French windows and into the garden, blinking at the pale amber of the September sun. The garden was in that curious autumnal state: half abundant, half moribund, offering up the last of its bounty while the leaves fell and everything began to die back. She loved the smell, the sharpness of the cold air mixed with the earth that still contained the warmth of summer. There were apples, pears and plums to be picked, the late-ripening raspberries, onions and potatoes to dig up . . . Then bulbs to plant for spring. Her heart wasn't in any of it. She stomped past the greenhouse and the tangle of the little orchard just in time to see Kanga coming out of her door. She looked exhausted and drained, more like her age than the strong, caring woman who had taken charge of her last night.

'Kanga?'

'Oh, darling. I was just coming to see if you're all right.' Kanga looked tearful, which was unusual. 'I haven't slept much.'

'What's the matter?'

'I didn't tell you yesterday because I didn't want to worry you, but Ivy had a fall on Friday evening and broke her hip.'

'Oh no!' Laura loved Ivy. Everyone did. She had been Laura's honorary godmother, as her mum hadn't believed in such things. She always bought over-the-top presents – huge flagons of perfume and glittery purses and furry slippers. 'Why didn't you tell me?'

'I didn't want to worry you. Not after yesterday . . . How are you?' Kanga was uncharacteristically flustered, obviously overwhelmed by her friend's condition but mindful too of Laura's plight.

'Don't worry about me. Ivy's far more important. What have they said?'

'They did an operation to pin her hip. But she's very frail. Very confused. I'm off now to go and see how she is.'

Laura hated seeing her grandmother so distressed. She knew how close Ivy and Kanga were. They'd been friends since they were small girls, and even though they were wildly different and didn't live in each other's pockets, they were defiantly proud to still be propping each other up at the grand old age of ninety-three.

'What about her daughters?'

Kanga's lips tightened. 'Beverley was the one who found her. She was going to phone Kim in Australia. And Nadine came in yesterday but she's got enough on her plate with the salon so she won't be much help. You know what they're all like. They need Ivy to tell them what to do.'

'I can imagine.' Laura knew Ivy was the archetypal matriarch and that her family leaned on her heavily.

'Have you heard from Dom?' asked Kanga, anxious. 'I'm so sorry, darling.'

'Not yet. And I'm OK. Let's talk about it later. You've got enough to worry about.'

'I want to get back to the hospital so I can be there when the doctor comes.'

'I can take you if you like?'

'No, I'll be fine.' She looked at Laura. 'You need to talk to Dom. Sort things out.'

Laura didn't want to draw Kanga into her own drama right now.

'I will. I've got a few other things to sort out first. Sam Budge is coming to do the Aga.'

'Your marriage is more important than the Aga.'

'That,' said Laura, 'is where you are very wrong. Nothing is more important than the Aga.'

She watched her grandmother head off through the back gate and her heart contracted with pity. Laura would have gone with her but she knew Kanga wouldn't have allowed it. She was ferociously independent, as was Ivy. For a moment she smiled, imagining them as youngsters. They must have been a formidable pair.

II

1942

'The bastards,' said Ivy as the sirens went off again that night. 'The dirty stinking swine. Come on.'

She shoved at Jilly to get her up, gathering everything they needed: blankets and pillows. The two of them scurried as quickly as they could, down the stairs, down into the dank gloom of the cellar. There was no electric light, but a stack of candles and a box of matches. There were three fraying armchairs to sit in. They bundled themselves up in their bedding to keep as warm as they could, but the damp was freezing and still needled its way in. They could feel the boom of the bombs as they dropped. They sounded even louder tonight.

'Oh, what shall we do?' said Jilly, trying to control her distress. She clasped her hands together. 'Maybe we should pray?'

'There's no point in bloody praying,' said Ivy. 'When did that do any good? Where's God when you need him? If he wanted us to be all right he wouldn't have invented the Germans.'

Jilly laughed. Ivy's vision of the world always cheered her.

'I'm not sure that's quite how it works,' she said. 'But I agree.'

'We'll sing instead. Singing is much more useful than praying.'

Ivy began to croon in her tuneless little voice, swaying backwards and forwards in time, a rather mournful song about declaring undying love for someone.

'Can we sing something else?' asked Jilly, abruptly. 'Something jollier?'

The words had awoken something in her. Something she didn't want to think about. Had she declared her love to him, in the hot, sweet heat of that moment? Surely not. Surely you didn't say 'I love you' to someone you had only just met. But she didn't know how else to describe how he had made her feel. It had been quite overwhelming. All-consuming. It had made her feel alive; the complete opposite of how she felt now – heavy and empty.

She wasn't going to think about him. Not now. Everything had changed. There was no place for Harry Swann in her life, whatever he had been, however he had made her feel. He was going off to learn to fly. He didn't belong to her. He belonged to the war.

It seemed to be taking everything from her, the wretched war. But she still had Ivy. She put out her hand to grasp hers. Their fingers entwined and they held on tight to each other as they sang, the sound of the bombs providing a rhythmic counterpoint that in any other circumstances would have been immensely satisfying. For hours they sang their hearts out, exhausting their entire repertoire.

The next day, it soon became apparent that the first raid had been a mere warm-up, a reconnaissance mission, a chance for the Germans to expose the city's underbelly.

They'd only used incendiary devices the first night, which by contrast had wreaked only havoc, not devastation. The second night they'd used powerful explosives that gave no time for fire-fighting. The destruction was relentless and the loss of life inevitably higher. The townspeople were shaken and bewildered, any adrenaline from the first night evaporating as the true horror became apparent.

As Bath emerged dazed into the aftermath, the fires burned on and the air was thick with smoke and soot and dust. It was going to be all hands on deck. There wasn't time to bemoan what had happened. There was no time to stand and stare.

Ivy and Jilly came up from the cellar to wash and gulp down a cup of tea and a piece of toast before they headed back down into the centre of the city to see if they could help. Yet again there was no detail on the wireless to put them in the picture. But they had heard the bombing. They knew they would be stepping out into a different world.

In the rush, Jilly knocked her mother's favourite cup onto the quarry tiles: a pretty bone-china cup covered in strawberries. She went to grab it but it smashed into tiny slivers, scattering itself all over the kitchen floor. For some reason this was the last straw. A symbol of what she had lost. She slumped into her chair at the kitchen table and sobbed. There was nothing normal she could hold on to. Everything was slipping through her fingers.

Ivy gave her short shrift. She swept up the shards and made another cup of tea, plonking it down on the table.

'You can let those Nazis win,' said Ivy. 'That's what they want: to see us all in despair. You can let them laugh at you. Or you can pull yourself up by your bootstraps and help people worse off than you.'

Jilly stared at her. What could be worse than losing both parents in one night?

'There'll be people who've lost their loved ones *and* their homes. People with nowhere to go. So stop grizzling.'

'Grizzling...?' Jilly felt wounded by Ivy's hardness. 'Ivy, my mum and dad are dead. They're never coming back. I'll never see them again. Either of them.'

She had to breathe to stop a wave of panic engulfing her. She didn't want to get hysterical.

Ivy's tight lips softened. She sat down.

'I know, sweetheart.' Now Jilly could see the anguish in her eyes. 'I know. But we've got to keep going. There'll be plenty of time for crying later.' Ivy swept away the bread crumbs with a flourish. 'While you're sorting yourself out I'm going to pinch your dad's bike and go and see if my lot are all right.'

'Won't they want you with them?'

'They don't need me to look after them. Mum's got my two big brothers if she needs anything doing. They only need me for my wages.' Ivy was flippant, but Jilly could see that underneath her bravado she was agitated about her family. 'I'll be back in two shakes of a lamb's tail.'

After Ivy had gone, Jilly stepped out again into the back garden. The apple blossom was coming out, the espaliered trees stretching their branches along the walls as if to say *look at us – look how pretty we are*. There would be weeding to do and potting up and planting. Things to attend to in the greenhouse. Her mother and father spent an hour together in the garden every day, chatting companionably, conferring. Jilly lent a hand sometimes but she had no real idea of the timetable they adhered to. Only that even a momentary lack of attention could have grave consequences. Words whirled around her head: black spot and greenfly and potato blight. All things she would have to familiarise herself with if the garden was to remain as bountiful as it had been under their care.

That was not for now, though. The garden could wait for a while. There was no point in worrying about black spot if they were all going to get blown up.

Yesterday's strategy of 'keep calm and carry on' was not so apparent later that morning when Ivy and Jilly set off to go into the city. Panic was now setting in, and many people who had stood firm the night before were losing their nerve and preparing to flee the city.

The streets were choked with buses stuffed with distraught families taking as many belongings as they could with them, hoping to find refuge elsewhere – anywhere – not wanting to risk yet another night of sustained attack.

'Yellow bellies,' sniffed Ivy, who had been relieved to see her own family had escaped unscathed. They were staying put, resolute, and she felt proud of them.

The city was in a state of bewildered shock, but there was a system in place, teams of people ready to restore order: police, firefighters, nurses, messengers... Everyone stepped up to do their bit and there was a spirit of co-operation and self-sacrifice that was reassuring in itself. Some emergency workers had been at work since the very first bomb had dropped the first night. How could you stop, when people needed you? Beneath them were reams of volunteers and helpers, and no job was considered too small or unworthy.

Nevertheless, it was a daunting task to organise everything that needed to be done to restore order. The search for survivors among the wreckage was the priority, but also to make buildings safe and to put out fires. Then help for those whose homes had been destroyed or people who had been hurt or injured.

Everyone was aware that precious daylight hours were slipping away.

No one knew if the Germans would come back again.

But the disaster brought out the best in people. Help poured in from all corners. Buildings were commandeered as rest centres, supplies were shipped in, donations and offers of assistance were boundless. Counteracting that were terrible tales of loss and tragedy. Finding enough space to store the dead quickly became a crisis as the mortuaries were overflowing.

Jilly and Ivy became more and more sombre as they walked through their beloved city. It was almost surreal, walking along a road you knew and loved to find that an entire house had been wiped out while the others around them stood oblivious. Some of the bombed houses were still burning; others lay sprawled out across the pavement and into the road, slumped in defeat. The mess, the chaos, the crowds of dazed and displaced people not knowing what to do were distressing, but there was no point in standing by and gawping. That wasn't going to help anyone.

'Why?' asked Ivy as they hurried along the high pavements. 'Why did they do it? I don't understand.'

'Of course you do. Because they can. Isn't that the

point? To unsettle us. To frighten us. To make us feel that nowhere and nothing and no one is safe.'

'All these innocent people. Look! Just ordinary people living in a house, minding their own business.'

They could see a body covered in a tarpaulin. A woman looking on, weeping, being comforted by her neighbours. Rescue workers dug through the rubble, the look on their faces indicating they didn't hold out much hope. A small girl in a yellow dress came out of a house further down the street to stare. She was clutching a doll in one arm and had her thumb in her mouth.

'She looks just like my little cousin Maisie,' said Ivy, distressed. 'That's the terrible thing. It could have been my own little cousin. Or any of us.'

For a moment, somehow, she had forgotten about Jilly's parents. Then she stopped in her tracks.

'Oh, Jilly, I'm so sorry. I'm so stupid. It's all of this – it's stopping me thinking straight.' Ivy's eyes were wild in her narrow face. She was rubbing at her arms, cold in the thin dress she had put on, her hair tangling in the breeze, vulnerable in that moment, even her indomitable spirit crushed by what they were seeing.

Jilly, conversely, felt braver now she had seen the destruction. Had her parents perished in isolation, it might have been harder to bear, but they were two among many. It didn't take the pain away, but it gave her a distraction from her grief, the idea that she might be able to make a difference to someone else who had suffered.

'Come on,' she said to Ivy. 'There's no point in weeping and wailing. There's work to be done.'

She hooked her arm in her friend's and they carried on. As they walked, Jilly realised they were taking the same route she and Harry had taken the night they met – the moonlit tour she had given him, in blissful ignorance of what had been about to happen. She had been so proud of her city and its grace and beauty. Bath would rise up against this destruction, she was certain of it.

There was a fire engine outside the church hall near the Assembly Rooms. The pumps were dry, drained from the demands already put on them. They watched as the flames ate the brick with a voracious appetite, scarlet and orange and black licking the yellow stone. The firemen were weary and frustrated. They had been on their watch since the raids began the night before. And what could they do without water?

'Blimey O'Reilly,' said Ivy, her eyes wide. 'We were only in there Friday night. It seems like a lifetime ago. I had three port and lemons.' She turned to Jilly. 'You buggered off. I came to find you and you'd gone. You missed a right knees-up.'

Jilly just smiled. Ivy poked her with a sharp elbow.

'You've got to stop being such a boring old wallflower. You might have met the man of your dreams.'

'I doubt it,' said Jilly. Half of her longed to tell Ivy that she had. It would be a welcome distraction. But the other half wanted to keep it all to herself. She still wasn't sure how to feel or what to think. Harry might have felt like the man of her dreams, but she had banished him from them for the time being. At the moment, she didn't want to dream at all.

They walked to the rest centre they'd helped at the day before. It was even more chaotic, and it soon became apparent that last night's bombings had doubled the severity and created a crisis. The death count was in the hundreds now, with many more missing, and there were terrible stories of families ripped apart: fathers walking out of the door and not coming back, children crushed by falling masonry, half a hotel's guests burned to death while the other half remained unscathed. It was a lottery; a game of chance.

Jilly's head swam as she took in the gravity of the situation. She didn't know whether to count herself as a lucky survivor or an unfortunate victim. All she did know was that it was her duty to help. She might have been bereaved, and in the most brutal way, but she was still in one piece, as was her house.

'I'm going to take in a family,' she said to Ivy. 'I've got two big rooms at the top of the house. Plenty of space. They can stay there as long as they like, until they get back on their feet. I can feed them. Look after them.'

'You're bloody mad.' Ivy looked at her in horror. 'You don't know who you'll get.'

Jilly shrugged. 'Someone who needs refuge. Someone who needs comfort. It's the least I can do.'

'I think you'll be sorry.' Ivy crossed her arms.

'It's what my parents would have done. I know they would.'

Jilly was sure of that. Her father would have been working tirelessly to tend the injured, with her mother either helping him or finding her own rescue mission. They would have been cheerful and indefatigable and reassuring and just the people you would want around.

'Yes, but they had each other,' Ivy pointed out. '*And* you. You're on your own. And are you sure you feel up to it? After what's happened?'

She didn't say the words, but Jilly knew what she meant. She squared her shoulders.

'What's happened is the *reason* for doing it. And what else am I going to do? My father's gone so my job's gone. I don't want to rattle about in that huge house.'

Ivy shook her head. 'You've always been a much better person than I have.'

'No, I haven't. It makes sense, that's all.'

Ivy looked around at all the people in the room; their weary patience. Elderly couples looking dazed, young children clinging to their mothers.

'Well, don't think I'm leaving you on your own with a houseful of strangers. I'd better move in.'

'Actually,' said Jilly, 'I'd love that. If you're sure your family won't mind?'

'You're joking, aren't you? They'll have my bed before my back's even turned.'

Jilly felt happy with the plan. Ivy was a whirlwind and had her own way of looking at things but she had an energy to her that was contagious, and Jilly feared that without her in the house she might not want to get up and face the day, which had been part of her reason for taking in a family. There would be no malingering with Ivy around.

The council offices were mayhem. There were queues of people in varying states of emotion: distressed, dazed, demanding. The trauma affected everyone differently – some were agitated, some compliant. One woman was shouting, hysterical, demanding that something be done to help her right now this instant. Another was incapable of speech, mute with shock, quite helpless. There was no one in charge of managing the crowd because everyone was needed to deal with the administration.

Jilly had to queue for ages, because there didn't seem to be any system and the staff were overstretched and under pressure. They weren't prepared for this chaos – how could they be? It was impossible to put a contingency plan in place for a disaster of this scale. She finally spoke to a harassed-looking woman who was delighted when she offered accommodation rather than ask for it.

'Oh, that's wonderful. I've got just the family for you. The whole house came down around their ears last night. Mum and the kids were under an upturned sofa and had to be dug out. They're in shock, but not hurt.'

'I can't begin to imagine,' said Jilly. How were you supposed to cope with an experience like that?

'They've lost everything. They've got the clothes they were wearing and nothing else. They've sorted them out with some bits and pieces at the WVS – nappies for the baby and so on.'

'I'm sure I can find some basics. And I've got plenty of bedding and towels.'

'That's wonderful. People have been so kind but it's hard to find room for a family this size and of course they want to be together. And mum doesn't want to move out of Bath – she got quite hysterical when we suggested Bradford on Avon...'

The woman was shuffling around endless pieces of paper. She finally found the one she wanted. She looked at Jilly, worn out, her face pale as milk. 'I hope they don't come again tonight. We're barely managing as it is. Address?'

'Number Eleven Lark Hill. Lansdown.'

'It's a fair old walk. I'm not sure the smalls would manage it. Or mum, come to think of it.' The woman frowned. 'She is quite... fragile.'

Jilly wasn't sure what she meant by fragile, but she thought it might be a euphemism. She remembered the big black Austin in the garage at the bottom of the garden.

'I've got my father's car. I could go back and get it, then come and fetch them?'

She didn't mention she didn't really know how to drive. Living in a city, there was barely any need: she walked everywhere. Her father had needed it for visiting patients out in the countryside, and of course speed was of the essence in his occupation. It was a familiar sight. Everyone knew Dr Wilson's car.

'Oh, that would be perfect. You are an angel. Now as I said, they've lost everything including their ration books. But they'll be able to pick up new ones in the next few days.'

'It's not a problem. Not for the time being. I'm in a good financial position. I'm happy to be able to help.'

The clerk spread out the paperwork in front of her.

'They're the Norris family. From Kingsmead. Mum and three little ones. The husband's away fighting so I'm sure they'll be very grateful. We'll be doing all we can to house them permanently but it won't be for a while. As you can imagine, we're very short of accommodation.'

She stamped the papers with a bang then moved on to the next person in the queue. There wasn't time for niceties. As far as the clerk was concerned, that was one family taken care of among many others to deal with.

12

Somehow, after Sadie had gone, Laura managed to get showered and dressed, although she felt sure that if she hadn't got Sam Budge coming to mend the Aga she might have been tempted to stay in her pyjamas despite her friend's directive. She felt light-headed from lack of sleep, agitated and nervy, her mind flipping from wondering how Willow was to poor Ivy in hospital and trying to avoid thinking about the real elephant: her marriage.

She had no idea what to do. If only she hadn't found out. Maybe they could have gone on for ever, her living in blissful ignorance. She'd had no inkling, after all, that Dom was unhappy with her or being unfaithful. There were no clues. He seemed to love her and appreciate her. And they still had sex – good sex. As often as anyone their age, she imagined.

What had he told Antonia? What had they spoken about? How had they justified what they were doing? To themselves? To each other?

Laura forced herself to put on some mascara. She looked in the mirror: she had quite a round face and plump skin, which hadn't aged badly. She didn't look so very different from when she was first married. A few strands of silver in her hair, and she was certainly a stone or two heavier . . .

Her mobile was ringing. It was Dom. She braced herself. She would be businesslike. She would not cry. She picked up the phone gingerly and answered.

'What?'

'Laura. Darling. We need to talk.'

'No. We don't. And don't "darling" me.'

'I need to see you.'

'Why?'

'Well . . .' He sounded nonplussed. 'To explain.'

'I don't want to know.'

'We can't just do nothing.'

'Why not?'

'You mean that's it? I don't get to—'

'No, Dom. You don't. I didn't have any choice in this, so you don't either. You can come and pick up whatever you need from the house.'

'That's crazy.'

'No, it's not. It's a perfectly rational reaction.' She could imagine the expression on his face so clearly. Bewilderment. It used to make her laugh when Dom was flummoxed by a situation. Now, his bewilderment hardened her heart. 'Let me know what time you're coming and I'll make sure I'm out.'

She hung up. Her hands were trembling and she felt as if her stomach had been turned inside out. She put her phone down on the table. It rang almost straight away and she nearly jumped out of her skin.

'Bugger off!' she shouted at the phone, then saw it was Sam Budge. She snatched it up. She couldn't afford to miss him.

'Hello?'

'I'll be with you in about half an hour, Mrs Griffin. Get the kettle on.'

Sam Budge was as broad and sturdy as the Agas he serviced, and had a voice like cider and Laurie Lee – slow and sweet and countrified. In a trice he had dustsheets all over the kitchen and the innards out and had started fettling all the intricate and mysterious parts with an assortment of cloths and brushes and screwdrivers, making a glorious mess.

While he worked, Sam kept up a monologue of hilarious anecdotes, part Young Farmer japes/part stag-night malarkey, that had Laura weeping with laughter despite her mood. He had a descriptive way with him and a wry sense of humour and was obviously high-spirited once he'd had a few. Laura wasn't sure she would want to bump into him on a stag night, but he was very conscientious and good-humoured and, above all, kind.

'Anyway, Deggsy got done for drink-driving the next morning,' he told her. 'They pulled him over on the Yate road. Locked him up till teatime – he was twice over the limit.'

She tutted. 'He'll lose his licence.'

'Idiot. Everyone knows not to drive the next morning after a skinful. I always get Hayley to drive on a Sunday. She never has more than three Smirnoff Ices.'

Laura heard the front door open and shut, and Dom call out. She immediately tensed.

'I'm not here if he asks,' she told Sam, who looked puzzled, but it was too late. Dom was standing at the kitchen door. Laura didn't know what to do. She looked towards

143

the French windows as if to make her escape, then pushed past Dom into the front hall. He followed her.

'What are you doing here?' She turned at the bottom of the stairs to face him, resting her arm on the curve of the newel post. On the wall behind, she could see rows of photos she had put in matching frames: the story of their life, her and Dom and Jaz and Willow, black-and-white photos in frames she had carefully painted in hot pink and burnt orange and acid yellow, pops of colour on a fashionably grey wall.

'What do you think?'

'I said to tell me when you were coming so I could be out.'

'We have to talk. Please.'

'I don't want to listen to the clichés.' She put on a pretend whine. '*It's not like that. It just happened. It didn't mean anything.*'

'But that's all true. It *didn't*—'

'Great. So you sacrifice our twenty-something-year marriage for something that didn't mean anything. That makes it worse, not better.'

Dom scratched his head, despairing. He was laying traps for himself. 'Laura—'

She pointed at him.

'This is the deal. You stay away from this house. You can get your stuff now and if you need anything else, let me know and I'll leave it in the garage for you.'

'Where am I supposed to go?'

Laura shrugged. 'I don't care.'

He sighed and went to head up the stairs. 'I'll get my stuff then.'

She stood in front of him, blocking his way.

'And this is the most important thing. No one can find out about this. You better not tell *anyone*. Because I don't want the girls finding out. I especially don't want Willow to find out.'

'Of course not—'

Laura could feel hysteria rising up inside her. She fought it down. Hysteria was no good at all, because then she'd be in a position of weakness and irrationality. She breathed right down into her diaphragm and kept the panic at bay. Her voice trembled slightly but it was firm.

'I don't want Willow upset. I don't want her to have an attack because she's distressed. You know how fragile she is. Something like this could . . .'

She didn't want to think about it. It was her dread, her fear, that Willow would have a setback. She knew most of the triggers were physical – cats, colds, calla lilies – but stress could be a factor. Willow would be devastated if she knew what her dad had done. She relied heavily on both of her parents. Laura when she was properly poorly, because Laura did all the practical stuff, but she turned to Dom when she was on the mend, for encouragement and reassurance.

Jaz was more pragmatic and independent. She would be shocked, but she wouldn't miss a beat. Jaz was solid and focused and matter-of-fact. Laura had always been in awe of Jaz's commitment. She didn't think Jaz had ever missed a practice or a match; had never tried to slide out of something because she didn't feel like it; never pulled a sickie. She would take it in her stride.

But Willow . . .

'I won't tell anyone,' said Dom. 'Who would I tell? It's not something I want to broadcast.'

'I'm guessing *Antonia* knows that I know?' She gave her name heavy italics.

He gave an awkward half-nod.

'Well, tell her to keep it to herself. Tell her not to blab to her friends.'

'She's not like that,' said Dom quickly, then realised his mistake. Laura wouldn't want to hear him defending Antonia.

She looked at him coldly.

'Tell her from me this is not to be common gossip.'

Dom nodded. He was scared of this icy Laura. He had seen her before, when she was fighting for Willow, confronting the consultant who had dared to belittle her asthma and implied it was 'one of those things' and 'they'd have to live with it'. Icy Laura had come out then, an immoveable force, kicking up a fuss until they had found a consultant prepared to work with them to manage the asthma better. It was easy to think of Laura as warm and easy-going and a pushover, because mostly she was. But Dom had seen the warrior, the woman you wouldn't want to mess with. And that was who he was dealing with now.

'You have my word. She won't say anything.'

'Ha.'

He closed his eyes. Whatever he said, even if he just breathed, it would be wrong.

'Can I get my things now?'

'Sure.' Laura stood to one side.

He went to walk past her, then stopped. 'I'm so sorry.'

He reached out to touch her but she pushed him away. 'Don't.'

The door to the kitchen popped open and Sam stood there, hands covered in black oil.

'Have you got any—' He stopped mid-sentence, frowning, as he saw their body language. 'Is everything OK?'

'Fine.' Laura stepped aside and nodded to Dom to carry on up the staircase, then followed Sam back into the kitchen. 'Have I got any what?'

'Liquid soap. My hands are covered.'

She found a bottle under the sink. 'Here. Hold your hands out.'

She pumped a few dollops into Sam's open palms then turned the tap on for him.

'Are you all right?' he asked.

'No.' She swallowed. 'Not really.' She shut her eyes. 'I've just kicked him out.'

'Mr Griffin?' Sam looked shocked. 'What the hell? Why?'

'Usual cliché.' Laura realised she sounded bitter. And that she had broken the very commandment she had just made. 'Some bimbo half my age.'

Sam looked at Laura in utter disbelief. 'Who in their right mind would cheat on you?'

She almost laughed. Sam was so sweet and genuine and baffled and concerned. He seemed almost more upset than she was. She felt numb, still nowhere near processing what had happened or what was going to happen. She was on automatic pilot. It was a mode she was used to. It was the mode she went into when Willow was ill, not letting anything else penetrate her, just freezing so she could get through the trauma.

It was afterwards she would fall apart, once Willow was back at home, breathing easily and sleeping soundly, the colour back in her cheeks. Then Laura would cry with relief, letting out all the bottled fears.

The door opened and Dom stood there.

'I'm off, then.'

'OK.'

They stared at each other. Laura turned away, handing Sam a towel to wipe his wet hands on.

Dom shut the kitchen door quietly and a few moments later they heard the front door go.

Sam looked awkward. 'The Aga's back on, anyway. Should be running as sweet as a nut.'

Laura cleared her throat.

'Sam – I'd be really grateful if you didn't tell anyone. About me and Dom.'

Sam knew a lot of people she knew in Bath. Apart from anything, he spent a lot of time in the kitchens of the great and the good, tending their Agas, and he loved a chat while he worked. This piece of gossip could be around the city in no time. She had to appeal to his better nature. He was quick to reassure her.

'Listen, people tell me their stuff but I never repeat it. I've got dirt that would shock you to the core.' He grinned. 'You'd be amazed how many women try it on with me, for a start.'

Laura giggled. 'That's outrageous.'

'And then there's the women that are still in bed at two o'clock in the afternoon. The ones that are pissed by ten o'clock in the morning. And the men are no better. I've seen them snorting coke off their worktops with their coffee. They think I don't notice.'

'Stop.' Laura couldn't help laughing.

'Anyway, I keep everyone's secrets. I'm like a priest. One day I'll write a book. When I retire. *Confessions of an Aga Repair Man*. But until then . . .' He indicated pulling a

148

zip across his mouth. 'And if you need anything, I know people.'

'People?'

'You know. If you want . . .' He gave a knife-slashing motion. 'You know, tyres. That kind of thing.'

'Oh!' She wondered what kind of car Antonia drove. And just for one moment imagined her coming out of her house in the morning and seeing her tyres all slashed. It was, she had to admit, quite tempting. But what would that change? Nothing. 'No. No, I don't think so. That's not really my style.'

'Fair enough. But anything you want. Anything. Around the house, even. I can give you a hand.'

His round face was earnest and concerned.

'Thanks, Sam. I'll be fine. I think.'

Why did kindness make you want to cry more than cruelty?

When Sam had gone, the house felt incredibly quiet. It wasn't an 'everyone's at work and school' quiet. It was a mocking quiet, a 'you're all on your own now' quiet that made her feel deeply uncomfortable. If only she had a job, she'd be at work now, distracted by the minutiae of an environment where people had better things to do than discuss your private life. What a luxury that would be.

She picked up her phone. A voice in her head told her not to do what she was about to do. But when did a voice in your head ever stop you from doing something? She called up her browser and typed into the search bar: *Antonia Briggs solicitor Bath*.

Her heart thumped as she waited a few seconds for the results to come up, then clicked on Images. There she was, staring back at her. Antonia Briggs, conveyancing solicitor at Kettle and Sons, smiling at the camera as if it was something she was being forced into (and she probably was; no one liked a compulsory work photo). She had a narrow, bony face, a brown shoulder-length bob parted in the middle, glasses, a navy-blue blouse with white birds on it. She looked very straight, very sensible and very dull. A bit mousy, if anything. Not like a predatory husband stealer. Just . . . ordinary. Not someone you could hate. Laura felt flummoxed. She'd been expecting someone more high-flying and confident. Glossy and corporate and pleased with herself. At least then she would have understood the attraction.

She put the phone down, utterly at a loss as to what to think.

Then she called up Antonia's image again. 'You might be half my age,' she told her, 'and you might be a solicitor with letters after your name, but I'm not taking this lying down. So watch out.'

13

D om stood in front of Wellington Buildings. The root of all his problems. In his hand he held a bag with as many of his clothes as he had been able to stuff in, given Laura's hostility and the fact he couldn't really think straight, as well as his wash stuff and some paperwork.

The house stretched up in front of him towards a blue September sky. Seven floors of Georgian elegance, it oozed confidence, brimful as it was of history and heritage and perfect proportions. It had a side view over the lawns that fronted the Royal Crescent, where a sprinkling of sheep were contentedly grazing, the ultimate in *rus in urbe* – country in the town. The Georgians had always wanted the best of both worlds, and that legacy lived on.

He remembered the first time he had set eyes on the house, and how he had fallen head over heels in love with it and done everything in his power to claim it as his. That had been his mistake. It was like the most toxic love affair. The building he had seen as perfect was hiding a multitude of cracks and flaws, like a beautiful woman masking her neuroses and insecurities. The deeper he dug, the more flawed the building turned out to be. It almost seemed to be laughing at him as defect after defect became apparent. A vast proportion of his money had gone into rectifying these faults, rather than investing in improvements. He never seemed to be able to move the project on.

He had turned a corner recently and progress was being made. But time was running out. His development loan ran for just eighteen months: a non-negotiable deadline after which the bank would call the money in. Which meant the apartments had to go on the market the minute Christmas was over, and they would have to sell like hot cakes if he was to repay his loan by the deadline.

He felt sick when he thought of the consequences if they didn't sell straight away. He would be in massive trouble. Sometimes he couldn't believe he'd done it, but it had seemed so logical and easy at the time – using Number 11 as collateral for the loan.

Now, as he stood in the street and looked up at the building, the realisation hit him hard. If he didn't pull it off, then their family home would have to be sold.

He'd been in no doubt when he took out the loan that he would be able to repay it. The project had made perfect sense. He had experience, a great team, a vision – and luxury apartments in Bath were hugely sought after. While he knew it would be a challenge, it had seemed like a logical step up for him.

Now, he realised he'd been a deluded fool. It was far too ambitious for him to manage on his own. He was wrangling up to twenty different tradesmen at any one time, some of whom were great – conscientious and professional – others of whom were slapdash and delivered late, but still wanted paying on time. There'd been the new interior staircase that had been out by a few crucial centimetres; the scaffolder who'd smashed through an original Georgian window; the stonemason who'd destroyed the steps into the garden with a jet washer. No one took the blame or apologised or wanted to put things right at their own expense when they'd cocked up. He took up the slack every time.

He was exhausted. He never switched off for a moment. Everything whirled around in his head from the minute he woke up – if he had actually managed to sleep at all.

And underneath was the sick guilt of what he had done to Laura. While she refused to speak to him or see him he couldn't atone or explain. He was trapped. And the worst of it was it was all of his own making. He'd been greedy, overambitious, weak . . . *Ugh*, he thought. He couldn't afford himself an ounce of sympathy.

Worse than that was the thought of what she would say if she knew Number 11 was in jeopardy. They owned the house jointly, as officially they'd had to buy it from Kanga when she gave it over to them to avoid complicated tax issues, and it was Dom's income that had secured them the original mortgage – a pittance now by today's standards. And over the years he'd extended that mortgage to raise development money. That was how you made money, after all – by borrowing on what you already had; your assets. And he'd been transparent with Laura. She had to sign the paperwork, after all. But she never really paid attention to the figures, she signed on the dotted line without querying the amount. So when he'd borrowed more money than usual for Wellington Buildings, he hadn't been dishonest – she could see the numbers. But if she knew the truth, she would be horrified.

And on top of his current transgression, he was hardly going to get any support or sympathy. He couldn't tell her.

Of course, the easiest thing to do would be to ditch Wellington Buildings right now. There were several people waiting in the wings who would take it off him. A quick trip to the Wellington Arms on a Saturday lunchtime and he would have a deal by the end of the week, he knew that. It was stuffed with estate agents and property developers and entrepreneurs who would take it off his hands.

But if he did that he would lose a huge amount of money. By the time he had paid back his loan, he would be down a quarter of a million. He'd lose the stamp duty he'd paid on the original purchase, the structural survey fees, the architect's plans, the listed building schedule: none of these came cheap.

And he would lose his pride. His professional integrity. His reputation.

He pushed open the door of the house. He needed to get upstairs and get his bag hidden away before any of the workmen clocked it. He ran up the wide stone staircase that had so beguiled him on first viewing. Normally he would stop to chat on each floor, to see how things were progressing, but today he ran all the way to the top of the house, to the room where he had a makeshift office. He could barely breathe by the time he got there. Shit, he was really unfit. He'd stopped going to the gym while this project was on. He didn't have time. Jaz had bugged him about it over the summer. Tried to get him to come for a run. But he was knackered by the time he got home and a glass of wine seemed infinitely more enticing than putting on his running gear.

Oh God. He couldn't think about the girls. It made his skin crawl with shame. How could he even begin to explain? How Antonia had gradually moved from someone he took advice from to someone much more than that. How the physicality of their relationship gave him something he needed. How he had been so sure he could ring-fence his relationship with her because he knew she didn't want more than he was prepared to offer. Of course he would never have done it if he'd thought Antonia was expecting some kind of commitment.

They'd been in this very room when he'd stepped over the mark. They had stood by the window, looking out at the view, and something had changed. Something he couldn't ignore or resist. He was pretty certain she had made the first move. Reached out her hand—

Dom gave a tut of impatience and told himself to stop trying to justify what he had done. He was a fool and a cliché and selfish. A sorry excuse of a husband and a dreadful father and an appalling role model. He'd let everyone down. Himself, Laura, Jaz, Willow, Kanga, Antonia... The list was endless.

He sat down in the orange plastic office chair to recover his breath. He looked around at the charts and timetables and plans and drawings that surrounded him. He'd pinned them all neatly to the wall, so he could double-check measurements or regulations or costings. Once upon a time they had made perfect sense but now they seemed to mock him. They all blurred into one, swimming in and out of his line of vision. He wiped a bead of sweat from his forehead. He needed some water. He felt like death.

Get a grip, he told himself. If he took his eye off the ball now, he would lose everything. Wellington Buildings, Number 11, Laura... The whole bloody lot.

14

Ivy lifted the custard cream as if it was a house brick and nibbled the edge.

After her operation, she'd been moved onto a general ward. She was out of danger, but the worrying thing was her lack of fight. Kanga would have had money on Ivy badgering the nurses to be discharged, giving them hell, flirting with the consultant, calling for the tea trolley, asking for the channel to be changed on the telly. But seeing her lying there, her eyes milky, her skin papery, with none of her usual spirit, made Kanga anxious.

'Is there anything you want me to bring you?'

Ivy reached out and touched her hand with a smile. 'Nothing, love. I'm fine.'

'Are you in pain?'

'I can't feel a thing.' There was a shadow of a smile. 'I'm on so many painkillers I can't even tell if I need the toilet.' There. A faint glimmer of her old spirit.

'You need to eat. Get your strength up.'

Ivy put her custard cream back down on the tabletop in front of her.

'I'm not hungry. I could do with some squash, though.'

Kanga got up to fill her glass with water, and poured in a glug of Robinsons Barley Water.

'There you go.'

Ivy sipped at her drink, then handed her the glass, lying back on her pillow. She seemed exhausted.

'All right, Mum?' Beverley had been out to get a KitKat from the vending machine.

Ivy didn't answer. Her eyes were shut. There was a tiny custard cream crumb on the side of her mouth. She seemed to sleep about eighteen hours a day, waking sporadically, like a newborn baby.

'I think she's dropped off again,' said Kanga, wiping the crumb away gently. 'Shall we go and have a chat?'

They sat opposite each other in the family room on either side of a plastic table. Beverley looked terrible. She hadn't even bothered with make-up, which was a first – Kanga had never seen her without false eyelashes and red lipstick – and the strain was starting to tell.

'The consultant says there won't be much more they can do for her here in a week or so,' said Beverley, snapping the KitKat finger in two. 'But she can't go home. She won't be able to walk properly for at least a month. She's so frail. And what if she falls over again?'

'Couldn't you look after her? Just while she gets better?'

Beverley looked aghast.

'I'm not a nurse,' she said. 'I wouldn't know what to do. And I'm still running the salon six days a week. It would fall apart without me. Nadine might be able to do balayage but she can't do a balance sheet to save her life.'

'You could get some professional help. It would be much nicer for her to be in her own home, surely?'

'I honestly don't think that's what Mum would want.' Beverley shook her head. 'She wouldn't want to be a burden. She's always said that.'

'No.' Kanga knew Beverley was right. Ivy would never want to be a nuisance or a drain. 'So where will she go?'

'I've been speaking to her social worker. There's a care home in Frilmington that has a place. It's only a mile away from the salon so we'll be able to visit as often as we like. Just while she recuperates. If she gets proper care then maybe she'll be able to go home again.'

Frilmington, Kanga knew, was a miserable overspill on the very outskirts of Bristol which had nothing to recommend it. She was fairly sure any care home in its environs would be insalubrious at best.

'Frilmington?' She made a face.

'It's the only place with a bed available at the moment. It's a recommended care home. It's on the list.'

'Yes, but some of those places can be awful.' Kanga had seen the programmes on television. And read the papers.

'We haven't got much choice.' Beverley looked distressed. 'Oh God. I hate this. This decision-making. I told Kim not to come back until we'd settled things, but part of me wishes she was here. I feel so responsible.'

'I know how hard it must be. If there's anything I can do to help, just let me know.'

Kanga was dying to take over, but how could she? She was just a friend, not family. She had to respect Beverley's position.

'Would you come with me to the home? To have a look? At least then I could have someone to talk to and help me decide.'

'Of course. We need to make sure your mum gets the best care. That's what she deserves.'

'Thanks.' Beverley was folding the foil the KitKat was wrapped in, scoring lines in it with her long red nails. She didn't speak for a moment, then she looked up. 'I feel so guilty that I don't feel capable of looking after her.'

Kanga thought for a moment. She needed to be tactful with her next suggestion.

'Maybe you could sell the flat?' she suggested. 'If you released some capital, that might give you a bit more choice about what to do.'

There was an awkward silence.

'There isn't any capital,' said Beverley eventually.

'There must be. The flat's worth quite a bit now, surely?' When she was widowed not long after Kanga lost Jocelyn, Ivy had bought a flat in an area of Bristol that had been very unfashionable at the time, but was now being gentrified – prices had shot up and flats like hers were being snapped up and renovated by young couples. 'I'd have thought the sensible thing to do would be to sell the flat and use the money to finance somewhere really nice for your mum. Maybe a warden-controlled flat?'

Beverley looked as if she was choosing what to say next very carefully.

'Mum released the capital in her flat about ten years ago. To one of those companies.'

'An equity release scheme?' Kanga's heart sank. No wonder Ivy hadn't told her. She'd have stopped her straight away. She frowned. 'But where did all the money go?'

'You do know Mum had quite a few gambling debts?'

'Gambling?' Kanga knew Ivy liked what she called the gee-gees, but she didn't think she was a gambler.

'She liked a flutter. Well, more than a flutter.'

'I didn't know.' She knew Ivy could be a dark horse, but it seemed there was a lot she'd kept hidden from her best friend.

Beverley gave an exasperated smile.

'We've had our problems with her, you know. It was Dad's fault – he gave her a taste for it. But once he died she didn't have his tips – he was in with all sorts of stable lads – so she ended up losing most of the time.'

Ivy's husband, Reggie, had been a bit of a wild card – a second-hand car dealer who loved the high life. He'd never been short of cash but it slipped through his fingers. It had been Ivy who harnessed his money and made sure they bought property. They'd been a colourful couple – they loved the races and cruises and flash hotels. It had always been amusing when the four of them went out, Kanga remembered with a smile. Her own husband, Jocelyn, had been the polar opposite of Reggie – quiet, thoughtful, contemplative – but in a funny kind of way they had got on, and respected each other. They'd always had fun – Reggie made sure of that, from the very first bottle of what he called 'shampoo', and he was always overanxious, making sure they were having a good time and always, always picking up the bill. Jocelyn wasn't in the least offended, but Kanga found it grated on her. Reggie obviously had no idea that Jocelyn was a shrewd and successful businessman himself – he just chose not to flash his cash. She never said anything though. It was Ivy and Reggie's way, conspicuous consumption.

'She likes to gamble and she likes to spend. Have you seen her bedroom? It's full to bursting with stuff she's never worn.' Beverley shook her head in despair. 'Coats. Shoes. Handbags. All designer stuff.'

Kanga wanted to stifle a smile. She could remember that from when they were young. Ivy loved to wear something new. The latest fashion. She hadn't been able to indulge during the war but afterwards...

'I know how generous she is,' said Kanga. 'She's the queen of birthday presents.'

For her last birthday Ivy had bought her a magnificent Wedgwood teapot and insisted on taking her out for lunch at the Royal Crescent Hotel. If she'd released the equity in her flat no wonder she'd been able to afford it.

'Yeah. She didn't just spend the money on herself. She wanted to help us all out while she could. Me and the kids and the grandkids. You know, a few family treats. A few things to make our lives a bit more comfortable.'

Now things Ivy had told her that had struck her as extravagant at the time were starting to make sense. A big family holiday to Australia to visit Kim and her family in Perth, no expense spared. The salon Ivy had handed down to Beverley and her daughter Nadine getting a big makeover. A new conservatory for Beverley...

Kanga did the maths. All of these could add up easily to the amount of equity Ivy would have been able to release from her flat. By the time the interest was added on, there'd be nothing left over. Ivy wouldn't be able to benefit from her own house going up in value.

It was almost criminal. She knew perfectly well that Ivy would have been persuaded into it by some smooth-talking salesman. If only she'd mentioned it. But she wouldn't have, because she knew Kanga would have talked her out of it, and she would have thought it was a great idea, because all Ivy ever wanted to do was give. She knew there was nothing her friend would have loved more than getting all of her children and grandchildren and great-grandchildren onto that plane to Australia.

She remembered her talking about it – the holiday of a lifetime! – and now she understood the pride she'd had in her voice, because she'd been able to make it happen. And Ivy lived for the moment. It wouldn't stop her even now, knowing there wouldn't be anything left over for her care. She would do it all over again.

'I'm not going to know anything about it, am I?' Kanga could imagine her saying. 'No point wasting the money on me at my age.'

Kanga wanted to cry. She wanted to cry for her wonderfully good-hearted, misguided friend, who suddenly seemed so frail and vulnerable.

'I'll come with you to look at the home,' she told Beverley. 'Then we can talk about the best thing to do.'

15

1942

'If they're from Kingsmead they'll be rough as badgers,' said Ivy, her voice dark with foreboding.

'You don't know that,' said Jilly, bright with enthusiasm for her new project. Anything, she thought. Anything to stop her thinking about what had happened. Looking after the Norris family would keep her busy, for the time being at any rate.

The two girls had gone back up the hill to fetch Jilly's father's car. Luckily Dr Wilson had backed it into the garage when he had last used it, as Jilly wasn't sure how to put it into reverse. They clambered in, sliding over the cold of the leather seats.

Jilly tried to remember the instructions her father had given her when he'd attempted to teach her to drive a couple of years ago. It hadn't been a huge success. He had teased her when she hadn't got to grips with it and she had been indignant, then furious, then thrown a tantrum and got out of the car in the middle of the road, and eventually they had both agreed it wasn't worth them getting cross with each other.

'You need someone other than your father teaching you,' her mother had said. 'He's impossible.'

He hadn't been impossible; he was just hopeless at teaching and couldn't resist pulling her leg. He wasn't being patronising. It was just his way. Now, Jilly tried to remember the little he had taught her. She pulled out the choke, turned the key, put her foot on the clutch, crunched the car into first, let off the handbrake then put her foot on the throttle.

The big car bunny-hopped out of the garage and along the road while Jilly tried to put it into second gear. It stalled almost immediately. She started it up again.

'Push the clutch in harder. Any fool knows that!' Ivy instructed from the passenger seat.

'I've got it now!' cried Jilly, grappling with the gearstick. There was an awful crunching sound, then the car lurched forward. 'There we are.'

For a few hundred yards they glided forward gracefully. Then Jilly turned left into Lansdown Hill and accelerated downwards.

'Oh my God!' Jilly wanted to shut her eyes as the car gathered speed, remembering the terror from her lessons.

'Keep your foot on the brake!'

'I should have let you drive.' Jilly hated the sensation of panic. 'I can't do this.' She didn't feel in control at all, although the car did seem to stop when she applied the brakes, which was reassuring.

'No fear. I'm not crashing your dad's car. You can do it, Jilly. Course you can.'

They edged down the hill, past the high pavements of Belvedere with its black railings, Jilly breathing in a sigh of relief when they reached the safety of the Paragon at the bottom. She stopped to take stock, her hands gripping the wheel. This was almost worse than listening to bombs dropping all night long: her heart was pounding and her palms were sweating. A car behind her sounded its horn.

'Oh God.' Jilly fiddled with the gearstick until she got the car into first and edged off again. Ivy clapped in delight and Jilly couldn't help laughing as she turned right and picked up speed along George Street, travelling sedately between the Georgian buildings. It was a moment of triumph and levity after the darkness of the past two days.

'Wooo hoooo!' screamed Ivy, throwing her head back. 'Off we go!'

Where there was laughter, thought Jilly, there was hope.

The rest of the journey was difficult to negotiate. So many roads were blocked off that Bath was almost impossible to get around. The traffic was heavy with emergency vehicles and buses crammed with people fleeing the city.

'Cowards,' said Ivy.

'You can't blame them.'

'We're all in this together. You can't just run away.'

Jilly moved the car up into third gear. She had barely got out of second up until now.

'I think I'm getting the hang of this.'

By some miracle they reached their destination without crashing into anything. Jilly slumped backwards in the seat, exhausted. She could see a family waiting outside the council building: a diminutive woman with a baby balanced on one hip flanked by a small boy and girl of about school age. They all looked exhausted and dishevelled. There was one small bag at the woman's feet.

'Is that them?' asked Ivy with distaste. 'They'll have nits, I'm telling you that now.'

Jilly jumped out of the car and went to greet them.

'Are you Mrs Norris?'

The woman nodded. 'Yeah.'

'You're coming to live with me for a while. I hope you'll be comfy with me. And I'm so sorry. About your house. It's awful. It's all awful.'

She felt quite emotional. Seeing this family made it all real. The poor woman must have been terrified.

'I'm Jilly, by the way,' she said, holding out her hand.

Mrs Norris just moved her baby onto the other hip. She stared at Jilly dully, not offering her name or a hand. She was wraith-like and beautiful. No bigger than a child herself, with a tangle of dark hair to her waist and large dark eyes that looked as if they had been burned into her face with a hot poker.

Jilly tried again.

'I can't call you Mrs Norris. It's far too formal. What's your name?'

The woman thought long and hard for a moment, as if it was a trap, before finally divulging her name.

'Helena.'

'Hello, Helena. I'm Jilly. And what are the little ones called?'

Helena touched each child on the head as she named it.

'Colin and Julie. And this is Baby Dot.'

'Short for Dorothy?'

'No. Just Dot.'

There wasn't even the glimmer of a smile. Jilly supposed she must be in shock. She bent down to Colin and Julie. They looked grubby, with too-long ratty hair and chapped lips. It must be hard, she thought, bringing up three children in wartime in poverty, with your husband away fighting.

'Hello, you two. You're going to be staying with me for a little while. I'm hoping I might be able to dig you out some toys.'

They gazed at her solemnly with their mother's dark-brown eyes. They seemed bewildered by the situation, but Jilly supposed they must be in shock like their mum.

She stood up.

'Well, the car's just here so shall we head off? I'm not very good at driving but don't worry. We haven't got far to go. And this is my friend Ivy.'

Ivy was leaning against the passenger door, smoking a cigarette. Helena looked at her warily.

'All right?'

Ivy dropped her cigarette and gave a nod. 'Come on then, you lot. Hop in.'

Jilly could sense there might be trouble between Helena and Ivy but this was no time for rivalry. There was a war on.

Jilly stalled five times heading back home as driving uphill proved much harder than going down. She tried to laugh about it but Helena remained impassive in the back seat, her arms wrapped round the children. Ivy tried to catch her eye in the rear-view mirror.

'I've got a pig in my garden,' said Jilly, trying to jolly the journey along. 'So I'm hoping one of you will help me with him.'

'Pigs stink,' said Colin.

'Mungo does smell a little bit, I admit. But he's very

nice. I've got some chickens too. Who wants to be in charge of collecting the eggs?'

There was a silence. Jilly could see them all looking at each other as if she had suggested something quite out of the ordinary, like collecting dinosaur eggs.

'Me, please,' piped up a little voice in the end, which she assumed was Julie.

The Norrises walked through Number 11 with awe. They stepped reverently onto the tiled floor, staring up at the high ceilings and the Bath stone staircase with the black iron bannisters as if they were visiting a cathedral. Jilly had never thought of the house as particularly grand – to her it was comfortable and homely – but maybe it seemed palatial if you were used to being crammed into a tiny terrace. She knew some of the houses in Kingsmead were bordering on slums, so they probably were a bit overwhelmed.

'What a beautiful house,' said Helena eventually. Her voice was very faint, little more than a whisper.

'Are you rich?' said Colin.

'Colin!' Helena jabbed him with her elbow.

Jilly laughed. 'No. Not at all. Very ordinary. But we are lucky.'

She ushered them through into the kitchen as it was probably less daunting than the rest of the house. It was bright from the late-afternoon sun that poured in through the big windows looking out onto the garden. There were dark-red quarry tiles on the floor and a big scrubbed pine table in the middle with a selection of wobbly chairs that didn't match. A jug of tulips her mother had picked a few days ago stood on the dresser, the blooms drooping as if they had heard the sad news. Jilly felt her throat tighten, then snatched up the kettle to fill it at the butler's sink.

'Sit down. You must be exhausted.'

Helena sank down into the flowery armchair by the Aga. Jilly flinched: that had been her mum's roost. She'd sat there at breakfast, trying to wake herself up, and in the afternoon when she got back from a day's teaching, kicking off her shoes and tucking into a piece of cake. Her mum had been unashamed about enjoying her comforts and was quite happy for Jilly and her dad to wait on her. It wasn't that she was lazy or couldn't look after herself. It was what they did. There was plenty she did for them in return.

Jilly turned away and fetched the stout brown teapot down from its shelf. She didn't mind Helena sitting there. It was strange, that was all, to realise that she was never going to see her mum in that chair again. She felt a lump rise up and swallowed it down. There was no time for self-pity.

'How about boiled eggs?' she said brightly. 'The hens laid me exactly three this morning.'

Even amidst the chaos of the bombing the hens had done their duty. It had been a small reminder that life goes on. A comfort.

Colin and Julie looked at each other and then at their mother. Helena jiggled Baby Dot up and down on her knee.

'We love eggs,' said Colin. 'But they make Mum want to puke.'

Ivy raised her eyebrows.

'Colin . . .' Helena looked embarrassed. 'I'm sorry. Eggs aren't my best thing.'

Ivy went to say something but Jilly flashed her a glance. 'I've got a tin of sardines?' she offered.

'That would be nice.'

Jilly made the children boiled eggs and toast on the Aga and gave up her butter ration for them. They needed something hot and plain but delicious to feed them up, and she didn't have much else in. Then she found some leftover rice pudding and gave it to them with a blob of jam. Colin and Julie scraped their bowls clean and asked for more.

Helena prodded at her sardines, listless.

'You must eat,' Jilly urged her. 'You need your strength.'

Helena pushed the plate away. 'I can't.'

Jilly picked the plate up and took the sardines away. She understood. What Helena had been through must have been terrifying. And now dusk was approaching and the once sunny room was becoming gloomy.

'We need to get the blackouts up,' she said, snapping on a lamp. 'And I need to show you the cellar, just in case . . .'

She didn't want to say in case of what. But even at the suggestion, Helena seemed to shrink into herself. She went the colour of dirty dishwater. Jilly scooped Baby Dot off her lap and knelt down next to her.

'It'll be OK. You'll be safe here, I promise.'

She knew it was a promise that was impossible to keep, but it didn't stop her making it. She would do her best to keep this straggly little family safe.

After tea, and when the blackouts had gone up, Jilly took them up to the top floor, where there were two spare bedrooms. They hadn't been used for a while and the rose-covered wallpaper was faded and the carpets rather threadbare, but there was a double bed in one and two singles in the other, and although they looked a bit gloomy with the blackouts up, they would be very different in the daytime, with the curtains drawn back and the windows open. And gloomy could soon be turned into cosy, with a bit of imagination and a good clear-out. There was quite a bit of clutter – old suitcases and cardboard boxes full of goodness knows what – but it was only a morning's work to transform them.

'I know they don't look very welcoming at the moment, but this is all a bit sudden. We can sort them out properly over the next few days,' said Jilly. 'Get them aired out a bit, find you some books and toys for the children. Some things to make you feel at home.'

Helena looked anxious. 'Can we all sleep in one room? In one bed? I don't want to be apart from the children.'

'If that's what you want.' Jilly wasn't going to argue, and the children were only small; there was probably just enough room for them all to squash up together. In time, perhaps Helena would feel ready to sleep on her own, but for now Jilly understood her need to keep her children close. Her need to protect them must be overwhelming. 'I've got plenty of bedding, so you should all be as snug as a bug.'

She found an extra eiderdown and two thick cream blankets with a satin edge and two more pillows, and by the time she had piled them all onto the bed it looked like rather an inviting nest. She wondered if the children would have nightmares after the night before, but decided it was more likely that Helena would be disturbed by the memory than them: they seemed to have forgotten everything and were squabbling over who should have the biggest pillow.

She also wondered about giving Helena one of her father's tablets to help her sleep, but decided against it. Everyone needed their wits about them in case the sirens went off again. She didn't want Helena dead to the world. With luck, she was exhausted by everything and would fall asleep naturally. With even more luck, Jilly would too. She couldn't believe it was only Monday and her life had changed beyond recognition.

This time on Friday night, she had been pulling on her lilac dress, the butterflies in her tummy only slight as nothing ever usually happened to her at dances, only Ivy. Three days later, she had lost her virginity and her parents, and was landlady to a motley crew of strangers.

Who knew what the next few days would bring?

Helena lay Baby Dot on the bed to change her nappy. Jilly had worked out that Dot must be nearly two, and probably old enough to be potty trained, but now was hardly the time to bring that up. Dot was waving her chubby legs about and laughing, and Helena was struggling, exasperated rather than amused by her daughter's antics. Jilly could sense she was reaching the end of her tether.

'Let me do that while you go and have a bath.'

Helena look surprised at her kindness.

'That would be lovely. I feel as if I've got dust everywhere still. In my hair and in my teeth.'

'I'll lend you a nightie. It'll swamp you – you're much thinner than me.' It was true. Jilly felt enormous next to Helena, who, despite having had three children, was painfully thin. 'The children can sleep in their vests and pants and we'll get them pyjamas from somewhere tomorrow.'

Helena stared at her, her eyes swimming with tears.

'Are you all right?'

Helena nodded. 'It's just . . . I'm so scared. And I really miss Tony. My husband. I wish he was here. I'm terrified something's going to happen to the kids and it will be my fault.'

Jilly touched her shoulder gently.

'Listen. I'm scared too. But we're going to be all right. I promise you.'

She had no right to make that promise. The night was getting nearer. The black night that might be full of fire and noise and destruction and death. Or might not. But if it meant Helena resting easy in her bed with her little ones, she didn't care about lying.

16

A few days later, Laura made her way up the stairs to the top floor with a roll of bin bags and a notepad and told herself, *You can do this*.

Dom had texted her every day this week, pleading to meet, and every time she had refused. Eventually he had sent her a final message:

> OK. I won't text you any more. Please don't be in any doubt that I love you. Just let me know when you are ready to talk because we can't not talk for ever. Dom xx

She still couldn't bear the thought of talking to him. In the meantime, she was determined to get on with her new plans. She had to prove herself to *herself*. She had to prove that she was more than just a mum with an empty nest. That she could make a plan and see it through, and be a success on her own terms. Edmond's encouragement rang in her ears as she stood on the landing.

There were two bedrooms and a shower room on the top floor, but they were rarely used. If the girls had guests they stayed in their rooms on the second floor, and there was a spare room next to Laura and Dom's room on the first floor for adult guests. So the attic rooms had become glory holes and dumping grounds.

They must have been the servants' quarters once, with their smaller windows tucked into the eaves, but they were each a decent size by today's standards. One had a big old brass bed and the other had two cast-iron singles. It must have been years since anyone had slept in either of them.

Other than the beds, there was not much furniture, just boxes of clutter that must date back to her grandmother's ownership – Kanga had only taken the things she really wanted with her to Acorn Cottage – and all the things that the family had grown tired of but didn't want to get rid of just in case. Dom's accounts were in here together with games and jigsaw puzzles, bits of gym equipment, fishing rods, a sewing machine, photo albums, a travel cot and a Moses basket full of cuddly animals, two boxes of LPs and a hi-fi system.

Laura felt a little daunted by the task in front of her. How could she turn these two dusty, dreary rooms into somewhere people wanted to stay – and, more importantly, would pay good money to stay in? At the moment they were less than inviting.

She thought it would take her at least a month to get them up to scratch. They would need to be painted, new curtains put up at the windows (they would need cleaning; she must find a window cleaner as she didn't fancy leaning out this high up), fresh mattresses put on the beds and bedding purchased. She peeled back the faded burgundy carpet and saw floorboards underneath. If they were in good order they would need painting too, otherwise she'd need new carpet.

She started to make a list. She'd need rugs, towels, toiletries – it was going to cost a fortune. How would she pay for all that? She and Dom had a joint account all the bills came out of, and there was always money for food; anything she wanted she put on a credit card. But she didn't actually have her own money and now she wasn't sure how she felt about plundering the joint account to finance her new idea ... How was it all going to work?

How was it all going to *end*? Would it end in divorce? The very word made her skin prickle. It might not even be up to her. Dom might leave her for Antonia. And that might mean selling Number 11. She would never allow that to happen.

But she wouldn't have any choice. Dom would be entitled to his half of the house; she knew enough about how divorce settlements worked to know that. Even if he was the transgressor, there was no blame. It was fifty-fifty. And no way could she afford to buy him out. Number 11 had shot up in value since they had bought it from Kanga.

The more she thought about it the more she realised she didn't even have a clue how much money they had in the bank or how much Dom was set to make from Wellington Buildings. She didn't suspect him of hiding anything from her – he was totally transparent – but she'd never taken any interest or paid any attention to the details when he outlined things to her. She trusted him, signed whatever he asked, then forgot about it. Irresponsible, she realised now. And it left her very vulnerable.

Her mouth went dry and she began to sweat. This was worse than she had imagined. It wasn't simply that Dom had been unfaithful. It was that their lives might never be the same again. She might lose her home, her beloved home, the home that went back as far as her great-grandparents... She was a fool. If Dom left her, she'd have nothing to call her own. No income, no career, no way of supporting herself... What could she buy with her half of the house? If she got half – she knew they still had a mortgage. How much was that? How much would be left? She simply had no idea.

Instinctively she reached for her phone. She could call him right now, ask him to come back. Then everything would be back to normal. She would be safe and secure, and they could keep Number 11 and she could carry on with her plans.

She was about to text him. Then she told herself: *no*. That wouldn't change anything. All that did was signal to Dom that he could behave as he liked and she would put up with it. Something needed to change before she had him back, and that was her.

She needed to learn to stand on her own two feet. It was more important than ever. The future was a very different place from what it had appeared to be. She would play her part in determining what happened next. Dom was right – they couldn't not talk for ever but she had to arm herself first. She had to be independent and know she had a future that didn't depend on Dom.

It could include him, but it mustn't depend on him. That was the only way she could move forward. On her own terms.

Could she manage it? She went and stood at the window, and when she saw the panoramic vista over the city she thought yes, she could. People would love this view of the church spire, the green hills the other side of the city, the curved crescents and terraces. She would make the rooms cosy and comfortable, with little homely touches. Her guests would be tucked away up in the eaves and she would hardly know they were there, but she would be able to realise an income pretty quickly.

It was a start.

By six o'clock, she was filthy. She had filled four bin bags: two to go out with the rubbish, two for the charity shop. It had been tough, emotional work, going through the detritus of their family life and deciding what to do with it all, but she had been ruthless, somewhat motivated by both fear and anger.

She lugged them downstairs and put them in the hallway, then washed the dust off her hands and face and went into the kitchen.

It smelt delicious and homely: she had put a chicken in to poach earlier, sloshing in all the ends of the unfinished bottles of wine in the pantry and handfuls of herbs. She took down the little recipe box from the shelf and leafed through the cards until she found the one she wanted. She knew the recipe by heart, but somehow she needed the ritual of finding the card with her mother's writing on it. Even after all these years it was a connection to Catherine, the mother she had lost when she was only four.

Catherine had been a free spirit, by all accounts, and had spent her late teens and early twenties travelling, constantly in search of the sun. She had come back from Greece with a tan and a baby bump that had turned out to be Laura. Despite her parents' broad-mindedness – Kanga and Jocelyn had made it very clear Catherine was welcome to live at Number 11 – she had been determined to be independent. She'd lived with a clutch of other free spirits in a communal squat in Walcot Street, which had been a bit of a hippy enclave in those days. Laura had dim memories of a household full of music and barefoot children that smelled of patchouli and dope and curry powder. Her mum had worked in a wholefood shop at the end of the road, scooping out muesli and lentils for other like-minded health-food nuts, as they were regarded in those days. And then one day she'd been knocked off her bicycle by a delivery lorry turning right straight into her path. She had died instantly.

Laura remembered being scooped up by her grandparents and taken to Number 11. She was used to spending a lot of time there, because relations between her mum and her grandparents had always been good, even if they hadn't seen eye to eye on everything. And Kanga – as Laura had rechristened her – had made sure she never forgot her mother. There was a dreamcatcher in her bedroom her mother had made, several of her paintings on the wall, two colourful patchwork cushions she'd sewn. Even now she still had her mother's collection of records and an armful of silver bangles.

And the recipes she had brought back from her travels, including the avgolemono, which was the Griffin family's favourite comfort meal.

Before she started to make it, she texted Kanga:

Come for supper? 7ish Xx

It took only seconds to get a reply:

Lovely.

She took the chicken out of the poaching liquid and strained it, then put on two handfuls of basmati rice to boil. She zested and squeezed the juice of three lemons, and separated three eggs. She was just pouring herself a glass of wine when her phone went. As ever she tensed before she saw who it was, then smiled at Willow's name on her screen. They'd texted a few times, but hadn't spoken properly yet – Laura didn't want to pester.

'Darling!'

'Hi, Mum.'

'How's it going?'

'Brilliant. Totally ace.'

'What have you been up to?'

'Oh, the usual fresher stuff. Drinking myself stupid. Staying in bed all day. Signing up to societies. Taking loads of Es.'

'Willow!'

'OK . . . I haven't signed up to any societies.'

'What are you like?'

Willow laughed. 'Honestly, Mum. It's cool. It's fun. And I've been to all my induction sessions and met all my tutors and stuff.'

'Have you made some new friends?'

'Yeeeees . . .'

Laura could sense the eye-roll and smiled.

'Eating properly?'

'Yeeeees . . .'

'Taken your inhaler?'

'Oh, wait . . . Um . . . yeeeeees.'

'So when can I come and see you?'

'Maybe leave it a couple of weekends?'

Laura could hear panic. She laughed.

'Don't worry. I'm not going to turn up unannounced.'

'How's things at home?'

Laura hesitated. At least she had something to tell Willow that would deflect from the situation. 'Oh, it's a bit sad. Ivy had a fall and broke her hip. She's in hospital so Kanga's been trying to sort what happens when she comes out.'

'Oh no – poor Ivy.'

'Yes. And I'm just doing Kanga supper. Avgolemono.'

'Oh.' Willow sounded wistful for a moment. 'I wish I was there. Miss you, Mum.'

'Oh my God, I miss you too.' Laura felt her defences lower as her need for her daughter tugged at her insides.

Then Willow cut across her.

'Listen, I've got to go. We're going to a fancy dress. There's eight of us going as Crayola crayons. I'm the blue.'

Laura laughed, a little shaky. 'Well, good luck with that. And have fun.'

'OK, no probs. Love you.'

'Love you too.'

She hung up. Thank God Willow hadn't asked about Dom. She wasn't sure how she was going to deal with that at all.

Fortified by a glass of wine, Laura finished off the avgolemono, beating the egg yolks and lemon juice into the chicken stock, then whipping the whites before folding them in along with the cooked rice. The creamy yellow concoction never failed to soothe her, and Kanga arrived just in time for her to dollop several spoonfuls into two bowls, then scatter finely chopped parsley, a sprinkling of lemon zest and black pepper on the top.

'This is just what I need,' said Kanga. 'Beverley and I are going to look at a home for Ivy next week.'

'Can't she go home?'

'Not in the state she's in at the moment. She's going to need full-time nursing care with her hip, and none of her family are up to looking after her. They're all too busy with the salon. And she's terribly frail. I think this has probably been coming for some time. I'm just cross I didn't see it.'

'Kanga, you don't have a crystal ball.'

'No, but she's been getting frail and doddery. She hides it so well, that's the trouble. You know Ivy – last time I saw her she was still in lipstick and three-inch heels!'

'A home, though. That seems drastic.'

'At least she'll be properly fed and looked after, and if she falls again they'll know about it. And if she makes a good recovery she can go back to her own home...'

Laura sensed that Kanga didn't think she would. After all, how often did old people go into nursing homes and come out of them again?

'At least you can help Beverley make the right choice.'

'At the moment, there isn't a choice. Just a place at a home in Frilmington. And the really awful thing is Ivy's released all the equity on her flat so there's no money.'

Laura was shocked.

'That's terrible! How could they let her do that?'

'Well, I think perhaps there might have been something in it for them. You know what her family can be like. They do take advantage a bit.'

'A bit?' Laura raised her eyebrows.

'I'm not going to judge. Beverley's doing the best she can.'

'Well, at least Ivy's got you to fight her corner. I'm not sure I'd trust Beverley to choose my care home.'

'Don't you worry,' said Kanga. 'I'm going to make sure she gets the best care possible.'

17

1942

Jilly could just make out the face of her bedside clock in the gloom. It was five in the morning and Ivy was deeply asleep in the bed next to her, her breathing gentle and rhythmic.

The Germans hadn't come back.

She slumped back onto the pillow with a sigh of relief. When she had gone to bed at eleven she hadn't thought she would sleep, but she must have done. She lay there for a few minutes, and as the relief faded the cold hardness of grief slipped in and lodged itself somewhere in her chest, familiar after only two days.

It was Tuesday. Usually in two hours she would be getting ready to go with her father to the surgery. She felt overwhelmed by the thought of everything that needed to be done: funeral arrangements, all the people her parents worked with notified, decisions to be made – perhaps she shouldn't have taken on the responsibility of a family to look after? But that was how the city was going to get over this: by helping each other, by going above and beyond and putting other people first. The administration would take care of itself eventually. For now, everything was in a state of chaos.

She thought if she could just restore order to Number

11 and make it a safe place for everyone, she could cope. After all, the very last thing she wanted at the moment was to be on her own. She was grateful for Ivy, even though she was a potential liability. She was grateful to the Norris family, for giving her a purpose. Without all of them she would be alone in this big house with nothing for company except desolation.

She slipped out of bed and peeped behind the blackout to see a pale-pink dawn creeping over the roofs below. No plumes of black smoke; no flames. Bath still slumbered, luxuriating in a much-needed rest after the horrors of the last two nights. No one would be able to sleep in for long as there was still much to be done to get the city back on its feet, but at least there were no more casualties, no more destruction. That was no guarantee they wouldn't come back another night, but at least they could make progress today.

Jilly crept out of the bedroom to go down to the kitchen. The stone stairs were cold beneath her feet so she ran back up and into her parents' room, where she found her mother's slippers by the bed. She stood for a moment staring at them. They were a dark red, in a velvety fabric, with sheepskin inside. Was it morbid, to wear her dead mum's slippers?

She didn't care if it was. She slipped her feet inside and straight away their soft warmth made her feel better. They were a tiny bit big, but it didn't matter. She stood up and put her shoulders back, standing tall. Maybe they were magic slippers and would give her the strength she needed. They would give her all her mum's qualities, her kindness and calmness and her humanity. Her way of knowing just the right thing to say or do. She could see her face so clearly: round, with her smiley eyes and pink cheeks and the smoothest skin that made her look much younger than she was.

Jilly could sense a wave of desolation coming. She turned quickly to dodge it, running out of the bedroom and down the stairs as fast as she could until she reached the kitchen door. She ran in, slamming the door behind her as if to shut out the demons of despair.

She filled the kettle, lifted the hob on the Aga, put the kettle on to boil and climbed up to take down the blackouts and let the morning in. Then she ran outside and down the garden to let the chickens out of their coop. She breathed in the spring air, deep gusts of it. Yesterday had smelled scorched and acrid, but today she smelled blossom and damp grass and hope. She heard Mungo give a deep, rich snort of greeting and she smiled: you couldn't not smile when there was a pig on the premises.

Five minutes later she sat at the kitchen table, a steaming cup of tea in front of her, the teapot on standby for a top-up, covered in the yellow knitted cosy she had made when she was eight, the pompom slightly lopsided. She had a piece of paper and a pencil and started to make a list of what needed doing:

Funeral
Ration books
Clothes for Helena/children
Toys
Money?

Money was a poser. She had her own, from her job, and there was always a float in her father's study, in a cash box in the top drawer of his desk. She'd go and look for that later. In the meantime, she pulled out the kitchen drawer and there was her mother's purse, a red leather pouch with a metal clasp. She snapped it open. Two pound notes and an assortment of coins. She emptied the purse out and put the money on the table.

She would have to see Mr Kettle the solicitor. See if she had access to her father's bank account. She realised she had no idea how much money they had. They'd never wanted for anything but presumably it wasn't a bottomless pit. Never mind money, she thought. Food was the most important issue at the moment: she had six mouths to feed.

She could hear Ivy coming down the stairs. Her peace was going to be shattered, and now the day would begin, and they would all have to face the future – the future that was so uncertain and fraught with peril.

'The buggers never came back then,' said Ivy, stretching and yawning as she came into the kitchen, still in her dressing gown. 'Thank goodness. I needed that kip.'

'It doesn't mean they won't come back again, though, does it? Maybe they're lulling us into a false sense of security.'

Ivy stared at her. 'We can't look on the black side. We've got to believe that it's going to be all right in the end. We've got to.'

Jilly couldn't answer. She was doing her best, but some-times it was terribly hard to keep buoyant. She wasn't so worried about her own survival as how she was going to face life without her parents. It would almost have been easier if she'd died with them. But she knew that attitude wasn't going to help. Misery and gloom were catching. She didn't want to spread them. She had to smile, even though she wanted to go back to bed and put the covers over her head.

The door burst open and Colin barrelled in, still in his vest and pants.

'Mum's still asleep. She says you'll give us breakfast!' he shouted.

Julie sidled in behind, thumb in her mouth, wearing a blanket as a cape.

'How about porridge?' asked Jilly.

Colin's nose wrinkled. 'I don't know if I like that.'

'Well, if you don't, we can give it to Mungo. He loves porridge more than anything.'

Ivy frowned.

'They'll bloody well learn to like it. We don't want waste.'

Jilly pulled out a saucepan from one of the cupboards and reached down a jar of oats.

'What about Dot? Is she awake? Why don't you go and fetch her down and we can let your mum sleep a bit longer?'

The two children left the room to go and get their sister.

'Why does she get special treatment?' asked Ivy when they were out of earshot.

'Ivy, we must treat Helena with a bit of compassion. What happened to her was terrible.'

'What about what's happened to you?'

'It's all right. I'm fine. I don't think Helena's quite as tough as I am.'

'Don't you believe it. I know her type. They play helpless but they're not.'

Jilly knew her friend needed a firm hand. When Ivy took against someone it was impossible to change her mind, but she wasn't having her being hard on Helena.

'Don't start, Ivy. I'm doing my bit.'

Ivy put her hands on her hips, indignant.

'Well, you want to be careful. You'd be best off hiding any valuables. I've seen her looking around.' Ivy wiggled her fingers. 'She might not be able to keep her mitts off.'

Jilly just laughed. 'You're being ridiculous.'

Ivy looked furious. 'Don't come crying to me when she pinches the family silver. She's Kingsmead and they're all thieving guttersnipes.'

'We're not, actually.'

The two girls turned to see Helena standing in the doorway with Dot holding her hand. She shook back her hair, looking fierce and proud.

'I've never nicked anything in my life. I can leave if you want. I'll go back down the council. They'll have to find me somewhere else.'

Jilly flashed a glare at Ivy, warning her not to say anything.

'No, no, no. Don't be silly. I love having you here. Come and sit down and have some porridge.'

Helena walked past Ivy towards the table. The two women locked eyes for a moment.

Ivy tossed her head and made for the door.

'I'm going to go and get dressed.'

Once Ivy had gone, Jilly sat down next to Helena. 'Don't mind Ivy. Her bark's worse than her bite, you know.'

To her surprise, Helena smiled.

'Oh, don't worry. I know all about Ivy Skinner. Who doesn't? She can bloody talk about nicking things. She's stolen more men than I've had hot dinners.'

Helena plunged her spoon into her porridge. Jilly

189

passed her a pot of raspberry jam with a sigh. There was definitely a war still on – under her own roof.

After breakfast, Jilly went back up the stairs and braved her parents' bedroom. She opened the wardrobe to see if she could look out some of her mum's old dresses. When she was younger her mother had been tiny and had been known for the pretty frocks she ran up on her Singer. It was only in later years she had become thicker in the waist and hips and dressed more like the schoolteacher she was, although she still liked to dress up for an occasion.

Jilly steeled herself as she opened the wardrobe. It smelled of her mother's scent. It was as if she had walked into the room. She could almost hear her voice: 'Hello, poppet. What are you after? You don't want any of my clobber, surely?'

She wasn't going to be mawkish. She wasn't going to start fondling her mother's old clothes and end up sobbing into them. She braced herself and began to dig about at the back of the wardrobe where her mum had kept the older stuff. She found a selection of things that might be suitable for Helena: some skirts and a couple of cardigans and blouses. And there were two floral dresses made of silk, with tiny covered buttons. She held them up, admiring her mother's dressmaking skills. She would never be able to fit into them herself. She swallowed. She couldn't be sentimental about keeping them. This was an emergency. Helena needed clothes.

She took them down to the kitchen where Helena was spooning the last of a bowl of porridge into Dot. Most of it seemed to be on the table or in Dot's hair. Ivy was washing up the breakfast things.

'Look,' said Jilly. 'I found these. I think they would fit you. They're so pretty. You'd look lovely in them.'

She held them out, showing off the brightly coloured silks. They were a breath of fresh air: everyone still seemed to be wearing the sombre colours of winter, as if war was dictating the sartorial mood.

Helena looked at the dresses longingly.

'Go on. I'll look after Dot if you want to go and try them on.'

Helena reached out and took them from Jilly, then left the room without a thank you.

'She is so bloody rude!' exploded Ivy.

'Shhhh. She's been through a lot.'

'It doesn't excuse rudeness. You're the kindest person anyone could ever wish to meet. I don't know how you can have her under your roof.'

'It doesn't matter,' said Jilly. 'It's not for ever.'

'Let's hope not,' said Ivy. 'Let's hope the council get their finger out and rehouse her quickly.'

Dot banged her spoon on the table and glowered at Ivy, as if she knew Ivy wasn't keen on her mother.

'Come here, you,' said Jilly. 'Let's get that porridge off you.'

She dampened a tea towel and scrubbed at Dot, who scrumpled up her face. She was a funny little thing, but made Jilly's heart melt rather as she pushed her mouth out into an exaggerated pout and breathed deeply in and out through her nose.

'You're a pickle,' said Jilly, giving her a hug.

Five minutes later Helena appeared in the doorway in a green dress sprinkled with yellow flowers. It was a little too long but fitted her perfectly otherwise. She looked like a fashion plate, as if she was heading out for a romantic encounter, but for her clumpy lace-up shoes.

'Oh,' said Jilly. 'You look like something out of a magazine.'

It was the first time Helena had smiled since she'd arrived.

'Thank you wouldn't hurt,' said Ivy.

'Thank you,' said Helena shyly, and burst into tears. 'Thank you. You've been so kind . . .'

In the afternoon, Jilly had planned for them all to walk into town to find out where they could get replacement ration books for Helena and the children.

Helena was reluctant.

'I'll never make it up and down that hill. My legs won't manage it. Can we take the car?'

'That's a waste of petrol. I don't think there's much left in the tank. And I'm not very good at driving, so I'd really rather not.'

'Can't we go tomorrow?'

Jilly sighed. 'OK. You might have more energy then. And I expect there'll be endless queues today. We've got enough food to keep us going for the time being. We won't starve just yet.'

Helena seemed nervous and on edge.

'I'm so tired,' she said. 'Dot kept me awake all night wriggling, and I was waiting. Waiting for the bombs. I didn't sleep a wink.'

'Go and have a lie down. I'll look after the children.'

'Would you?' Helena shut her eyes. 'I just need to rest. I keep feeling dizzy.'

Jilly sat in her mum's armchair and pulled Dot onto her lap.

'I don't mind. Honestly. Go and have half an hour.'

Later, Ivy came into the kitchen to find Jilly fast asleep with Dot in her lap and the bigger two playing out in the garden. She picked Dot up and Jilly woke with a start.

'I was just looking after them while Helena has a rest.'

'You're the one that needs a rest,' said Ivy. 'You look exhausted. Go on – go and have a nap. I'll look after this rabble.'

Ivy waited until Jilly had gone upstairs to her room and was asleep, then carted Dot up the next set of stairs. She rapped on the door of Helena's room and walked in without waiting for a reply. Helena sat up in bed, startled. She'd taken off the dress and laid it carefully over the back of a chair, and was just in a slip. She crossed her arms over her chest.

'Oi! What are you doing in here?'

Ivy plonked Dot on the bed, who rolled over next to her mum and stared balefully up at Ivy.

'I've come to say I'm sorry for being horrible,' Ivy told her.

'Oh.' Helena looked wary. 'Well. That's all right.'

'Jilly's my best friend, you know. I've known her since I was Julie's age.'

'That's a long time.'

'And there's something you should know.' Ivy sat down on the bed. 'Jilly lost her mum and dad Saturday night in the bombing. She's being bloody brave and bloody kind and I get upset.'

'She lost her parents?'

'Yeah.'

'I didn't know. She never said.' Helena looked distressed.

'Well, you wouldn't because Jilly doesn't moan. And they were the nicest people you could ever meet.'

'That's terrible. And she's so kind.'

'That's because she's a good person. Not like you and me.'

Helena looked at her sharply, nettled. 'I'm not a *bad* person.'

'I don't want you taking advantage, that's all. You shouldn't have left her with the kids.'

'She offered,' said Helena. 'And I'm so tired. I haven't slept properly since it happened.'

'None of us have. We're all in it together, this war,' Ivy finished. 'So you've got to do your bit. And if anyone needs looking after, it's Jilly.'

'Of course,' said Helena. 'I'm sorry. It's all been so topsy-turvy.' She bit her lip. 'I know I lost my house, but losing your parents? Poor Jilly.'

'Well, now you know. But don't tell her I told you. She won't want pity.'

'I'm glad you did.' Helena smiled at Ivy, unsure. 'Thank you.'

'Truce?' said Ivy, holding out her hand.

Helena looked at it for a moment.

'I'm not a thief, by the way,' she added. 'I know I'm Kingsmead, but it doesn't make me a crook.'

'Good,' said Ivy. 'Don't take it personally. It's my job to look out for Jilly. When you're nice like she is, people take advantage.'

Helena nodded and took Ivy's hand.

'Truce,' she said, and the two of them shook hands on it.

'Piggy,' said Dot, and gave a little oink.

'Come on, you,' said Ivy, scooping Dot up again. 'I'll take you to see the piggy while Mummy gets dressed. But she'd better make me a cup of tea later.'

She gave Helena a wink and was gone.

For tea, Jilly eked out the few sausages she had to make toad-in-the-hole and made a pan of mash to fill everyone up. As she pounded at the potatoes with the back of a fork, Helena drifted into the kitchen. She looked more anxious than ever.

'Whatever's the matter?'

'I've just come to say . . .' Helena stumbled over her words. 'I'm really sorry about your mum and dad, and I'm sorry I've been so awful. It's just . . .' Her eyes became glassy and her voice broke. 'I really thought we were going to die. Me and the kids. I thought that was it and I was going to die, with Dot in my arms and the other two beside me, and they'd find us all curled up together under that settee—'

'Hey, hey, hey!' Jilly put the fork down and took Helena in her arms. 'You haven't been awful.'

'And I miss my husband and I'm so afraid I'll never see him and it's going to happen again.'

'It won't. We've got the cellar. No one can get hurt in there. It's as strong as anything. I promise you.'

'I'm just so scared. I can't bear it when the night comes.'

'I know. I know. Me too.'

To her consternation, Jilly found that tears were coursing down her cheeks as well. The two of them stood in the kitchen, strangers who barely knew each other, gripping on tightly for comfort.

'Tell me it won't happen again tonight,' Helena begged. 'I know they didn't come last night but I couldn't bear it if they came back.'

'I promise they won't,' said Jilly. And even though she didn't believe in God or life after death or magic or the power of prayer, she sent a message up to her father: *Dear Dad, tell whoever's up there to get Hitler to leave us alone. He's made his point. There's no need to come back for more.*

Afterwards, Jilly felt overwhelmed by the emotion of her exchange with Helena and went into the larder to escape. It was down a corridor by the back of the kitchen, a cool dark room with stone walls painted white, a smooth marble worktop and rows of wooden shelves. There was a meat safe with a mesh front, and another one for cheese. Strings of onions hung from a hook on the ceiling, gleaming pinky gold. She could remember her father in the greenhouse, a piece of string hanging in front of him as he twisted the onions together and layered them up. They filled the air with their sharp pungency.

On the shelves were rows and rows and rows of jars. As soon as she saw them, Jilly remembered the kitchen filled with the sharp smell of vinegar or the sweet scent of sugary fruit coming to the boil, her mother standing at the Aga stirring the contents of her jam kettle with a wooden spoon. She would show Jilly how to draw the spoon through the chutney to see if it parted: if it did, then it was ready. Or to dollop a blob of jam onto a cold plate and then push it with your finger: if it wrinkled then it was thick enough to be put into jars.

There was a rhythm and a ritual that was governed by what was in the garden, from raspberries to runner beans. Ruby-red crab-apple jelly; bright yellow piccalilli; sharp green apple chutney; dark-purple blackcurrant compote: no meal was complete without a spoonful of one or another to bring out the flavour and liven up the dullness of wartime fare. Pickled onions, the white globes spinning in the golden liquid – there would often be one or two on the side of their lunch plate, together with a triangle of sharp cheddar and a slice of brown bread. She could imagine the crunch as she bit into one. Deep-burgundy slices of beetroot: woe betide if any of the juice got on your clothes, as the stain would never come out. And her own favourite, sticky damson jam, which she loved on hot buttered toast for breakfast, tea or last thing at night. She would play with the stones: tinker, tailor, soldier . . . pilot?

Everything her parents had grown in their garden was contained in these four walls. They had left her a wonderful legacy, she realised. The garden was starting to come to life after the long winter and would offer up its bounty over the next few months. It was up to her to harvest what had been planted, and to preserve it as best she could for the following winter. And to carry on what they had begun by replanting. She felt daunted. Although she sometimes helped them in the garden, she had paid little attention to what was planted where and when, or when was the optimum time to pick. She had taken it all for granted; gone about her own life while they weeded, dug, planted, pruned, harvested, dried, bottled, preserved.

On one of the shelves was a small brown box, achingly familiar. On the front were printed the words 'A Family Recipe' in copperplate script. Jilly opened the lid and inside were stored dozens of index cards, all covered in her mother's writing, in blue ink. She pulled one out:

Apple and Date Chutney

1lb apples, peeled and cored
2lbs stoned dates
½lb sultanas
1lb chopped onions
1lb treacle
2 tbs sugar
4 oz salt
pinch cayenne pepper
2 ½ pints vinegar

Put onions, apples, dates and sultanas through the mincer.
Combine all other ingredients and bring to boil.
Add fruit and onion mixture then cook gently for an hour or until nicely thickened.

She could almost taste it on her tongue: sharp and sweet, the last windfalls of autumn boiled down for the coming months, to be served with a thick slice of cold ham or a pork pie. All the recipes she would ever need were in there, with careful notes: *Very greedy for sugar! The longer kept the better. Don't pack too tightly.*

She closed the box gently and held it to her heart. This would be her guide to life over the next few months. The garden and the kitchen would give her rhythm and purpose, and somehow she felt her parents would live on in what she was doing.

18

September slid into October, the daylight gold and the night soft velvet. Laura looked down at the pot of plums bubbling on the hotplate, breathing in their rich fruity sweetness. She spooned away a layer of froth and gave the plums a stir to make sure they weren't sticking, then double-checked the recipe to see how much sugar she needed for the next step. It was her great-grandmother's recipe, she thought from the writing, but both she and Kanga had added notes to the index card: Laura had put in the metric measurements because she found she was starting to think in grams and kilos these days.

She strained the plums through a fine sieve, squeezing out every last drop of juice, then put it all back in the pan with the sugar. It would boil down until it was unctuously thick and ready to be put in the jars she had sterilising in the Aga.

By the end of the day she would have a dozen jars gleaming deep dark red behind the glass. For a moment she felt her heart sink. This was one of her signature accompaniments: she made the plum cheese every year and always plonked a jar onto the cheeseboard when she had a dinner party and her guests would usually see off the whole thing over the course of an evening. She was always giving people a jar to take home with them, they loved it so much.

But with no Dom there had been no parties at Number 11 since he had left nearly a month ago, and she had none planned. She didn't feel inclined to entertain on her own. Nor had she felt like going out. She – they – had been invited to several social occasions, but she'd made excuses. She couldn't face either lying or explaining his absence. Usually she said she was going up to York to see Willow, and that seemed like an acceptable excuse. She hadn't been caught out yet. But neither had she been to York. Again, she couldn't face the lying. Pretending everything was all right when it wasn't. Between them, she and Dom had obfuscated so the girls didn't suspect anything was amiss.

As she took the warm jars out of the Aga, she wondered what on earth she was going to do with them all. There was only so much plum cheese you could eat on your own. Then she thought – maybe she should sell them?

For years she'd sold her jams and pickles and preserves at the table-top sale every Christmas at the girls' school. She had always sold out before everyone else and had made a profit – not for herself, but whichever charity the school had chosen to support that year. She'd made a couple of hundred pounds, usually. Everybody raved about her preserves. She used the old-fashioned recipes from the recipe box that had been handed down, but often gave them a modern twist.

So why not do them on a commercial basis? She could start small, see what the response was. After all, she needed another source of income. She needed to be ambitious. The Airbnb was a start: she'd managed to clear the rooms out. They weren't exactly *House & Garden* standard yet, but they were empty of clutter. She'd rolled up the old carpets and dragged them down the stairs – that had been more effective than going to the gym – and the old sagging mattresses too, then phoned a man with a van to come and take it all to the tip, together with the rest of the junk she didn't want. She'd been ruthless. She didn't need a set of purple plastic dumb-bells or a broken music stand or a mouldy old rucksack. She'd boxed up all Dom's paperwork into date order and put it in the cupboard on the next landing.

Then she'd gone to the out-of-town industrial estate, where the DIY shops and home superstores were, and ordered several tins of paint for the walls and floorboards, floor-length velvet curtains, bed linen, cushions, bedside lamps: it was all going to be delivered next week, ready for the grand makeover.

It had been really tempting not to bother adding it all up, to just slam it on the credit card as she drifted from shop to shop, but she was determined to do things properly, so she'd done a budget and kept a meticulous record. Nevertheless she felt a bit queasy when she saw the total. It was nearly two thousand pounds, and that didn't include the new mattresses.

She reminded herself the rooms had to look and feel luxurious if she was going to charge good prices. She should be able to have them ready to rent out in the next couple of weeks. The day before she'd had a long FaceTime session with Jaz, who was going to build a simple website for her and set her up on Airbnb.

'You're quite the entrepreneur, Mum,' Jaz had teased.

'But you need to get your head around the tech. You should go and do a course at the college.'

'Why would I do that when I've got you?' Laura bantered back.

'You can run the whole thing from your phone, but you need to know how it works. I'll show you next time I'm home.'

Happy that she was set fair to launch in plenty of time for the Christmas shoppers who descended on Bath, Laura decided it was time to add another string to her bow. She went over to the dresser and picked up the old recipe box. She could use this as her brand. *A Family Recipe*. Get the logo scanned off the front of the box and have some labels made up. Isn't that what people wanted? To feel as if something had been handed down through the generations? That it had some history to it? This box certainly had that. She could even do a press release. Get a story in local magazines and newspapers, about how the recipes had kept everyone going through the war and were still being used . . .

Where could she sell them, though? She couldn't exactly go down to Waitrose and give them her homespun spiel. She had to start small, try out different flavours, grow the business carefully. Even Jo Malone had started small, she thought. She'd be the Jo Malone of jam.

She could hardly wait for the mixture to cool down before pouring it into the waiting jars and screwing on the lids. She knew exactly where she should start. She felt a frisson of anticipation: it was exciting. More importantly, it stopped her thinking about Dom. What he was doing. What he was thinking. What was going to happen . . .

She ran upstairs to her – their – bedroom and threw

open the wardrobe door. She didn't look at Dom's end where his remaining shirts hung. Instead, she flicked through her own clothes. She remembered something she had bought in Sadie's Christmas sale and hadn't ever got round to wearing. It was a pale-grey suede biker jacket, and Sadie had given it to her for next to nothing because someone had tried it on and got foundation on the collar. Laura had used a wet wipe to get it off, and it was as good as new. But until now, she hadn't worn it because she'd feared she wasn't really able to pull it off.

Today, however, she felt as if the jacket was perfect for her new image as a go-getting entrepreneur. She pulled on fresh jeans and a long sleeved white T-shirt, and she slipped the jacket on over the top. Then she ruffled her hair up a bit and tied it into a side ponytail, put on a flick of eyeliner, mascara and bright-red lipstick.

She looked in the mirror, turned up the jacket collar and grinned at herself.

'Get you,' she said, and nearly doubled up laughing.

Then she pulled on a pair of ankle boots and headed out of the door.

She loved her city, she thought, as she made her way down Lansdown Hill. Bath suited autumn. The leaves were turning a golden yellow that matched the stone of the facades. She wandered along the pavement with its black iron railings, high above the road. She had a bird's-eye view of black slate roofs and chimney pots, the windows glittering in the afternoon light, the Doric columns surrounding the front doors standing proud as soldiers.

At the bottom of the hill by the traffic lights, she turned right along George Street then left into Milsom Street, which led gently down to the centre of the city. With its upmarket shops, restaurants and flagship department store, the pavements were milling with shoppers and every window was a temptation. Boots for the upcoming winter in tobacco suede, dark-blue velvet, burgundy brocade, black patent, with heels in every height and thickness: leg-lengthening wedges, vampy stilettoes, dainty kittens. Men's shirts and ties, from classic stripes and funky dots to psychedelic. Gorgeous coffee-table books on every subject, from Russian churches to Venetian tapas to coastal birds. Intricately decorated bottles filled with lotions and potions and perfumes and unguents. A florist, its buckets stuffed with roses in glorious colours: pale green and lilac and the deepest blood-red crimson. Every shop was subtly lit and beckoned you inside.

Laura appreciated these shops but she wasn't seduced by them. She preferred the smaller, specialist shops off the beaten track, down the narrower side streets with their uneven pavements and cobbles. The deli with its strings of salami and wheels of pungent cheese and bowls of shiny black olives. The chocolatier that smelled of cocoa and vanilla and temptation. Her favourite was the kitchen shop, with the Italian gadgets she lusted after but could never justify: elegant coffee machines and pasta makers with dizzying price tags. There were shops that sold candles, antique maps, gentlemen's hats, thick black fountain pens waiting to write letters of life-changing importance. She lingered as she looked, wondering if any of the owners of these shops had felt like she had today, about to start out on a new venture. *Ad*venture.

And then she turned the corner and there it was in front of her. One of the places she loved best in the world, that gave her inspiration and comfort and might just be the key to her future, if she played her cards right.

The Lulgate Weekly Market was held in a tiny square at the end of a crooked lane. The stalls were clustered around a mighty oak tree and surrounded by a range of quirky shops and small businesses.

It was Laura's favourite place in the world to buy food, especially if she wasn't in the mood to actually cook. There was always something new to try, something you hadn't heard of, a new culinary fashion or a twist on something old. There was a baker who made every kind of bread you could think of, and some you couldn't, in every shape and size: sourdough, crusty white, focaccia, ciabatta, soda bread. A specialist in infused oils and flavoured vinegars. A charcuterie stall – she always bought a chunk of fennel salami to nibble on with a glass of wine before supper. Local cheese, of course. Sausages and cider and oysters. Tacos and paella and porchetta rolls. It was Laura's idea of heaven, and she loved how the customers and the stallholders interacted, often deep in conversation making comparisons. There were always little samples to try – a new flavour combination or texture to experiment with.

She bought a takeaway latte from a coffee stall called El Beano.

'Is that to rhyme with El Niño?' she asked the stallholder, who was as enticing as the coffee he sold: tall, with wild dark curls and a smattering of stubble. He was wearing a tight black T-shirt with the company logo on it, and his arms were muscular. She could see what looked to be a tattoo of an angel wing peeping out from under his sleeve.

He gave her a self-deprecating grin.

'I know, it's a terrible name. I was under pressure at the time. But you know what? People remember it, and that's the important thing.'

He handed her a thickly ridged cardboard cup. She could smell South America in its steam, rich and dark and exotic. She sipped at it as she wandered around the stalls. Everyone took huge pride in how their food was displayed. The stalls were rustic, built out of old pallets, but each trader made their stall their own, dressing it with exquisite plates and bowls and baskets, slabs of white marble or polished wood platters. The labels alone were often works of art, with intricate lettering and delicate illustrations.

As well as edibles, there were culinary-themed wares: vintage mixing bowls, crystal glasses, bone-handled cutlery and bundles of snow-white table linen. Picnic baskets. Jelly moulds. A stall full of antique cookery books.

Her mouth watering, Laura bought a *flamiche aux poireaux* – leeks set in golden wobbly cream in a rectangular tart – a loaf of bread thick with nuts and seeds, a bag of bitter salad leaves and a punnet of pale-gold apricots. She added a pat of creamy butter wrapped in a twist of brown paper and tied with string, and two tiny pots of rich dark chocolate mousse.

When she had visited every stall, she sought out the organiser, Freya, a dreamy girl with long blonde plaits and pink cheeks in a pinafore dress. Freya had started the market three years before with a single stall selling handmade pastries – croissants and pains au chocolat and palmiers and friands, apple turnovers and Portuguese custard tarts – that soon gained cult status in Bath. People made a trip to her stall on a Saturday for their weekend treats and the market had grown from there. She reminded Laura of Heidi – she'd found her childhood copy of the book when she'd cleared out the attic rooms – but she suspected that underneath the winsome image there was a shrewd businesswoman.

She'd read an article recently where Freya had explained the ethos of the market; how the traders were handpicked by a small team of passionate young entrepreneurs who encouraged traditional methods and artistic integrity. They valued stallholders with exacting standards, and in return they offered support which lured a stream of customers with money to burn. The market Instagram feed was renowned for being stylish and aspirational. You could even buy willow shopping baskets stamped with the market's 'LWM' crest to take your wares home with you.

For a moment, Laura felt shy. OK, so she could make jam – but could she make it and present it to the standard expected? All the stallholders looked as if they knew exactly what they were doing. Did she really have the confidence to go and set up her own stall, her own label, her own brand? This was a commercial enterprise, not the school fete, after all. These people were professionals, not kitchen amateurs.

But presumably they had all started somewhere. Presumably they'd all had the germ of an idea, like she had. They would have been nervous about taking the risk.

You can do it, she told herself.

Apart from anything, there was no one else doing jams and pickles. She had to at least try. She smoothed down her hair, turned up the collar of her jacket and approached Freya.

'I'd like to inquire about renting a stall,' she told her. 'Have you got any available?'

'We've got two possible plots left,' said Freya. 'We're nearly at capacity but we're always looking for exciting new produce. What is it you want to sell? We only have one of each kind of thing – there's no duplication. So – one cheese person; one sausage person.'

'Jam,' said Laura. 'Jams and pickles and chutney. Basically anything you can put in a jar.'

Freya smiled. 'Cool! We don't have a preserve person at the moment. Our last jam girl moved up to London just before the summer.'

'Great,' said Laura. 'What do I need to do?'

'We do have a strict selection process, I'm afraid.'

'Of course.' Oh God. Was she going to fall at the first fence?

'The best thing is for you to make an appointment and bring me some samples. And a list of what you're going to sell, with prices. And a visual plan of your stall and an example of your packaging and presentation.'

Laura gulped. She had ideas, certainly, but they weren't fully formed yet. She was going to have to recruit Jaz's help again. But it was doable. 'OK.'

'And presumably you have your hygiene certificates?'

'Yes, I've got all of those.' Luckily she had, from selling at the school.

'I know it sounds strict but it's why the market brings in so many customers. Because everything looks and tastes better here than it does in the supermarket or on the high street. We're all about quality and individuality.' She laughed. 'Sorry. I'll get off my soapbox. But we're really passionate.'

'I know. And that's what I love about the market,' said Laura. 'I'd love to be part of it.'

Freya gave her a card and told her to call her later in the week to make an appointment.

'It's not just me you have to impress.' She pointed over at the El Beano coffee stall. 'It's Herbie too. He's the real stickler. He was the one who came to me with the idea for the market, when he bought a croissant off me once.'

Laura eyed him from afar. He was talking to a customer, and once again she was struck by how he stood out. 'He looks like Poldark.'

Freya rolled her eyes. 'It has been said,' she grinned. 'But don't be fooled. He's not just a pretty face. He won't accept anything except the very best. He's one of the reasons why this market is such a success.'

Laura looked over at Herbie again and put Freya's card in her pocket.

'I'll call you,' she said, and felt a tingle. It would be a challenge, but she was bloody well going to do it.

Tucked away in the corner of the square, in a crooked little building with wonky wooden floors and bow windows with glass so thick it distorted everything, was the Reprobate Bar. Laura wasn't sure quite how she ended up standing outside at three o'clock in the afternoon, but it had a certain *Alice in Wonderland* allure. It drew you in when you least expected and made you do things you shouldn't. Edmond had bought the building, with its renovated flat above, off Dom, who had free drinks for life as a consequence.

It had been one of Dom's favourite projects, restoring the building and wondering what it might become, and they all agreed Edmond had been the perfect owner. That was one of the problems with walking around the city. Everywhere she looked there was a building Dom had worked on. She wasn't allowed to escape him even if she wanted to.

She decided on impulse to go in for a drink. Edmond was probably in there, and she wanted to thank him again for being so encouraging about the Airbnb idea. At least, that was the excuse she gave herself. Secretly, she wanted to do something she would never normally do, to celebrate the new Laura. Laura the entrepreneur. Laura the jam queen.

Inside, the Reprobate was decorated like a Dickensian bordello crossed with an opium den. It had teal blue wallpaper covered in erotic drawings, wall lights in the shape of enormous clam shells, shelves stuffed with risqué vintage books and taxidermy: ravens and peacocks, and rats and kittens dressed up as pirates. The chairs were deep and squashy and covered in soft velvet, and the tabletops were foxed mirrors so everything was reflected back at you yet seemed slightly blurred – or was it the drink that made you feel like that? The Reprobate was naughty, fun and immensely popular, not least because of its list of potent and imaginatively named cocktails.

And there was Edmond, the eponymous reprobate, wearing his trademark velvet suit. Today's was midnight blue, almost black. Edmond loved the latest luxuries and always introduced you to something that would make you swoon, a scent or a drink or a taste. Last time he had fed her salted caramel chocolates drenched with passion fruit. He was like a deadly cocktail of the Mad Hatter, Byron and Bowie – and just the person she needed to give her an excuse to behave completely out of character.

'Laura!' He smiled as he saw her and looked her up and down. 'My God, I am loving the leather jacket and the red lipstick. You look positively Parisienne. What can I get you? I'm thinking Marmalade Martini. Something very pure but with a comforting kick – just a dollop of Frank Cooper.'

'That sounds perfect. And very appropriate.'

'How so?' Edmond dodged behind the bar and pulled a frosted glass out of the fridge and a bottle of vodka from a bucket of ice, then set about making her Martini, mixing up the vodka, lemon juice, Cointreau and ice.

'I've just pitched to sell my preserves at the market. I've got to jump through a few hoops but I'm really hoping they'll have me.'

'Well, they'd be mad not to.' He looked up from his handiwork. 'And how's my Willow? I miss her terribly, so you must.'

He was so sweetly concerned, and quite genuine. He was a self-proclaimed sybarite, but he understood the importance of family.

'Willow's great. Really great. Every time I speak to her she's off to another party or club. I'm not entirely sure she's getting any work done.'

'Isn't that what the first year's about?'

'I suppose so. The main thing is I don't think she's had an asthma attack.' Laura held up crossed fingers.

He added in a spoonful of marmalade, then held a match to a circle of orange zest, squeezing the burnt oil into the glass. Then he held the glass out to her.

'Has something happened to you, Laura? You really are

looking ... I don't know ... a bit scary. In a good way. You're not having an affair?'

She had to laugh at the irony. 'Absolutely not.'

'Good. You're my favourite couple. I couldn't bear it.'

For a moment she was tempted to confide in him. She wanted sympathy and consolation, and there was something beguiling about Edmond: he would say the right thing and make her feel better about herself.

'It's the red lipstick,' she told him, and went to get her purse out.

'Don't you dare,' he said. 'It's on the house.'

He watched her as she sipped.

'Laura,' he said. 'I'm not buying into your story. Dom's been in here a few times. Drinking more than a happily married man should do on a week night.'

She coughed as she swallowed down a bit too much of her drink. 'He works late and he likes to wind down.'

Edmond reached out and took her chin, turning her to face him. He stared at her.

'If you want to talk, darling.'

She shook her head. 'Everything's fine,' she lied. 'And guess what? I'm going to be ready to rent those bedrooms out in a fortnight or so. So thank you for encouraging me.'

'Neatly dodged,' said Edmond, his eyes burning into her. 'Do you know, Dom says exactly the same. *Everything's fine.* But I don't believe either of you.'

He leaned towards her and she looked into his grey eyes. They were caring and sincere.

'Talk to me if you want to,' he said. 'I won't judge. I can't judge! I'm lots of things but I'm not a hypocrite.'

Laura took another sip of her Martini. It was dulling

the edges of reality. Maybe if she had another, she could forget about everything altogether.

'I don't want to talk about it,' she said. 'I'm trying to concentrate on my business plans at the moment.'

Edmond's eyes were shrewd but he didn't press her. 'Fair enough,' he said. 'But I'm here if you need me.'

Two Marmalade Martinis later, Laura wandered back out into the street in a slight blur. She was going to cut through a nearby square and walk up the back way, via the park, but then she remembered: that would take her past Kettle and Sons. She wanted no reminder of Antonia Briggs. So she went back the way she'd come.

Several shots of neat alcohol on an empty stomach made the journey back up the hill quite arduous. She felt a little unsettled by Edmond's suspicions. If he had noticed, had other people? Probably not – most people in Bath were too wrapped up in their own stuff, and Edmond was particularly eagle-eyed about these things.

She tried to bat the conversation out of her mind and focus on her new projects. There was an awful lot to get done, she thought, recalling Freya's brief. She wasn't just playing shop. She'd need a business plan as well as everything else. She realised she had no idea about pricing. She couldn't just pick an arbitrary amount to charge for a jar of jam. She had to work out her costs and her profit margins.

She had a mental image of Dom surrounded by quotes and bills and estimates, working out his next building project. He did that kind of thing all the time. He'd be able to help her. He'd know about other things too. Insurance. She'd need insurance.

And reassurance. Suddenly, more than anything, she wanted Dom's encouragement. She could imagine his voice. 'Darling, you'll be brilliant. They'll be queueing round the block.'

But Dom wasn't here and she couldn't call him.

Oh God. What was she letting herself in for?

19

Kanga pulled up to the care home in Frilmington with a heavy heart. Not just because she suspected that she wasn't going to like what she found, but because she had no idea of what to do if that was the case. It was a difficult situation, and delicate. And Beverley, she knew from Ivy, could be tricky when faced with a reality she didn't care for. She was going to have to be firm with her from the start. Beverley was *not* a coper. She was a panicker.

Beverley was waiting for her in the entrance hall. The home had been converted from a sprawling Victorian house with a sweeping staircase and high ceilings.

'It's nice and airy,' said Beverley doubtfully.

'Draughty,' said Kanga. 'Imagine it once it gets colder. We haven't had a cold snap yet.'

She wasn't fooled by the grandeur of the entrance. She could see out-of-date posters on the wall and dust on the skirting boards.

'I'll get someone to show you round,' said the receptionist. 'But it's a busy time for us.'

'We do have an appointment,' Kanga pointed out. 'We were hoping to see the manageress.'

'She's with the governors today.'

Kanga frowned, unimpressed.

They waited fifteen minutes before someone got hold of a care assistant. She was extremely young; still in her teens, plump and bespectacled. Her name badge announced her as Lia.

'Have you worked here long?' asked Kanga as she led them down a long corridor.

'Three months, since I left school,' said Lia.

'And do you like it?'

Lia looked at her in astonishment. Then realised that she probably wasn't supposed to tell the truth. 'Yes,' she said, not very convincingly. 'I love old people.'

'How would you feel if your granny was to move in here?'

'You can't ask her that,' said Beverley.

'Why not? It's a fair question.'

Lia shrugged. 'I dunno,' she said cheerfully. 'My gran's dead.'

Ivy and Beverley exchanged glances. Piped music blared out, as if the notes could cover up the fact that the carpet was rather worn and the paintwork grubby. Occasionally they passed an open door, but there was no time to look inside properly.

'I'll take you to look at Mrs Graham's room,' said Lia. 'It's the same as the one you'd be having.'

'This isn't for me,' said Kanga. 'It's for my friend. Ivy.'

'My mum,' said Beverley, but Lia didn't seem to care who it was for. She tapped on a door and opened it.

'All right, Mrs Graham?' Lia sang out. 'Got some visitors to have a look at your room.'

Mrs Graham's room was tiny, with only just room for a single bed. Mrs Graham gazed at them blankly from under her duvet, her hands gripping the edges. There was hardly any space for the visitor's chair. Next to that was a sink with a lone toothbrush sticking up out of a glass. The carpet was corded and grey and needed hoovering. There were no pictures on the wall, and no sign of Mrs Graham's personal possessions.

'Doesn't she have any things?' asked Kanga, sotto voce.

'She doesn't like clutter,' said Lia. 'Do you, Mrs G?'

There was no response.

On Mrs Graham's bedside table was her lunch, on an institutional green plate. Two slices of processed meat, pinky beige, impossible to tell what it was. And a dollop of baked beans roughly the same colour, clumped like baby mice in a dried-up orange sauce. No vegetables. No potatoes. No greens. Next to it was a bowl with a splat of wrinkled custard covering a square of sponge.

'Isn't someone going to feed her?'

'I've got twelve patients and there's only me. Sorry – guests. We're not supposed to call them patients. I'll be back along to feed her in a minute.'

'What do you usually serve for breakfast?'

'She has Rice Krispies. Don't you, love? Or there's toast.'

'And supper?'

'Bread and jam and cake for tea. Then soup and sandwiches for dinner. They have their main meal at lunch.'

'There seems to be a lot of bread.'

'Well, it's easy, isn't it? Fills them up.'

'Thank you, Lia. We'll leave Mrs Graham in peace. I think you should give her her lunch.'

'Don't you want to see the lounge? There's entertainment in the afternoons. Music, dancing, cards, crafts . . .'

'I think we're fine,' said Kanga. 'Unless . . . ?'

She looked at Beverley.

Beverley shook her head. 'No, thank you. I think I've seen enough.'

Afterwards, the two of them stood next to their cars, which were parked together in the car park.

'Well, Mum can't go there. And that's that,' said Beverley.

'I'm so glad you think so.' Kanga looked relieved.

Beverley looked surprised that Kanga might have thought she would think otherwise.

'Of course she can't. If she ends up in there she won't last five minutes.'

'Yes. I mean, I'm sure it's fine and they do their best, but they seem overstretched. And it was very . . . tired.'

'She'd hate it.'

'So what are you going to do?'

'I'll have to talk to her social worker. See if there are any other places available or if we can get some home help. I'll see if I can rejig things at the salon so I can get some time off. Or get Kim to come over from Oz – but that would cost a fortune.' She fiddled with her car keys. 'I'm not prepared for this. I suppose I thought Mum would go on for ever.'

'I know. You forget how old she is.' Kanga grimaced. 'How old *we* are.'

Beverley bent her head and turned away from Kanga so she wouldn't see the tears glistening in her eyes.

'I really appreciate your support,' said Beverley softly. 'This is so hard.'

'Oh dear,' said Kanga. 'Please don't cry. Things will sort themselves out. They do have a way of doing that, you know. If my age has taught me anything it's not to give up hope.'

*

As soon as Kanga got in the car, she had a little weep herself.

It took a lot to make her cry these days. But she sat in the car park of the care home and wept for Ivy. She wept for her plucky and funny and unashamedly flawed friend, who had shown her unflagging loyalty for the best part of a century. She wept for a country that had fought the bitterest of wars but now couldn't afford to look after its own with a modicum of dignity.

Then she picked up her phone and dialled her financial adviser. He had looked after their money when Jocelyn was alive, and did an excellent job of making sure Kanga got the best return on her investments.

'I want to cash in one of my ISAs,' she told him.

Of course, he wasn't happy to hear that.

'Whatever for?'

'I need funds. Straight away.'

'May I ask why?'

'I have a friend who needs to go into care. She's broken her hip and she needs looking after while she recuperates.'

As she expected, he grilled her further and protested and tried to persuade her that what she was about to do was not her responsibility. She remained steadfast.

'It's not my responsibility but it is my duty. I am paying her back for years of friendship. And, as you know, Jocelyn left me very well provided for.'

'Yes. But you'll be eating into your capital. And you may need that money for your own care one day. We've planned for it. Very carefully.'

Kanga could hear panic in his voice.

'I may not. And I'm prepared to take the risk. Ivy needs

looking after right now. I might never need that money. It's what I want to do.'

Her adviser sighed. He knew there was no point in arguing with that generation once they had made up their minds.

'Very well.' It was the expression people used when they were being forced into something they didn't agree with. 'I'll arrange to have the money transferred to your current account immediately.'

The next day Ivy seemed a little brighter, and lit into the box of Lindors that Kanga had brought her, unravelling the bright red twists of paper as fast as her fingers would allow.

'I've had enough in here,' said Ivy. 'When can I go home? They're being very funny about it. They keep fobbing me off. I know when I'm being fobbed off.'

'Well, it's difficult,' said Kanga. 'Beverley's trying to make arrangements. And you need to stay here a bit longer. We don't want you falling again.'

'I'm sick of having to watch everyone else's rubbish on the telly. Beverley said she was going to bring in an iPad but she keeps forgetting.'

'No, I do not,' said Beverley, who had appeared at the bedside. 'It's here. I've even remembered the charger.'

'Oh, good,' said Ivy, reaching out for it. 'Earphones?'

Beverley rolled her eyes. 'Old people today,' she said. 'They are so demanding. I forgot earphones. But I can probably get you some from the hospital shop.'

'Grand,' said Ivy, popping another Lindor into her mouth. 'There's racing at Ascot this afternoon. I don't want to miss that.'

'Have you put a bet on?' asked Beverley, suspicious.

'How would I do that from here?' demanded Ivy, eyes wide with innocence. 'I'm not a bloody magician.'

They left Ivy later that afternoon, plugged into the iPad and scoffing the rest of her Lindor.

'She seems much brighter,' said Beverley.

'Yes,' said Kanga, wondering how best to approach a delicate subject. As they reached the exit, she decided she would take the plunge, and stopped by the automatic doors. 'Beverley, I don't want you to take this the wrong way, but I'd like to pay for Ivy's care. I'd like to find her somewhere lovely where she can recuperate in comfort.'

'What?' Beverley looked astonished.

'Jocelyn left me fairly well-off. He had quite a few properties around Bath which he sold off before he died. And I've got everything I need at Acorn Cottage. The interest on the savings more than covers my living costs.'

Beverley was silent as she thought. Eventually she turned to Kanga.

'I don't understand. Why would you do that? She's not your relative. It's going to cost you a mint.'

'Ivy was an incredible friend to me. She got me through the darkest time of my life. I would never have managed without her. Every day, she found a way to make me laugh and see the light. I never thought I would be able to repay her. This is the very least I can do. She is my friend and I love her. That's the reason.'

'What will Laura say? She won't be happy, surely?'

Kanga imagined Beverley picturing her own family's reaction to a gesture that would eat into their inheritance.

'Laura will be delighted. I promise you.'

Kanga could see that Beverley was overwhelmed by her

offer. They stood in the entrance as the doors opened and closed, letting patients and visitors in and out, the light outside starting to fade.

'But what if . . .' Beverley looked away, awkward. She couldn't voice what she was thinking. 'I mean, you said yourself, you're the same age as Mum . . .'

'What if I die?' asked Kanga, gentle. 'I will make provision for the fees in my will.'

'I'm sorry. I didn't mean to sound ungrateful. It's just I know we couldn't afford it. If you stopped paying.'

'Beverley, it's fine. I understand.'

Beverley looked out of the doors, at the street lamps coming on and the headlights of the cars flashing past.

'I don't know how to thank you. That's the most wonderful thing anyone's ever done.'

'I can never repay what Ivy did for me as long as I live.'

Kanga and Beverley spent the next week looking at potential homes. Talking to managers and cooks and helpers and nurses. And patients. And relatives. It was the homes with transparency that they were drawn to. The ones with an open-door policy, who welcomed them with a smile.

In the end, it wasn't the most beautiful home they went with. And some of them were stunning, in gracious buildings with extensive grounds. The setting wouldn't matter to Ivy. It was the people who would matter. She needed kindness and caring and warmth. Not to be made to feel like a nuisance or just another set of fees.

Amhurst House was a nondescript building, purpose-built about twenty years before, but inside there was an energy to it, a sense of life. There was chatter and laughter and camaraderie among the staff and the patients. A feeling of trust and respect. It even smelled right: of fresh air and flowers and newly baked cakes.

'It's so difficult, this choosing process,' said the sympathetic manageress. 'And care homes have such a bad reputation these days. Which is why we try to be as open as we can. Yes, we make mistakes from time to time, but we keep the lines of communication open. If there's an issue, we deal with it. You are the client.'

A private ambulance moved Ivy to Amhurst House later that week. As she was settled into her room, with its jolly yellow walls, a jug of bright flowers on the windowsill, Kanga felt a huge sense of relief. She rearranged some of the things Beverley had brought Ivy from home on the dressing table – several flagons of expensive perfume, silver-framed photographs of her grandchildren in Australia, her hairbrush and comb. It was a very pretty bedroom, she thought. Like a country-house hotel room, but with discreet additions – a bell for emergencies, the en suite done out with handrails and an easy-access shower, an electric bed so the patient could be moved regularly to avoid bedsores.

'Who's coughed up for this then?' said Ivy, nestled inside a mound of comfortable pillows and covered in a pink velvet bedspread. 'This isn't council run.'

'I think it's overspill. There weren't any local authority places.'

Ivy looked at her beadily. 'If I find out you've got anything to do with this...'

'Oh, it's none of my business. I'm just visiting. I've got no idea what the arrangements were,' Kanga said airily. She knew perfectly well Ivy would kick up a fuss if she knew the truth.

'Well, I shan't be here long, anyway. I intend to be home by Christmas.'

'Then I'm sure you will be,' Kanga told her. 'But for the time being, it looks as if you'll be well looked after here.'

She felt a wave of emotion as she remembered how Ivy had looked after *her*, all those years ago, when they were still running scared, when something had happened to turn her world, already upside down, into even bigger confusion.

20

1942

The Baedeker Raids, they were calling them. After the Baedeker Guides used by tourists. They said the Germans had got hold of them and were picking out the five-star towns as targets, bombing the heart out of them to lower morale. Bath had five stars, and was paying for its beauty: nearly four hundred dead and a chastened population working overtime to restore order, no longer complacent enough to think they wouldn't be hit.

There was a mass burial for the dead: a silent congregation lined the edges of a hastily dug grave that stretched as far as the eye could see. Everyone knew someone who had died. Doctors, firemen, the elderly, a pregnant woman, babies, teachers, schoolboys, shopkeepers – no strata of society went unscathed. The only good thing was the Germans hadn't come back since that weekend. They'd done their worst. Bath could get back on its feet, although it would never feel safe again.

Jilly was lucky to have the money and the contacts to pay for a private funeral for her parents, two weeks after they died. The undertaker had removed their bodies from the morgue and had spared Jilly some time to arrange the ceremony: he was overworked and traumatised even though he was used to death. He had never seen anything on this scale or dealt with the logistics of so many corpses. Of course, he had known Dr Wilson through work, and expressed his sincere condolences.

Jilly was gratified by how many mourners were there. They held the service at St Stephen's, the church round the corner from Lark Hill at the top of Lansdown Hill. Despite everything that was going on, people still had time to come and honour her parents. It was a bright day in May, and she pulled the most gaily coloured blooms from the garden to make a wreath, with fat peonies and ranunculus and apple blossom from the trees in the tiny orchard at the very bottom of the garden. There were patients and former pupils and colleagues and, of course, her parents had had many friends.

Jilly chose the most uplifting hymns she could. Everyone needed to feel cheered. And although a tear trickled down her cheek when everyone burst into 'Glad That I Live Am I', she felt it was suitably rousing, the perfect riposte to all that had happened. '*After the rain, the sun...*' She wasn't sure about growing nearer to God on high, not at all, but the spirit of the hymn was in keeping. She wanted everyone to leave with a spring in their step, not sombre and downhearted.

She stood on the steps outside the church as everyone came out. It took two hours for them all to leave. Each one said something heartfelt, about her father or her mother or both. Each comment lifted her heart a little, and she felt proud, and determined to be as kind and wise and thoughtful as her parents before her. She knew they were good – of course she did – but not everyone was, in this life. If the funeral showed her anything it was that her mother and father had made a difference to a lot of people.

Afterwards, she and Ivy went to the churchyard where her father had judiciously bought two plots long ago. They watched, arms linked, as the coffins were lowered into the ground. That part didn't seem real; Jilly found little comfort in the ceremony. It didn't seem as if it was her mum and dad in the pale oak boxes. As the clods of earth went in on top of them, she tossed the apple blossom from her wreath into the grave: a symbol of hope and a reminder of their home. She left before the hole was filled, tears streaming down her cheeks.

She had been left plenty of money. Her father had had a good income and her mother's had been a bonus on top of that, and they were never spendthrifts. They had what they needed for a comfortable life, and had put plenty to one side. It seemed, for the time being at any rate, that Jilly would not want for anything, according to Mr Kettle, the family solicitor.

'It's no consolation,' she told Ivy, looking at the savings books piled up on her father's desk.

'Yes, it bloody is,' said Ivy, fierce. 'This would be much worse if you didn't have any money, I can tell you. You don't know what it's like to scrat around for pennies.'

Jilly felt chastened. Ivy was right. Of course she had no idea what it was like to be desperate for money, to scrabble for food, to live in poverty. She sometimes forgot her friend's circumstances, because Ivy rarely pointed out the difference in their fortunes. Jilly knew that Ivy paid for the clothes on her siblings' backs from her wages, that she was the provider of hot food and little luxuries, and went without herself as a result. Ivy looked like a good-time girl, but she was a grafter underneath.

Jilly turned away. It was so hard to keep your spirits up

when your heart was aching, but she had no choice, and what was the point in wallowing? There *were* people worse off than her. She had a beautiful house and a bountiful garden and the opportunity to help people.

'This too will pass,' she whispered, and tried to ignore the pain of loss that felt no nearer to healing. It was something her mother used to say to her, when she was feeling dejected, and she knew it to be true. Although her childhood dejection had been trivial in comparison: silly little schoolroom injustices and adolescent frustrations. But somehow her mother's voice sounded in her head and she clung to it for comfort and put on her brave face, yet again. She feared she might wear it out before long.

At Number 11, the strange little household fell into a routine as they headed towards summer. Ivy went back to work at the hairdresser's, and Julie and Colin went back to school, so it was just Jilly and Helena and Baby Dot in the house during the day.

It soon became apparent that Helena had no idea how to cook. Her understanding of basic nutrition was sparse and she watched in wonder as Jilly plundered the garden. It was starting to offer up more bounty, enabling her to make meals from scratch from their own fresh fruit and vegetables and their combined rations.

Jilly wasn't an adventurous cook, but she had learned all the basics from her mother and was going through the recipes in her little box, looking for inspiration. Her mother had written in lots of tips she had gleaned from snippets of newspaper articles and listening to the radio, about how to make food go further and how to cheat. She had been a genius with leftovers. Helena was fascinated, watching in awe as Jilly produced bubble and squeak to go with a small side of bacon.

'How did you manage if you don't know how to cook?' asked Jilly.

'I don't know. I just opened a tin. We eat a lot of bread.'

'Well,' said Jilly. 'I'd better teach you how to cook properly. It's actually jolly good fun, once you put your mind to it.'

She was shocked that Helena barely knew how to peel a potato. She held the knife awkwardly and peeled off thick strips of skin.

'That's a terrible waste,' said Jilly. 'You're throwing away all the goodness. Look, keep the knife very close to the surface. You should almost be able to see through the skin when it comes off.'

Eventually Helena became more accomplished. Jilly taught her to make pastry and Yorkshire pudding and dumplings, how to eke out a sponge pudding with mash and bulk out stews with parsnips and turnips and swede. When Helena made her first pie – rabbit mixed with onion and apple and celery – she brought it to the table with pride. Even Ivy pronounced the pie delicious and asked for a second helping. She and Helena were rubbing along, though there were still moments when Ivy was sharp with Helena if she thought she wasn't pulling her weight, but all in all it was as happy a household as it could be, given the circumstances.

As May came to an end the weather got hotter, and as the temperature rose, Jilly felt more and more limp. She could barely get through the day. An overwhelming fatigue dragged her under. She wondered if she was sickening for something. She took her temperature and felt her glands but could find nothing wrong.

Then one morning she took a sip of her tea and was overcome with nausea. There was nothing she could do to stop herself: she ran to the sink and vomited, retching until she was empty.

'Perhaps that ham was a bit off,' she said, clinging to the edge of the sink, looking down at the yellow bile.

Ivy was eyeing her thoughtfully.

'There's another reason I can think of. But that's impossible.'

Jilly felt sick again. A chill crept over the back of her neck. It suddenly made sense.

'No, it isn't.'

'What?'

'If you mean what I think you mean, it's not impossible.'

Ivy frowned. Then gave a half-laugh.

'Don't be silly.'

'I'm not being silly.'

'You know what I'm on about? I'm on about you being up the duff.'

'Yes. I know.'

Jilly bent over the sink and washed her face and rinsed out her mouth.

'But you can't be pregnant. I mean, you've never—'

Jilly stood up.

'Yes, I have.'

She could see all the fillings in Ivy's teeth as her mouth dropped open.

'What? When?' She was outraged. She put her hands on her hips.

'The night of the blitz. That first night Bath was bombed. I went to meet someone.'

This wasn't the story she'd wanted to tell Ivy about her first time. This version of the story had such a terrible ending. She'd always imagined regaling her friend with a very different tale, and them laughing about it.

'Who?'

'I met him at that dance we went to. The night before.'

'But you buggered off. Like you always do. Left me dancing with that bloke with the huge Adam's apple and the wandering hands.' Ivy shuddered as she remembered. 'He was a good dancer but he wanted more than he was getting.' She frowned. 'You went home. I remember looking for you when I'd got rid of him.'

'No. I didn't.' Jilly sat down at the table, feeling as if she couldn't hold herself up any longer. 'I was going to go home. But I met this boy outside. We got talking. We just ... clicked. Straight away. We made each other laugh. And he was so handsome.'

'Who was he? What was his name? Why didn't I see him?'

'He was at the dance with his friend. They were going off to train as fighter pilots. It was their last weekend of freedom. He wasn't really bothered about the dance. He wanted to go home too, like me. But we went for a walk together.'

'Bloody hell.'

'We only talked the first night.'

'Really?'

'Well, we kissed a bit. And Ivy – it was ...' Jilly couldn't find the right word. She shook her head as she searched.

'It was heaven,' she managed finally, but the word was inadequate.

'Oh my Lord!' Ivy put her hand over her mouth. Her eyes were wide with astonishment.

'Then we arranged to meet up the next night. That's why I wasn't at home when the raid started. I was meeting him in Hedgemead Park. In the bandstand.'

'The bandstand?'

Jilly nodded.

'And you did it? You actually did it? In the *bandstand*?'

Jilly felt slightly hysterical, both at the memory and the consequences.

'I know it was madness, but he was leaving the next day and it was our only chance. We might never have seen each other again. We ... had to.'

'And you've kept that quiet from me all this time?'

The initial flush of excitement at the memory died away as Jilly remembered what came afterwards. She looked down, crestfallen. She didn't want to remember the planes, the bombs, her running away.

'I want to forget it. I want to pretend it never happened.'

Ivy looked at her stomach. 'Well, you're not going to be able to do that now.' She reached forward and prodded Jilly's chest.

'Ow!'

'Are they sore? Do they feel bigger than usual?'

Jilly looked down at her bosoms. 'Well, now you come to mention it. Yes.'

Ivy sat back in her seat and folded her arms. 'After everything you've heard me say. Did you never listen? Didn't you use anything?'

232

'We didn't think.'

'Jilly – you're a doctor's daughter!'

'I know.' Jilly was pink with embarrassment.

Ivy looked totally shocked.

'If that was going to happen to anyone I'd have thought it would be me. What are you going to do?'

Jilly put her hand on her stomach. 'I've got no idea.'

Gradually the reality was sinking in. She and Harry had been swept away, and had taken a huge risk. Ivy pressed her lips together. Eventually she spoke and her voice was curt. Jilly wasn't sure if it was because she was cross to have had the secret kept from her or because she disapproved.

'Well, I know a woman. We'd have to get the bus to Bristol. And you won't be good for much for a couple of days. It won't be nice. And it will cost money.'

Jilly looked horrified. 'No. I can't do that.'

'But you can't have it. You're on your own. No mum and dad. No fella.'

'That is absolutely definitely not the answer. No. This is a baby. It's not the baby's fault.'

'It's not a ruddy baby. Not yet. You can't think like that.'

'It is to me.' Jilly pulled her cardigan tightly round herself as if to protect the child inside her.

'Bloody hell,' said Ivy. 'It takes a lot to shock me, but I am. I'm shocked.' She looked at Jilly in wonder, as if she was a peculiar museum exhibit.

'Sometimes I think it was a dream. Sometimes I *wish* it was a dream, because then everything that happened afterwards wouldn't have happened.'

'So what *are* you going to do?'

'There's not much I can do. Just . . . wait, I suppose.'
Jilly was determined not to panic, although her mouth felt rather dry.

'You have to tell him.' Ivy looked very decisive. 'Whoever this bloke is. Harry. It's his duty to look after it. And you. You have to tell him.'

'How? I just ran off when the bombs started and I haven't seen him since.'

'Do you know his name?'

'Harry. Harry Swann.'

'Harry and Jilly. It's a match made in heaven,' mused Ivy. 'And he was going off to fly?'

'Yes. He'd joined the RAF. He was going to Devon. Paignton.'

'Well, there you go. That's all we need. You can write to him.'

'Do you really think I should?'

'Yes. I do. It takes two, Jilly.'

'I know . . .' For a moment, Jilly went a bit dreamy, remembering.

Ivy leaned forward.

'Was it worth it?' she asked with a wicked smile.

'Is that how it's supposed to feel?' asked Jilly. 'As if someone's let off fireworks inside you?'

Ivy threw back her head and laughed.

'Oh my,' she said. 'He did do his job properly then. Yes, my darling girl. That's what it's supposed to feel like. That's what all the fuss is about. But they don't all make you feel like that. They have to be special. Or very attentive. Some of them make you feel like a lump of dead meat. But some of them . . .' Her eyes went misty. 'Some of them make you feel like nothing on earth. Those are the ones you shouldn't let go.'

'But I did.' Jilly remembered sliding out of his grasp.

'We'll find him.' Ivy sat up straight. 'Come on. Get a piece of notepaper and let's compose a letter.'

Jilly thought about it. The idea of seeing Harry again made her feel . . . well, something, at least. She wasn't sure what, but it was better than the dead emptiness she had been carrying around with her. For some reason, she wasn't alarmed by the thought of having a baby. There was no one to judge her, after all. No one to chastise her. Although she didn't think her parents would have chastised her if they'd found out. They might have been upset that she had scuppered her plans for the future, but they would have supported her.

She sighed. There might be no one to judge her, but there was no one to look after her either. Maybe that could change.

'If you don't mind, I'd rather write it on my own,' she said to Ivy. She needed to get her thoughts straight. This was the most private and most delicate letter she had ever had to write. She didn't want Ivy, well-meaning though she was, breathing down her neck and telling her what to put.

She crept into the drawing room and sat down at her mother's writing desk. They rarely sat in here, any of them. They all preferred the warmth and cosiness of the kitchen. There was nothing wrong with the drawing room, but it did feel stiff and formal in comparison, with its brocade sofas and heavy oil paintings. It was quiet, though, and that was all that mattered at the moment. She pulled open a drawer and found a sheet of blue notepaper, then unscrewed the lid of her fountain pen.

She began to write:

Dear Harry
I hope this finds you well and you are enjoying learning to fly.
It must be awfully exciting. I hope the exams aren't too hard.

He'd mentioned being worried that he wouldn't keep up with the studying, even though he had done well at school.

She chewed the end of her pen. What on earth should she say next?

I expect you're surprised to hear from me. We never got a chance to say goodbye properly. The Germans took good care of that. You must know everything that happened in Bath that night, and the night after. Very sadly, I got home to find both my parents had been killed. It has been very hard but there are people who have suffered worse than I have.

At that point she had to break off for a moment from writing as there was every danger her tears might fall onto the page and smudge the ink. She waited for a few seconds to compose herself, then carried on.

But that night was not just about death and bad news. And that is why I am writing: I am expecting a baby. It was probably as much of a shock to me as it will be to you. I am not asking for anything from you — I have been left quite well off and have a large house, so the baby will always be safe and well looked after and will want for nothing. But I think

236

we felt something, that night we met. Something that went quite deep — at least it did for me — so I felt you should know.

I will look after the baby, whatever happens. But if you would like to be involved, please do write to me. My address is at the top.

Keep safe in the sky, Harry, and I hope perhaps to hear from you. What a funny world it is — how one moment can change everything. But I am grateful for my moment with you.

Yours truly,

Jilly (Wilson)

She didn't put a kiss. It seemed too frivolous for such a serious letter.

She read it back and thought she had hit just the right tone. She folded the notepaper in half, found a matching envelope in a pigeonhole and slid the letter inside.

She held it in her hand, allowing all the fantasies that she had been suppressing about Harry to be set free. Before now, she had closed her mind whenever he popped into her head, not allowing him to have any significance; never giving herself any hope. Now, she gave her imagination free rein. She imagined a joyful letter winging its way back and landing on the doormat. Harry getting leave and jumping on a train to come and see her or, better still, arriving in a sports car. He would run up the garden path and knock on the front door, and when she answered he would fold her in his arms and she would have that glorious swirling feeling inside once more.

She pictured coming home from the hospital with a dear little baby in her arms, wrapped in the white silk shawl with the fringing that she knew was in one of the drawers in the chest on the landing outside her parents' bedroom. She and Harry leaning over a cot, holding hands, watching their baby sleep. Its hair would be a deep chestnut – not ginger.

She knew even as she fantasised that she was being foolish. That life was never the same as it was in your dreams. That Harry probably had another girlfriend by now – or worse, had already had one that he hadn't mentioned. That her letter was the last thing he wanted arriving at his barracks. That he would feel he had no choice but to do his duty but would be sulky and resentful and ignore the baby – and her. That the baby would be ugly and red-faced with ginger hair and wouldn't stop crying…

She shook herself out of her daydream. She couldn't control what was going to happen. The only way she could influence the future was by posting the letter, to the flying school at Paignton. She licked the gum along the flap of the envelope and stuck it down, before Ivy came in and demanded to read it. She turned it over and wrote his name on the front then found a stamp in her mother's little wooden box. She put it in the corner as straight as she could.

Before she could change her mind she took the letter and went outside, walking down the road to the postbox at the top of Lansdown Hill. Mr Archer came out of his house as she walked past.

'How are you doing, Jilly, love?' He tried to come across as solicitous, but Jilly knew he was just being nosy.

'Very well, thank you, Mr Archer.'

She walked on and she smothered a tiny smile as she thought of what she could have said: 'If you must know,

I'm expecting a baby. It was conceived in the bandstand at Hedgemead Park.'

She laughed out loud at the thought of the expression on Mr Archer's face as she pushed the letter into the postbox.

The next few days oozed by as slowly as treacle. Jilly found the mornings sheer purgatory and couldn't face so much as a cup of tea until midday, so she tended to stay in bed listening to *Kitchen Front* on the wireless. Ivy was more excited than she was and rushed out to intercept the postman before she left for work every morning. She was very attentive, and hovered over Jilly, as anxious as if it was her own baby Jilly was incubating. Jilly found her attention quite claustrophobic. She wanted to be left alone. There was a lot of thinking to be done as she lay in her bed: about her parents, about the baby. She was putting the past behind her and thinking about what was to come. It was hard to make plans and have dreams when there was a war on, but maybe one day that would end and they could all come out from underneath the dark cloud and the sun would shine once more.

Two weeks went by before she finally saw a letter on the doormat. It had arrived in the second post: a blue envelope like the one she had sent to Harry.

Her mouth was dry. This was the letter that would decide her future. She was about to find out whether she was going to face her future alone or with the father of her baby.

Whether she was going to see him again.

She knelt down to pick it up – it was still early days but she found it difficult to bend over already as it made her dizzy. She turned it over and saw her own writing on the front, a line through the address she had written so carefully, and three words written in thick red pen: RETURN TO SENDER.

She could see the envelope had been opened and taped up again. The contents must have been read, then the letter put back inside. The message was loud and clear.

He didn't want her. He wasn't interested.

She felt her heart float downwards, dropping like a stone into her boots. Her disappointment was crushing, and it was only now she realised how much she had believed that the power of that night would work its magic.

You silly girl, she thought. *There's no such thing as fairy tales.*

She went into the kitchen, opened the door of the Aga and dropped the letter into the fire. She knew the chances of her fantasy becoming reality had been slim. But she had hoped he would remember the fiery brightness of what had happened between them, the intensity, the wonder...

Her hope went up the flue as the pages of her letter burned.

She was still sitting at the kitchen table when Ivy came home from work. She smelled of cheap perfume and hairspray and it made Jilly want to be sick.

'What are you doing sitting here all alone in the gloom?'

Jilly shut her eyes and held her breath, not wanting to make an outburst. She replied in a monotone.

'Return to Sender.'

Ivy understood immediately.

'Bastard,' she breathed. 'Oh, the utter bleeding bastard. Oh, my lovely girl.'

Jilly shrugged. 'You can't blame him. He's out there learning how to fly; he's going to go and fight for his country, high up there in the sky. He's got enough of a job on his hands. He doesn't need another responsibility. And I suppose he thinks he has a high chance of dying...'

'He's a chicken.'

'No. I understand. He doesn't want a life sentence in return for five minutes of...'

Of what? Fun? Pleasure? Ecstasy?

She wasn't going to think about it. She couldn't find the right word. For her, it had been momentous. But maybe it had meant nothing to him. Maybe it was like that for him every time and not something to get excited about. Maybe it was just like eating a piece of chocolate – delicious but unimportant. Something sweet that was readily available if you knew where to look for it.

She sighed.

'I don't know what to do now. Maybe your woman in Bristol is the only answer.'

Ivy looked appalled, her eyes widening in horror at Jilly's suggestion.

'No.' She was vehement. 'If it was anyone else in the world, I'd have you on the number eighteen bus tomorrow afternoon. But it doesn't seem right. I've been thinking about it. You're just not that sort of person. Are you?'

Jilly shrugged. 'I don't know. I'm not sure now. I suppose I had got my hopes up. Had visions of a happy family. It might be the easiest thing.'

'No. You'd definitely regret it.' Ivy was definite. 'This

baby's meant to be here. I think it's been sent to you. To make up for what you've lost.'

Despite herself, Jilly began to laugh. 'Don't be silly. Of course it hasn't. It was a mistake—'

'No! Think about it. That baby is part of your mum and dad. A reminder of them. And it's not as if you're some useless baggage like Helena. You're fantastic with her children. You're a natural. You'll take the baby in your stride. You won't bat an eyelid. And there's always people around who'll help you. Me for a start.'

Jilly smoothed her hand over her jumper. She looked around the kitchen, trying to picture her own baby sitting in a high chair, dozing in a pram outside the back door, taking its first steps across the quarry tiles. It was a little bit daunting, of course, as any new idea is, but it wasn't impossible to imagine.

She certainly couldn't imagine the alternative. A bus ride to Bristol, a stranger, a dark room, pain, blood, guilt, tears.

'I'll always give you a hand,' said Ivy. 'Auntie Ivy.' She grinned and gave a wicked chuckle. 'I'll teach them all the tricks they need to know to get on in life.'

Jilly nodded. 'You're right. I know you're right. I'm just disappointed.'

'You really thought he would do the right thing?' Ivy looked exasperated. 'Haven't I taught you anything? Never expect anything from a bloke and you won't be disappointed. And trust me: having no man is better than having a man who doesn't want you. Having no man is better than having a no-good coward. You don't want a yellow-belly in your life. He might think he's something

242

special, but a flying jacket and a pair of goggles doesn't make you a hero.'

Ivy sat down in a chair, exhausted by her diatribe. She was nearly running out of steam, but she jabbed a finger at Jilly to emphasise her point.

'In the meantime, you are not settling for second best or giving a damn that he can't step up. He has no idea what he's given up. He'll never meet anyone as good as you.'

'You're right,' said Jilly. 'I know you are.'

Jilly knew that she had no choice. She would never be able to live with herself if she took the easy way out.

'I am,' said Ivy. 'Only next time, take precautions, will you?'

'There won't be a next time,' sighed Jilly. 'Never ever.'

'Yes, there will. You'll meet your hero one day. I know you will. Someone who deserves you and will look after you.'

Jilly sat there, feeling a little bit dazed. She was going to have a baby, without a father, all on her own. Ivy took her hand in hers.

'I'm proud of you,' she said softly. 'You're the strongest person I know.'

'I'm not strong,' said Jilly. 'I'm a wet blanket. I still cry every night.'

'That doesn't make you a wet blanket,' said Ivy. 'It makes you real.'

Jilly nodded, gripping her friend's fingers. They were an unlikely coalition, the two of them, so different in background and attitude and ambition, but somehow they balanced each other out perfectly. Ivy gave her courage and helped her see the world for what it was, and she kept Ivy in check and gave her a sense of security. They would be friends for ever, she felt sure.

The two of them looked up as Helena walked in and broke the moment. She looked at them sharply, because they both looked guilty; complicit in something clandestine.

'What's up?'

'Mind your own beeswax,' said Ivy.

'Actually,' said Jilly, 'she might as well know.'

After all, Helena had had three babies. Maybe she could give her advice. And what was the point of keeping it secret? It only added to the difficulty of the situation, and it would become pretty obvious before long.

'Know what?'

'The thing is . . .' said Jilly, looking coy.

'Oh,' said Helena, waving her hand towards Jilly's stomach. 'That! That's obvious, isn't it? I've known for ages.'

'How?' Ivy was furious.

'Yes, how?' Jilly was curious.

'You can see by how you carry yourself. Everyone starts to waddle a bit, even before they show. And I can tell by what you look like in the morning – all washed out and a bit green. And here.' She patted her chest. 'That's always a giveaway.'

Then she smiled.

'Don't you worry about it. You're going to be a lovely mum. Really lovely.'

There was obviously no question in Helena's mind about whether Jilly would have the baby. Nor did she seem to view it as a catastrophe. This unspoken vote of confidence made Jilly feel a little stronger. Maybe the future wasn't so terrifying after all.

21

Antonia and Dom weren't supposed to contact each other, except in working hours about business. That had been the deal. But of course they did, because old habits die hard. Antonia called Dom because she cared and worried about him, and Dom called Antonia because he didn't have anyone else to offload on.

'Laura still won't speak to me,' he said. 'What am I supposed to do? We can't go on like this for ever.'

Antonia looked out of her window. The clocks had gone back and it was defiantly dark and chilly. For a fleeting moment, she debated getting Dom to bring round a takeaway. What harm would it do? She missed him and his solid warmth.

She walked away from the window and sank into the sofa. She wasn't going to cave in. She must stick to her principles.

'Tell her if she won't talk to you, you'll file for divorce,' she suggested.

'I can't do that! It's not true for a start.'

'Well, someone's got to make a move. You're right – you can't stay in stalemate indefinitely.'

'It's awful. And I hate lying to the girls. Every time I speak to them I have to pretend I've just left the house or I'm on my way home. I'm living a lie.' Dom hated the shame of hiding what had happened from his daughters. He'd always had such an open and loving relationship with both Jaz and Willow. Knowing he was duping them filled him with even more self-loathing than he already had.

'What's Laura said to them?'

'Nothing. She's adamant she doesn't want them to know, in case Willow gets stressed.'

'OK, then tell her if she won't talk to you, you'll tell the girls.'

'Oh my God, no way! She'd kill me. *They'd* kill me.'

Antonia sighed. Didn't he understand this was a game of chess and you had to make moves? Even if you were bluffing? She reminded herself he hadn't had the benefit of her training.

'And everything's falling apart at Wellington Buildings,' Dom went on. 'The landscape gardener can't get to me for another three weeks because she's been held up on another job. The slate guy put the wrong template on for the basement kitchen but he says it's my fault and because there's no record I can't prove it – that's eight hundred quid down the pan.'

'Can't you repurpose the slate?' asked Antonia, practical as ever.

'Yes, but that's not the point. I still have to pay him or he won't do me the amended worktop. And I don't know where to put the old one really. It's all just stress.'

'So why isn't there a record?'

'Because I'm fucking useless and I should never have taken this on.' Dom sighed. 'I feel like jumping into the river. Then at least the life insurance would cover it.'

'Don't say things like that.' She knew he was joking but it wasn't funny.

'Well, it would if I had any.'

'You don't have life insurance?'

'Nope. Too expensive.'

'Oh for God's sake.' Antonia loved Dom, but he could be totally irresponsible. And of course Laura wasn't the sort of wife who would badger him about things like life insurance. If Antonia was married to him...

But she wasn't, and she never would be, and the more she discovered about him she realised it would never have worked. Their relationship had only thrived as a clandestine bubble, with neither of them responsible for each other.

Only she felt partly responsible for what Dom was going through. If it hadn't been for her encouragement, right at the beginning, he might not be in such a precarious financial position, hugely stressed, with his marriage in tatters.

Ironically, what had gone on between them had had no impact on Antonia's private life or career or financial position. It was as if Dom had never happened. She was carrying on as normal.

But then, he'd taken risks and she'd had nothing to lose.

Was it her fault?

Yes. She'd enabled him. She knew she had. She knew there had been moments he could have turned his back, both on Wellington Buildings and their affair, but she had egged him on. Yet again, she was aware she had the power of persuasion; that she'd been trained to take the

facts and twist them to suit. She was an arch manip-
ulator.

OK, she thought, maybe the time had come for her to
use that skill elsewhere.

Antonia felt as if she was walking the plank as she went
up the path towards the front door of Number 11. *Crunch,
crunch, crunch* went her pristine white suede trainers on
the chippings, the windows staring at her as she approached, hostile and wary.

The house was as perfect as she'd imagined it. The
house you would choose if you were offered any house
in Bath. Imposing and impressive but not intimidating or
unmanageable, it was tucked away with enough garden
around it to stop curious tourists peering in.

A home. A family home.

The front door, which was to one side of the shuttered
sash windows, was tall and wide and pale yellow. Antonia
knew straight away she would never have thought of pale
yellow for a front door, but as soon as she saw it she knew
it was just right and the door could not have been any
other colour.

She hesitated for a moment before pressing the white
porcelain button of the doorbell. She jumped at the
sound. It was loud and much more aggressive than she
expected; she would have preferred a gentle *ding dong* to
announce her arrival. But of course the house was huge
– four storeys – so it had to reach every corner.

It was a while before she heard anything, but then a
voice called 'Coming!' and there were footsteps and she
thought about turning and heading back down the path.
Or suddenly thinking up a lie. She could be a charity

canvasser. Or have got the wrong house. She couldn't do this.

And then the door opened and Laura was standing there. She was in jeans and an old sweatshirt, her hair half up, half down, her face pink from running to the door. She seemed to have paint on her hands and in her hair. She smiled with polite puzzlement, as you did when answering the door to a stranger you thought perhaps you recognized but weren't sure where from.

'Hello?'

Antonia stared.

She was startled by Laura's beauty. The simple beauty peculiar to people who had no idea how alluring they were: plump smooth skin, shining hair, bright eyes. How had Dom described his wife to her? He'd said she had long dark hair and didn't wear much make-up and was conscious about her weight, so Antonia had pictured someone dumpy and frumpy. She had always managed to resist looking at photos, because she wasn't a clingy, needy mistress who wanted to make comparisons.

But now Laura was standing in front of her she wondered how on earth Dom could have chosen her over this creature. Then she remembered he hadn't chosen her *over* Laura at all; he'd simply had his cake and eaten it. Laura was the cake, toothsome and moreish. Antonia was just the crumbs by comparison. The dry sponge to Laura's thickly iced showstopper.

Laura was frowning. Then a look came into her eyes: recognition mixed with suspicion.

'Oh,' she said. 'It's you.'

Of course she knew who Antonia was. The power of Google. What woman didn't do a search for her husband's mistress online? Antonia wondered what Laura had thought when she saw her photo. She'd probably been mystified and wondered what on earth he saw in her.

'Can we talk?'

Laura's expression was hard. 'I have nothing to say to you.'

'No, of course not. I completely understand. But there is something I need to tell you. It's really important.'

Laura leaned against the doorjamb with her arms crossed. 'Go on.'

She was intensely hostile. She wasn't even going to ask Antonia in. She couldn't blame her. Why would she? She was surprised though – Dom had always described her as gentle and passive. Someone who wouldn't say boo to a goose. She hadn't expected to feel frightened of Laura herself, only of her reactions.

She swallowed, plucking up the courage to carry on, when all she wanted to do was run back down the garden path.

'I've never been so ashamed of anything in my life. It's not the sort of person I am—'

'Oh God,' said Laura. 'Spare me. I honestly don't care what sort of a person you think you are.'

She spat the words out with distaste. Antonia flinched.

'I understand why you feel like that. I would too.' Oh God, whatever she said sounded so limp. 'But what I want to say isn't about me. It's about Dom. And you. Dom adores you. He absolutely does. Whenever he spoke about you, I felt jealous. Jealous because I knew I would never, ever make him feel like you do. You're his world. You and the girls and this house. He wasn't ever really interested in me.'

She looked Laura straight in the eyes. It was the hardest thing she had ever had to do, because she was afraid of what she would see in there. Disgust. Distaste.

'I am not worth you losing your marriage. Please don't throw it all away because of me. I am nothing and no one. And you – you're everything to him. Please believe me.'

'Oh,' said Laura in surprise. 'Well. That wasn't what I expected. I expected some sort of plea for me to let him go, so you could be together.'

'Oh my God. No. No, no, no.'

'Well, I hear what you're saying. But if what you say is true, I don't understand why. Why he did it. What was the point? I mean, really? What was the point?'

She looked Antonia up and down as if searching for a clue, but could clearly see nothing that shed light on the mystery.

Antonia looked miserable. She couldn't give Laura an answer. Not without going into unnecessary detail.

'I suppose,' she ventured at length, 'everyone makes mistakes sometimes.'

'Hmmm,' was Laura's only response. Dismissive rather than thoughtful.

Antonia could see she wasn't going to achieve what she came here to do without upping her game.

'I *made* him need me,' she blurted out. 'I made out the legal problems he was having with his properties were much worse than they were. I promised him I'd sort them out. Sometimes I would make it look as if he was going to lose a deal. Then I made it look as if I was responsible for saving it. He was grateful to me. I took advantage of that.'

As she said the words, she realised it was partly true.

251

Not that she had ever quite lied, but she had played up her part in smoothing things over. Because she wanted to impress Dom. She wanted his gratitude. She loved seeing the relief on his face, and knowing she had brought that about. Oh God, she thought. She was a controlling psychopath. How had she not recognised how wrong her behaviour was? She'd enjoyed the power she had over him, and manipulated him to make up for her own insecurities.

And ruined his marriage as a result. It was a terrible thing to have done, and the only thing that mattered now was convincing Laura to forgive him.

'He's miserable,' she said. 'Utterly miserable. Don't think for a minute he's gone running into my arms. Quite the opposite.'

Laura was looking down at her fingernails, scraping a bit of paint off. She seemed almost bored. 'Do people know you've got a habit of screwing your clients?' she asked casually.

Antonia looked alarmed. 'No. I promise you, it's not common knowledge. I've never said anything to anyone.' She paused, then added in a small voice, 'And it's not a habit.'

'Kettle and Sons has been our family solicitor for three generations. I'd have expected more professional behaviour. I wonder what James would say if he knew?'

Antonia drew herself up and faced Laura. 'I'm not sure he needs to know. How will that help?'

There was steel in her voice.

Laura chewed on her thumbnail for a moment.

'I'm sorry,' she said. 'I can't carry on this conversation. I've got things to do.'

Then she shut the door firmly in Antonia's face.

Antonia was left staring at the yellow door. She had never felt so humiliated in her life.

Laura ran back up the stairs to the rooms she was painting. By the time she reached the top, she was breathless. She felt sick. If only she'd ignored the doorbell, but she'd thought it might be a delivery: stuff had been arriving all week.

What a bloody nerve the girl had, turning up on the doorstep! It had taken her totally by surprise. Laura hated confrontation; hated being backed into a corner. She should have slammed the door in her face. It was an invasion of privacy. And totally unfair, to take her by surprise like that.

She plonked herself down on the top step to mull over what had happened – the two rooms were bare except for the bed frames and the odd bit of furniture, so there was nowhere to sit.

Her primary reaction was amazement at how un-mistressy Antonia looked. Laura wasn't bitchy, but she was rather shocked by her nondescript appearance: she was even more normal and ordinary and mousy in the flesh than in her photograph. But perhaps that was an act? Perhaps underneath her neat navy-blue clothing she was wearing crotchless knickers and a push-up bra and did all the magical things in bed that Laura would never dream of nor initiate. Not that Dom had ever complained or looked bored or hinted at anything more risqué or daring than she felt comfortable with. She had her minxy moments. She smiled at the memories, then felt a bit sad. It hadn't been enough . . .

Laura couldn't quite believe how cruel she had been, mentioning James Kettle. It wasn't in her nature to make people squirm. But she had hit a raw nerve. She could see by the anguish on Antonia's face that she minded more about being called unprofessional than immoral. She wondered if everything she had said was true, about painting herself as some sort of conveyancing guru. Dom would have fallen for that hook, line and sinker, she knew. He hated the legal side of the job. He would love someone who took all that stress away from him.

As she sat there, she realised that was what Antonia had given him that she hadn't. Reassurance. Something that Laura knew she couldn't. She hadn't a clue about any of it. She would just murmur 'I'm sure it will sort itself out' whenever there was an issue with a project; whenever he came home ranting about a loophole or a structural defect or a piece of missing paperwork. What help was that to a man under stress?

She'd neglected him. As a wife, it was her duty to take an interest and support him. But she'd been too wrapped up in Willow and hospital appointments and prescriptions to worry about indemnities and completion certificates. It wouldn't have killed her to get more involved, would it? No wonder Dom had found solace with Antonia. She had given him the support he needed, and he was grateful.

Hang on a minute, thought Laura. *Why am I suddenly taking the blame for this?* Being grateful to Antonia didn't give Dom the right to have an *affair* with her.

Coming face to face with Antonia was finally forcing Laura to confront what she was up against. She'd spent so much time in the past few weeks burying herself in plans and projects, avoiding the issue. She had so many conflicting emotions – doubt, fear, worry, despair – that it seemed easiest to avoid them. She had even, for a tiny moment during their exchange, felt pity for Antonia. It must have taken quite a lot of courage to come and knock on her door, and she was impressed, despite herself. It showed a certain sort of backbone.

But then a thought occurred to her. Had Dom persuaded her to do it or even actively coerced her? Had he made her feel so culpable for wrecking his marriage that he'd managed to get Antonia to come and beg Laura's forgiveness on his part, by twisting her arm and laying on the guilt?

No, she thought. That wasn't Dom's style. He wasn't manipulative or scheming.

Mind you, she hadn't thought he was adulterous.

Oh God. It was all so confusing. What was she supposed to think? What was she supposed to *do*?

She decided to call Sadie. She had kept her personal life to herself as much as she could, but sometimes you needed the cavalry, to stop yourself going mad. And at least she would have the fun of the drama; she could imagine Sadie's face when she told her about Antonia's impromptu arrival. Sadie would be outraged and indignant, and it would go a little way towards comforting her, in her raw state.

Sadie turned up at seven with a rescue package: a Thai meal from the best takeaway in Bath and a bottle of Waitrose champagne.

'We're not celebrating, obviously,' she said, easing out the cork. 'But champagne is very good for drowning sorrows in.'

'What about for drowning mistresses in?' said Laura, putting the takeaway cartons in the warming oven to heat through.

'I think "mistress" is glamorising her.' Sadie looked at the picture of Antonia on Google. 'You are ten million times hotter than she is.'

'But I don't think Dom wanted hot,' said Laura sadly. 'That's the whole point. He wanted supportive.'

'No. I know this type. It's always the quiet ones,' said Sadie, tapping Antonia's face with a painted nail. 'The psychopaths who look for a man's weak spot before homing in. They are clever and dangerous. Much more trouble than silly tarts like me who look predatory but are actually pussycats. I would never touch a married man. Never.'

Laura smothered a smile. Sadie's memory was a tad selective, she thought, but she didn't pull her up on it. Those transgressions had been a long time ago.

'She was absolutely adamant I should have him back, though. I have to say, I quite admire her for her bravery. How did she know I wasn't going to scratch her eyes out?'

'So what *are* you going to do?'

Laura nibbled on a prawn cracker while she thought.

'I don't know. I just don't know. What are the rules? What are the choices? Forgive and forget? Or divorce and take him for everything he's got? I want to go back to not knowing. I want to go back and start again – to not be the sort of wife he wanted to cheat on.'

'Laura – stop blaming yourself.'

'Oh, let's change the subject.' Laura was starting to feel uncomfortable. She didn't want her marriage under the microscope. 'Look at this.' She reached behind her onto the dresser and picked up the recipe box. She put it on the table between them.

'These are our family recipes. It goes right back to my great-grandmother's recipes from the war. Mostly for jam and marmalade and chutney – they had an amazing vegetable garden here. Kanga said it kept all of them going during the war – her and Ivy and the family she looked after.'

'Wow.' Sadie leafed through them. 'They're so sweet. Look at that tiny neat writing. And all the comments.'

'This,' said Laura proudly, 'is part two of my plan for world domination. But I'm not going to tell you the details until I know it's going ahead.' Laura put the lid down and grinned. 'You'll have to wait and see. Anyway, I've got two rooms to finish painting out first. I'm nearly finished. It's taken much longer than I thought. It's all the bloody woodwork.'

'You're unstoppable. You're a one-woman reality television show. *Dragon's Den* meets *The Apprentice*.'

Laura took a swig of her champagne. 'You just don't know with life, do you? Look at Kanga. Ivy's had a fall and has had to go into a home. They're ninety-three, Sadie. Ninety-three.'

'Your grandmother is a legend. After everything she's been through. The war. Losing her parents. Your mum. Your grandad.'

Laura didn't reply for a moment. Sadie was right. Kanga was so strong and dignified. She realised Kanga must have been around the same age as Laura was now when she'd lost Laura's mother, her daughter, Catherine. Laura couldn't begin to imagine the pain. But she had never let the four-year-old Laura see her grief and suffering. She

257

had been calm and kind and endlessly patient. As had Jocelyn. Laura knew Jocelyn wasn't her real grandpa – that he'd scooped Kanga up after the war – but the details of how and why had been something that Kanga had never shared with her. And you didn't intrude on Kanga – you just didn't. She thought it was probably out of respect for Jocelyn that she had never shared her story, who to all intents and purposes had been Catherine's father.

'I know. She's an inspiration.'

'Has she said anything about Dom?'

'You know Kanga. She doesn't judge. But she's really supportive. She's there when I need her.'

'Just like me then,' twinkled Sadie.

'Do you think we'll still be going strong when we're that age? Still mates?'

'I hope so,' said Sadie. 'I'm banking on you to be doing the cooking. I'll be fit for nothing by then. Raddled with booze and ogling the window cleaner.' She laughed, but something flickered across her face. 'At least you'll have your children to come and visit you.'

Laura looked at her friend. It wasn't like Sadie to be bitter. She had always been defiant about not wanting a child.

'Are you OK?' she asked, frowning.

Sadie drained her glass. 'I just feel sad. That it's come to this. I thought you had everything. Everything I wanted, anyway.'

'But you love being single. You love being the girl about town.'

'I did,' said Sadie. 'But then it kind of became a habit. And I gave out the wrong messages. Secretly, I long for all this.' She waved her hand around the kitchen. 'This beating heart of a house, and a family.'

'Oh, Sade.' Laura sat down opposite her friend and put out a hand. 'I had no idea.'

'I don't think I did. Until now.' Sadie looked tearful. 'Oh God. Don't listen to me. I've drunk too quickly on an empty stomach and I'm getting all emotional. But maybe what I'm saying is don't throw it all away. You don't know how lucky you are.'

Laura was astonished. Sadie had always been the glamorous single career girl without a responsibility to anyone but herself. She'd had no idea she was harbouring such longing.

'It's not too late for you, Sade,' she said softly.

'Oh, yes, it is,' said Sadie. 'There are no single men my age who'd look at me. They all want a younger model.'

There were bright tears in her brilliant blue eyes as she poured the last of the champagne into their glasses.

'Yes,' said Laura ruefully. 'You're right there.'

'Oh God,' said Sadie, starting to laugh. 'Sorry. I didn't mean . . . Oh God. I've put my foot right in it.'

But Laura was laughing too. That was the beauty of a great friend. You could say terrible things to each other and it didn't matter.

22

'You didn't tell me she was beautiful.' Antonia hated herself for saying it, even as the words came out of her mouth.

'It's not the sort of thing you say,' said Dom. 'But yes. In a very natural way, Laura's stunning.'

It was Sunday morning and Antonia had been for her run. In the end, she couldn't stay away. She'd run through Victoria Park and found herself pounding along the pavement in front of the Royal Crescent, admiring the burnt-orange leaves on the sweeping lawns, and then before she knew it she'd been in front of Wellington Buildings.

Now, here they were in his makeshift office. Taped to the walls were all the plans for the house: the electrics, the plumbing, the cabling, the fire doors. Diagrams for every single plug and light-fitting and smoke alarm. At the far end of the room it got more interesting: the kitchen and bathroom layouts, swatches of carpet, colour schemes, and pictures of all the appliances – state-of-the-art cooker hoods and whisper-quiet dishwashers and top-loading American-style washer-dryers. The people on track to buy these apartments would want every modern luxury.

Dom hadn't long got up. He'd been sleeping on a blow-up mattress in the corner of the office, in a sleeping bag. He was making himself a coffee from a nasty jar of powdery instant. He was still in his lounge pants and a ratty T-shirt.

'Isn't that the best kind of beauty?' she asked. 'Who wants to be beautiful in a fake way?'

'I don't know.' Dom didn't want to be reminded. He shook a milk carton hopefully. The lumps banged against the sides; there was no fridge. 'Bugger. The milk's gone off. So what did she say?'

'Not a lot, really. I'm so sorry. I thought it might help.'

She'd told him about going to see Laura the day before. He hadn't seemed pleased. On the contrary, he had looked at her as if she was mad when she'd told him.

'Of course it didn't. No woman wants to meet the other woman.'

'But I'm not the other woman. That's the point. Not any more, anyway.'

She'd done the wrong thing, realised Antonia. And now Dom was cross with her. Though he was trying not to show it. She was worried about him. He'd gone into a total decline. He looked awful. His face had a grey tinge to it. At first she had thought it was building dust, but then she realised it was his skin colour. And he didn't seem to have shaved for a few days. And he smelled as if he had been drinking – she wondered which pub he had been to. He'd been trying to stay away from his usual crowd so they didn't find out about him and Laura.

'How did she seem?'

'Well, I don't know her, so it's hard to say. But she seemed quite together. I think she was painting. She had paint in her hair and on her hands.'

'Paint . . . ?' Dom frowned in bemusement. 'But she seemed OK?'

'Well, she was up and dressed and doing things.' The remark was a little pointed. Dom flashed her a suspicious glance to see if she was getting at him. Maybe she was. The confrontation with Laura had shaken her more than she cared to admit. She had found her so far away from what she had imagined. Not that Dom had ever said anything to justify the image she'd had of Laura in her head, of someone middle-aged who didn't really bother. He'd only ever talked about the emotional side of their relationship, not what she looked like. He'd talked about the strain of Willow's illness and the impact it had on their marriage.

But it was his inability to deal with it all, rather than Laura's, that had made it a problem. And why he'd turned to Antonia.

'I wish we'd never started this,' Antonia said in a very small voice. 'I think I thought I was helping you, when it began. But there wasn't anything wrong, was there? Not really?'

'Don't say that,' said Dom, his voice sharp. 'You're making me feel even worse. It was awful, Willow being so ill. And I stopped confiding in Laura about the business because I didn't want to worry her, because it all seemed so trivial next to whether Willow might . . .' He didn't want to say the word *die*. 'But it's been bloody hard, keeping it all together and pushing the projects through and making enough money for us all. And Wellington Buildings is a nightmare. I wish I'd never bought it but I thought I was being clever. I'm in too deep now.'

'It's starting to come together,' said Antonia. 'Isn't it?'

It certainly looked to have moved on since she was last here, although it was a long way from being ready to put on the market. He didn't have long. She wasn't going to remind him. He knew well enough.

'I am so sorry,' said Dom. 'I've used you. I've used your strength and your certainty and your knowledge to prop me up, because I'm too bloody pathetic to handle it without someone cheering me on.'

'You haven't used me. I knew what I was letting myself in for. I used *you*,' she said.

He looked askance.

'I'm too much of a coward to have a proper relation-ship with someone,' she went on. 'I don't like compromise and I don't like sharing and I don't like commitment. So it suited me. To have a time-share in you.'

A smile flickered across his face at the metaphor. 'A time-share?'

'What's the Stevie Wonder song? "Part-Time Lover"?' she asked. 'I knew that's what I wanted and I set you up for it.'

'I'm not going to let you take the blame, Antonia,' said Dom. 'It's very gallant of you to try and let me think I had no choice. Of course I had a bloody choice. I'm a cowardly little shit. I don't deserve to get Laura back. And you shouldn't be here either.'

'I wanted to see if you were all right.'

Dom crossed his arms.

'I'm fine. I'm going to get showered and have a shave and then get to work. I've got piles of paperwork to get through.'

She nodded.

'It's bloody cold in here. Do you want to have a bath at my place? I've got real coffee. And milk.'

For a moment he hesitated, and she wanted to implore him. She wanted the comfort of his presence. She felt insecure. She missed him.

'I don't think that's a good idea. Do you?'

She shook her head, miserable. 'No.'

He sighed. 'I just want to say thank you,' he said eventually.

She looked puzzled. 'Thank you for ruining your marriage?'

'No. For trying to save it. Not many people would have done that.' Dom looked at her. 'You are quite unique, you know. You deserve someone special.'

She looked away. She was going to cry. 'I don't feel as if I do. I just wish I was normal.' Her throat felt tight.

Dom's instinct was to comfort her, but he didn't think body contact would be helpful right now. Luckily she recognised that too, and walked away without saying any more, her footsteps echoing in the emptiness of the enormous house.

23

Antonia didn't want to go home. She didn't want to go back to that bloody perfect anodyne flat and wonder what to do with the rest of her day. The day that stretched out, empty and pointless.

Almost as pointless as she was.

Self-loathing bubbled up inside her. Seeing Laura had shocked her. Had made her feel the lowest of the low. If only she hadn't taken the risk. It had been totally out of character. But Antonia feared going back to the person she'd been before: the controlled, vanilla, sensible, boring creature who never stepped out of line. That Antonia, she realised, had never felt anything. How could she go back to a life devoid of passion? Of reckless abandon? Of spontaneity? All those wonderful things her affair with Dom had made her feel?

There was only one person who would be able to kick her out of this self-destructive mood. She put her hands in her pockets and headed across Bath. She hoped he'd be in. He'd probably still be in bed – he'd have been out the night before.

Antonia thought her brother was probably the most infuriating person on the planet. But the really annoying thing was that no one knew her better. No one else could hone in on her faults, tell her where she was going wrong and then tell her what to do about it, quite like Herbie.

She arrived at the gates of Hedgemead Park and made her way through the trees to the tiny row of villas where Herbie rented the end house. Around the back of the house was a row of ramshackle outbuildings where he stored his coffee roaster and sacks and sacks of coffee beans.

She was so proud of how far he had come, and of her part in that story. And now, maybe, it was Herbie's turn to show her the way. They were like chalk and cheese.

He hadn't been christened Herbie. His real name was Martin. But from the age of fourteen he had been the purveyor of illicitly grown substances to everyone who needed it in the dreary little town they'd grown up in ten miles outside Bath, and he had a lot of customers, because that was one of the few ways to escape. Someone had nicknamed him Herbie and it stuck – it suited him.

It had been Antonia who had picked him up by the scruff of the neck ten years ago and frogmarched him to Bath, where she had kept him captive in the flat she was renting at the time. Her parents weren't going to do anything about him, she could see that. While he was quietly stoned in his bedroom he wasn't going to ask anything of them, which suited them perfectly. Their mother, certainly, whose only interest in life was dog rescue. She didn't give a fig for humans, it seemed, if her disinterest in her own children was anything to go by. And their father was their mother's lapdog, who did everything she asked and never thought for himself. He ran the pet-food shop which financed the rescue charity. They had no time for anything or anyone else.

To Antonia's amazement, Herbie had turned himself around under her iron rule. It seemed all he had needed was a few boundaries and a bit of bossing about. He'd found a job as a barista and had fallen in love with coffee. In six months he had branched out on his own, started importing coffee beans and had found the house near Hedgemead Park to rent. He had a roasting machine in the garage, and bagged everything up in there. He did all his own design and marketing and distributing. He was a one-man band and happy with his lot.

And although he'd sorted himself out, he hadn't compromised himself. He was still Herbie. He was vibrant, funny and so unbearably good-looking it hurt – his hair and his stubble were just the right length to give him a tousled rock-god look, his triangular torso poured itself into his skinny jeans. There weren't many people who didn't love him at first sight.

But like Antonia, he couldn't commit. He gave willingly of his heart repeatedly – he was a deeply loyal friend – but never all of it. He always held back when it came to relationships. She wondered what it was about their upbringing that made them both so wary and unable to share themselves with others.

Now her affair with Dom was over, she felt she could confess it to her brother, because she wanted his advice.

'Oh my God!' said Herbie, when he'd given her a big white cup full of Nicaraguan coffee that made her heart pound. 'So you're not perfect after all?'

'I'm awful,' said Antonia, sinking into his ancient sofa. 'I'm horrible and evil.'

'Stop blaming yourself,' he told her. 'He was a married man. He knew what he was risking.'

'But I knew it was wrong,' Antonia protested. 'And his wife is . . . just lovely.'

'Maybe she's got a dark side? No one *is* perfect, Toto.' He used her childhood nickname. 'I know how hard you try to be.'

'I feel so guilty.'

'Guilt never changed anything. It's the most useless emotion there is.' Herbie never felt guilty about anything. Or if he did, he didn't show it. He was completely unashamed, sprawled in a beanbag, his feet bare, a cup of coffee in his hand. He was so at ease with himself, so chilled.

'How come we're so different?' Antonia asked him. 'How come you're so out there and I'm so uptight, but we're both so screwed up?'

'Mum was a narcissist,' Herbie told her. 'We never got any love from her. All she was interested in was that bloody charity. Casting herself as the heroine over and over and over again. I responded by rebelling and doing whatever I liked; you kept your head down, desperately hoping you might get some attention one day if you were good enough.'

'Wow,' said Antonia. 'That kind of makes sense.'

'I'm on a constant quest for love and attention. You've always been too scared to look for it. But maybe this affair with this guy is a breakthrough. Maybe you can finally admit to yourself that you're human.'

He waved his cup at her.

'You need to get out of Bath. You need to get out of that bloody solicitor's and go and see the world. Come with me to Mexico for Christmas. That'll rub the edges off.'

He was taking a month off at the end of the year to go travelling. He could do that, because he had no real ties or responsibility. Antonia felt a twinge of envy.

'I can't. I can't take that much time off work.'

'For God's sake. It's conveyancing. Not high art. Someone else can do it.'

Antonia bristled for a moment, but she knew Herbie was right. If she didn't want to stay as she was for the rest of her life, she should get away. Have some adventures, get dirty, take some risks.

But she couldn't, because she had to see the sale of the apartments through for Dom. She couldn't delegate that task to anyone. But she didn't tell Herbie, because he would say she was sabotaging her chance of change. That she was clinging to Dom even though she knew the relationship was wrong.

And it was true. She was in a trap she couldn't get out of. She longed to be more like Herbie. They came from the same parents. It couldn't be that difficult, could it?

24

'Oh, Laura.' Kanga looked around the bedrooms in amazement. 'It's wonderful. You've totally transformed them.'

They were up on the top floor, and Laura was showing off the fruits of her labour: two double bedrooms waiting for her first guests. It was the beginning of November and they were ready bar a few minor details.

The decor was warm and cosy and soothing: simple comfort rather than showy luxury, done in pale mauve and heather. The beds were dressed with pale-grey stone-washed linen then layered up with cable-knit throws and velvet cushions in plum and mulberry. Everything smelled of delicious lavender and fresh laundry; the windows were sparkling clean.

On the wall, Laura had stencilled some literary quotes about Bath:

Bath is the worst of all places for getting any work done – William Wilberforce

Bath is a place of gallantry enough; expensive and full of snares, where men find a mistress sometimes but very seldom look for a wife – Daniel Defoe

'Do you think they're a bit much?' she asked anxiously. 'I think the second one might be a bit close to the mark. Life imitating art . . .'

'I think they're a brilliant touch,' said Kanga.

'And I used a power drill,' Laura grinned. 'I put those curtain poles up myself. They are straight, aren't they?'

'They're perfect. It's all perfect. Like home from home but without the clutter. You've thought of everything.'

'I'm not doing televisions. People can watch stuff on their iPads if they need to. They've got the Wi-Fi code.' She'd hung up a little chalkboard with the code on it, next to a bookshelf with a row of paperbacks inspired by Bath: Jane Austen and Georgette Heyer, mostly. 'The two rooms have to share a bathroom which means I can't charge top whack. It's bed and breakfast, not a five-star hotel.'

'People understand that. And it's very comfortable. Luxurious, really.'

'Oh yes. Fluffy white towels and constant hot water. I'm going to take some pictures tomorrow and Jaz is going to load it all onto the website. Then I can start taking bookings.'

Kanga hesitated before asking. 'What does Dom think?'

Laura's eyes hardened. 'I've no idea.'

'Darling – what is going to happen? What are you two going to do? What about the girls? I mean, it's fine while they're away at university because they have no idea. But Christmas isn't far off . . .' Kanga looked anxious. 'And money. What about money? And what's happening with Wellington Buildings? Is he anywhere near finishing? He needs to get those apartments on the market by the New Year.'

The trouble with Kanga was she didn't miss a trick. You

271

couldn't fob her off. She knew how things worked. She was nobody's fool.

Laura sat down on the bed. She picked up a velvet cushion.

'I don't know. I honestly don't know about any of it. Which is why I'm trying to figure out who I am and what I want to do with my life. Then I can see where – if – Dom still fits in. I didn't have a choice in this happening. So it's my turn to choose what's happens next. It has to be on my terms.' She looked up. Her face was determined, her jaw set. 'Does that make sense?'

Kanga knew her granddaughter wasn't as tough as she was making out. That she was putting on this bravado to hide all the hurt she was feeling inside. She could tell by the way she was hugging the cushion to her, clinging on to it for comfort. Maybe it was better for her to be in denial than to do something impulsive that she regretted. And she did seem to be taking positive action. Letting out the bedrooms was a stroke of genius. And the kitchen at Number 11 was filled with glorious smells – sugar and vinegar and fruits and spices – as Laura experimented with what she was going to sell at the market.

'As long as you're not being an ostrich about it,' Kanga told her. 'Problems don't tend to go away just because you're ignoring them.'

'I know that. And maybe I'm punishing Dom in my own way. Though I keep asking myself where I went wrong. I didn't see it coming.'

'No. None of us did. But you didn't do anything wrong, darling. It's a sad fact that people don't always behave as well as they should. It doesn't always make them bad.'

Laura ran her fingers over the intricate cabling. 'I think

I could forgive a one-night stand. I get that, in a funny way. That you might find someone irresistible and it might be just too tempting. But this was more than that. They have – had – a relationship.' Her eyes suddenly filled with tears. 'He *needed* her.'

Kanga sat on the bed and slid her arm round Laura, squeezing her tight.

'I am proud of you, darling. You've been very dignified. Not many women would have been so composed.'

For some reason, this made Laura unravel.

'Oh God,' she said. 'I don't feel composed. Not inside. Mostly I want to dump all his things right outside Wellington Buildings for all his workmen to see. Or tell James Kettle she's been shagging one of her clients – what do you think he'd say if he knew that? Part of me would love to get revenge.' She paused for a moment. 'But I've always told the girls to walk away and hold their heads high if people behave badly. So I have to set an example. Even if they don't know what's going on.'

'You've set a very good example.'

'What – by messing about with a few paintbrushes and jam pots?'

'Lesser women would have fallen apart. Or taken to the bottle.'

'Or turned into a bunny boiler?' Laura smiled. 'I suppose there isn't a right answer.'

'Sometimes you have to go with your heart.'

'But I don't know how I feel or what I want. That's why it's taking me so long. The girls coming home will force me into doing something eventually. So I'm hoping the answer will come.' She sighed. 'Anyway, you don't need

273

to listen to my stuff when you've got Ivy to worry about. *That's* a real problem, not stupid mid-life crisis affairs.'

'Ivy's settled in,' said Kanga. 'She's sorted for the time being. There's not much I can do to help you. But I can listen or give you advice. Any time. So come on. Let's see some of that fighting spirit.'

'I'm seeing the market people this week,' Laura replied. 'If I get the thumbs-up, my first stall will be the week after. And I might get some bookings in. That's my focus at the moment. That's all I care about.' She paused, then tilted her chin up defiantly. 'Me.'

There was no need to say anything for a few moments. As she held Laura in her arms, Kanga looked around the room again.

She could almost see the ghosts. Helena and the little ones: these very rooms had brought shelter and comfort to those who had needed it at a terrible time. She had done her part in repairing the damage to the heart and soul of her city. It had been a small gesture, but the most she could do, a young girl bereaved herself. Looking back sometimes she wasn't sure how she had coped. But you did. You just did.

25

James Kettle's office at Kettle and Sons looked just as it might have done two hundred years ago. A gleaming desk, a plush carpet, a clutch of portraits staring down and the smell of money, tradition and a little bit of provincial power. As one of Bath's longest practising firms of solicitors, Kettle and Sons was party to most of what was going on in the city: wheeling and dealing, property purchases, divorces and lawsuits – some petty, some founded.

James was as charming as his father had been, and his grandfather before that, thought Kanga. He treated her like royalty, because she was probably their oldest client. She was sure he had far bigger fish to fry than sorting out her affairs, but he hadn't let her feel that for a moment. There had been no question of her being assigned to a junior member of staff. She was led into his office, given a china cup and saucer with coffee and a piece of shortbread and his undivided attention.

James was dressed in an immaculate navy-blue suit that screamed Jermyn Street. His Patek Philippe watch and the Paul Smith tie whispered money and style. She felt very safe in his hands. Both her father and Jocelyn had used Kettle and Sons. They knew how to look after you.

'How can I help you, Mrs Ingram?'

Kanga gave him a rundown of what had happened to Ivy, and the arrangements that had been made.

'I want to make provision for Ivy's care in my will. If I should die before her I want to make sure she's looked after. I've spoken to my financial adviser. He's suggested ring-fencing some of my capital – the interest should cover the fees, and then when Ivy dies the capital can pass on to Laura.'

'That's very generous,' said James. 'I can liaise with your FA and set something up. I suggest we revisit the arrangement every year to make sure you are still happy with it.'

'Yes. I also want to redo my own will. I want to put Acorn Cottage in trust for my granddaughters. And I want you to advise me on the rest of my assets.' She looked at James piercingly. 'What I don't want, if there is a divorce in the future, is for my son-in-law to walk away with any of my money.' She cleared her throat. 'I like him very much, but my money belongs to Laura, not him.'

'Is a divorce likely?' James steepled his fingers.

'Well,' said Kanga. 'You never know, do you? I'd rather put things in place now.'

'There are several ways of organising things. Let me have a word with my colleagues and we'll draw up some suggestions. If you make an appointment to come and see me in a week or so, we can talk it all through.'

'Perfect.'

'Is there anything else I can help you with?'

'Actually,' said Kanga, 'yes. There is.'

Afterwards, she drove over to Amhurst House to visit Ivy.

'I don't know if it was a bug she picked up in hospital,' said the manageress. 'But she's been very quiet. She's

276

sleeping a lot.' Her face was genuinely concerned. 'We'll call in the doctor if she doesn't perk up by tomorrow. Unless you'd rather we called one now?'

Ivy looked very small in her little bed. But Kanga was pleased the room smelled fresh and clean, and the sheets were crisp, and although she was asleep she was a better colour than she had been in hospital – her cheeks were pink. Unless that was a fever.

'Is she eating?'

'She had some lunch. Some fish pie and some sweet-corn. And some syrup sponge. She's got a sweet tooth.'

'She has.' Kanga smiled. She remembered Ivy getting her hands on an illicit supply of chocolate. The Fry's factory in Bristol had donated free chocolate bars to the city of Bath after the Blitz, and somehow Ivy had managed to secure more than her fair share. She had brought it home and handed it round, even to Helena. 'Let's have it all now,' said Ivy, her eyes bright with greed and pleasure. 'Let's eat it till we're sick.' They had feasted until they could eat no more. 'Let's see how she is in the morning.'

'She might just be sickening for a cold. It's that time of year.'

Kanga went and sat in the upholstered chair next to Ivy's bed. She swallowed down a lump in her throat. Events were hitting her hard today, after the adrenaline of the hospital and then the move. She was worried about her friend, and her granddaughter. She'd done everything she could to protect them, she told herself. James Kettle would make sure of that.

She'd brought in a framed photo for Ivy to put on her dressing table. Earlier in the year, they had both attended the seventy-fifth memorial of the Bath Blitz. It had been a clear April day, and they had stood together, arms linked, heads bowed, as a young girl played the Last Post on the trumpet, by the memorial gate in Victoria Park. They were two of only a handful of survivors to attend.

A journalist had taken a picture of them for the local paper: Kanga in a navy-blue overcoat with her mother's brooch on the lapel, Ivy in defiant red with a beret at a jaunty angle, still in high heels. Ivy had put two fingers up at Hitler for the photo, and Kanga had to tell the journalist quite firmly that he wasn't to use that one.

'Four hundred and seventeen. Four hundred and seventeen of the poor buggers,' Ivy had told him, and Kanga had wiped her eyes at the memory of her mum and dad. Seventy-five years since she had seen them, that last night, over a supper of lamb and boiled potatoes. What would she have said to them if she had known that was the last time she would see them? She'd been so busy thinking about her rendezvous with Harry Swann, she couldn't remember what they'd talked about. But she comforted herself knowing that there had never been any rancour between them, that although she had been preoccupied she would not have been rude or unkind, and they would have gone off to bed knowing she loved them.

And Harry. She'd seen his name in the paper too, towards the end of the war. Shot down over Italy somewhere. She'd wept when she'd read it: that handsome young man, so full of promise. What a waste of a life.

Ivy had scoffed. 'He wasn't much of a gentleman. You're better off being looked after by me,' she said. 'I won't ever let you down.'

It was true. Ivy had never let her down. Though sometimes she had tried her patience. She shook her head, a smile on her lips as she remembered Ivy's antics. She'd been a handful. She had never quite known what her friend would get up to next. It was never dull, life with Ivy.

26

1942

A few weeks later, another letter arrived on the door-mat.

Helena ran into the kitchen waving it excitedly.

'He's coming home. He's got leave. My Tony will be here in less than a fortnight!'

She was crackling with the excitement, her eyes sparkling as she reread the letter in her hands.

'Oh, that's fantastic,' said Jilly. 'I'm so pleased.'

She had often thought how hard it must be for Helena, not knowing if, let alone when, she might see her husband again. Scouring the paper every day for news of battles and fatalities. Always slightly dreading the ring or knock on the front door in case it was a telegram.

Helena's face fell for a moment.

'It will be all right for him to come and stay here, won't it? Only there's nowhere else we can go. I'm not going to his mum's. She doesn't like me. We don't get on.'

'Tony would be very welcome here,' she reassured Helena. 'I'll prepare a special lunch to welcome him home. There might be a war on but it won't stop us celebrating.'

The relief on Helena's face was palpable. She held the letter to her heart.

'Oh, thank you. I can't believe I'm going to see him. Just you wait till you meet him. He's a dreamboat, my Tony. And so handsome. I sometimes don't understand why he picked me, but he did.'

The children were like over-inflated balloons the day their father came home, so excited they might pop. Even Baby Dot, who probably had no proper memory of her daddy, had very carefully helped Jilly make two dozen jam tarts, and together they had rolled out the scraps and put a pastry letter on each tart, arranging them on a big white plate to spell out WELCOME HOME DADDY.

'You clever thing!' Jilly told her, and Dot clapped her fat little hands.

'Daddy!' she crowed, because they'd all been getting her to practise saying it.

Helena was sitting in a chair in the middle of the kitchen. In the excitement of Tony's return, Ivy had offered to do her a shampoo and set. The two women seemed to have settled into an uneasy friendship, though Ivy was always sure to remind Helena she was top dog. Jilly was pleased, even though she wasn't entirely sure how hygienic it was – Helena's long dark hairs got everywhere as it was – but she looked around the kitchen and felt pride at how far they had all come since that dreadful night.

'Right,' said Ivy to Helena when all her hair had been neatly rolled onto curlers. 'Let's go upstairs while that sets and do your face. And get you changed.'

Jilly was happy to stay in the kitchen and look after the three children. They were occupied in making a big 'welcome home' sign to put over the fireplace. Even Dot was scribbling furiously on the edge in blue crayon. Jilly had to chastise Colin when he got agitated.

'She's ruining it.'

'There's room for all of you to do what you want. It doesn't have to be perfect.'

'Yes, it does!'

'That's your corner of the poster there. Don't worry about Dot's. It's from all of you.'

Jilly managed to restore peace by distracting them with a few of the broken jam tarts.

Half an hour later, the kitchen door flew open.

'Ta da!' Ivy stood back and revealed her handiwork.

Everyone gasped.

Helena's hair was coaxed into an elaborate roll on top of her head, then fell in thick, smooth curls down to her shoulders. Her arched eyebrows were painted black and her lips were ruby red to match the red silk dress Jilly had found packed away in another wardrobe. She had put on a little bit of weight while being at Number 11, thanks to Jilly's home-cooking, and the extra pounds suited her. She looked less gaunt. Even better, she had lost that haunted look. She didn't jump any longer at every loud noise or continually look over her shoulder.

'You look like a film star!' said Jilly.

Helena beamed, and at that moment there was a loud *rat-a-tat-tat* on the door.

'That's my Tony,' she said. 'That's his knock. I'd know it anywhere.'

Tony Norris wasn't a particularly tall man, but he filled the room with his personality the moment he walked in. He was charming and quick-witted and funny, with a boxer's broken nose and dark eyes that gleamed with mischief. The sort of person who kept you going when your morale was flagging, he missed no opportunity for a joke. The house rang with his laughter as soon as he stepped over the threshold.

He disappeared under a sea of children when Helena brought him into the kitchen. They clambered all over him, and he dangled them upside down by the ankles until they screamed for him to stop. Dot was overawed by his presence, but wouldn't leave his side.

'My little monkey,' he called her.

Helena rushed around helping Jilly serve up the 'welcome home' dinner they had made: a great big Irish stew. They'd saved up their meat rations to get as much mutton as they could, then filled it out with potatoes and leeks and onions from the garden, and Helena had made some dumplings as well. She carried it proudly to the table and the rich scent of gravy filled the air as the lid came off the pot.

Jilly looked around the table as they ate. She'd made a difference, she thought. The children were much calmer and better-mannered than they had been when they arrived, and they were more confident. They also got on better; it would be impossible to expect small children not to squabble, but now they played together nicely and shared, where once there would have been snatching and tattle-telling.

The only thing that unsettled her was Tony. There was a hunger in his eyes she recognised when she saw him looking at Ivy. She sensed trouble on the horizon. She would say nothing, for the time being. Hopefully Tony would be distracted by his wife. Helena was glowing under his attention. It was as if someone had thrown fairy dust over her and brought her back to life.

The atmosphere in the house changed dramatically once Tony had arrived. Perhaps it was the presence of a male in the house – the rumble of a deeper voice, a heavier tread on the stairs, the scent of tobacco – but it felt quite different to Jilly. Although Tony was very amiable – and particularly charming to Jilly, as the hostess – she wasn't sure he made her feel comfortable, perhaps because he was so different from her father, who had been mild-mannered, considerate and, above all, helpful. Tony seemed to think that being on leave meant he needn't to lift a finger. Once or twice Jilly had asked him to help her mend something or bring something in from the garden and he had obliged, but he didn't think ahead or do anything more than he needed to.

He was only here for a fortnight, so she didn't confront him about it. But gradually his upbeat persona began to tarnish. He was irritable with the children and ignored Helena. All he wanted to do was sit with a glass of beer and a cigarette, reading the paper, or fall asleep on the settee in the drawing room. He liked it in the drawing room, but he told the children they weren't to come and disturb him while he was in there.

Basically, thought Jilly, as long as no one demanded anything of him, and he was kept fed and watered and left to his own devices, he was charm personified. But that wasn't how life worked. And it made her sad, as she could see Helena drooping visibly, losing her sparkle too. She became almost downtrodden when he snapped at her or, worse, took no notice of her. The honeymoon period seemed to be over. Helena became more and more withdrawn. In the meantime, Tony seemed to focus his attention on Ivy, teasing her, telling her jokes, asking her questions. To be fair to Ivy, she treated him the same way she treated everyone else, with her good-natured banter. But it was obvious Tony found Ivy beguiling.

On the middle Sunday of Tony's leave, Ivy was cutting his hair in the kitchen and giving him a wet shave. He was sitting in the chair with a towel round his neck. As Ivy took care to scrape the last of the shaving cream from his cheeks and was smoothing his hair into place, Tony was enjoying the attention.

Helena was sitting at the table peeling potatoes for lunch, looking more and more miserable. As Ivy poured some balm onto her hands and patted it onto Tony's cheeks, Helena slammed down the vegetable knife and ran out of the kitchen.

'What have I done now?' asked Tony. 'I've just been sat here. How can I have done anything wrong?'

Jilly looked at Ivy, who just shrugged. She pulled away the towel that had been round Tony's neck.

'There you go, handsome,' she chirruped. 'Go and see to the missis. Put a smile back on her face.'

There was no point in having a go at Ivy, Jilly thought afterwards as she swept up Tony's curls from the floor and put them in the bin. Tony had a game going on with Ivy and Helena, Jilly could see that, and it wasn't a nice one. But it wasn't fair to castigate Ivy, who was just being herself. She suspected Ivy didn't always understand the extent of the power she had over people, probably because she wasn't technically pretty, and so thought little of herself. But she had something more animal, that men liked and women feared. Jilly herself was immune, because she knew Ivy inside out, almost like a sister, and they had never competed. But she didn't like the way Tony was playing Ivy and Helena off one another. It was unsettling.

Exasperated, Jilly decided not to bother cooking Sunday lunch after all. What was the point? It was supposed to be a time when everyone got together round the table and enjoyed each other's company, not a war zone. The piece of bacon she was going to boil could wait for another day. The parsley she'd snipped for the sauce would keep fresh stuck in a glass of water. She would make potato cakes for the kids instead with the spuds Helena had peeled.

She went out to feed Mungo, who gave her a sympathetic grunt.

'I don't know, Mungo,' she sighed. 'Seems to me people aren't happy unless they are causing trouble. Give me a pig any day.'

A couple of hours later Tony came down into the kitchen looking miserable.

'I don't know what's the matter with her,' Tony told Jilly. 'I don't know what more I can do to make her happy. It's not my fault there's a war on. I can't just leave and come home. And I know we haven't got a place of our own yet, but she says she loves it here. Says it's the happiest she's ever been.'

'I think the bombing was pretty frightening,' said Jilly, handing him a cup of tea. 'I think it's had a bit of an effect on her. You should remember that. She thought they were all going to die.'

'I know. But they didn't.' Tony looked disgruntled. 'Maybe I should get her something really nice for Christmas. A ring or something? Do you think that would help?'

'No,' said Jilly. 'I don't think it's as simple as that.'

'The fucking war.' Tony looked up, shamefaced. 'Sorry. I didn't mean to swear.'

'It's OK. I agree with you. The fucking war.' She handed him a Garibaldi biscuit. 'Just be patient and kind. She misses you.'

'She's got a funny way of showing it.' Tony looked down into his tea, gloomy.

'And you shouldn't play up to Ivy.' She was going to say it. She wasn't going to let him get away with it.

Tony looked up, his eyes wide with innocence.

'I don't know what you mean.'

Three days later, Jilly went up the stairs with a pile of clean clothes for the children. She'd laundered and ironed them herself because it was quicker than trying to get Helena motivated: she was very distracted and hard to manage while Tony was around, and Jilly didn't want to put her under pressure. She was surprised she had managed to go out today, but she'd decided to walk the children to the school with Baby Dot in her pram, then take her to Hedgemead Park to play before coming back for lunch.

She knocked on the door before going in. She didn't know whether Tony was still asleep or not. She jumped as the door opened suddenly and Ivy came out, pulling the door shut behind her with a bang.

She was in a pale-green silk dressing gown, loosely tied at the waist.

'What are you doing here?' demanded Jilly. 'You should be at work.'

'Off sick. With a headache.'

'What were you doing in there?'

Ivy put her hands on her hips, her dressing gown falling open to reveal a bare shoulder.

'What are you saying?'

'Ivy – you have to admit, it looks suspicious, you coming out of there half-dressed. I've seen the way Tony looks at you.'

'Yes,' said Ivy. 'So have I. And I went in there to put him straight. He's got to pay that poor girl more attention. Be a bit more kind. OK, yeah, so he's off fighting, but she's been through it as well, and he doesn't seem to realise. Those kids are a handful and he does nothing to help her out. He's a selfish pig and he needs to snap out of it.'

'Oh,' said Jilly, realising she had underestimated her friend. 'I'm sorry, Ivy. I got the wrong end of the stick.'

Ivy glared at her.

'Yeah. Well. You obviously don't think much of me.'

She pushed past her and ran off down the stairs.

Jilly was dumbfounded. Before she could decide what to do, the bedroom door opened again and Tony stood there. He was in his trousers, bare-chested, and Jilly could see every muscle in his arms, his skin smooth. His hair was swept back, just one lock falling over his eyes.

He had the grace to look embarrassed.

'I'm sorry. I've been a bit of a . . .'

'Yes,' said Jilly. 'Poor Helena. I've been meaning to say something but I wasn't sure it was any of my business.'

'Well, your mate did it for you. Gave it to me with both barrels.'

'You do understand what Helena went through was very traumatic for her?'

'Yeah, I do. And I'm doing my best to make it right.

But there's only so much I can do, and Helena – she doesn't seem to want to know me . . .' He looked down at the floor. 'If you know what I mean.'

Jilly nodded. He didn't have to spell it out.

Tony looked up at her.

'I just want to be held. To feel like I matter. To feel that there might be a point to going back into war and maybe getting killed. To feel like there might be something to come back to one day. I can't just be shut out. I love Baby Dot but she's in the bed with us still . . .'

He looked anguished.

Jilly sighed. 'I know it's difficult, with everyone living on top of each other and no privacy. What if I take the children out for the day at the weekend? Give you some time on your own. You can talk and . . .'

She blushed. Tony reached out and put a hand on her shoulder.

'You're a diamond, you are. I reckon that would help no end.' He sighed. 'Hopefully when the war ends and I get back, we'll have a place of our own again.'

Jilly went back down to her room and lay on the bed staring at the ceiling. The incident had unsettled her, and unlocked memories. She remembered that glorious feeling; the feeling that would make anyone throw caution to the winds. She had only felt it once, and found it hard to believe it could ever happen again. It made her heart ache to think that might have been her only chance. She understood only too well what it was Tony was yearning for.

As she lay there, wallowing in her gloom, she suddenly felt something. A flicker, deep in her belly. As quick as a tiny mouse. She couldn't be sure if she had really felt it or not. She lay as still as she could, concentrating, and then she felt it again. This time it was stronger and went on for a little longer.

It must be the baby. It was all it could be. She wondered what it was doing, whether it was waving a tiny arm or turning a somersault or kicking out to say 'Hello, I'm here'.

'Oh,' she said, putting a hand on her belly. She couldn't feel anything through her skin. The baby was obviously too deep inside her. 'Hello, little one,' she said. And it gave another flutter in response.

Somehow, it made her feel better. This was new life, a tiny new life, and surely that had to give anyone hope.

27

Antonia was being ushered into James Kettle's office by his personal assistant, who had sent word that he wanted to see her.

While she waited, she went to stand by the window and looked out at the handsome square where the offices had been since 1812. The trees were November-bare, so she could see the row of identical Georgian houses opposite, their brass nameplates winking in the autumn sun: rival solicitors, estate agents, a swanky private dentist, an ad agency.

'Antonia.'

She turned to see James walk into the room. He had recently taken over from his father, and had already injected a little twenty-first-century pizazz into the firm. His office had remained traditional, but the offices elsewhere had been updated with sleek glass and wood flooring and every technological innovation possible. There was a canteen with the ultimate in healthy food, and yoga classes twice a week.

He was as smooth as the cup of coffee his assistant had made for Antonia to put her at her ease.

He pulled out his chair then indicated she should take the one opposite. He sat back, resting his elbows on the chair arms, eyeing her thoughtfully. She knew he was ruthless. She'd heard stories about him playing hard ball during takeovers. Ambitious, too. He had aspirations for Kettle and Sons.

Eventually he leaned forward, resting his chin in his fingers.

'The word is, Antonia,' he said, his tone light but Shere Khan deadly, 'that you're having an affair with one of our clients.'

She sat up a tiny bit straighter, her mind racing. 'Oh?' She frowned. 'I'm not sure how anyone can possibly suspect that.'

'So it's not true?'

She stared at him. 'I'm not having an affair with one of our clients, no.' That wasn't a lie. It was long over.

James laughed. His perfect white teeth had no doubt come from the clinic over the square. 'But you *were*?'

No one could prove it. Unless they had actually been in the room watching her and Dom have it off, it was all just supposition. The lawyer in Antonia knew this, and this was her career at stake.

She allowed herself a hint of a smile. 'How is this relevant?'

'Well,' said James. 'That's a good question. It's not as bad as if you were a doctor screwing a patient, no. Or a teacher screwing a pupil. But...'

He paused for a moment, thinking.

'I can see you as a partner, Antonia. You're smart, diligent and you go the extra mile. I'm looking to grow our conveyancing department. As you know, the property market in Bath is ever buoyant. I would hate you to scupper your chances of a great career with this firm because of a bit of idle gossip. I like my partners squeaky clean. This is still a small town.'

Antonia looked at him, wondering if he was squeaky clean himself or if he had a discreet mistress tucked away, maybe up in London. She had seen his wife, in her uniform of jeans, loafers and camel-hair coat, the type of woman who looked thirty at forty and forty at fifty thanks to money and lack of stress.

'You will hear no more gossip, I can assure you. I am very happily single and I love working at Kettle and Sons. I don't want to jeopardise my position here in any way.'

'Excellent.' James nodded, then his gaze hardened slightly. 'Just don't screw it up for yourself, Antonia, OK? This is a family firm, not a fucking soap opera.'

Ralph Fiennes. That's who he reminded her of. Classy and suave with a deadly edge. She met his gaze, bold and resolute.

'You have my word.'

No one looking at Antonia would have realised anything was wrong. After her meeting with James she glided around the office with the most serene of smiles. Anyone might think she had been offered a partnership.

At lunchtime, her smile disappeared, she slipped on her trainers, bolted out of the door and walked as quickly as she could to Wellington Buildings. She pushed open the door, walking past an electrician up a ladder rewiring the light fittings in the hall, a glazier putting a fresh pane of glass in a window frame, two chippies cutting out a template for a kitchen work surface. Everything was covered in a fine layer of dust – brick dust, wood dust, plaster dust. There were three different radio stations blaring, workmen arguing, bantering, whistling. There were flasks of coffee, cans of Coke, Tupperware boxes of sandwiches, bags of crisps perched around the building. It was supposed to be no smoking but she could smell roll-ups and at one point something more suspicious, but she had learned intervention was pointless. You had to let them get on with whatever they wanted to do if you wanted the job done. It was chaos.

She ran up three flights of stairs until she found Dom. He looked up, startled, as Antonia bore down on him, only pausing for a moment to ascertain no one could overhear. She was a familiar-enough face on the site, but she was fairly certain no one was suspicious. After all, she didn't look like anyone's mistress.

'Someone has told someone at Kettle and Sons that we're having an affair,' she hissed. 'I'm not losing my job over this. That would not be fair.'

'What?'

'James Kettle just accused me of knocking off one of my clients. He didn't name you but who else would it be?'

'Shit. I'm sorry. Did he haul you over the coals?'

'He was not happy. Was it your wife?' Her tone was hectoring. She hated how she sounded. 'Was it Laura who told him?'

Dom frowned.

'I wouldn't have thought so. It's not Laura's style at all. It's really not.' That he was certain of. Laura wasn't a sneak.

'Then someone's been spying on us. Someone's been watching my flat.'

'Who, for heaven's sake? This is Bath. Not Cold War Berlin.'

Antonia walked over to the window. As always, the view took her breath away, the orange leaves, half still on the trees, half on the ground, adding a layer of bright colour to the landscape.

'I can't deal with you any more,' she said. 'The contracts, I mean. I'm going to have to hand them over to someone else.'

Fear flittered across Dom's face.

'No. You mustn't lose your nerve, Antonia. I need you on the job. I don't trust anyone else.'

'But this is compromising me.' She felt near to tears suddenly. She had tried so hard to limit the damage on this. She had been the least needy mistress on the planet.

'If you give the files to someone else, it makes you look guilty.'

'I can easily hand them over. I do it all the time. I always shove stuff I don't want to do onto my juniors.'

'Don't give this to a junior!' Dom felt rising panic.

'I can still oversee it.'

'Just another few weeks and I can get the agents round and get these on the market. Once they're sold you can close the files and you need never see, hear or speak to me again.'

Antonia looked doubtful.

'You'll be lucky if they get snapped up straight away. If you don't get the prices right it could be weeks. Months.'

'I know. You don't have to tell me.' He ran his hands through his hair. She swore there was grey in it that there hadn't been a week ago. 'Antonia. I need you.'

'If I lose my job...'

'You won't lose your job. No one can prove anything.'

'Laura might.'

'She won't. I give you my word.' He'd have to phone her. Beg her. Explain the implications. Because if the sales didn't go through smoothly, Laura was going to lose everything she loved as well. 'Our home is at stake. You know that.'

He couldn't think about it. It had seemed logical and sensible at the time, to use Number 11 to raise the money. Now it seemed rash and foolhardy. What the hell had he been thinking?

'And that's more important than my job, is it?'

Dom tried to steady his breathing. He could feel panic rise up, just like the panic Laura had described to him on so many occasions. It was awful.

'It's not in her interests for you to be fired. Just keep your head and hold your nerve. It will all be fine.'

He could feel his heart pounding from the pressure. He had to get this house finished so it looked perfect: three aspirational apartments that combined Georgian splendour with twenty-first-century luxury. Right now, it looked like a bombsite.

He was never going to do it. It just wasn't possible.

28

Laura had done six different samples for the market to try: the original plum cheese that had been the inspiration; bramble jelly, from the tangle of berries at the bottom of the garden; black butter, a delicious dark concoction made from apples and cider and black treacle; and hot and sweet chilli jam, using the last of the tomatoes. Then two marmalades: grapefruit and Campari, which gave a delicious bitter edge to your morning toast, and endlessly useful caramelised onion – Laura lobbed a spoonful of the last into almost everything savoury to give it a kick.

She included a list of more adventurous and unusual recipes, as well as some suggestions for Christmas. It was the beginning of November so it was only round the corner. Strawberry jam with golden glitter. Mincemeat drenched with Cointreau. Port and cranberry relish – you could put a spoonful of that in gravy or in with your slow-cooked red cabbage...

She'd lined a wooden crate with dark-purple tissue paper. Nestled inside were half a dozen jars and a folder full of drawings showing the artwork she was going to use if she got the go-ahead. Again with help from Jaz over FaceTime, she'd scanned the logo from the recipe box, and she'd mocked up some labels that perfectly captured vintage nostalgia and modern graphic design. If they said yes, she could order the labels over the Internet and they would be there in three days, ready to stick on the jars.

As well as that, the rooms were now up on the website and live on Airbnb. It was just a question of waiting for the first booking. If it all took off, she wondered if she was going to manage. If she had the market on a Saturday and guests arriving, how would she juggle that? For a moment she felt daunted, then told herself she'd have to get help. It was all possible, but she had to take it one step at a time. She hadn't got a booking or the market stall yet.

Her phone started ringing just as she was about to pick up the box and leave. It was Dom. She ignored it. Eventually the ringing stopped but the phone rang again straight away. She frowned. Which part of her not wanting to talk to him did Dom not understand? She pressed 'decline' and picked up the box, but it rang again. She sighed. She supposed she should answer it. It was irresponsible not to. It might be important.

'Yep?'

'It's me.'

'Yes. I know.'

'Did you tell James Kettle about me and Antonia?' Dom blurted out.

'What? No!' Laura almost laughed. 'I told you. I don't want anyone knowing. We're supposed to be keeping it a secret, remember? So the girls don't find out.'

'Yes. I know. I just thought maybe . . .'

'Why would I do that?' Laura tucked the phone under her ear as she looked for her car keys. 'Unless I was about to undertake divorce proceedings, I suppose. Then I might tell him.'

'You're not, are you?' Dom's voice was shaky.

'No.'

'Well, someone's told him. He called Antonia into his office.'

'I'm sure he'll keep it to himself. It's his job to be discreet.'

'She might lose *her* job because of it.'

'My heart bleeds.' Was he honestly expecting her to give a damn?

'Not that we're in touch any more,' Dom added hastily. 'She messaged me to ask if I knew who it was.'

'I don't care if you're in touch or not.' She tried to keep any trace of emotion out of her voice. But it was hard.

'Laura, can't we talk? Please? I miss you and I want to explain and see if we can—'

'I haven't got time. Sorry.'

She rang off. She stood in the middle of the kitchen. Hearing Dom's voice unsettled her. It was so familiar. It was part of her. The voice she had listened to for more than twenty years. He was still her husband. Her Dom. And she could tell both Kanga and Sadie thought it was time to take action.

But she couldn't get past what he had done. She couldn't face hearing about it. Just him mentioning Antonia made her nauseous. He was obviously still protective of her. She was his primary concern, clearly. He was only worried Antonia would lose her job.

She felt shaken. This was not what she needed today. She needed to feel confident when she went to see Freya and Herbie. She needed to be knowledgeable and enthusiastic about her product and persuade them she was worthy of a stall at the market. Instead she felt vulnerable and wobbly and on the verge of tears.

She flumped down into a chair and put her head in her hands. She couldn't do it. Who was she trying to kid, that she was some sort of kitchen-table entrepreneur who was going to make her fortune out of jams and pickles? Prove to the world that although she had done bugger all for the best part of twenty years, she was a formidable businesswoman? Yes, she could slop a few old tomatoes into a saucepan and make a nice chutney. But anyone could. She was nothing special.

She wouldn't bother. She'd phone Freya and tell her she'd changed her mind. She'd stick all the jars on a shelf in the larder. They wouldn't go to waste.

Then she looked up and saw her grandmother's recipe box, sitting on the dresser. She thought about the Blitz and everything Kanga had been through. Losing her parents. Looking after that family. Her friendship with Ivy that had kept her going all through the war. Kanga hadn't ever given up. She'd faced up to all the hardship and forged ahead. And still had the grace to face heartbreak with dignity. Kanga was never self-pitying. Kanga never gave up.

She was pathetic, thought Laura. Falling apart just because a phone call had rattled her. Where was her bloody Blitz spirit? She wanted to do this. She wanted a stall at the market, to be part of that vibrant and exciting food scene. To share what she had made with people. To imagine her little jars of goodness winging their way into people's pantries and onto their tables. Putting her jam on their crumpets, her chutney on their cheese toasties, her relish in their sandwiches.

She picked up the box, threw back her shoulders and swept out of the front door without a second thought.

29

'We're not going to bite,' laughed Freya. 'Don't look so terrified.'

The preserve-tasting was held in the back office of a café in Lulgate Square. Freya supplied them with pastries and Herbie supplied their coffee, and the café saw the market as something that would enhance their reputation and get them new customers, so they supported the enterprise and provided the office free of charge whenever Freya and Herbie needed it.

Freya had lined up a row of saucers with a blob of each of Laura's preserves and two spoons.

'I don't know where Herbie is,' she frowned. 'I told him three, but he's a bit of a law unto himself.'

'I'm sure he'll turn up,' said Laura. She was surprised how nervous she was. This really mattered to her. She eyed the saucers critically – did everything look as inviting and delicious as it could? She thought so. All the preserves had kept their colour and were a good texture. It was so easy to overcook things or for them to be too runny . . . She tried to snap her attention back to what Freya was saying.

'There's only one more stall available now – we are nearly at capacity. There are a couple of other people who've applied, so we won't be able to let you know straight away.'

'Oh.' Laura felt increasingly nervous now she knew she had competition. And that made her want the stall even more.

Suddenly the door burst open and Herbie appeared. Up close Laura was all the more aware how attractive he was, with a kind of wild-boy dishevelment to him; more Che Guevara than Poldark, perhaps. He looked as if he'd been up all night, with his dark hair all over the place and a fair bit of stubble. He smelled of bitter coffee and burnt oranges.

'I'm really sorry. I put some beans on to roast at lunchtime and I couldn't leave them. The roaster is like something out of *Chitty Chitty Bang Bang* and I don't trust it not to burst into flames the minute I turn my back. Hi. You must be . . .' He pointed at her, trying to remember. 'Either the dried fruit lady or the jam lady. You're definitely not the oyster man.'

'I'm the jam lady,' Laura smiled, utterly beguiled. 'Otherwise known as Laura.'

'You're late, Herbie,' Freya chided him.

'I'm always late. We know this. I'm glad you're jam, Laura. I'm a sucker for a good marmalade.'

'Well, it goes well with coffee, I suppose,' said Laura, realising she was simpering and hating herself for it.

'Yes. We're very symbiotic.'

The thought of being symbiotic with Herbie made her blush.

'Shall we start?' asked Freya, used to the effect Herbie had on even perfectly sensible women.

Herbie grabbed a spoon and looked at the six saucers.

'So what have we got?'

Laura tried not to stammer as she ran through her selection. She felt as if she was on a television show, being judged in front of millions of viewers, as Freya and Herbie tried each sample and asked her questions. It was worse than an exam. Far worse, because she never remembered caring about exams and this mattered to her very, very much.

'Wow. The Campari is perfect in the marmalade.' Herbie wagged his spoon at it. 'What a stroke of genius. You can get drunk at breakfast without anyone knowing. Stealth boozing. I love it.'

'I'm afraid the alcohol cooks off during the process,' laughed Laura. 'So it won't get you drunk.'

'The membrillo is delicious,' said Freya, giving the pronunciation a very Spanish flourish. 'I'm definitely taking some of that home.'

'Actually, I call it plum cheese. Strictly speaking, membrillo is made from quince.'

'Well, it's *all* bloody delicious.' Herbie chucked down his spoon. 'Laura's in as far as I'm concerned.'

'We can't say that,' panicked Freya. 'We haven't seen the other candidates yet.'

'I don't think prunes and sultanas are going to do it for me. And I think Laura will go down a storm. Her stuff complements so many of the other stalls. You need jam with bread, pickle with cheese, relish with sausages . . .' He spread his hands. 'It's a no-brainer, isn't it?'

'Yes, I agree, but it's a bit naughty when we haven't seen the others.'

'Just let me know,' said Laura. 'Honestly. I can wait until you've seen them.'

'There's no reason why we should. It's up to us to decide who we have.' Herbie was trenchant. 'I think you should start straight away.'

'Herbie, you are a nightmare.' Freya turned to Laura. 'I'm so sorry, this is really embarrassing. The market's not really run like this. We're very professional.'

'This is professional. It's saving us from having to chomp through bits of rubbery old dried fruit. This is a great product with great packaging.' Herbie looked at Laura's artwork. 'It's totally what we are all about. I'm in, as they say.'

Freya held up her hands. 'Well, I can't say no, then, can I? You're a monkey, Herbie. Luckily, I happen to agree with you.' She turned to Laura. 'Can you start as soon as possible? Say next Saturday? There's loads of paperwork, I'm afraid. And you'll need public liability insurance. I'll give you a welcome pack with all the bumph. It'll make you lose the will to live but we have to follow the rules.'

'So I'm in?'

'Welcome to Lulgate Market, Laura,' said Herbie cheerfully. 'You'll be part of the family in no time.'

'Just call me if you've got any questions,' said Freya.

'Wow.' Laura looked down at her jars, thrilled to bits. 'I better start brushing up on my mental arithmetic. Thank you both so much. I'm really delighted.'

Herbie looked at his watch. 'It's a bit early, but we could go for a drink to celebrate. The Reprobate's open.'

'Count me out,' said Freya, picking up her bag. 'I've got yoga tonight. I need a clear head.'

Herbie looked at Laura, raising one eyebrow in question. She felt her pulse quicken. Something inside her longed to go for a drink with him. It would be lovely to have a celebratory glass; to feel that reckless warmth that afternoon drinking always gave you. But Edmond would be in there, and what would he think if he saw her with Herbie? They could explain they were celebrating her joining the market, but she knew she would look guilty. What she was thinking deep down inside would be written all over her face and Edmond would know – he was terrifyingly perceptive.

'I better not,' she said. 'I need to get back.'

She didn't. Of course she didn't. There was nothing and no one to get back for. But she had a feeling Herbie might lead her astray and would add yet another ingredient to the slightly toxic cocktail of emotions she was already feeling.

'Oh,' he said. 'I thought you were going to be fun.'

'I am fun,' protested Laura. 'Just ... not today.'

She picked up her box and walked away, feeling slightly regretful but nonetheless certain she had made the right decision turning him down. She'd have to make do with a few more episodes of *Suits* on Netflix for her thrills.

30

The house was quiet and dark when Laura got home. She felt a curious mixture of elated and deflated. Elated because she was thrilled to be starting the market next week, right in at the deep end, just as everyone was beginning to gear up for Christmas.

And a little deflated, because she didn't have anyone to share her news with.

She tried calling Jaz, because she'd been so much help and she couldn't have got everything together without her, but she wasn't answering. And neither was Willow.

She could go and find Kanga. Or she could ring Sadie. Sadie would be excited for her but really, next to running a glamorous boutique, selling a few jars of jam at a market was no great achievement. Sadie had won Bath Business-woman of the Year twice now. Laura had a long way to go before she was anywhere near as accomplished.

Although obviously Sadie's accomplishments were just a veneer. Laura still hadn't properly processed her revelations. She wondered what Dom would say – he and Sadie had always been quite close. Had she ever revealed her longing to him, when they'd stayed up late finishing off their wine after Laura had gone to bed? Dom would have been kind and given her good advice.

Suddenly, Laura missed Dom with a physical ache. She longed to open a bottle of fizz with him, to celebrate the market and talk about Sadie. She longed to share her achievement with him and debate what to do about her best friend. And hear his triumphs and worries in return. That was what marriage was about. That's what she had had that Sadie envied.

Maybe the time had come for them to talk. What would he be doing on a Friday night? She realised she had no idea.

Then she reminded herself that for all she knew, he was tucked up with Antonia. They had both insisted the affair was over, but perhaps Laura's refusal to talk to Dom had pushed them back together again?

She felt a familiar tightening in her chest and a swirl in her belly at the thought of talking to him. That anxiety she had come to know so well. She'd managed to keep it at bay over the past few weeks. She didn't want to give it any opportunity to sneak back in.

No, she thought. She needed to be stronger before she saw Dom. She was taking steps to build a new Laura, but she wasn't quite there yet.

She heard the doorbell go and wondered who it could be. Someone interesting, she hoped. Someone she could lure in and tell her news to. She headed for the door, pausing for a second to look in the hall mirror. She still had make-up on from earlier – not too bad.

She thought she could hear laughing. Maybe it was some kids playing Knock Down Ginger? She opened the door.

'Surprise!'

Two figures threw open their arms. Two figures in hoodies and beanies and skinny jeans.

'Oh my God!' Laura put a hand to her mouth, not able to believe her eyes.

'Muuuum!'

Jaz and Willow hurled themselves against their mother in a flurry of giggles and explanations.

'We decided to surprise you.'

'We thought you'd been sounding a bit down.'

'And I've missed you.'

'Willow got the train down to me and I drove.'

'We're just here for the night.'

'Are you surprised?'

Laura was laughing and crying.

'Oh, my darlings. This is the best surprise ever. I've got so much to tell you. And so much to show you. Oh, goodness – what am I going to cook for supper?'

'It's OK. We've got it covered. We've ordered pizza for eight o'clock.' They were pulling off their hoodies and hats, hanging them on the pegs. She breathed in the smell of them.

'We didn't want you to have to cook. We know what you're like.'

'And we brought wine.'

'You've thought of everything.'

Suddenly the house was filled with life again. Laura felt her heart lift. Her beautiful girls. Willow looked so well. Taller, perhaps.

Then Jaz turned to her with a smile.

'We were worried you guys wouldn't be in. But you are. Where's Dad?'

Laura ran up to the bedroom as soon as she could,

telling the girls she needed to put on a jumper. She shut the door and pulled out her phone, dialling Dom's number.

Please answer, she thought, thinking of all the times she'd ignored his calls. It would serve her right if he ignored her.

'Laura.' He'd answered. Thank God. 'Is everything OK?'

'You've got to come home,' she told him. 'The girls are here. They've surprised me. I had no idea. You've got to come home and pretend everything is normal.'

He didn't need her to explain.

'I'll be as quick as I can.'

She sat in the quiet of the bedroom for a moment. How wonderful if she could walk downstairs and for Dom to walk in and for everything to be as it had been pre-Antonia. Just them, their normal family, him and the girls and her, laughing and talking and scoffing pizza and pouring wine and flipping the lid on bottles of beer and turning up their favourite songs, all round the kitchen table.

It wasn't going to be like that. It was going to be one massive, exhausting lie, with her worrying every moment that the truth would come out. She breathed in and out slowly. She had to carry it off. She had to let Jaz and Willow believe everything was normal, just as it had been the night before they left.

She felt tears well up. She was overwhelmed. With joy at the wonderful surprise, but also fear. The effort it was going to take. She wasn't even sure she could look Dom in the eye. The girls would guess.

They mustn't. She had to summon up the strength from

somewhere. She grabbed her phone and called Kanga. She needed an ally. Safety in numbers.

'Willow and Jaz are home. They wanted to surprise me,' she told her grandmother. 'I've told Dom he's got to come back and pretend nothing's happened. Will you come? The girls have ordered pizza. I need you.'

To look at Dom, no one would have realised anything was wrong. He sauntered in less than half an hour after Laura had called him, laughing as the girls jumped all over him, dropping a kiss on Laura's forehead as she sat at the table gripping her wine glass with a forced smile on her face.

While they were waiting for the pizza to arrive Laura told the girls about the market, and Dom had to pretend he already knew all about it; she could see surprise and admiration in his eyes as he looked at her.

Willow found 'Jamming' by Bob Marley on her iPod and they all started singing along.

Dom chinked his wine glass against hers.

'Congratulations. That's brilliant news.'

Laura didn't know what to say. Before she could reply, Kanga came into the kitchen and the girls jumped up again.

Only the most observant person would have noticed Kanga's froideur towards Dom, and the fact that she chose to sit as far away from him as she could.

By ten o'clock there were four cardboard boxes open on the table, and most of the pizza devoured except for the more challenging crusts.

'Mum! Mum Mum Mum!' shouted Jaz, who'd been scrolling through her phone. 'You've got a booking. You've got your first booking!'

Dom looked at Laura. She knew he could have no idea that she'd got the rooms renovated and on the website. The last he'd heard, it had been an idle plan. She met his gaze, willing him not to show any surprise or he would give the game away.

'When are they booked in for?' she asked.

'Next weekend. Two nights. That's nearly two hundred quid!'

'Well done, darling,' said Dom valiantly. 'Your first booking. I knew it would be a success.'

He really was a good actor and a good liar, thought Laura. No wonder she'd been duped for so long.

They all went to bed just before midnight.

'We've got to go back tomorrow,' said Jaz. 'I've got a hockey match on Sunday.'

Conscientious Jaz would never countenance missing a match.

'Oh, that's a shame,' said Laura. 'Only I know Daddy's got to get up early and go to work anyway, so it would just be me.'

She looked at Dom, who raised his eyebrows. Laura smiled at him sweetly.

'Can we have pancakes for breakfast, before we go?' asked Willow.

'Of course. Whatever you want.'

'I've tried making them for the house, but they're not as good as yours.'

Laura went to kiss each of her daughters good night in their rooms. All that mattered, really, more than her marriage – their marriage – or her happiness or money, was that the two girls were happy and healthy. And they seemed to be.

'Are you settled?' she asked Willow. 'Are you happy?'

'I love it, Mum. But I do miss home. I miss our banter. Our madness. I miss you and Dad.'

'We miss you too, darling. It's not long till Christmas.'

Oh God, thought Laura. Christmas. Something would have to be done by then. This mess would have to be sorted out.

Afterwards, she popped in to see Jaz.

'Thank you so much, darling. It's been a lovely surprise, and I know it was your idea.'

Jaz was cross-legged on the bed, her back straight. She looked at her mother. 'I was worried about you.'

'Really?' Laura tried to keep her voice light.

'Every time I spoke to you, you sounded as if you were pretending to be all right.'

'Well, I'm fine. You can see that.' Laura smiled brightly.

Jaz smiled back. 'Yes,' she said, but she didn't seem sure.

'Honestly. It's just been a bit odd, having an empty house. I'm not used to it. I keep making too much spag bol and having to throw it away. I'm OK. Honestly.'

She was definitely protesting too much. She hugged Jaz and left the room before she saw through her obfuscation.

As she headed across the landing, she realised Dom would have to sleep in their bedroom for the night. It would be very odd for him not to. Unless she banished him to the spare room with some cock-and-bull story about him snoring and her not being able to sleep. But she didn't have the energy either to argue with him about it or to lie. It seemed much easier if they slept together.

He was rifling through his drawers, looking for a pair of pyjamas.

It was as if he had never been away.

She got into bed and lay stiff and quiet, her eyes shut, as Dom climbed in beside her. She felt the bed dip, the familiar squeak of the springs.

'Laura. Can we talk?'

'No.' She wasn't going to let him turn the situation to his advantage. Especially when she'd had several glasses of wine. She'd only cry. 'And can you make sure you're gone first thing in the morning?'

She could feel him next to her. His warmth. She could smell him. She could hear him breathe. Her Dom. Her husband. It would be so easy to reach out, slide into his arms, his familiar embrace, his strength, his tenderness.

But he'd betrayed her. He'd been unfaithful. She couldn't get past it, the thought of him with Antonia, the thought of him kissing her, caressing her, sliding into her.

'Tonight was wonderful.' There was a crack in his voice as he broke the silence and the darkness.

'I know,' she said, and turned her back on him.

31

Laura was surprised how nervous she was about receiving her first B & B guest the next weekend.

The guest's name was G. MacBride. Two nights, arriving Friday. Departing Sunday. She had no more information than that. She hadn't felt confident enough to message to ask for more details. It seemed rude.

When the doorbell went, she smoothed back her hair, put on her shoes – it wouldn't do to answer the door barefoot – and strode out into the hall, assuming a confidence she didn't feel.

She answered it to a man of about her own age, with a head of thick salt and pepper hair, light-green eyes and a confident smile.

'Hello.' She held out her hand. 'I'm Laura. Welcome to Number 11.'

'I'm Gino,' he said, and she thought – Gino? She'd had her money on George. Or Gillian.

'Scottish Italian,' he grinned, seeing her surprise. 'My mother's from Naples.' He looked around the hall. 'This is wonderful. What an amazing house. It kind of hugs you when you walk in.'

She had gone out of her way to clear the clutter and make it welcoming, with a massive vase of autumnal orange and yellow flowers, some warm light bulbs and a pomegranate candle from Jo Malone. She had to admit it did look like something out of a magazine.

She stole a closer look at her guest while he was admiring the photos on the wall. He wore a charcoal grey V-necked sweater over a white T-shirt and faded jeans, and very expensive-looking sneakers. He was carrying a battered brown leather holdall that looked as if it had been around the world with him a few times. No jewellery.

No wedding ring.

Fashion conscious in a good way – understated, confident.

'Is this your first visit to Bath?' she asked.

'No. My wife and I have been here a few times. My daughter's at the uni. Second year.'

'Oh. Lovely.' That would be a good market, she thought. Visiting parents. Maybe she could advertise at the university.

'This is my first trip on my own, though. My wife and I separated a few months ago. And I miss Sasha desperately.' He gave an awkward smile, as if he had been rehearsing declaring his new status.

Laura smiled back at him. 'I know the feeling. My youngest started at York in September. I'm counting the days till the end of term.'

'I thought I'd come and do a bit of early Christmas shopping.'

'Don't mention the C-word!' It was funny, thought Laura. One minute you were putting away the sun cream, the next everyone was obsessed with mince pies and stocking fillers.

'I know. Sorry. Guilty as charged.'

He was charming, thought Laura. Her mind started ticking over. 'Shall I show you the accommodation?'

She felt very nervous as she showed him the rooms. What if he turned his nose up? What if, after all her hard work, they weren't what people expected these days? Standards had risen so high. Everyone expected all the luxury and all the mod-cons. She hoped she had done her best to supply comfort and style within her – and their – budget.

'This is lovely. Just what I want. Quiet and cosy and comfy,' Gino told her, and she felt relieved. He was her idea of a perfect customer. Someone who knew what they wanted but had good manners.

She scampered back down to the kitchen as soon as he had chosen his room. She texted Sadie.

Laura: OMG my first guest is called Gino. He's a total silver fox. He is PERFECT for you. Separated. 40 something. Drop Dead Gorgeous!

Sadie: Take a picture!

Laura: I can't. That would be weird.

Sadie: I'm coming over.

Laura: No. I've got my first market tomorrow. I can't risk a hangover.

Sadie: Spoilsport.

Laura: I'll do some digging and let you know. Supper tomorrow night?

Five thumbs-up emojis pinged back.

'Will you be wanting dinner?' she asked politely when Gino came down to collect some fresh milk. 'I do offer a three-course meal. Or two courses. Or just one. Whatever you like.'

'I'm going to hit the sack – it's been a bit of a drive. But maybe tomorrow? I'm taking Sasha out for the day, but I expect she'll want to be rid of me by the evening. It's not very cool to have your dad in tow on a Saturday night.'

Laura laughed. He was funny and kind and self-deprecating, with a really attractive soft Scottish lilt.

'OK. Well, I'm out at the market all day but I could have something on the table for eight if that's not too late?'

'That sounds perfect.'

She gave him a key and a map of Bath she'd got from the tourist office and showed him where to find the breakfast things so he could help himself. He disappeared off with a cheery good night.

Had she been wrong to give Sadie the heads-up? Surely there was nothing wrong with a bit of matchmaking? And Gino looked more than a match for her: a sophisticated grown-up. He certainly didn't look as if he was going to go out and pull a thirty-year-old.

There was hope for Sadie, thought Laura. There had to be.

Laura was at Lulgate Square by seven o'clock the next morning. Cars were allowed in to unload, but she had to leave her boxes of jars while she went and parked. She saw Herbie and asked if he would keep an eye on them.

'Hey, listen, everybody has this problem and nothing's been nicked yet. Probably because it's too early for any light-fingeredness. But don't worry – I'll stand guard.'

She thanked him and drove to the nearest car park as quickly as she could.

Was it going to be difficult doing this all on her own? She wished Jaz or Willow were here to help. They would love it. Oh God, she missed them. She could imagine the pair of them bossing her around and reorganising things how they thought fit. They had the confidence of youth that she lacked. She was dreading even simple things like counting out change. Things that the young didn't find daunting in the least – she remembered watching Willow add up drinks bills at the Reprobate in her head, taking the customer's money and dishing out change while she was already on to the next customer. Laura was worried she was going to dither.

She got back to her stall in record time and started unpacking.

Herbie brought her a coffee – he gave a free cup to all the stallholders as they arrived.

'I remember you're a latte girl,' he said.

She took it gratefully – there'd been no time for anything before she left the house.

'Amazing. Thank you. It's so cold.'

'You'll be like a block of ice by the end of the day.' He pointed. 'Can I buy a jar of that Campari marmalade before it goes?'

'Have one. Please. You've been so kind.'

She handed him a jar. Her hand was shaking, but it wasn't from the cold. She had no idea she would be this terrified.

Gradually her confidence grew as the other stallholders stopped by to introduce themselves and look at her stall.

They all took the time to admire it, even though they were busy themselves.

'Hey,' said the bread girl. 'I should display some of your jars on my stall. They're so cute. Let's talk later.'

'Great!' Laura felt the warm glow of belonging.

Even if she said it herself, her jars did look wonderful, neatly arranged in serried ranks. The labels had arrived just in time. They were the colour of old-fashioned brown paper, *A Family Recipe* written at the top, then the individual flavours written in a retro typewriter font, and underneath, slightly offset, a perfect circle cut out to show the product inside.

She laid out some square plates with tasting samples, and had bought a box of disposable wooden spoons. She had a bag of change and some brown paper bags with strong handles in case anyone bought more than one jar.

It was half past eight. Time for the market to open. Customers were already arriving, the hardcore market aficionados who wanted the best choice. There was nothing worse than arriving to find your favourite raspberry friands had sold out.

It was hard work. The cobbles under foot were freezing and Laura made a note to wear thermal socks next time, and maybe even fingerless gloves. Her voice was hoarse from talking. People loved to ask questions about the food they were buying: how it was made, the story behind it. They seemed to love knowing that the plum cheese came from plums in her garden. They even asked her for advice on making their own jam and she wondered if maybe she should provide recipes – it probably wouldn't stop people from buying from her, but it might just inspire them, and it was all about developing a relationship.

And she sent people to other stalls to buy things to go with her range.

'This raspberry jam would be perfect on a piece of soda bread.'

'This relish would go with a chunk of Comté. Or a wedge of Somerset brie.'

'Try making a Marmalade Martini,' she even urged one customer, who seemed delighted with the idea.

By two o'clock she had very nearly sold out. She couldn't believe it.

Bloody hell, thought Dom, standing stock-still in the cold autumn air. He was at the end of one of the little streets that led into Lulgate Square.

He'd been up since six, working at the house, and because it was Saturday and there were no workmen he could actually think. He had gone through the house carefully from top to bottom, making notes on what had been done and what needed to be done. He did this every week, a kind of stocktaking, because it was the only way to make sure nothing had been forgotten. Then he would go back upstairs and put everything into a spreadsheet.

Although it was taking shape, and was a million miles from the dilapidated, crumbling wreck he had purchased, it had a long way to go before people were going to be convinced that Wellington Buildings was *the* address in Bath. It was a masterpiece in co-ordination, like bringing all the members of an orchestra together for a crashing finale.

It was crucial for the agents to be on board and get the apartments to market in the New Year. There were windows of opportunity in marketing property, and he couldn't afford to miss this one. That wasn't an option. The bank had made that *very* clear.

His snag list today had taken all morning. He was starting to look ahead to the finishing touches, because if he didn't get them ordered they would get caught up in the craziness of Christmas and wouldn't arrive in time. And he needed to schedule them in. Things had to be done in the right order. You couldn't put a new knocker on a front door that hadn't been painted.

And even the bloody front door had its own to-do list: apart from the new knocker, it needed three new doorbells wired in and the brass plates over the doorbells put up; a period-appropriate boot-scraper needed to be sourced; two trees chosen to go either side of the door in big lead planters – olive or bay? So many decisions . . .

How the hell was he supposed to do all of this on his own? Never again, he vowed. It was too much for one person. He had to make all the decisions and had no one to delegate to. Not even to go and buy light bulbs. His light-bulb list was enormous. Different watts, different shapes, different sizes, different colours . . .

By lunchtime he realised he hadn't eaten anything since a lukewarm pasty the day before. He needed some fresh air, to clear his head, so he'd decided to walk to Lulgate Market and treat himself to a decent coffee and something delicious from one of the stalls.

He knew Laura would be there. She wouldn't talk to him, but he wasn't going to spend the rest of his life pussyfooting around Bath trying to avoid her. She wasn't being fair. He wasn't going to pretend not to exist. As he headed for the market, he felt bullish. He had every right to be there, didn't he?

But as soon as he saw her there, behind her stall, confident, laughing, interacting with customers, doing something he hadn't been party to – it took his breath away. His heart was actually aching, he realised. He felt pain, a heavy pain, right in the middle of his chest.

He wanted to be there, next to her, supporting her. There was a big queue, and she could have done with help, he could see that. He should be by her side, his beautiful wife. He knew how passionate she would be about what she had made, how people would be hanging on her every word.

He should walk over and say hello. Congratulate her. Give her a hug. Why shouldn't he? If she was feeling confident and uplifted, she might look kindly on him. Perhaps they could have a truce. Maybe he could ask her for a drink later. Or even dinner.

He was about to step into the square when he saw a man come over to her, dark and devilish, and the two of them laughed, and the man gave her a hug, and the pain in his chest turned into something sharper, like a serrated knife slipped in between his ribs. He could barely breathe.

Oh Laura, he thought. *What have I done to you? What have I done to us?*

32

L aura was as high as a kite when she got back home
from the market. She was exhausted, but she was too
full of excitement and adrenaline to care.

'I can lay you a place in the dining room for supper,'
she told Gino. 'Or you can eat in the kitchen with me
and my friend Sadie. We won't bite.'

Gino laughed. He was reeling from a day spent with
his daughter, being dragged around the shops. 'I'd love to
eat with you. I'll walk down to the off-licence and buy a
nice bottle of wine.'

Laura made a face. 'That would be lovely. But I'll feel
awful charging you for supper. It doesn't feel right.'

'No. It's great. I get it. It's your business. It's a bonus,
to be made to feel part of the household. Don't make the
mistake of treating your guests as friends. You'll never
make a profit.'

'It's a new venture for me. I'm just getting used to it.'
She grinned. 'And I'm sure I'll have guests that I don't
want to welcome into the kitchen.'

'Oh God, probably.'

When he got back from the off-licence, he presented
Laura with a chilled bottle of Pouilly-Fumé. Laura passed
him the corkscrew.

'Open the wine and I'll get cooking. Sadie will be here in a minute.'

Sadie arrived, super-glamorous in a black satin shirt, skinny faded jeans and silver Chelsea boots, clutching another bottle. She swooped in on Gino.

'Hi, hi, hi, everyone. Hello. You must be Laura's first guest. What an honour. For her, not you, I mean.' She laughed. She was nervous, thought Laura. Sadie was never nervous.

'Oh no – the honour's all mine. You must be Sadie. I'm Gino.'

Sadie started singing the Dexy's Midnight Runners hit, then stopped, blushing. 'God, sorry. I bet everyone does that.'

'No,' said Gino, deadpan. Then he laughed. 'Yes.'

Laura swore afterwards that she could see the zap of electricity that passed between them, a palpable current of pleasure and recognition, almost a white light connecting them. She smiled to herself. She'd been right. They were perfect for each other.

She let them sit at the table talking while she cooked: big fat duck breasts that she pan-fried, a compote made from the last of the plums, little squares of sautéed potato and a big pan of spinach.

Once they'd finished their supper and the second bottle of wine, Sadie looked at her watch and gave a mischievous smile. 'Let's go to the Reprobate Bar.'

'But it's gone ten o'clock,' Laura protested.

'That's the perfect time to go. I'll get Edmond to save us a table.'

'What's the Reprobate Bar?' Gino was laughing, swept up by Sadie's enthusiasm.

'It's the coolest bar in Bath. They serve absolutely wicked cocktails. You'll love it.'

'I'm guessing I don't have a choice?'

Sadie shook her head with a grin.

'Not really. Laura, I'll call Edmond; you call a cab.'

Gino was staring at Sadie in bemused admiration. Laura could tell he was already smitten.

'Are you sure I'm not going to be a gooseberry?' she whispered to Sadie as Gino went to the cloakroom before they left.

'No. You're coming with us. You need to let your hair down and celebrate your sales.'

'My profit will be gone after just two cocktails at the Reprobate.'

'This is only the beginning, darling. You are going to be on every table in the country. Trust me.'

Sadie's eyes were glittering. There was no stopping her when she was on a high. *God help Gino*, thought Laura, then thought – *no, he's going to love it*. He could totally handle Sadie.

He shouldn't have started on the Scotch. He knew it was going to make him feel terrible. He'd bought it because it was so bloody cold in Wellington Buildings and he put a nip in his coffee just before bedtime. But once Dom had started on it, he couldn't stop.

And three shots in, he suddenly felt the need to call Antonia. For reassurance. As ever. She always gave him reassurance when he needed it, so why not now, when he felt utterly wretched about the mess he'd made of his life?

It hadn't given him the nerve to call Laura, although that's what he'd wanted it to do.

Antonia would do instead. He fumbled for his phone, then felt his chest tighten again. It had been doing that on and off all evening. He thought it was the bloody awful takeaway he'd had on the way back from the market. He hadn't had the nerve to go and browse the stalls, so he'd wolfed down a saveloy from the chippy instead.

He lay down on the blow-up bed and pressed Antonia's number. Ouch. He knew saveloys were made of all sorts of awful things but he wasn't sure he deserved this amount of pain for resorting to junk food for once in his life . . .

The Reprobate was heaving by the time they got there. It catered for an older, more sophisticated crowd than some of the bars in town, so it was full of Bath's movers and shakers, glamorous and beautiful and out for a good time. Sadie pushed her way through the crowds towards the bar with Laura and Gino behind her. She waved furiously at Edmond, who beckoned them over to a table for four right in the corner. Laura could see people looking at them, wondering what made them so special: tables were at a premium.

They settled into the crushed-velvet banquettes. Edmond sent them over Violet Femmes, with gin and egg white and crème de violette.

'Maybe I could get used to this single life after all,' said Gino, raising his glass to the two of them. 'It's been a rough few months.'

'Don't look back,' said Sadie, chinking her glass to his.

Laura bit her lip before taking a cautious sip of her drink. This was kind of crazy fun. She hadn't been out like this for years. Sometimes at Christmas she and Dom came into town, but they usually hung out at home. It felt weird. But it felt good too, she told herself. She wasn't too old for a night out on the town with the beautiful people.

After two cocktails, Laura's head was spinning a little. She thought she'd go to the loo and step outside for some fresh air. As she pushed her way through the crowds, she felt a hand on her shoulder. She gave a little shiver as its warmth rippled through her. She turned.

'Hey.'

He was leaning against the wall, holding a glass with a dark amber liquid swirling in the bottom.

'Herbie!' She felt a rush of pleasure.

'Do you come here often? This den of iniquity?'

'Not very often.'

'Have you got a drink?'

'Yes. But thanks. I'm at a table over there.' She grimaced. 'I feel like a bit of a gooseberry, to be honest. I think my friend's hitting on my B & B guest. Though it is my fault. I pretty much set them up.'

They looked over at Sadie and Gino, who were locked in conversation, oblivious to anyone around them.

'Well, talk to me, then,' said Herbie, and hooked an arm round her shoulder, pulling her in towards the wall.

Laura swallowed. She wasn't used to this level of intimacy. Herbie felt warm and smelled gorgeous. She knew she was drunk and she was pretty sure he was too. She leaned into him.

'What are you drinking?' she asked.

'A Sazerac.' He held the glass to her lips and made her drink. It burned her throat.

'Oh my God,' she spluttered. 'What's in it?'

'Rye whisky, bitters, absinthe. And now you've drunk it, it will make you do *terrible* things you shouldn't.'

He was looking at her mock-seriously. She couldn't tear her eyes away from his. Somewhere, deep inside her, a pulse began.

'Like what?' she asked. She was asking for trouble. *He* was trouble. The crowds were pushing them closer together. Her chest was against his. She could almost feel his heartbeat through his shirt. She smelled coffee and burnt orange again, and the tang of his sweat. He leaned in closer and she put her head up. Their mouths were almost touching. Just two millimetres and she would be able to taste the remnants of the Sazerac on his lips.

She looked over her shoulder as he whispered in her ear.

'Come home with me.'

A thrill bubbled up inside her as she laughed. 'I bet you say that to all the stallholders.'

'No.'

'I can't. I've got a paying guest.'

'Give him a key.'

'He's a stranger.'

'Let me come back with you, then.'

She felt something dangerous unspool inside her and stepped away from him.

'Don't be ridiculous. I'm a respectable pillar of Bath society.' She put on her best Jane Austen air, but she was smiling, unable to tear her gaze away.

'No, you're not.'

He leaned back against the wall, crossing his arms. His eyes were teasing. She swallowed. She looked across the room to Sadie and Gino and as she did she caught

Edmond's eye. He was looking at her, his eyebrow raised. Was his disapproval directed at her? She gathered her thoughts for a moment, trying to grip on to reason through the blur of wine and cocktails.

What the hell *was* she doing? She was mad, flirting with Herbie in public. It might be irresistible right now, this second, but she was still married to Dom. She felt a tug inside her. Despite the intoxicating pull, what she really wanted was to feel safe. Not out of control. Her head was spinning; her conscience was needling her. Maybe she should leave the bar and walk home, before she got herself into big trouble.

She felt her phone ring in her pocket. She pulled it out. It was Dom. She smiled. Maybe he knew she was in trouble. Maybe he would rescue her. If he was at Wellington Buildings he was only a few minutes' walk away. Maybe it was time for them to talk.

She answered the phone.

'Hello?'

'It's Antonia.'

She could hardly hear. 'What?' She pushed her way through the crowds to go outside.

'Antonia. I'm on Dom's phone. I think he's had a heart attack.'

Laura could barely make out what she was saying. Had she heard right? She pushed the door open and stepped out into the square. 'He's what?'

'He's had a heart attack. He called me about fifteen minutes ago because he felt ill. I called an ambulance. I'm going to follow him to the hospital.'

'Oh my God!' Terror gripped Laura. 'Is he ... is he OK? Is he ...?'

'I don't know. The paramedics were working on him.' Antonia sounded tearful.

'Shit. I can't drive. I'm way over the limit. And I'll never get a cab.' Laura put her hand to her head, looking wildly around for help.

'Where are you? I can come and get you.'

'Would you really? I'm at the Reprobate. Lulgate Square.'

'I'm five minutes away. Wait for me outside.'

Laura's own heart was pounding as she tried to make sense of what Antonia had told her. A terrible sick fear flooded through her. For a moment, she thought she might puke on the pavement as adrenaline swirled with the cocktails. She tried to go back over what Antonia had said. What did she mean? Did she mean Dom was dead? That the paramedics were resuscitating him? She couldn't call her back. She'd be driving. Oh God. If he died, what then? He would die thinking she'd hadn't forgiven him. Thinking she hated him. She had to get to him.

She pushed open the door of the bar, tears blinding her, elbowing people out of her way, stumbling through the crowds until she reached Sadie and Gino. They looked up.

'We thought you'd pulled,' Sadie began to say, then saw Laura's face. She stood up. 'What's happened?'

'It's Dom. He's had a heart attack. Antonia's just called me.'

Gino stood up too. He put his arm round Laura and moved her through the crowds until they got outside.

'OK, now what do you want us to do?' He was very calm and kind.

'Antonia's coming to get me. We're going to the hospital.'

'Do you want us to come with you?'

'No. I'll go with Antonia.'

'Is that a good idea?' Sadie frowned.

'It's fine.' It was odd. Somehow Antonia felt like the person who should be in charge.

'We'll go back to Number 11 and wait to hear from you,' Sadie told her, and hugged her tight.

Laura felt strangely disconnected from the situation. She had thought the worst had happened. But this was far worse. The thought of losing Dom altogether was terrifying. She gave a choked sob. It was her fault, for being so bloody stubborn. She should have talked to him when he came home, when the girls were back.

'Here,' said Gino, handing her a handkerchief. She took it gratefully as Antonia's Golf appeared at the end of the street that led into the square.

'She's here,' said Laura, and raised a hand in farewell as she rushed towards the car.

'Let us know what happens,' Sadie called after her, but Laura had already opened the car door.

Inside, Antonia looked as white as a sheet as Laura scrambled into the passenger seat. As Laura shut the door she slammed the car into reverse and backed up the street like a demon. She turned the car round, knocked it into first and drove off, throwing Laura back into her seat with the force of her acceleration.

'Let's go. I don't care if I get a speeding fine.'

33

Antonia stared at the road ahead while she drove, and filled Laura in on what had happened.

'A heart attack?'

'That's what the paramedics thought. We won't know exactly till we get to the hospital.'

'So what happened?'

'He called me about an hour ago. He sounded terrible. To be honest, I thought he was drunk. He said he was in pain. That his chest hurt. I told him to take some painkillers and get some sleep.'

'But a heart attack?' said Laura. 'He's pretty fit, Dom. And he's not old. He doesn't smoke. He goes to the gym. Goes running.'

'He hasn't been. He's been too busy. And it's the worry of everything.' Antonia looked sideways. 'He hasn't been sleeping, for a start.'

'You don't have to tell me. It's always like this at the end of a job.' Laura looked at her sharply.

Antonia didn't reply for a moment.

'Listen. Laura. Dom and I – we're not a thing any more. You must know that. I do talk to him because of the legal stuff. In a professional capacity. That's it.'

Laura nodded. She believed her. 'OK.'

'But he does still tell me everything he's worried about. Because he doesn't *have* anyone else.'

She couldn't keep the accusation out of her voice.

'I can't talk to him, can I? After what happened?' Laura was defensive.

'Yes, but you never did.'

'What?'

'That's always been the problem. He told me you never listened. That you were too caught up with Willow and he felt he couldn't burden you with his problems.'

'What? Because of my child being ill?' Laura's voice rose in indignation.

'I'm not getting at you, Laura.' Antonia's voice was gentle. 'I'm trying to explain. This project was a step too far for Dom but he wanted to prove himself. He thought he could handle it but it was a nightmare from the start.'

Antonia slowed down at the roundabout, looking at the signs. Laura pointed.

'That's the quickest way to the hospital at this time of night.'

'I'm not trying to excuse what happened between us. I'm just putting you in the picture. And I think the thought of losing you ... you not talking to him, not finding a way to make it work ... it was too much.'

'So it's my fault.' Laura was tearful.

'No. It's not. The complete opposite. It's actually my fault. For encouraging him. For telling him he could do it. For getting him to take out the loan on your house.' She sighed. 'I suppose I had too much faith in him.'

'The loan on our house?' said Laura. 'What loan?'

Antonia frowned.

'You knew about that. You signed the papers? I told

333

him he had to have your agreement. You're joint owners, so he couldn't do it without your permission.'

'I don't remember. Maybe he mentioned something. I'm always signing stuff, I never take any notice.'

Antonia raised an eyebrow. 'Well, you should. If he doesn't sell the apartments by the time his loan expires, your house will have to be sold to pay back the loan. So he's been desperately trying to finish it to get them on the market.'

Laura's voice shook. 'You mean we could lose Number 11?'

'Yes,' said Antonia.

'I had no idea,' said Laura. 'That it was all such a big risk.'

'Of course it was a big risk. You don't make big money with dead certs.'

'Why the hell didn't he say something?' As Laura spoke the words, she knew that Dom had tried. Maybe he hadn't spelled it out clearly enough, but the signs had been there and she had just ignored them. And that stress might kill him. 'Oh God, what if he dies?'

'He's not going to die,' said Antonia firmly. 'He's going to be OK. I know he is. He has to be.'

In that moment, Laura could see what it was that had drawn Dom to Antonia. It was her certainty and her confidence. She had provided that at a time Laura hadn't given him the support he needed. She'd been totally wrapped up in Willow, neurotic and needy and difficult, constantly full of anxiety. She could remember him looking at her thinking *Is she going to have a meltdown?* It can't have been easy to live with.

334

It was only now – now Willow was better, and she was starting to see a future – that she felt stronger.

As they swung into the hospital car park, she realised just how strong she was going to have to be.

34

The hospital was a blur. A blur of sliding doors and lifts and reception desks and people looking at lists while they tried to track down where Dom was.

'I don't know whether to call the girls. Should I call the girls?' Laura looked at her phone as they hurried along yet another endless corridor. She didn't want to wake them in the middle of the night. They were both too far away to get here quickly. There was nothing they could do anyway.

'There's no point in worrying them yet. And I don't think Dom would want you to worry them.'

'But what if...?'

'We'll know more in a few minutes.'

They reached the Critical Care unit and were directed to seats in yet another endless corridor to wait for news.

'He can't be dead,' said Laura. 'Or they'd have told us.'

'He's not dead,' said Antonia.

A clock with a white face and black numbers stared down at them, expressionless, as its hands moved slowly round. The two of them sat together in silence. Laura texted Sadie to say there was no news.

'This is unbearable.'

Antonia cleared her throat. 'If you want me to go...' she said. 'I know it's not really appropriate for me to be here.'

'No. I don't want to wait on my own.' Laura looked at her. 'And it was you who called the ambulance. I need to thank you for that.'

Antonia gave her a quick smile, then offered her a bottle of water out of her bag. Laura drank from it gratefully. She must still be pretty drunk, she thought, though events had sobered her up quickly. But her thoughts were jumbled and her mouth was dry.

'I'm glad we've called a truce,' said Antonia. 'Because whatever happens, you're going to have to step in. Those apartments need to be finished by Christmas and they're not going to do it by themselves.'

Laura looked alarmed.

'Surely the bank will understand? If we explain Dom's ill?'

Antonia grimaced. 'Yes, they'll understand. Then they'll extend your loan at crippling interest rates you won't begin to be able to afford.'

'But that's not fair.'

'No, it's not fair. It's business.'

Laura rubbed her face, trying to take everything in.

'I don't think I can talk about this right now.'

'Sorry,' said Antonia, looking flustered. 'I shouldn't be talking about business. It's nerves, I think.'

'It's OK. It's better that I know the truth.'

Antonia put a hand on her arm.

'I'll do whatever I can to help. You know that.'

Laura looked at her. 'I think you've done enough. But thank you.'

She didn't mean to be sharp, but in that moment she felt Antonia was overstepping the mark, and she felt the need to pull rank.

Antonia's face crumpled at the barb, her composure gone. She looked incredibly young suddenly. And for all her bravado, out of her depth. She must be frightened, thought Laura.

'Sorry,' she said. 'This is a weird situation.'

Antonia composed herself.

'I guess I feel it's all my fault,' she admitted.

Fault, thought Laura. It was such a strange word. How could you point the finger at any one person or any one thing or any one moment and apportion blame? Maybe it was everyone's fault. Or perhaps it was a perfect storm. A crisis that meant order could be restored.

She took in a breath, realising that her anxiety was nowhere to be seen. She felt calm. And she was the strong one now. She had to be. She had to step up, for Dom, for the girls, for the family. For the business.

'There's no point in blaming anyone,' she said.

They both turned towards the double doors as a woman stepped out into the corridor. She was in a grey trouser suit, about Laura's age, attractive but authoritative.

'Mrs Griffin?'

Laura stood up.

'That's me.'

The woman came forward with an outstretched hand.

'I'm Mary Beauchamp. I've just examined your husband. He's stable now but we are going to have to operate first thing tomorrow. He's going to need a stent fitted as soon as possible.'

'But he's going to be OK?'

'I think we've acted just in time. He's going to need to take it very easy for a while.'

'Of course,' said Laura. 'Thank you,' she added politely. 'Can I go and see him?'

Mary nodded.

'You can have five minutes. But he needs to rest.'

Laura turned to Antonia, whose eyes were tight shut. There were tears of relief trickling down her cheeks. Laura reached out and put her arms round her.

The two women held each other tight, united in their relief.

'Go and see him,' whispered Antonia. 'Go on.'

Laura sat, very gingerly, in the seat next to Dom's bed. The ward was dimly lit and quiet. There were big round suction pads on his chest and endless wires attached to the machines next to him. He looked tired and vulnerable. Not like Dom at all. She felt a surge of tenderness.

She reached out a hand and laid it on one of his, lacing their fingers.

His eyes opened slowly. He looked over at her.

'Hello,' she whispered.

'Laura.' He seemed surprised. 'I didn't think...'

'What?'

'I didn't think you'd come.'

'Of course I have.' She squeezed his hand. 'Antonia called me.'

'Oh.' He shut his eyes as if to block out this information.

'She's a good girl,' Laura told him, and he gave a wan smile.

'I've messed everything up,' he said.

'Shhh. We don't need to talk about it now.'

'I have. I've messed the house up. I've messed us up.'

'No,' said Laura. 'You haven't. It's all going to be fine.'

'Have you told the girls?'

'No. We'll see how you are tomorrow and decide then what to tell them.'

She was surprised how calm she felt, how in control she was. How the right thing to do and say was presenting itself logically. Everything was slotting into place. Everything was in perspective.

Dom didn't say anything for a moment.

'I'm sorry... for everything.'

'Well. I am too.'

He frowned, not understanding.

'You don't get to take all the blame,' she teased.

'I thought I was going to die,' he said. 'And I thought – at least Laura will be rid of me.'

'That's a terrible thing to say.'

'Can you ever forgive me, do you think?'

'Now, that's really not fair. You're lying there all wired up and you ask for forgiveness? That's emotional blackmail.'

Her tone was light, but she saw tears spring into his eyes. She bent forward to kiss him.

'Just get better,' she whispered. 'Get well, Dom, and we'll sort everything out. Together. You and me.'

He looked into her eyes.

'I love you, you know,' he said. 'None of this was because I didn't love you.'

She looked down at him. There were patches of baldness on his chest where they'd shaved it. She ran her finger over one of them.

'I love you too,' she said. 'But more importantly, I love *us*. You and me and the girls and Kanga and everyone...'

'Oh God. Me too.'

'And that's what I don't want to lose. That's what's special.'

'We won't. We can't.' His face crumpled. 'When I was staying at Wellington Buildings, all I could think about was being in our kitchen. Banter, music, cooking. I even missed the arguments...' He looked up at her. 'We can get it back, can't we?'

She nodded. A lump had come into her throat, because he had described exactly what was important. She wanted to tell him about Gino and Sadie tonight – he'd have loved being part of her matchmaking conspiracy. But now was not the time.

'I think that's enough now.' A nurse came over, slightly apologetic.

Laura stood up.

'I'll come back in the morning. What time is he in theatre?'

'We won't know until tomorrow. But he's urgent, so it should be first thing.'

'Thank you.'

She took one last look at Dom. He was fast asleep. She was taken back to all those years ago, to the hospital in the ski resort and the hours spent with him, when she had very first fallen in love with him. That *had* been her fault, the accident. Or had it? She'd always blamed herself, but now she knew life wasn't that simple; that culpability wasn't cut and dried; that there were a million sides to every story. And if it wasn't for the accident, for that time spent together, they probably wouldn't be together. Everything happened for a reason.

All that mattered now was that she loved him, her big mountain of a husband.

When Laura went back out into the corridor, Antonia was nowhere to be seen.

35

The following Monday, Laura stood looking up at Wellington Buildings. The sky above was that special cobalt blue that only winter can produce. Against it, the gold of the stone shone bright. The facade had been painstakingly cleaned – the last time she had seen it, it had been streaked with sooty black and murky grey. Now, it looked as splendid as the day it had been built. The casement windows had been freshly painted white, the guttering was black, the front door a pale pinky biscuit. The glass of the windows glittered and winked.

She felt a swell of pride. Dom had restored the tired, neglected building to its former glory with love and care. It was a triumph.

There was, of course, still work to be done, the final details, the snagging; and they were still waiting for the delivery of some of the bespoke fittings. Laura was determined to see the project through. There was no way she was going to let Dom fall at the last fence.

And she felt confident. Somehow, her minor achievements had combined to give her a self-belief she hadn't felt before. A sense that anything was achievable if you wanted it enough and worked hard enough for it.

She walked inside. Her breath was taken away. The

stone staircase curved in front of her, the same gold as the facade. The floor tiles had been restored and polished, intricate jewelled patterns in blue and black and pink. A magnificent chandelier swing overhead, its droplets shimmering.

He had done this. Her Dom had done this. It was up to her to make sure every ounce of blood, sweat and tears he had put into it paid off.

She walked into the drawing room of the ground-floor apartment. All the workmen employed on the project stood in a shuffling cluster. They exchanged bemused glances as Laura came in.

'I feel a bit like a headmistress,' she told them, laughing. 'But I'm not here to tell you off. Far from it. Firstly, I want to thank all of you. I know Dom loves working with you, because that's why he's chosen you to be part of his team. And what you have all done here is amazing. Truly amazing. I hope you are as proud of it as we are.'

She looked around at them all.

'As you know, Dom went into hospital at the weekend. He suffered a heart attack. He had a stent fitted yesterday, and he's going to be in hospital for a few more days, then home to recuperate. He's not going to be on site for quite some time. So you have the pleasure of me at the helm.' She smiled. 'I'm going to have to trust you guys to get me through this. Come and tell me if you've got any problems. If this is a success, we can go on to greater things, all of us. I really hope you can pull together, to do this for Dom. It would be great if we could get this signed off by Christmas. I've booked us all in for a slap-up Christmas dinner at the Wellington Arms in anticipation. I want us all there, job done, raising our glasses. I know it's going to be hard work, but I'm not afraid, and I hope you aren't either.'

Afterwards, she walked through the house, talking to each of them in turn about what they were doing and what needed to be done. The response was heart-warming. Their affection and respect for Dom was palpable, and again she felt pride.

At the top of the house, she found the blow-up bed and sleeping bag Dom had been sleeping in. Swiftly, she deflated the bed and rolled up the bag, stuffing them into a black bin liner. She'd throw it in the skip on the way out.

That part of their lives was over now.

'I need some time off,' said Antonia. 'Not exactly compassionate leave. Or sick leave. But it's important to me. For my . . . personal development.'

James Kettle looked at her across the boardroom table.

'Right. Do you want to elucidate? Only it's useful for me to put this request into context so I can make a decision.'

'I think if I carry on I'm in danger of burning out. It's not that I can't manage the workload. It's for . . . personal reasons.'

'I'm guessing this is related to what I called you in about?'

Antonia held his gaze. 'Can I plead the fifth amendment? On the grounds that it might incriminate me?'

He looked around the room for a moment while considering his response.

'And if I say no?'

'I'll have to hand in my notice. And I'm owed at least three weeks' leave so . . .'

James Kettle was a reasonable man. He knew perfectly well that Antonia was invaluable, but also that they could manage without her for a short period of time. And actually, if you were going to lose a valued member of staff for a couple of months, over Christmas was probably a good time to do it. Yes, it was frantic just before, but there were weeks afterwards when no one expected anything to have been attended to. If she could be back in saddle by the spring . . .

'How long do you want?'

'I was thinking three months. Long enough for me to get my head together.'

'And for the dust to settle?'

'Maybe.'

'If I grant you this leave and you come back with a clean slate . . .'

'That's what I'm hoping.'

'OK. Just give us enough time so we can reassign your workload and you can brief everyone on what you've been handling. Then I'll see you back at your desk in . . . March?'

She stood up. 'Thank you.'

'Don't let me down.'

'I won't. I love working here. You know that.'

James nodded. 'What are you going to do?'

'I don't know.' She managed a smile. 'That's the whole point, though. Every day for the past ten years has been mapped out and scheduled and organised. I need to learn to let go.'

'Just don't let go too much, OK?' James smiled.

345

'I don't think there's any danger of that.'

She flashed him a grin, and for a moment he saw a glimpse of another Antonia, and he thought she was doing just the right thing. It was important, in life, to recognise your faults and weaknesses and address them. He just hoped she wouldn't fall in love while she was away – not with a person, necessarily, but perhaps a place or another way of life.

He watched her as she left the room. James admired Antonia. He could tell she was on her way to the top, and he had no doubt whatsoever that she would make it, once she'd cleaned up her act.

Everyone was allowed to make a mistake. Just one.

Antonia knew this was the only way. For her to get out of Bath while the Griffins repaired their marriage. It was no good if she was on the periphery. If she was handling the conveyancing. If she might bump into Dom or Laura at any moment. She had to get as far away as she could, for as long as she could.

And maybe, just maybe, she would find a new Antonia while she was away.

36

Two weeks later, Kanga took a call from the managess at Amhurst House at eight o'clock in the morning. As soon as she heard her voice, she knew. It had that consummately professional mixture of sympathy and matter-of-factness. She was very sad to tell her that Ivy had passed away at 4.38 a.m.

'She deteriorated rather yesterday afternoon, and we got the doctor to come out. He was worried she was getting a chest infection and gave her some antibiotics. She didn't suffer. It was very peaceful. She really did just slip away.'

Kanga hung up the phone after agreeing to come over to the home to make arrangements. She shivered, even though the heating went on in her little house at seven. The world seemed a colder place altogether. She could feel that Ivy was no longer there. She really could. Desolation descended, icy and unforgiving.

She wanted to cry, but she couldn't. She had no tears, it seemed. They would come, no doubt, but for now she felt numb. She gathered her things together to drive over to Amhurst House.

Then, for a moment, she wavered. She wasn't sure, this time, that she had the strength to manage on her own. Now it was over, and she didn't have Ivy left to fight for, she felt vulnerable. She hesitated. She wanted comfort. Someone else's strength. She wasn't used to asking for it.

But she decided she would. There was nothing wrong in admitting defeat and asking for help. The home wouldn't mind if she was late. It wouldn't affect anything. They had called the undertaker.

She went out to her front door and stepped into the garden. There was frost on her front step and glittering across the lawn, and she reminded herself to get some de-icer. She couldn't afford to fall, like Ivy.

She walked tentatively and carefully along the path, then opened the French door that led into the kitchen. The warmth embraced her, and the scent of coffee. She stood in the doorway, unable to think, unable to speak, utterly overwhelmed.

A figure at the Aga turned. It was Dom. It wasn't Dom she wanted. She was glad he was back, but she was still cross with him. They hadn't had the conversation yet, although they would at some point. He knew she was disappointed in him, but he was still convalescing. There would be time for the conversation when he was stronger.

'Kanga?' He put down what he was doing and came over to her. 'Kanga, what's the matter?'

'Ivy . . .' She couldn't say any more, but she didn't need to.

And the next moment she found herself folded up in Dom's big arms. He scooped her up and brought her into the warm, and suddenly what he had done didn't matter so much because he was there for her, comforting her, making her feel safe. And then Laura came downstairs.

'Oh, darling,' said Laura. 'Oh, Kanga. Lovely Ivy.'

'I'm sorry,' said Kanga, her weeping overtaking her.

'Don't be sorry,' said Dom. 'We all loved Ivy. They broke the mould when they made her.'

It took her an hour to gather herself. Dom made her hot sweet cocoa, and even that made her cry, remembering the cocoa Ivy had made her that first night, here in this very kitchen.

'It's OK to be sad,' said Laura. 'It's OK to be sad.'

Kanga agreed that Laura should drive her to Amhurst House. She felt as if she might be a little in shock, so it wasn't a sign of weakness.

She embraced Beverley in the reception hall, next to the Christmas tree that had been put up on the first day of the month.

'My mum,' said Beverley, distraught. 'My little mum. She drove us mad, but we loved her to bits.'

'Of course you did,' replied Kanga. 'She was one in a million.'

'Listen,' said Beverley, and Kanga paused. A carol was spilling out of the speaker. 'The Holly and the Ivy...'

'Oh,' she said. 'How perfect.'

It brought the years spinning back. That first Christmas after her parents had gone. And the most important thing Ivy had ever done for her. The most precious memory of all.

37

1942

The horrors of the Blitz had gradually slipped further and further behind them at Number 11. Of course, they would never fade from memory completely, but as each day passed without any further bombings, everyone became a little less tense. Life was returning to something resembling normality as the city rebuilt itself.

The house was a little quieter once Tony had gone, his leave over. But they had muddled through, the three of them. Once her sickness had abated, Jilly got bigger by the day. She had kept herself busy throughout the autumn, harvesting everything that the garden had offered up and preserving it for the months ahead, then preparing the ground and replanting seeds to ensure a plentiful supply of food for next year.

She was proud of the larder. The shelves were groaning with jars and pots of pickle and chutney and jam. She followed her mother's recipes carefully, although as she grew more confident she made little changes which she marked on the cards in red pen to show they were her addenda. A different spice, a little less sugar, a more daring mixture of ingredients: she loved the science behind it, but also how experimentation could lead to pleasant surprises.

Helena helped too. Ivy wasn't interested. She didn't

have a domestic bone in her body and wasn't interested in food or where it came from, but Helena found it soothing and therapeutic. She was incredibly neat and particular: cutting green beans into exact lengths, slicing cucumber with precision, choosing the perfect berries – she was far more diligent than Jilly, who chopped with gay abandon and found herself chastised by her pupil.

'It's as much about how it looks as how it tastes,' said Helena.

And now their handiwork was displayed in the larder, Jilly had to agree it was worth making the extra effort. Every time she went in there, she had an enormous sense of satisfaction and order. There was so much bounty, they were able to wrap some of the wares as presents: a jar of raspberry jam and a jar of green tomato chutney were a welcome addition to anyone's household.

The house looked and smelled glorious as Christmas galloped nearer. The children were semi-hysterical with excitement. Jilly was determined to make it particularly special for them after everything that had happened. She loved everything to do with Christmas, so it was no hardship to totally indulge in preparations.

She took the children up to the woods and they gathered as much holly as they could, lugging it back in a little four-wheeled truck. She made a wreath for the front door – not a very good one but it was made with love – and tied bunches of holly with red ribbon to the bannisters. She trailed ivy along the mantelpiece in the drawing room and set up the Christmas cards in between the carriage clock and the Staffordshire china dogs.

That had been difficult. Cards started arriving from the middle of December from people who didn't know what had happened. If there was an address on the back of the envelope Jilly took the time to write and tell the sender the sad news, but sometimes there wasn't one. Was she going to have to face this every Christmas until the end of time? Cards to her mum and dad from people who didn't know?

They spent one afternoon making paper chains in orange and red and yellow and green. Jilly put as many candles as she could spare around the drawing room on Christmas Eve and they sat by the tree singing carols. So, as Christmas approached, the terrible sadness Jilly had been feeling started to fade as everyone's excitement grew.

On Christmas morning she woke feeling exhausted before she'd even got up. Her back and legs were aching, but she'd been doing an awful lot over the past few days to get everything ready, delivering Christmas cards by hand around the neighbourhood, queueing early at the butcher to get the last few things they needed. She pulled herself out of bed; the meat needed to go in, the potatoes needed peeling. She thought perhaps she'd strained her back the day before, moving the Christmas tree into a better position to get the presents underneath. There was a sharp twinge whenever she moved. She'd have to start taking it easy. She couldn't go lugging things around in her condition.

In the end, it was worth the effort. Christmas lunch was a triumph, even if she said it herself. She and Helena had worked hard to make everything as delicious as they could, despite rationing. They had decided to save all the sugar and butter for the pudding, and go without a cake, as the pudding was the dramatic centrepiece.

In the kitchen, Jilly had to steady herself before she lifted the steaming pudding in its cloth out of the saucepan. She felt the pains again, and thought how ridiculous not to be able to lift a pudding any more. She took in a few breaths and moved herself around until the pain eased, then plopped the pudding onto a big silver tray she had polished for the purpose.

Jilly laughed as she brought the pudding to the table, decorated with holly and blazing with brandy flames.

'This looks just like me,' she said. 'I am a Christmas pudding!'

As she bent over to put it on the table, she felt a sharper pain, lower down this time. She put her hand out to support herself, then gasped as the pain travelled round and squeezed the very breath out of her.

'Ooowwwww,' she moaned.

Ivy jumped up and came to her side. 'What's the matter?'

Jilly could hardly speak. 'Ah. It hurts. Oh. Oh my goodness. Oh dear.'

She looked down.

'That's your waters gone,' said Ivy. 'Oh my. We're going to have a Christmas baby.'

Helena's eyes were as round as the pudding.

'Not in the kitchen!'

'Come on,' said Ivy, holding Jilly's arms. 'Lean on me and let's get you in the lounge. In front of the fire. There's plenty of room on the floor.'

'What about the carpet?' panicked Jilly.

'Bugger the carpet,' said Ivy.

'Get blankets and pillows,' Helena told the children.

'Shouldn't we call a doctor? Or the midwife?' asked Ivy.

'It's Christmas lunch,' said Ivy. 'No one's going to want to come out.'

'Well, I had my three at home. I know what to do. I suppose.' Helena looked doubtful.

'And I was there for most of my cousins. We'll sort it out between us. Though you could have waited till we'd had pudding,' Ivy teased Jilly.

'And what about presents? We were going to do presents after – ooooowwwwwww!' The next contraction nearly brought Jilly to her knees.

'You'll have your own little present before long,' said Ivy.

'Come on. Let's get you lying down,' coaxed Helena. 'We don't want baby dropping out and landing on its head, do we?'

Three hours, it took. Helena held her hand and talked her through every contraction while Ivy stood over them, eyes wide with empathy, wincing every time Jilly howled with pain. They had sent the children up to their bedroom, but they were lined up on the staircase, one, two, three, waiting with bated breath.

And then suddenly, with a final effort and a terrible bellow from Jilly, Ivy was pulling the baby from her, laughing with glee and delight.

'A baby girl!' she cried. 'A darling little baby girl. Oh, you clever thing, Jilly. You clever, clever thing.'

And she laid the baby gently on Jilly's chest.

Jilly was exhausted and dazed, but she put her hand on the baby's head.

'You'll have to call her Holly,' said Ivy.

Jilly shook her head.

'Catherine,' she said. 'My mother's name. Baby Catherine.' She looked up at her friend, her Christmas hairdo all unravelled and her lipstick smudged. 'Baby Catherine Ivy.'

38

From the *Bath Chronicle*:

A memorial service takes place on Thursday giving thanks for the life of Mrs Ivy Bennett, nee Skinner. Mrs Bennett died peacefully at the age of 93, leaving two daughters, Kim and Beverley, five grandchildren and a number of great-grandchildren.

Mrs Bennett lived through the Bath Blitz and was a well-known hairdresser in Bath for many years. She was one of the few survivors of the Blitz to attend the 75th anniversary memorial service in Victoria Park. She is pictured here with her close friend Mrs Jilly Ingram, nee Wilson. Mrs Ingram said:

'Ivy and I were the firmest of friends, and it was her spirit that kept me going throughout the Blitz, when both my parents were killed, and the rest of the war. She lived with me at Lark Hill and even delivered my daughter, Catherine, on the living-room floor, on Christmas Day 1942. I feel very lucky to have had her as a close friend all of my life.'

39

There was a man standing by the mantelpiece in the drawing room of the Royal Crescent Hotel.

They had all agreed it was the perfect place for Ivy's memorial: she had loved to come here for lunch, as a treat, and look out over the lawns at the front; she had loved the grand furniture and the paintings, and to pretend to be posh for the day. Kanga had often shared birthday lunches with her here. Sometimes with all her family. Sometimes just the four of them – Reggie would always order the most expensive champagne on the menu. And lately, just the two of them.

She stood, with a cup of tea, wondering just who the man was. He looked reticent, and wasn't with anyone. He must be about the same age as her and Ivy, Kanga thought. He was old, though not entirely frail, and he had on a very nice suit. He moved with the confidence of a man with class. A secret admirer, perhaps? Though he didn't seem Ivy's type. She had always gone for the rogues, the silver-tongued rascals, and this man looked more of an establishment type, with a silk tie, the last of his silver hair still well-cut and swept back.

As she went to catch his eye, perhaps smile at him and ask if he wanted a cup of tea, she suddenly stopped.

There was a look about him that seemed familiar. The way he held himself, the smile, the look in his eye. He was walking towards her as if he recognised her. There were not many people he could be, given that most of the people she knew of her age had passed on.

As he got closer, she stared harder at him. There was one possibility. Though that wasn't a possibility either. She'd seen his name. She knew she had. In the list of people who'd been killed in action. So it couldn't be him, but it was so like him. Now he was almost in front of her, she could never forget those eyes.

'Jilly.'

He said her name – the name that barely anyone used any more – and she thought her heart might stop.

'It can't be you,' she said. 'I saw your name. In the RAF casualty lists. Harry Swann. You died in action.'

'Well, yes. Sadly, Harry did die.' The man drew himself up. 'I'm not Harry Swann. I think I owe you an explanation.'

He swept his hand through the remains of his silver hair.

Kanga looked around at the rest of the mourners. She couldn't have this conversation here.

'Shall we step outside? Into the garden? This is rather a shock.'

'Of course. Will you be warm enough?'

He was chivalrous. She liked that. He took her arm, and the two of them walked out through the hotel and into the walled garden at the back. She turned to him.

'How did you find me? Why here? Why now? I don't understand.'

He took out a silk handkerchief and dabbed at his forehead.

'It's probably more than seventy years too late, but it's the thing I've been most ashamed of all my life.'

'You had no reason to be loyal to me. It was one night. Why should you be ashamed?'

'Because I lied. I lied to you. And I knew. I knew the consequences of that night but I was too much of a coward...'

There was pain in his eyes. Kanga frowned. 'Consequences?'

He sighed.

'I told you a lie that night. I wasn't going off to learn to fly. I was supposed to. I was all packed and ready. But at the last moment, I failed the medical. Bloody asthma. They wouldn't let me train. It was out of the question.'

'Asthma...' Kanga echoed, thinking of Willow.

'I was so ashamed. I wanted to fight for my country. I wanted to be a hero. And when I met you, I wanted to be a hero in your eyes. I lied to you. I gave you my friend's name. Harry's name. Harry Swann was doing the thing I wanted to do so badly. For one night with you, I was him. I was the person I wanted to be.'

'Oh.' Kanga understood. Only people who had lived through those terrible times could understand that level of patriotism. She put a gentle hand on his arm. 'Well, it doesn't matter. We were young. Swept up in the moment.'

'It does matter. I let you down. Horribly. I've lived with the shame all of my life. Because I knew...'

She frowned. 'Knew what?'

'I knew about the baby. I knew about your letter. The one you wrote to Harry. And he sent it back to you. Of course he did. He had no idea who you were. But when he was on leave, he told me he'd had a letter. From a girl expecting his baby. He laughed about it. But I knew straight away it was you.'

Kanga caught her breath. She remembered the envelope landing on the mat. *Return to Sender*. The crushing disappointment. The sense of being let down. But the letter had gone to the wrong person.

And yet he had known all along. The father of her baby had known.

'If you knew, why didn't you come and find me?'

'I did.' He looked at her. 'I came, after the war. I found your house. I was going to knock on the door. But as I was plucking up the courage, I saw you come out. You were with a man. A tall man, quite a bit older than you. With glasses. But I could see, you were in love. The way you looked at each other. You laughed and he kissed you . . .'

Kanga nodded. 'Jocelyn. My Jocelyn.'

'And a little girl came out and he scooped her up and put her on his shoulders. There was no doubt in my mind that you were a family. That she might have been my child, but she belonged with you and him, not you and me.'

'I don't know what to say . . .' Kanga felt a little dizzy.

'I'm sorry if I've shocked you.'

'Why now? Why tell me now?'

He looked out across the gardens. There was a bleakness in his face.

'I suppose we don't have much time left, and I wanted to atone. Explain and atone. As I said, it has been something I have wrestled with all my life. For years, I thought you were better off without me. Who wants a coward? A liar?'

'You were young. So young.'

'I happened to see the picture of you and Ivy in the newspaper, when her death was announced.' Ivy's death had been picked up on by a couple of the nationals, as she was one of the last survivors of the Bath Blitz. 'I thought you would be here. I thought it was time to put the record straight.'

Kanga pulled her coat further around her. She had so many questions.

'If you're not Harry Swann, then what is your name?'

'Rufus. Rufus Hammond.'

She hesitated for a moment, then held out her hand. 'Well, it's very nice to meet you again, Rufus.'

He took her hand in his. There was a look of enormous gratitude in his eyes. 'You are very gracious. Very forgiving.'

'I never forgot you.'

How could she? She'd had the ultimate memento.

There was a pause.

'Our daughter?' he asked, his eyes full of questions.

Kanga looked away.

'Our daughter was wonderful. Catherine. Jocelyn was a wonderful father to her. He brought her up as his own.' She faltered for a moment. 'She was a free spirit. A traveller. Full of adventure and wonder at the world. I'm afraid . . . she died. When she was thirty. She was knocked off her bicycle when she was going to collect her daughter from nursery. Thank goodness Laura wasn't on the back. That was the only saving grace.'

'I'm so sorry.' He looked stricken.

'It was a long time ago. And we had Laura. We brought her up. Catherine didn't have a partner – the baby's father was a one-night stand from her travels in Greece. We never judged her for that.'

The two of them stood in the late-afternoon breeze as the sun started to go down. They contemplated their mistakes, their memories, their losses. But, eventually, they exchanged a glance and a smile. At their age, thought Kanga, forgiveness was all.

For a moment, she imagined telling Ivy:

'You won't believe it, Ivy. He's come back. Harry Swann's come back to see me. Only he's not Harry Swann. He's called Rufus.'

She could imagine Ivy's wicked laugh. The toss of her head and the flash in her eye as she said, 'It's a bit bloody late now, tell him.'

40

1945

Jilly stood in the garden. The sun shone with a triumphant glow as if it had heard the news, announced by Churchill with his usually solemnity.

'The hostilities will end officially tonight, at one minute after midnight...'

The leaves rustled in the breeze as if to add their applause. Apart from that, it was quiet. She looked into the sky. Clouds glided overhead as if they were heading somewhere important. They had a sense of purpose she didn't feel.

Instead of joy, she felt despair. Suddenly everything seemed pointless. Without the war to battle against, what was she to do? She knew she should be jumping up and down cheering, waving a little flag like everyone else, but she felt an unbearable sadness.

It was all over. She had been so brave, fighting on, keeping up her own spirits and everyone else's. But somehow now the realisation hit home: they had gone, and they weren't coming back.

The longing swooped in and hit her, an ache that left a ragged hole right inside her more painful than any bullet wound. A bullet wound would heal, eventually, but Jilly felt as if the pain would never subside.

She sank to her knees with her face in her hands, hot tears sliding through her fingers. She imagined her father coming in with the news, a broad smile across his face; her mother grabbing him and whirling him around the kitchen in a dance of triumph. Maybe that's what they were doing, somewhere up above those very clouds. Maybe they were glad she was now safe.

She fell onto the earth, feeling its warmth but not comforted by it in any way. She smelled its rich dankness as she sobbed.

Then she felt a hand on her head. A gentle pat. She looked up to see Catherine's round face, her cheeks pale pink with sleep, peering down at her. She must have woken from her nap and trotted outside. Jilly sat up, brushing the dirt from her hands, trying to compose herself, not wanting to distress her daughter.

'Mummy sad.' Catherine patted her cheek. Her eyes were grave with concern.

'Yes,' said Jilly. 'Mummy is a bit sad. But not now I've seen you, darling.'

She scooped the little girl up in her arms, pulling her to her. She was deliciously warm, the light cotton of her dress soft around her. She nuzzled into her neck, breathing in her sweet scent, glorying in her presence. She nibbled at her skin with her lips, making Catherine giggle with delight.

'Mummy! Stop it!' she squealed, clearly not wanting her to stop at all. And Jilly laughed with her as she squirmed in her arms. The dark gloom lifted slightly. She would go back into the house, wash her face and brush her hair, put on a clean dress, perhaps even put on some lipstick, and push Catherine into town in her pram. Her parents, she knew, would have been the first ones to put up bunting and join in the celebrations. She wasn't going to wallow in her grief any longer.

She pulled out the prettiest dress she could. She combed out her hair and pinned it back up with a roll at the front, in an approximation of what Ivy would do. Ivy was in the bath, preparing to do herself up to the nines. She was still living at Number 11. Helena and the children had moved out a few months ago, rehoused by the council in a place of their own. It was quiet without them, so she was renting the rooms out on a casual basis, board and lodging.

As she got herself ready, she heard the brusque ring of the front doorbell, loud through the house. As a doctor, it had been important for her father to have a bell that could be heard above everything else. She picked up Catherine and ran down the stairs.

There was a young man standing outside. He had kind brown eyes behind his black spectacles and was holding a leather Gladstone bag.

'I was told you might have a room,' he said. 'I need one for at least a month.'

'Oh!' Feeling a bit silly that she was so done up, her cheeks grew warm. 'Well, yes. I've got two in the attic.'

'May I have a look? Or were you on your way some-where?'

'I was going to join the celebrations. But it can wait.'

He gave a smile. 'It's marvellous news.'

'Marvellous!' she echoed, wondering why one earth she couldn't think of anything more intelligent to say.

'Though we have a long way to go. Before things are normal.'

She nodded. His gravitas intrigued her. He had a seriousness to him, a thoughtfulness, that drew her to him. He was younger than he looked, perhaps. But when he smiled, his whole face lit up and his eyes twinkled.

'Why don't you come in and have a look? See if you like the room.'

He followed her up the stairs and explained to her what he was doing.

'I'm here for at least a few weeks. I'm an architect. I've come to help with the replanning of the city.'

'An architect? That's fascinating.'

'It is. It will be wonderful to work in a city like Bath. Try and restore it to its former glory.'

'We've got a long way to go. Here. You might like the room on the right. It's a little bigger.'

He walked across the room and looked out of the window. 'What a wonderful view.'

'Not everyone likes looking at chimney pots.'

'Well, I do. How much are you looking for? Per week?'

She gave him her rate and he nodded.

'That's half board,' she said. 'Breakfast and dinner. Plus bread and jam for tea if you want it. But I'll need your ration book.'

He put his bag down on the bed in agreement. 'Done,' he said with that illuminating smile again. It made her feel special. For a moment, she couldn't speak.

'Would you like a cup of tea?' she asked eventually.

'Lovely,' he said, and reached out a finger for Catherine to grab. 'What's the little one's name?'

'Catherine. She's quite quiet, so she won't disturb you.'

'And you?'

Jilly laughed. 'I'm very quiet too.'

'I meant your name.' His lips twitched with amusement.

Jilly's heart skittered a little. How had she gone from lying in the dirt sobbing to standing in a room with a perfect stranger who made her feel . . . well, she wasn't sure what he made her feel, but he was making her feel something, and that was certainly a change.

'Jilly.'

He held out his hand. 'Jocelyn. Jocelyn Ingram.'

His fingers felt as warm as a peach that has been lying on a windowsill in the sun.

She didn't want to let go.

While he unpacked his things and had a wash, she ran down the stairs to the kitchen. She popped Catherine down and grabbed the tiny mirror she kept on the dresser, peering in it to see what she looked like, smoothing her hair. She couldn't put on lipstick, that would be too obvious. Ivy would, she thought. But she wasn't sure Jocelyn was the sort of man who cared about lipstick on a girl. She would do.

When he came back down, she had filled the old brown teapot and put some home-made scones on a plate with a dish of jam.

'I don't know if you're hungry.'

'I'm not. But I can't resist.' Jocelyn reached out and took a scone.

There was a clattering of footsteps along the corridor and Ivy whirled into the room. She looked radiant, her hair higher than ever, her lipstick brighter, her eyes sparkling.

'Come on,' she said. 'There's going to be dancing in the

streets. We can't waste another minute. Oh!' Her eyes fell on Jocelyn. 'Hello.'

He stood up and held out his hand. 'Jocelyn Ingram. I'm the new lodger.'

'Well,' said Ivy. 'Lucky us.'

'Lucky me, I'd say.' He twinkled at her.

'Are you going to come into town with us?'

'How can I possibly refuse?'

Jilly looked at him in fascination. She loved the way he held his own with Ivy, amused by her but not intimidated like some men. Yet not entranced either. She loved his teasing tone. His quiet confidence.

She slipped into the pantry and put some lipstick on anyway. She could use the celebrations as an excuse.

The four of them went down the hill into Bath, Catherine in the pram, Ivy dancing with impatience.

There was bunting and cheering and music and dancing and long trestle tables groaning with food down the streets. Ivy disappeared into the crowds and Jilly doubted she would be seeing her again before midnight.

It was wonderful, the atmosphere. Everyone hugged each other and cheered and waved. Catherine was given a little flag and brandished it from the depths of her pram.

By late afternoon, Jilly had had enough. Catherine was tired and needed a bath and her bed.

'Come on,' said Jocelyn. 'Let me get the two of you back. You look exhausted.'

'No, no, no. I can manage. I don't want to spoil your fun.'

'Don't be silly,' he said, taking the pram from her. 'I'll push.'

And later, when Catherine was tucked up in bed, he

poured her a glass of wine he had produced from nowhere and put it into her hands. He raised his own glass.

'To the future,' he said. 'To our future.'

She thought, at the time, he was talking generally, about the country's future, but looking back, she realised he had known straight away, and the future he'd been talking about was theirs, his and hers, the two of them. Together.

41

She looked for the tenth time at the departure board. When was the gate going to be announced? And would they have time to get to it? If their flight was on time, there wasn't long. She hated this not knowing. It was a long way to the gates if they were at the wrong end. She looked out at the planes on the runway to see if they could give her a clue.

'Will you just relax?' Herbie put a hand on her shoulder. 'There'll be plenty of time.'

'It's fine. I'm not worried,' insisted Antonia.

'I can see you. Checking and double-checking. Don't worry. They aren't going without us.'

Mexico. She was going to Mexico. With her crazy little brother. On a one-way ticket. Without a hotel booked, except for the first night, because she had insisted. She was way out of her comfort zone. Not in control at all.

But that was the point. This trip was her therapy. Her chance to let go a bit. Leave things to chance.

And although Herbie was maddeningly laid-back and disorganised, and left everything to the last minute, he would have her back. He knew the lie of the land, where they were going, he had mates. It would be fine, she told herself.

He'd laughed at her hand luggage. She had everything she needed. Headphones, travel pillow, eye mask, sleeping pills, books, Kindle, water, pashmina, spare knickers, chewing gum . . . all neatly packed and to hand, her travel documents in a special wallet, everything clearly labelled.

Herbie had a rucksack with a battered Ernest Hemingway paperback and his wallet and passport. That was it. She couldn't understand how he could travel so light. She bet he would start asking her for things halfway through the flight. That's what usually happened.

But she didn't mind. This was perfect for her. Just what she needed to leave the mess of the past few months behind her.

Suddenly the gate number appeared on the board. Her heart gave a little flip. It was real. Once she was at the departure gate, there was no going back. She picked up her bag.

'*Hasta la vista*, baby,' said Herbie. 'Let's go.'

42

It was the thing she loved best in the world. That quiet half hour in the kitchen before everyone arrived, when she put the finishing touches to the meal and made sure everything was perfect – but not too perfect, because actually there was nothing more annoying than perfection.

Laura counted up the places around the table again, looking at her list. She was obsessed with lists at the moment – how on earth would she have got through the last few weeks without them?

She'd gone from having an empty nest and nothing to do to running three businesses. The Airbnb had taken off like a rocket, with people coming to Bath to do their Christmas shopping. Her stall at the market was a huge success – she couldn't cook fast enough to keep up with demand. And Wellington Buildings was almost completed. There were a few cosmetic tweaks to add before they went onto the market, but she had got three separate estate agents to come and value the apartments the week before and Dom had been delighted with their estimates.

She cringed sometimes when she thought how easily things could have turned out differently. If Dom hadn't been so lucky – perhaps they had Antonia's intervention to thank for that? Or what if she'd gone back with Herbie, when he'd propositioned her at the Reprobate that night? She blushed even now at the memory.

He had apologised to her, charmingly, when she had seen him the next week at the market. Dom had still been in hospital, and she hadn't wanted to not turn up to man her stall. Dom was in good hands, after all.

'I was totally inappropriate,' said Herbie. 'I blame the Sazeracs. Though, of course, it's your fault for being so irresistible.'

'It's fine,' said Laura, not wanting to admit even to herself how near she had come to giving in to his charms. She would blame the Violette Femmes.

Today they were doing a big Sunday lunch at Number 11. She'd kept it simple. Smoked mackerel pâté which she would pass round on fingers of toasted soda bread while everyone arrived and had a glass of champagne. Then roast pork followed by floating islands – all recipes from her little box. Nothing fancy and gourmet, just plain home cooking with nothing that needed last-minute attention. And, of course, a huge cheese board – she'd bought lots at the market yesterday.

They were eating at the dining table rather than the island as there were so many of them. She'd laid it properly and it looked stunning, the silver and glass shining in the mid-morning sunshine that streamed through the windows. She counted up the places one last time.

Her and Dom.

Jaz and Willow, who had arrived back from uni and were probably upstairs fighting over the bathroom.

Sadie and Gino – who were inseparable. He had been back to Bath twice since they'd met. He had stayed at Sadie's the second time, even though he had booked in to stay at Number 11. He had insisted on paying his bill anyway.

And Kanga and Rufus. Kanga had come to tell her the story of Catherine's father, and they had both agreed that Rufus should be welcomed into the family. He wasn't intruding on Jocelyn's memory; it was part of their history, and there was no suggestion that he and Kanga were romantically involved. Today was his introduction: everyone had been briefed and Laura felt certain that he would fit in perfectly.

Half an hour later the kitchen was filled with guests. As she turned the roast potatoes over for the final time and slid them back into the Aga, Laura looked around the room.

Her heart squeezed with love as she watched Dom handing a glass of champagne to Rufus and raise his own glass of cranberry juice in a toast. Dom was on a fitness regime, and still tired easily after his operation. She kept a strict eye on him, but he was filled with resolve about the changes he was going to make to his lifestyle and how he worked.

Kanga was talking to Gino, obviously utterly beguiled by his charms. It was almost as if he had been part of the family all along, and he was good for Sadie. He kept her wilder streak at bay and made her feel secure, but it was also obvious that their relationship had the vital spark of mutual attraction.

The girls were both helping her, handing round the mackerel toasts, filling up glasses, chattering to everyone. Willow had a confidence about her she had lacked previously, and Laura was pleased that university had made her a little more independent. Jaz was talking to Rufus, making him feel welcome. It must be odd for him, being thrown into a cluster of people who were his blood relatives yet whom he hadn't known until now.

But he was lucky. Bloody lucky, thought Laura, to have ended up with all of them. She walked over to the table and lit the three beeswax candles in the middle, looking at the places that would soon be filled with all these people she loved. Of course, some people who should be there were missing, and the hole they had left would never quite be filled. But the other unexpected additions – Rufus and Gino – added a layer of richness.

It was unique, this gathering of people who meant so much to her and made her who she was. They made her, and each other, so happy.

It was the perfect family recipe.

If you've loved

A Family Recipe

Turn the page to discover
Veronica Henry's own family
recipe box

MY RECIPE BOX

Ever since I can remember there has been a small lidded box in the kitchen of whichever house we lived in (many, for my father was in the army) holding yellowing recipe cards.

It is a treasure trove: a diary, a family tree and a memory box all in one. Some cards are handwritten by my grandmothers, my mother or my dad; others I carefully typed out in a fit of efficiency when I was teaching myself secretarial skills aged about fourteen! Each card evokes a different time, a different place and a different set of people, but all of them bring me comfort.

I was the archetypal bookworm, but cooking was my other escape. On a Saturday morning I would beg to bake a cake or scones or flapjacks, and out would come the box. I still turn to these recipes now when I need to feel grounded and safe.

I have used the original weights and measures for authenticity.

Canadian Flapjacks

My maternal grandmother had a stash of post-war recipes, and this was one of the first things I learned to bake, along with the apple snow and peppermint creams from the *My Learn to Cook Book* (just looking at that cover even now throws up a mixture of emotions: nostalgia, excitement, comfort and a strong urge to cry). I could make these flapjacks almost unsupervised, standing on a chair with a wooden spoon. The biggest challenge was waiting for them to cool. I still make them today, when we need a stash of stodge, and they are very forgiving and accepting of whatever spin I want to put on them (usually dried apricots and pumpkin seeds which I kid myself makes them healthy). The recipe calls for margarine but I use butter: margarine seems like a relic from another age. I have no idea what makes these Canadian but that's what it says on the card!

RECIPE *Canadian Flapjacks*

Ingredients	Method
10oz Quaker oats *½ lb margarine* *2oz sugar* *2 tablespoons golden syrup*	*Melt the margarine with the sugar and golden syrup. Stir in the oats. Spread into a greased baking tin and cook for 30 minutes at 170°C.*

Soda Bread

My paternal grandparents were Irish, and I have nothing but the happiest of memories spent at The Shack – the dilapidated, ramshackle house they once owned on the coast of Kerry, overlooking the wild Atlantic. We slept in bunk beds, the inevitable damp from the endless rain dispelled by a peat fire that smelled sharp and earthy. My grandmother produced hearty meals three times a day for the ebb and flow of constant visitors: freshly-picked mushrooms, freshly-caught salmon, freshly-dug potatoes. And every day she would make a loaf of soda bread. Dense and cakey, it was a meal in itself, and if I could choose only one type of bread to have for the rest of my life, this would be it. I make it at Christmas to serve with smoked salmon, but it's also perfect with raspberry jam. Or just cold butter. Or dipped into soup.

RECIPE *Soda Bread*

Ingredients

4 teacups whole-wheat flour
1 tsp baking soda
1 ½ teacup buttermilk
salt

Method

Sieve the dry ingredients into a large bowl. Add buttermilk gradually until you can draw it all together – don't handle it too much. Pat into a round and put a cross in the top. Bake in the oven at 425°F for about 45 mins or until hollow when you tap the bottom.

Mezze

My parents met on a training course at Greenwich – my father was in the Army, my mother in the WRNS – and not long after they got engaged my father was posted to Cyprus. My mother went there to marry him. They had a tiny white house and she learned to cook, tentatively at first, from a copy of Elizabeth David. Their life revolved around tennis and drinks parties and bombing around the island in a Sunbeam Alpine (which they had to get rid of when I arrived . . .) They loved to sit outside the tiny restaurants by the harbour drinking liver-damaging glasses of brandy. This careful list of what to include in a mezze was written in my father's slanting hand, and I love to think of them laying it out on a table to eat in the sunshine with their dashing friends. It's redolent of a novel – Lawrence Durrell or Victoria Hislop – the glamorous young things in their Mediterranean paradise.

This is more of a list than a recipe, but I would get a huge big white plate and use the list as inspiration – it's quite old school and heavy on the offal and I have no idea what garlic meal paste is! The instructions are to serve on individual platters with brandy or wine, both with water – through I'm not sure if the water goes in the glass or is served separately. You decide!

Mutton kebab	Olive	Cucumber and tomato
Liver	Salad	Yoghurt
Sweetbreads	Radishes	Garlic meal paste
Kidney	Spring Onions	Dolmades
Fish	Hard boiled egg	Shoat (sheep and goat) sausages
Pork	Mayonnaise	Quail

Finish with a selection of baklava

Chocolate Chip Cake

When I was 11 years old, my father was posted to Washington DC. We left our dreary army patch on a rainy day and arrived in a land of sunshine. It was 1974 and we had a house with an intercom, a telephone on the wall with a ten-foot wiggly cord and a fridge that made ice. We were open-mouthed: it was like living in a high-tech paradise. We spent the summer at the swimming pool, unable to believe that each day dawned with a bright sun. We played John Denver and Neil Young and the Ozark Mountain Daredevils. But there was homesickness too. Some Army friends made us welcome and reminded us of home, and their mother made this amazing chocolate chip cake in a bundt tin. It became my go-to recipe at the weekends, with its mysterious ingredient of sour cream, and has been a family favourite ever since.

RECIPE *Chocolate Chip Cake*

Ingredients

¼ lb soft butter
1 ½ cups sugar
2 eggs
1 cup sour cream
pinch salt
2 tablespoons milk
2 cups pre-sifted flour
2 teaspoons baking powder
1 teaspoon baking soda
6 oz dark chocolate chips

Method

Mix everything together but the chocolate chips with a beater. Mix until smooth. Fold in chips by hand. Pour into a greased 10 inch tube pan. Bake at 350°F for for 45 minutes.

Marie Biscuit Chocolate Pudding

This no-bake pudding involving biscuits drenched with coffee was a dinner party staple during the 70s – very *Abigail's Party*! – and I lit upon it when I first started doing dinner parties as a teenager. My friends would come round dressed to the nines bearing bottles of Paul Masson and St Moritz, and I would produce my signature Hungarian goulash followed by this. There was nobody who didn't love its sickly chocolatey-ness – it's the original crowd pleaser. By the end of the night there were countless empty bottles and cigarettes stubbed out in the pudding plates. Decadence at its height!

RECIPE *Marie Biscuit Chocolate Pudding*

Ingredients

1 packet Marie Biscuits
4 oz butter
1 cup icing sugar
1 tablespoon cocoa powder
1 teaspoon vanilla essence
1 tablespoon milk
1 cup of strong coffee
1 tablespoon brandy
1 teaspoon baking soda
Tub whipping cream

Method

Make the coffee and add brandy. Beat together butter and sugar then stir in cocoa powder and vanilla essence until smooth, adding milk to soften. Dip one third of the biscuits into the coffee mix and lay in glass bowl. Cover in icing mix. Repeat three times. Spread with whipped cream and decorate with slivered almonds or silver balls.

About
VERONICA HENRY

Veronica Henry worked as a scriptwriter for *The Archers*, *Heartbeat* and *Holby City*, amongst many others, before turning to fiction. She won the 2014 RNA Novel of the Year award for *A Night on the Orient Express*. Veronica lives with her family in a village in north Devon.

Find out more at www.veronicahenry.co.uk

Sign up to her Facebook page
www.facebook.com/veronicahenryauthor

Or follow her on Twitter @veronica_henry
and Instagram @veronicahenryauthor